I0728674

# Babatunde's Heroic Journey
## From Nigeria to Ukraine via Russia

Nape `a Motana

RIVERSONG
BOOKS

An Imprint of Sulis International
Los Angeles I London

BABATUNDE'S HEROIC JOURNEY:
FROM NIGERIA TO UKRAINE VIA RUSSIA
Copyright ©2018 by Nape `a Motana. All rights reserved.

Except for brief quotations for reviews, no part of this book may be reproduced in any form or by any electronic or mechanical means, including information storage and retrieval systems, without written permission from the publisher. Email: info@sulisinternational.com.

Library of Congress Control Number: 2018953382
ISBN (paperback): 978-1-946849-36-6
ISBN (eBook): 978-1-946849-37-3

Riversong Books
An Imprint of Sulis International
Los Angeles | London

www.sulisinternational.com

# The Journey

For the reader's convenience, a glossary of Igbo, Pidgin English. and Russian words is located at the end of the novel.

For Pastor Sunday Adelaja, of the Embassy of God in Kiev, and
other faith warriors—known and unknown. *Pula*! Hallelujah!

'Adventures create heroes. When that happens, it is be-cause courage conquers fear.'

—Floyd McClung


'It is not great men who change the world, but weak men in the hands of a great God.'

—Paul Hattaway.


'Pray not for a lighter load to carry, but a stronger back to endure.'

—Liu Zhenying aka 'Brother Yun'

# PART ONE

## 1

At cock-crow that Monday morning, Babatunde Okoronkwo raised his head, stuck out his hand and pushed his blue and grey-chequered wrapper down to his chest. Sitting up on his buttocks, he lifted his knees, stretched out his arms and yawned aloud. Taking his time to stand up, he put on a pair of khaki shorts, threadbare at the bottoms. It was quiet in the hut that he shared with Nnamdi his male cousin. The only sound disturbing the graveyard silence was a loud snore from beside him. His female cousin, Adaobi, slept in a small hut adjacent to the cooking-shed.

Bare to the waist as usual, with the wrapper hanging around his neck oscillating across both his nipples, he shuffled out of the hut and strolled to the heap of firewood where he began chopping logs into thinner pieces with his machete. After that he swept the courtyard, a chore he usually did in the afternoons.

Before washing his face and armpits, he remembered to clean the wooden mortars and pestles for yam and cassava pounding. Then he stood in the doorway and surveyed what he had done, satisfied that his aunts [his uncle had two wives] would dispense nothing but praise.

His parents had sent him to work for his paternal uncle two weeks ago. It was the third week of January and the schools were about to re-open.

The previous Friday morning his cousins had told him they were not joining him on the farm as their father intended to take them to the nearest town, Port Harcourt, to buy school uniforms and stationery.

*What about me?* thought Babatunde. *Father said uncle Emenike is going to send me to school.*

Chopping firewood that afternoon, he saw his uncle's old charcoal Ford van entering the gate of the compound. When the chattering cousins showed him their school uniforms and stationery, he'd thought his turn would come: *I'm sure uncle will call me and give me my books and school uniform before we sleep.*

When that didn't happen, he thought the special moment would perhaps come on the Monday morning.

Before rising that morning, he had a dream: he was an adult wearing a blue and grey-chequered suit, walking towards his homestead; he heard next-door neighbours cheering, 'You are smart, *nkowe-oma!*'

As he entered the homestead, his mother and sister complimented him, 'Baba, you are smart!'

When he woke up and realised it was just a dream, he felt cheated.

That morning he dressed carefully. He remembered that as he stretched himself out on his grass mat, he could hardly sleep as he envisioned himself sitting in a classroom, learning fascinating things about this great mystery called education. He put on a clean white shirt, grey shorts and a pair of short grey socks which, when pulled up, barely reached his calves. He combed his short black hair and made his coffee-coloured face glow with *ude-aki*. He was now ready to meet uncle Emenike. He approached his uncle where he was sitting on an old garden chair under the kola tree, drinking from a gourd cup.

'*Dee* my cousins...' he hesitated, '...my cousins told me that they are going to the village school which opens today. Am I...going with them to school?'

Babatunde stood at attention, holding his breath, studying his uncle's face. His uncle finished drinking from his gourd cup and put it down on the tray lying on the ground beside him.

Babatunde clasped his fingers, '*Dee, biko...*'

'Hei *chi m o*! You don't understand,' uncle Emenike replied, shaking his head. 'Your father sent you here to learn to farm, not to go to school, my boy.'

Babatunde sighed, looking his uncle straight in the eyes for a moment, then dropped his gaze, trying not to show his disappointment.

'Farmers don't have to know how to read and write,' his uncle continued, 'and I can't afford to pay more school fees. Besides, you and I will be staying out in the bush for many weeks to do game-trapping soon. And when we come back, it will be time for the cassava harvest. Farm work never ends. So there is no time for school.'

Babatunde could not believe what he was hearing. He wondered if his father was misled or if his uncle was lying.

He dropped his face in his palms and sobbed. 'But my father...'

'I will speak to your father,' his uncle interrupted, 'and clarify the matter.'

Babatunde wiped tears away with the back of his hand. 'Is it possible that my father could pay my school fees and that I could start when I come back from the bush?' the boy asked, grasping at the last straw of hope.

'Where will your father get the money? Listen boy, your father sent you to farm, not to go to school.' Uncle Emenike beat his left palm with his right fist as he got to his feet. 'You can't learn to farm with your nose in a book. Now, hurry up and get to the farm. I want you to finish the cassava and yam harvest today.'

Uncle Emenike crossed the courtyard to bid goodbye to the children who could not wait to depart for school, leaving behind the dumbfounded and dejected boy.

*

Babatunde hurried to the boys' hut, took off his clean clothes, folded them carefully and put them away. Then he put on a ragged pair of khaki shorts for the field. He slaved all day picking the cassavas and yams, rivulets of sweat dripping off his body into the soil. As he worked his mind started slowly devising a plan. By late afternoon he'd finished the last row; he placed the huge basket of the produce on his head and began the trip back home with a look of determination on his face.

*If uncle Emenike won't let me go to school, I'll have to find some other way to learn*, he reflected. *I refuse to be a farm labourer for the rest of my days.* Confident that there had to be more to life than picking beans or harvesting yams, he told himself, *I will be a great person despite what's happening to me now.*

*

Once school had started, Babatunde's cousins, Adaobi and Nnamdi, no longer had time to while away their evenings playing games. They had lessons to write and arithmetic to understand. Instead of chattering in their native Igbo, they practised speaking and writing in English, as they were advised by their teachers.

Babatunde rose early and worked even harder in the days that followed, to ensure that his chores were finished by suppertime. The high point of his days was the early evenings, when his cousins sat in the courtyard, their school books spread on the ground, reciting the lessons they had learned at school. He sat beside them, his eyes gleaming with envy and curiosity. That was his classroom, his golden opportunity to learn, and he made the most of it. Although he was a houseboy without the privileges they enjoyed as son and daughter, his cousins loved him and delighted in helping him to learn.

One evening as they conversed in 'the Queen's language', they switched to Igbo when Babatunde joined them.

'*Hei speaky* English!' said Babatunde.

His cousins exchanged amazed glances when they heard a smattering of English emerging from his lips. Even more astonished were they when he recited the opening line of Psalm 23: *The Lord is my shepherd…*

'How do you know English?' Nnamdi could not suppress his curiosity.

'Before I came here, I did Grade One at the church school in my village. I also won the prize of a Bible at my school,' boasted Babatunde.

'How did that happen?' asked Nnamdi.

'Our teacher asked a question about the name "Nigeria" and I answered correctly: "The name Nigeria come from *Englishe* woman, Flora Shaw, in 1897."'

His cousins grinned at each other.

'*Nawa-o!* Our cousin is a brilliant boy,' said Nnamdi, 'I knew about the origin of the name of our country only when I was in Grade 3.'

Babatunde pointed to his chest: 'I will be a great person, one day!'

'How will you be a great person when you are not attending school?' Adaobi challenged him.

'I just feel it in my blood that one day I will be a great person,' Babatunde insisted. 'There has to be more to life than picking beans or harvesting yams.'

The cousins frowned. And after that day they treated him with great respect.

2

Weeks rolled by and soon it was June. Babatunde woke early as usual only to realise that he would not have serious chores as it was on Sunday. So he enjoyed the freedom of just relaxing; as a result, he felt refreshed on Mondays when he again started his work on the farm. His boy cousin, Nnamdi, liked to play soccer on Sunday afternoons; Babatunde looked forward to playing with him and with the children of their neighbours. He welcomed the day of rest as it provided a diversion from daily routine. He was one of the youngest players at age seven.

During the week his cousins sometimes returned home late in the afternoon because of school activities. Babatunde collected firewood and dropped it at the cooking-shed for his aunts and then swept the courtyard. In his spare time he would practise football alone; he learned the basic ball control skills such as kicking and balancing the ball on his feet, on his knees and then up onto his head. He was flattered when Nnamdi told him that he showed promising talent as a soccer player.

As he had spare time in the afternoons due to his hard work in the mornings, he invited other boys of his age as well as older boys to start a football team. Most of the children, whose parents practised African religion, availed themselves on Sundays. They started off playing football in the street, but when their numbers grew to more than fifteen, they moved to a nearby school yard.

*

During the second week of June Babatunde's cousins were busy preparing for their half-yearly examinations. On Saturday evening Babatunde heard his uncle calling to his cousins from his hut where he sat with his two wives. Babatunde had gone to fetch a straw broom that was leaning against the wall of the hut.

'The Great One, source of our fathers,' Babatunde heard his uncle say, 'here are my son and daughter, preparing for examinations. Please give them strength and wisdom so that they can write and pass with high marks.'

Babatunde could picture his uncle prostrating himself before the shrine and then parting with a gift of kola nut or a piece of yam.

A short while later when his uncle came out into the yard he ran into Babatunde who was on his way to the smallest hut which was used as a pantry.

'My brother told me that you are worshipping the Great One whom our forefathers worshipped,' said his uncle in a cheerful voice.

'That's true, sah,' responded Babatunde.

'I can assure you, nephew, you are doing a wise thing by following in our footsteps,' continued his uncle, 'unlike many young people today who are turning against our gods because they have been duped into believing that the god of white people is superior to The Great One whom we worship.'

'Yes, sah,' said Babatunde, nodding.

*

That Sunday afternoon Babatunde's team had just begun their soccer game when they heard the sound of singing coming from the small church adjoining the playing field. The windows were open and through the window opposite the goalposts they could see the back of the preacher's head.

5

The boys continued with their game, but they got distracted when the preacher started his sermon, as he became louder and louder.

'I've an idea,' Babatunde shouted, motioning to the other players to gather round. 'I'm going to kick the ball through that window and hit the preacher on the head! I'll put a stop to all that Christian noise that's disturbing our game.'

'Great idea, go ahead!' they encouraged him. 'I hate these people,' said Babatunde, 'who think that their god is better than our *Amadioha*!'

Stretching out his left arm, Babatunde raised his right shoulder as he dribbled past two defenders; when he got near the goalposts, he kicked the ball high towards the window. The ball hit the wall of the building and bounced back. He kicked again, and the ball hit the window frame and bounced back while the preacher continued with his sermon unperturbed.

'Try one more time, Baba; you can do it!' a teammate egged him on.

'I'll get him this time,' vowed Babatunde, the perspiration showing on his forehead. He kicked the ball again, harder than ever and at closer range. The ball again hit the window frame, but this time it bounced back and hit him on the chest, knocking him to the ground.

A few of the boys tittered.

'Come'n, Baba, stand up!' said one of the boys.

'How can a ball knock you down?' said another. 'What's wrong?'

'Baba, Baba!' shouted another teammate, Acho, running over to kneel beside him. Babatunde lay stretched on his back, the breath knocked out of him, too dazed to realise what had happened.

'Are you all right?' asked Acho, hovering over him.

Babatunde closed his eyes, appearing to have stopped breathing. Very worried, Acho felt the left side of Babatunde's chest. A few teammates gathered around, but most of them retreated to a safe distance, fearful of being implicated in the incident.

Acho pointed to one of the boys. 'Go and call the man of God. Quick! Before Baba dies!'


# 3


Acho raised his head to see a man whom he guessed to be the pastor walking towards them.

'I'm Pastor Ugochukwu. What happened?' asked the man.

'Pastor,' said Acho, gesturing towards Babatunde, 'he has stopped breathing. Please pray that he should not die. If he dies what are we going to tell his parents?'

The pastor muttered something and laid his right hand on Babatunde's head. He continued to pray. Suddenly Babatunde opened his eyes. He looked up to see a stranger standing over him. He observed that the man wore a concerned expression. Acho quickly explained to him what had happened.

Taking charge of the situation, the pastor motioned towards Babatunde. 'Let's take him into the church,' he said, in his strong voice.

Full of anxiety, Babatunde sat up on his buttocks and looked straight into the pastor's eyes. Then he got to his feet, shaking his head. 'Please don't take me into the church!'

At that moment a dozen members of the small congregation came out of the church and headed towards where Babatunde and the pastor were standing. Babatunde felt his sore chest and unbuttoned his shirt; the pastor took a closer look and pointed to a spot which was beginning to swell.

'We are going to pray for you in the name of Jesus,' said Pastor Ugochukwu, 'and ask God to heal you completely.'

*I wonder if he knows I was trying to hit him with the soccer ball*, thought Babatunde. *If he knew that, surely he wouldn't be praying for me to get well!*

The pastor put his hand on Babatunde's chest and prayed in a booming voice, while members of the congregation whispered their own prayers.

The pastor's wife put her hand on Babatunde's shoulder and said to the pastor. 'Let's take him to the vestry and give him something to eat.'

Babatunde shook his head. 'No, I'm not going in there!'

The pastor's wife pointed at one of the woman: 'Go and bring him a glass of orange juice.'

Pastor Ugochukwu smiled at Babatunde. 'Young man, what's your name?'

'Babatunde.'

'Okay Babatunde, tell us what happened when you fainted.'

'I heard very sweet music. I heard the words: "Hallelujah! Hallelujah!" I sat on green-green grass, and there were many beautiful flowers and trees full of fruits. Suddenly I saw a man dressed all in white; he wore something like an *agbada*…it was shining…'

'So he wore shining robes?'

'Yes, and he had something shining on his head.'

'It's called a crown. That's interesting; what did he say to you?' asked the pastor as

Babatunde paused to take the glass of juice.

'He didn't say anything. He just smiled at me and opened his arms.'

'He is King of Kings. Don't you want to accept him?'

Babatunde shook his head. 'No, no pastor!!'

With bulging eyes, Babatunde turned around, flexed his shoulders, brushed off the hands that tried to restrain him and walked quickly away; suddenly he started running home without looking back. Acho ran after him followed by the teammates. Pastor Ugochukwu stepped forward, gesticulating.

'Babatunde! Babatunde! Stop!' shouted the pastor.

Babatunde and the teammates continued to run.

The pastor hurried after the running boys. His wife tried to overtake him, striding briskly at his heels. As he broke into a run, she leapt forward too, managing to grab the pastor by his arm.

'No, Peter,' she said, 'you can't do that!'

The man of God broke loose from his wife. 'No,' he said, 'I must catch that lost sheep and take it out of the mouth of the hyena! Babatunde! Babatunde! I say stop!' he shouted as he ran. 'Listen, you are running in the wrong direction! Towards hell! Please return to the safe arms of Jesus, the great shepherd. Jesus is the only way, the truth and the life, can you hear me?'

Exhausted finally, the man of the cloth stopped running. He stood with arms akimbo, breathing hard, and looked on until the boys disappeared into a homestead about half a kilometre away.

*

When Babatunde got home, the teammates told his uncle everything that had happened.

His uncle shook his head, grinning. 'These church people can bewitch; how can football cause you to fall and result in you fainting?'

The teammates laughed aloud, very amused. After the teammates had gone, Babatunde's youngest aunt, Amara, gave him cooked yam, beans and pepper stew and he ate hungrily.

'Uncle, the swelling is getting smaller,' he said, feeling his chest.

'The god of our forefathers has healed you,' responded his uncle. 'He has protected you against the witches of the white people's god.'

*

One afternoon during the middle of November, Babatunde was busy chopping firewood when he saw his father enter the compound and dismount his bicycle. Throwing down his axe, Babatunde rushed to greet him. The news that Babatunde had nearly died had reached his father's ears.

Babatunde led his father to the hut where his uncle sat, drinking fermented palm wine. The two elders talked about many issues, starting with Babatunde's encounter with the church people. Babatunde's aunts and cousins also went to the hut to greet his father who was later given food. His appetite whetted by palm wine, he soon finished the mound that was in front of him.

Babatunde longed to spend a private moment with his father, intending to tell him that his uncle had reneged on his promise to send him to school. He took a broom and swept behind the hut where his father and his uncle sat chatting within his earshot.

'Nike,' Babatunde heard his father addressing his uncle in a serious tone, trying very hard not show that he was getting drunk, 'how can you do this to my son, treating him like a servant, not even giving him a moment to peep into the books?'

He heard uncle Emenike responding with loud laughter as if his father had joked.

'Listen Elleh,'—that was how his uncle addressed his father—'does work kill? Does school run away? A year is nothing! You and me worked for two years for our uncles and have we lost our arms?'

Babatunde could picture his drunk father's eyes losing the argument to the eyes of his persuasive uncle.

'I want to give him full training in farm work,' continued his uncle. 'My aim is to develop a work ethic that will help the boy when he's grown up. I want him to be so excellent that when we have all gone to the gods, he should know how to kill the hyena called hunger.'

Babatunde heard his father's lips slurping after taking another swig of palm wine.

'It's all right, Nike,' said his father, belching, 'the boy will go to school next year. My sister will help with the school fees.'

Babatunde knew that his father was referring to aunt Chimamanda, a nursing sister who stayed with her soldier husband in Kano in the north of Nigeria.

## 4

During the last week of November Babatunde's cousins wrote their final examinations. Whenever they wrote a paper, they passed it on to Babatunde in the evening.

One day while the children were at school, uncle Emenike came home from the market with a large bundle which he carried into his hut. Babatunde was sweeping the courtyard outside when he heard his uncle calling him. He went over to the door of his uncle's *obi* and looked in to see piles of new clothes for his cousins stacked on the bench.

It was the month of the Ekpe festival, the 'Christmas' of the tribespeople, the time of ceremonial dancing, exchanging of gifts, and making offerings of goats, chickens and kola nuts to Amadioha for good luck. Babatunde's cousins looked forward to the day, for their father always bought them new clothes at that time of year.

'Look, Baba,' his uncle said, holding up a simple white cotton undershirt from the top of the pile, 'I bought you this shirt at the market today. If you do your work well, I will give it to you for Christmas.'

'Yes, *sah – tank sah*,' Babatunde stammered, a bit bewildered. 'I'll do my best, sah.'

Babatunde had never received a Christmas gift before, so he did not know what to say.

He went back to his sweeping and household chores, trying harder than before to please his master. He knew that if it appeared that he shirked his duties, he might be denied the privilege of studying with his cousins after supper – a privilege more precious to him than any new shirt.

*

At last the long-awaited festival day dawned, and Babatunde heard his cousins squealing with delight as they received their new clothes.

'Baba, look,' Nnamdi shouted, running over to where Babatunde was chopping firewood to fuel the fire under the cooking pots tended by his aunts.

'See my new suit!' He strutted back and forth to show off his bright-blue jacket and trousers and chequered shirt. 'I even got new shoes,' he boasted, pulling up his trousers leg to show Babatunde the shiny leather and his bright red socks.

'That's very nice,' said Babatunde with a grin. 'You really look smart!'

Babatunde stacked the wood in a pile, wrapped a cord around it and carried it to the cooking-shed in the courtyard. The place bustled with activity as some women cooked rice, yams and pepper stew with beef and the children chatted and sang, eagerly waiting for the guests who were expected to arrive at any minute. Other women were kneading portions of ugba to thicken palm oil. As Babatunde put down the load of wood, he glanced at cast iron cooking tripods simmering with rice, stews and soups and as a result got hungry and swallowed saliva. He picked up an empty calabash and had started out of the compound to fetch water when he almost bumped into uncle Emenike.

'Good morning, sah,' he greeted in a low tone.

'Baba,' his uncle growled, 'I was just out looking over the yam plots yesterday. Lots of weeds growing there – I expected that weeding to be finished by now. What's the matter with you?'

Babatunde drew back as if he had been struck. 'I'm sorry, sah,' he replied. '*Dee*, please let me explain: it's because of the guests coming for the festival – the women gave me extra work to do here in the compound. But I'll begin work on the weeding tomorrow...'

'Well, *ogu-akwukwo* I think you've just been spending too much time with the books and neglecting work,' his uncle complained. 'Listen, I've decided not to give you that new shirt after all.' Without waiting for a response, his uncle strode across the courtyard and began greeting the guests.

Babatunde stood speechless, a sick feeling in the pit of his stomach. Painful thoughts turned in his mind.

*It's very clear that I'll never be able to please uncle Emenike*, he thought with bitterness. *But one day when I'm old enough, I'll get a job and buy a whole suit for myself. Maybe I'll even buy a new suit for uncle Emenike. Maybe then he will be pleased with me.*

With slower steps he continued his trek to the river to fetch water, still deep in thought. He dipped the calabash into the river to fill it, balanced it on his head and trudged back to the compound, his bare feet pounding the worn dirt path.

Looking at his own ragged clothes and remembering his cousins' new clothes and shoes, he wondered what it felt like to be able to dress like that. He had never worn a pair of shoes in his life; the few old clothes he owned were things his mother had sent him. He looked forward to getting a brand-new shirt. But he agonised more over his uncle's disapproving manner than over the fact that he would not get the shirt.

Back at the compound the festivities continued, with drums, children shouting and dancing, and palm wine flowing. His uncle's action dissipated his joy for the rest of the day. When the food was served, he took a bowl of rice and pepper stew and retreated to a quiet place away from the courtyard to eat in solitude.

He felt a stab of homesickness for his mother and the familiar Okoronkwo compound, but he refused to indulge in the futility of crying over it. Instead, he finished his meal then walked to the yam plots and resumed the endless task of pulling out the weeds. As he worked, he recited the addition and subtraction tables which he had learned with his cousins the week before: Two plus two is four! Four minus two is two! Three times two is six! Six minus three is three!

*

Children being children, the division brought by the Ekpe festival was forgotten by the following day. Life returned to normal between Babatunde and his cousins. They related to him as if their father's discriminatory treatment was a necessary thing that came and went. Free from the pressure of schoolwork, Babatunde and his cousins spent more time playing as they liked in the early evenings. Babatunde still saved a moment or two to read, however. He continued to wake early to start with chores such as chopping firewood and sweeping the courtyard. After washing his face and armpits he would take a book, sit in the sun and read. His cousins told him how much they missed their grandmother, Nwaboudu, who usually visited them once a year between Christmas and New Year. She was the mother of their father's senior wife, aunt Ifeka. Excited, they told Babatunde how they looked forward to the old lady's folktales.

'Last year she told us the tale of the Anwu [the sun] and Ikuku [the wind],' said Adaobi. 'I wonder what she's going to tell us this year?'

'Anwu and Ikuku ?' inquired a curious Babatunde.

'Can I tell Baba the story?' asked Nnamdi.

'No, let me tell him,' insisted Adaobi. 'I'm the one who came up with the idea.'

Adaobi turned to Babatunde: 'Once upon a time Anwu and Ikuku saw a man wearing an overcoat passing by. "Anwu, I can easily take away the man's overcoat," Ikuku boasted to Anwu, "I'm stronger than you; you are just a weakling! You can't..." Anwu interrupted Ikuku with laughter. "What are you laughing at?" asked Ikuku, "At your own weakness?" "No, at your stupidity," replied Anwu. "Listen, Ikuku, let's settle the argument once and for all! You go first! Take away the man's overcoat, within an eye's wink!"

'Without delay Ikuku descended on the man in full force, causing him to button up his overcoat and tighten the belt. The man also leaned against a tree trunk. Unable to remove the man's overcoat, Ikuku sighed, disappointed and shamefaced. "Now it's my turn," said Anwu; he quickly unleashed all the spears of heat upon the man, who soon took off his overcoat.'

Thrilled, Babatunde applauded.

# 5

Around the middle of December Uncle Emenike reminded the young trainee that it was time to go to the bush for their hunting expedition. To the book-hungry boy this was not good news. But he knew that to protest was futile; he had no-one to share his frustration with. So he quietly went about gathering the provisions they needed for the week-long excursion.

By early afternoon everything was ready, and the two set off. They trekked in single file, Babatunde a few steps behind his uncle. Babatunde carried the sleeping mats, a cooking pot, and a bundle of food balanced on his head. Soon the familiar sounds of the village were left behind them. The sounds of chattering monkeys and chirping birds echoed in the trees overhead, growing louder as they trudged deeper into the bush.

They arrived late at a spot where there were no trees and the grass was very short; there uncle Emenike had built a small mud hut. That became their home for a week; it would have been two weeks had grandmother Nwaboudu not indicated that she would visit her daughter and son-in-law before Christmas. As a result Babatunde missed the books for only a week.

Babatunde immediately set about making a broom of twigs to sweep out the hut. Later he spread their sleeping mats on the ground inside. He also went to cut a supply of firewood and hauled water from a nearby stream. He gathered the kola nuts that fell from the trees not far from the hut; these were their staple food while they worked in the bush in the days ahead.

That evening Uncle Emenike set a few traps not far from the camp, and he showed his nephew how it was done. Babatunde listened raptly as his uncle patiently guided him, repeatedly saying, *No be so. Na so.*

For supper they roasted yams over the open fire. Exhausted, Babatunde spread out his sleeping mat, his mind wandering to his cousins. *I wonder what game they are playing tonight*, he mused. In the distance he heard the laughing cry of the hyena and the occasional snarl of a wild cat as he gradually fell asleep.

It seemed he had barely closed his eyes when he heard his uncle calling, 'Wake up Baba, sleep doesn't buy a cow!'

*

As the sky began to lighten in the east, Uncle Emenike was ready for an early start for setting the traps.

Springing to his feet, Babatunde stuffed some kola nuts into the pockets of his ragged shorts and joined his uncle outside to begin the day's work. Observing with concentration everything the older man did, he learned the routine of setting and unloading the traps. He also learned how to skin the small game they caught and smoke the meat.

He realised that although he was far from his books, going out with his uncle on a hunting trip afforded him an opportunity to learn a new skill. Every morning a worker from home came to collect the skins and meat to take them to the market. At night uncle and nephew sat by the fire talking and eating the food Babatunde had prepared – usually a roasted rabbit or other small game with boiled yams. With no-one else to talk to, the older man seemed willing to treat his nephew more like a son. For the first time Babatunde saw his uncle's teeth as he laughed. His uncle began to praise him, something he was stingy with, and he also promised to give him the white shirt.

During their last night there, Babatunde was asleep when he was woken by his uncle. He lay on his back looking up at his uncle who stared down at him.

'Baba, what's happening? Were you dreaming?'

Babatunde sat up sleepily and yawned. 'I don't know, uncle.'

'You were dreaming. I heard you saying, "Uncle, I want to be a great person."'

Babatunde shrugged.

'You also said, "There has to be more to life than picking beans or harvesting yams,"' his uncle continued. 'Why do you say such things? Don't you appreciate that I'm teaching you work?'

'I'm sorry uncle.'

*

The short trapping season ended. The following day at midday Babatunde was delighted to return to the compound with his uncle.

When they reached home, he found that *Mama-Nnukwu* Nwaboudu had arrived. His cousins treated him like a hero and showered him with thanks and praise for the meat he and their father had provided. They paid him compliments about the muscles he'd developed in his arms and shoulders. Aunt Ifeka walked past them as they chatted, chewing the rib of a rabbit.

'I'm telling you, Baba,' said aunt Ifeka, 'your life will never be the same after this because you'll never starve. Your house will never be without meat. You've become an accomplished hunter!'

Babatunde received the unexpected compliment with a cheerful smile. When he asked for the books his cousins told him that there would be no time for books as they were about to listen to Mama-Nnukwu Nwaboudu's folktale.

The children gobbled up their food and a few minutes later went to sit in half a circle in aunt Ifeka's hut, all eyes fixed on their Mama-Nnukwu. She smiled, scanning them with her eyes.

'Remember, my children's children,' said Mama-Nnukwu Nwaboudu, 'after telling you this tale you shouldn't share it with anyone during the day. Fables are told only at night. If you tell them to anyone during the day, you will surely grow little horns.'

The children exchanged glances and burst out laughing. That was what the raconteur was looking for: to talk to a relaxed audience.

'Now listen, my children's children,' their granny continued, speaking in a charming old woman's tone. 'Long, long ago, deep in the forest of Nugwuchukwu, before the white men came to this land, there lived a lion who was a king, King Tau-ya-mariri. He had a large kingdom of Tau-ya-rora filled with all kinds of animals.'

'*Sala!*' the children responded in unison.

'One day when he awoke he convened a special meeting which was attended by all animals in his kingdom. When he cleared his throat, all animals knelt before the throne shouting, 'Hail the great King Tau-ya-mariri- the beast above all beasts!'

'*Sala!*' the children responded in unison.

'And the king's praise singer raised his spear and shield and chanted praises, "The Great Iroko Tree of our time, the mighty one who silences all beasts, the one whose bare paws and claws tear apart all who defy your throne, oh Priceless Gift of Tau-ya-rora kingdom!" And all animals cheered and applauded.'

'*Sala!*'

'The king then lifted up his spear, 'I King Tau-ya-mariri today decree that all the young animals shall be trained in warfare in the mountains, and all the old animals shall provide food during that military training. The decree of the king is the voice of the gods!'

'The word of the king is greater than us!' the animals roared in approval.

'After a year the King said to the young animals, "I King Tau-ya-mariri today decree that all the old animals should be killed because they do not work but they eat the grass that you the younger animals should be eating. The decree of the king is the voice of the gods!"'

'*Sala!*

'"The word of the king is greater than us!" the young animals roared.

'As a result, all the old animals were killed, except Kalulu the hare who saved himself by hiding in a hollow tree.'

'*Sala!*

'A few weeks later King Tau-ya-mariri fell asleep with his mouth wide open. A snake, which had travelled a long way and was very tired, thought that the lion's mouth was the narrow opening of a cave. It decided to rest in there. That awoke the king who told the snake to come out, but it refused. As the lion king grimaced in great pain, he asked the other animals to come and help him, but they replied, "Oh King Tau-ya-mariri, we are all young and do not know what to do; all the old ones who could have helped you are dead, for you instructed us to kill them."'

'*Sala!*

'Kalulu's son came to the king and said: "Oh the great and mighty King Tau-ya-mariri, if one of the old animals still remains alive and is able to help you, what will you do for him?" The king replied: "I will allow him to live and I will give him half of my large kingdom."'

'*Sala!*

'Kalulu's son told his father what the lion king said to him. Kalulu went into the forest where he caught a mouse. He then went to the king and asked him to repeat his promise. After the king had repeated the promise Kalulu told him to go to sleep and keep his mouth wide open.'

'*Sala!*

'When the king was asleep Kalulu put the mouse down on the ground next to his mouth. From inside the lion's belly the snake smelt the mouse; so the snake moved up the lion's throat. When he saw the mouse he came out of the lion's mouth to catch it. At that moment the lion woke up, and he was relieved of pain. Thrilled to regain his health, the king never hesitated to fulfil his promise: he gave Kalulu half of his kingdom. He never killed old animals again.'

The next evening Mama-Nnukwu Nwaboudu told the children how to play the game of 'The Hyena and the Children'.

## 6

One morning, two days before Christmas, while digging in the yam plot not far from the compound, Babatunde looked up to see two figures on bicycles approaching.

'That's my father and Kene, my older brother!' he exclaimed, dropping his hoe. Reaching the compound just as the visitors dismounted from their bicycles he knelt and touched the ground with one knee.

'Greetings, father,' he said, baring his teeth with great joy, 'you are welcome here!'

Just then uncle Emenike came striding across the courtyard to greet his brother and his nephew.

'You are welcome here, Elechi!' said uncle Emenike.

The two men embraced. His father turned towards Babatunde, taking note of how his growing boy was developing broader shoulders and work-hardened muscles.

'You are looking well, son,' he said with a smile. 'Life at my brother's farm has been good for you.'

Babatunde just nodded and grinned, too flattered by his father's words to know what to say. After the traditional greetings and pleasantries were exchanged, the two men sat down to talk and ate kola nuts. Babatunde and his cousins retreated to a discreet distance to play, but Babatunde managed to overhear his father saying the purpose of their visit was to take him home with them. His heart hammered in his chest at the prospect. He was about to see his mother again!

Out of a sense of duty Babatunde returned to his work in the yam plot but for some reason the digging job seemed easier than before.

That evening at supper it was confirmed: Babatunde would leave the next day with his father and elder brother. His cousins moaned when they heard the news. After the meal he gathered his meagre belongings for the journey home. His elder brother shared the sleeping mat with him and Babatunde bombarded him with questions about his mother, his siblings and the village. He found it hard to sleep with so many questions whirling through his head.

'Let's get going before the sun climbs to the top of the heavens,' said Babatunde's father early in the morning.

The two boys and their father set out on the four-hour journey home. Babatunde sat on the rear fender of the bicycle pedalled by his elder brother, his cousins waving goodbyes to him until he was out of sight. He had a good laugh as he waved back. Babatunde's extra load this time comprised a few books, an Oxford Learner's Dictionary, a white shirt, a school shirt, a pair of shorts, some yams, a few animal skins and dried meat. Babatunde was glad that peace between him and his uncle was now restored and that the past was history.

Bumping over the rough road under a boiling sun was not a pleasant excursion. But for Babatunde it was the trip of a lifetime. He was going home!

Just when he thought he was too weary to continue, his brother turned his head and said: 'We are almost there!'

A short while later they were approaching a small group of mud houses of Ijoto village. Babatunde saw his mother running towards them. He slid off the back of the bicycle even before it had stopped and ran to meet her.

'Baba! Baba!' his mother called with shrill excitement, stretching out her arms towards him as he ran into her embrace. She hugged him close for a few moments then held him at arm's length to appraise her growing son fully.

'How you have grown!' she exclaimed, her eyes brimming with tears.

'It's good to be home, mother,' Babatunde said, his voice choking with emotion. 'I have dreamed of this day for a long time.'

The Okoronkwos went to bed very late as they wanted to spend quality time with the family member they had missed for months. They listened to his many stories about his experiences at his uncle's place. They cherished bitter-sweet feelings when he told them about how his cousins had shared their books with him in the evenings. The highlight of the night was Mama-Nnukwu Nwaboudu's folktale about the lion king.

The following afternoon, the energetic Babatunde taught the children of the next-door neighbours the game, 'The Hyena and the Children'. He played the role of the children's mother, and Nnesinachi, his five-year-old female cousin who was the daughter of aunt Chimamanda, was the hyena lurking in the valley.

'My children, my children come home!' shouted Babatunde.

'We are afraid!' the children shouted back.

'Afraid of what?'

'The hyena!'

'The hyena has gone to nurse her children.'

The cautious children then crossed 'the valley' where 'the hyena' pounced on them and mauled them one by one, an action that caused them to shriek with laughter.

# PART TWO

## 7

Babatunde was so excited to be doing Class 2 that he woke up early to revise his homework before he walked to school. He was so happy to be a learner again that he sang the whole way to and from school. When questions were asked in class, he was always the first to raise his hand, ready to offer an answer. After the end of the class period he often remained to ask the teacher the meaning of an English word or a Geography or History item. The teachers noted that his vocabulary was better than that of other Class 2 pupils. At his class teacher's recommendation he was promoted to Class 3 at the end of the first quarter.

*

Months later Babatunde heard from his playmate and classmate, Chinua, that his uncle had been killed in the north of Nigeria. Arriving back at his home he greeted his mother and walked to the thatched-roofed hut where he removed his school uniform of white shirt and grey shorts. Bare to the waist, he put on his pair of khaki shorts – better quality than the threadbare ones he used to wear at his uncle's farm—and went with well-honed knife to peel the casavas next to his mother who was pounding *yam*.

'Mother, why are our people being killed in the north of the country?' he asked.

'It's true my son,' responded his mother. 'I don't know the whole truth, but it seems it's a matter of jealousy.'

'Are those soldiers from the north jealous of the Igbos?'

'Yes. Please wait for your father to tell you the whole story.'

Babatunde's father arrived before dinner. After they'd eaten Babatunde went to his father's *obi* and asked the question which his mother could not answer in detail.

'What you are asking about is in the news,' said his father. He was oiling his bicycle. 'But the government is not telling the truth.'

'What is the truth, father?'

'Perhaps you are too young to understand. Anyway, I'll try to explain to you.'

Babatunde sat on a sisal stool next to him, his arms folded, leaning towards his father as he spoke.

'We Nigerians were ruled by white people led by the Queen over the seas. In 1960, they gave us freedom to rule ourselves. But things did not go very well. The first president was a great man from our tribe, Nnamdi Azikiwe. In 1966 high-ranking soldiers from the Hausa tribe tried to take power from our president, but the leaders of the soldiers from our tribe crushed that military effort. A general from our tribe and high soldiers from our tribe took over the government. Months later, the Hausa military leaders grabbed power and killed the military leader together with some of the top soldiers. A new military ruler, called Yakubu Gowon, became the president, and he gave orders that the Igbos should be killed, and many were murdered.'

Babatunde kept quiet, thinking about Chinua's uncle.

'Mama told me that the Hausas are jealous of the Igbos. Why, father?'

'It's true, my son. When the white people came to this country, they built their offices and homes among the Igbos; so our people became the first people in this country to receive education from the white people. The whites brought the church and the Bible which were well received by our people, who converted to Christianity. The white people built schools and hospitals, and our people became the most educated among the Nigerians.

'So our people became teachers, nurses, doctors, traders and other professions. Some of these people went to stay in the north. Because the soldiers from the north are jealous of the Igbos, they are still killing our people; that's why our people are coming back to Iboland.' His father polished the spokes of the bicycle wheels. 'If things don't change, there's going to be a big, big war in the country.'

There was a moment of silence. Babatunde stood up, preparing to walk out of his father's hut.

'Perhaps people from your generation can change the way things are going in this country,' his father said.

*

Babatunde proceeded to Class 4 in 1967. He shared what his father had told him with his peers, who told him how their relatives were killed or maimed. At school Babatunde and other pupils heard the teachers talking about the possibility of war.

It was the first Friday of April. During the school break Babatunde and his fellow pupils saw army trucks entering the gates. Babatunde was playing with Chinua; he motioned towards the army vehicles. 'The soldiers! The soldiers!' he shouted. 'My father says there's going to be a war in this country!'

The principal came out of his office and watched as three trucks stopped in front of the building. He was not surprised to see the military visiting his school; he was part of the 'enlightened committees' comprising the secretaries of county councils, trade union leaders, student bodies and headmasters of primary and secondary institutions.

The pupils were also not surprised to see the army trucks, for they'd received information from the radio for weeks that 'war was coming' to their region and that the military leader and the soldiers were ready to defend the region.

The name of the military governor, Ojukwu, was on the lips of the young and the old, who lionised him. The youth often cheered when they saw his face in newspapers and magazines. There was talk in the streets, the homesteads, the churches and the markets that Ojukwu was the one chosen by the gods, and God, to be a liberator of the people of the eastern region.

At 13h00 when the pupils were about to go home, the principal instructed all the boys from age ten upwards to go to the school hall.

'Boys,' said the principal, 'we all know that war might come to our region. So tomorrow morning the army trucks will collect you in front of the school yard, and take you to the university, where Lt-Col Ojukwu is going to address the nation. I hope your parents will not object; they should know that anyone who does not support the new order will face the grim possibility of being branded a *sabo*.

*

The previous week had been eventful among the citizens of the region. It was disclosed in the newspapers and on radio that Lt-Col Ojukwu had tried to negotiate a peaceful secession of the eastern region without success at a meeting held in Accra.

Ojukwu told the 'new nation' over the radio: '*My officers and I have decided that in view of a history of dishonesty, corruption and the systematic killings of our people in the north, with the approval of the military ruler, we have no choice but to decentralise, or to put it bluntly, to secede.*'

As the truck slowed down as it approached the university, Baba saw a wide arch towering over them, bearing the words, *University of Nigeria Nsukka* in black, cut-out metal. The gates underneath the arch were flung open and manned by soldiers waving the trucks and cars through. He admired the ten young soldiers, all wearing khaki uniforms, their boots shining and a half of a yellow sun sewn on their sleeves.

Babatunde nudged Chinua standing next to him. 'I wish I was one of the soldiers.'

Chinua grinned and chuckled: 'Me too!'

The trucks proceeded to the sports stadium. Babatunde and his peers disembarked from the trucks, as students from the tertiary institutions arrived in buses, singing and stomping their feet, and raising their fists. The younger boys hummed along, following the older boys into the stadium.

A military officer who was the programme director stood up and introduced Major Ignatius Okpara to speak to the 'cubs and the young lions' of the eastern region.

'While waiting for His Excellency, the new head of the Eastern Region of Nigeria, I want to ask one of the senior students from the University of Nsukka to welcome you.'

A well-built student leader hastened to the microphone amid deafening applause.

'We Igbos have shed tears,' said the student, 'and rivers of our region are overflowing with the salt of our eyes. The waters of our rivers are turning red with the blood of our fathers, mothers, brothers, uncles and aunts. Now is the time to stop cringing in fear and fight back!

'The motto of our proud university is: "To restore the dignity of man". The question is: "Do we the Igbos have dignity at the moment?" No! The boot of Gowon has shattered it. So we must stand up and fight to regain our national dignity!' Loud applause broke out. We...'

Another loud round of applause interrupted him.

'...We are weighed down with a load as heavy as a mountain and our hands and feet are shackled with iron. Now is the time to shatter the chains. Now is the time to shake the stones off our backs. The time to wipe off tears and look into Gowon's eyes and shout: "Enough is enough!"'

The speaker gestured towards his listeners.

'Enough is enough!' responded the audience.

'Now is the time to resist Gowon and the Nigerian vandals in defence of our motherland!'

He grabbed an imaginary rifle and started 'shooting' around. The ecstatic audience rose to their feet and simulated soldiers shooting. At that juncture the sound of an automatic rifle interrupted the cheering.

Suddenly applause and shrill cheers filled the place as a green army jeep entered the stadium.

# 8

A bearded man standing in the cruising jeep, sandwiched by two gun-wielding soldiers, waved at the crowd and applause resumed. Everybody knew who the charismatic bearded man was: His Excellency, Lt-Col Ojukwu! The soldiers shot into the air and a frenzied cheering followed and was sustained until Ojukwu and the soldiers had taken their place on the make-shift stage.

'I greet you, young lions and patriotic people of this region.' Ojukwu paused, stroking his beard for a moment as he scanned his audience. Babatunde held his breath, his eyes focused on the man he admired with all his heart. He was awestruck by the leader wearing a belted army uniform, his shoulders wide, his eyes sharp, everything about him sparkling.

'You all know what's happening in the country,' Ojukwu continued after drinking from a glass of water. 'People all over the region are making a statement with their feet; they are lifting up their arms. They are raising their voices, saying, "Enough is enough!"'

'A full-scale war is coming closer and closer, and demonstrations are erupting everywhere in the region. The people of the region are a solid, united, angry block; the killings of our people have worked up the citizens of this region to a dangerously high state of excitement. This does not exclude the illiterate masses; everyone is affected. Call it mass hysteria. Everywhere in Iboland people are restless, praying for something to happen, anything to happen. But you young people can make things happen and change history!'

Babatunde recalled what his father had said to him a few days ago: *Perhaps people from your generation can change the way things are going in this country.*

'Young people, you must target foreign newspapers that are against secession. Take demonstrations to their embassies – embassies such as those of Britain, the US and the Soviet Union. I have praise for Nsukka University students; they've written to me, urging me to go ahead and not look back. They said they are prepared to trade their books for rifles and "fight to the last man". And patriotic teachers at the primary schools are eager to teach their students "the real history" of why the secession is absolutely unavoidable!'

The older students led applause.

'So we the soldiers, your protectors, came here to meet you today. This type of thing often happens in some countries. The citizens are mistreated and their toes are trampled upon because they belong to a certain tribe, or religion. When India became independent from Britain, the Moslems decided that it was going to be tragic if they were to be ruled by the Hindu majority. So they fought for their own state of Pakistan, and they won. There are many examples all over the world. When those in government become power-drunk and abuse power and become unjust and corrupt, then is time for those who are a target to stand up and say: "We've had enough!"'

Again the students from the tertiary institutions led applause which was augmented by thousands of other hands.

'The lives of the Igbos and other Easterners are no longer guaranteed inside Nigeria, especially in the Islamic North,' Ojukwu continued. 'In view of what has been happening over many months, when our tribes-people were being killed like rats, we have decided to draw a line; thus far and no further! All right-thinking Igbos and other Easterners including the leading intellectuals, writers, engineers, teachers and nurses are behind us, saying we are doing the right thing; that if we don't take this step, we have chosen blatant oppression, for which we shall be judged with gnashing teeth by generations to come.

'As we fight to reclaim our dignity, the Federal soldiers are not going to fold their arms. *Mba!* They are going to march with tanks to our new republic. Like other countries in other parts of the world which broke away and became sovereign states, we shall fight until we win the war. This is the risk we have to take. So this is what we are asking from any patriotic, right-thinking Igbos and other Easterners: be part of the solution so that years later you will be able to beat your chests as you tell your children, and your children's children, how you've sacrificed your sweat and blood, to establish a new state that will soon be named.

'As I'm speaking, our recruitment centres are swarming with thousands of soldiers and training camps are established all over the eastern region. A lot of your schools have been ear-marked as training camps. This means that principals who are *sabo*s will find their offices occupied by men in uniform. The soldiers we are recruiting will not be enough. That's why we are here today, to recruit you to increase the military manpower.

'At the last meeting of officers, we agreed to put 100 000 soldiers at the war-front at a moment's notice. Just before I came here this morning, I received information that the military leader of Nigeria has issued an instruction to seal off the eastern region by land, sea and air. Now is the time for us, for all of you, to defend the land against the invading Nigerian vultures!'

The audience applauded with gusto.

Again Ojukwu scanned his audience, and the soldiers standing behind him looked around the stadium as if searching for any intruding *sabo*.

'Before I leave this place I want to ask you this question: What shall we do? Shall we keep silent and let them force us back into Nigeria?'

'No!' the audience chanted.

'Shall we ignore thousands of our brothers and sisters killed like cockroaches in the North?'

'No!' roared the audience.

'Believe me, the Nigerians are certainly not going to fold their arms. *Mba*! And if they are going to declare war, I want to tell you now; it's going to be a long, messy war. Are you prepared?'

'Yes!' shouted the university students and the rest of the audience.

Ojukwu took a deep breath. 'Now, in view of what I've just stated, I came here today to make this important announcement to you and the nation in this part of Nigeria.'

He paused, and raised his hands: 'I, Lieutenant-Colonel Chukuemeka Odumegwu Ojukwu, Military Governor of Eastern Nigeria, by virtue of my authority and pursuant to the principles recited above, do hereby solemnly proclaim that the territory and region known as Eastern Nigeria, together with the continental shelf and territorial waters, shall henceforth be an independent sovereign state of the name and title of "The Republic of Biafra!"'

The audience applauded, whistled and chanted.

Ojukwu lit a cigarette, puffed at it and threw it on the lawn; it smouldered for a while before he quashed it underneath his gleaming black boot.

'Even the grass is going to...' he waved his right fist, '...fight for Biafra!'

'Yes!' The audience became ecstatic.

There was further applause and cheering while the soldiers brandished their rifles and shot into the air. Ojukwu saluted and strode towards the jeep.

As the journalists scrambled after Ojukwu, proffering tape recorders, the students stood up and marched around the stadium chanting, *Ojukwu nye anyi egbe ka anyi nuo agba!*

<br>

## 9

When Babatunde arrived home, he found his father standing in front of his obi. They heard the sound of a drumbeat: *Gom-gom-gom!* In a moment the chief's drum-beater appeared.

'A village meeting will be held tomorrow morning at the chief's homestead at 07h00,' announced the drum-beater.

*Gom-gom-gom!*

'Please bring or send boy-children from the age of ten years,' he continued. 'Boy-soldiers are needed to support the army.'

*Gom-gom-gom!*

Son and father saw the drum-beater disappearing.

'My boy,' said Babatunde's father after supper, 'like any father I love you and I want you to go to school and be educated more than I was. But because of what's happening in our country today, I have no choice but to let you go and become one of the boy-soldiers.'

Babatunde's mother spent the whole evening wiping away tears until she went to bed.

'I haven't seen enough of my son,' said Babatunde's mother. 'Baba stayed for some time at his uncle's farm; he came back and I spent the past year with him. Now he's going to war…'

'Baba's mother,' said Babatunde's father, 'if you cry, you are filling the boy's mind with discouragement. If there's one thing that Baba needs now, it's the assurance that what he's about to do is of national interest and that we know he's going to return a better person.'

*

The following morning at 06h00 Babatunde stood in front of his homestead, waiting for an army truck to collect him. His mother, with tearful eyes, gave him a tight embrace as she saw the truck approaching.

'May the gods of our clan protect you until you return, Baba,' she said, patting his shoulder. She pressed his cheeks with her palms and kissed him.

As Babatunde looked deep into his mother's eyes, his own eyes became misty and he began to cry. His father loosened his son's hands and lifted up his head before away from him.

'*Nna m o! Nna m o!*' said Babatunde as he looked and waved at his father, overcome by emotion.

'No Baba, you can't cry,' he said, 'you are now a soldier; so you must show your mother that you are going to survive.' He sighed. 'Listen boy, the gods of our clan are going to protect you. Do you hear?

'Yes, father.'

Babatunde put on a brave face and nodded. Although his eyes stayed dry, inside he was sobbing, affected by his mother's tears.

Babatunde turned around and began walking, forcing himself to hold back his tears, not to look back and forcing himself to resist the temptation to retreat back to his mother's arms.

Babatunde later joined other boys at the chief's homestead; he was one of over a hundred boys sitting on logs in front of the palace. Over a hundred village men also attended the meeting. Before the meeting started one of the courtiers counted the boys and handed a piece of paper to Chief Emeka, who was standing ready to speak.

'Thank you my people, for heeding my voice.' The chief adjusted his spectacles, smiling. 'A wise man from our tribe says, "When the men hear the voice of the king, they hasten to build a pen around it." We are living in a country during times which our ancestors haven't experienced; our fathers faced challenges that we don't know. It doesn't help to wish we were our fathers; we must thank God and the gods that we are living during these times. We can't drag our legs and let our hands stay idle when His Excellency speaks. *Mba*, we can't shirk our duty. Our leader was chosen by God and the gods. So we…'

Loud applause interrupted him.

'I am appreciating how…'

His attention was deflected; he was looking in the direction of the boys who were playing beside the homestead.

The chief grinned. 'They are playing a war game. They never cease to fascinate me. Let's wait for a moment and watch.'

Armed with mock guns made of bamboo, twelve boys of about eight or nine years old wore banana leaves on their heads. The longest automatic rifle belonged to the commander of the Biafran side, a tall boy with a stern, no-nonsense face.

'Advance!' the commander shouted.

The boys crept forward.

'Fire!'

'*Ra-tha-tha-tha-tha! Boom! Boom! Ra-tha-tha-tha-tha!*' the commander bellowed.

The rifles of boys on the Biafran side coughed fire and the Nigerian side fell about like flies.

'Stop the fire!' the 'commander' instructed. 'We've crushed Gowon and the Nigerians!'

Babatunde and the others who were watching laughed aloud.

'These boys are wonderful!' said the chief. 'Just give them arms and they'll surely drive back the vandals.'

More laughter followed.

The chief's face took on a serious expression. 'The boys have touched something deep inside me. Let the scoundrels come, we are ready for them! This village was never defeated by anyone during the tribal wars in the twenties – that's what my father told me – and it will never be defeated by Gowon and the Nigerians. Let the cowards flee, and the real men will stand up in defence of this place!'

The audience cheered. The chief paused to compose himself and gave a weak smile.

'I appreciate indeed the sacrifice you are making,' he continued. 'All over the continent and the world people have sacrificed their blood to make a better life for their children. My people, thank you that you've sent your boys to help the army. I am giving this venture my wholehearted blessing. Your effort will be blessed by God and the gods of our fathers. May plenty of rain fall on your crops and wash away ill omens as we fight for the freedom of Biafra.'

The audience gave him a rousing applause.

From Chief Emeka's compound Babatunde and his peers travelled in several trucks which took them to Enugu, where they found other trucks waiting and more arriving. An hour later about a hundred trucks drove for two hours until they arrived at a thick forest. After further travelling, they arrived at the banks of the Benue River, where Babatunde saw several army-green tents. The boys dismounted from the trucks.

# 10

That Sunday morning as they were awoken at about 04h00, Babtunde recalled how his uncle had once said to him, *Wake up Baba, sleep doesn't buy a cow!* They were instructed to take a 30-minute jog before having cold showers. They were then given tracksuits and takkies, khaki suits and matching caps and boots.

After breakfast they stood at attention in several rows, all eagle-eyed, facing their stern-faced commander.

'Chests out, heads up, and…' the commander bellowed.

As all the boys aimed at their heads with their hands, Babatunde gave a hand-quivering salute.

'Round-about-turn! Left-right, left-right…'

They marched to the bank of the river a kilometre away; they returned, marching to the biggest tent. There they attended their first church service. The chaplain read from the Bible—the book of Samuel, about how David defeated Goliath.

'We men of God have appealed for peace,' said the chaplain, 'and we have prayed for an amicable solution. But because the killing of our people is intensifying and because the Nigerian regime is against our secession, we are now praying for the army of the new nation to defeat the Federal army. And we want to remind Gowon that David is going to defeat Goliath!'

At the end of his sermon he prayed for them, and ended by saying: 'God, thank You for our Moses, Lt-Col Ojukwu. We are asking You to help him as he leads us to the Promised Land. Amen.'

After the service the boys were allowed a fifteen-minute break to stretch their legs. When they returned, they found that a canvas flag of Biafra had been unfolded between two posts. An officer who later introduced himself as Captain Onyekachi Achara stood before them as they sat down.

'A flag is the foundation and a source of pride for citizens of any nation,' said Captain Achara. 'So please look at it and absorb its detail as much as you can. By the end of the week you will be expected to draw it.'

He paused and scanned the boys.

'My duty today is to explain to you what the symbols mean.' He took a stick and pointed to the flag. 'Red is the blood of the Igbos massacred in the North, and black is for mourning. Green is for the prosperity of Biafra, and a half of a yellow sun stands for the glorious future of Biafra.'

He showed the boys how to salute. Then he asked them one by one to come to the flag and bow, salute, stand at attention and return to where they were sitting. Another officer handed them leaflets on which words were printed.

'It's the national anthem of Biafra; it was composed by the best writers of the nation, such as Achebe, Nwapa, Ike and Aniebo. Let us read through it slowly.'

> Land of the rising sun, we love and cherish,
> Beloved homeland of our brave heroes;
> We must defend our lives or we shall perish,
> We shall protect our hearts from all foes;
> But if the price is death for all we hold dear;
> Then let us die without a shred of fear.
>    Hail Biafra, consecrated nation,
> Oh fatherland, this be our solemn pledge;
> Defending thee shall be a dedication,
> Spilling our blood we'll count a privilege;

The waving standard which emboldens the free
Shall always be our flag of liberty.
　We shall emerge triumphant from this ordeal,
And through the crucible unscathed we'll pass;
When we are poised the wounds of battle to heal,
We shall remember those who died en masse;
Then shall our trumpets peal the glorious song
Of victory we scored over might and wrong.

Captain Achara read the anthem with them and asked them to read it again in the afternoon after lunch and also in the evening and the following morning.

'Remember,' the captain said in parting, 'you are no longer Nigerians, but proud Biafrans.'

# 11

On Monday morning after breakfast the boys were instructed to go to the big tent, where they stood and chatted in small groups. Babatunde stood next to his friend and classmate, Chinua. A commander stood on a chair in front of the big tent and clapped his hands twice to attract their attention; silence descended. He asked them to enter the tent and sit on camping chairs.

Babatunde expected to see the pleasant-faced Captain Achara. But the man who introduced himself as Colonel Zerubbabel Ohochuku was stern-faced. Another officer distributed leaflets to the boys.

Babatunde was horrified to see the picture of a huge headless corpse, with the heading at the top: THIS IS GENOCIDE.

'That's another victim, and part of the Northern massacres,' said Colonel Ohochuku. 'As you begin military training today, you must remember that this is taking place as demonstrations by the citizens of Biafra are increasing. More young people have stopped working and are asking to join the army. Even old people want to be trained and given rifles. So thank you for sacrificing your youth for the liberation of Biafra.'

Colonel Ohochuku paused and scanned them. 'Biafra shall be free!' He raised the volume of his voice, 'And if anyone or anything stands in her way, he or it shall be crushed; so you are going to do the crushing.' Surveying them again, he paused. 'We are going to teach you how to do that!'

Colonel Ohochuku turned to his left and shouted, 'Commander!'

A soldier stepped forward, a rifle tucked under his left arm, pointing downwards; he saluted and stood at attention in front of Colonel Ohochuku: 'Yes, colonel!'

'Your duty is to give these boys hearts of lions,' said the colonel.

'Yes, colonel!'

'You can't stand against Gowon and the Nigerians,' the colonel continued, 'if you have the heart of a rabbit.'

'Yes, colonel!'

The commander saluted as the colonel walked towards the first row of the boys. Holding his rifle with two hands, he pointed it upwards and shot into the air.

'Welcome to the training camp as soldiers who happen to be boys. I repeat: soldiers who happen to be boys,' said the commander. 'When I speak, you must respond: "Yes, commander!" Is that clear?'

'Yes, commander!' responded the boys.

For a brief moment Babatunde recalled how his father had said to him as he was about to get into the army truck: *You are now a soldier; so you must show your mother that you are going to survive.*

'You've received political education. That was very important because the mind is a person's engine. But a politically educated mind in a weak body is of no benefit to Biafra. That's why you need to develop a competent body to defend Biafra, to defeat the enemy and win the war. So you are going to be exposed to physical and mental activities that are going to transform you from being boys into real soldiers. Understood?'

'Yes, commander!'

The commander looked at his wristwatch. 'Today, until lunchtime, you will be taught how to walk and run like soldiers. Let's go.'

They were given rucksacks filled with sand and commanded to march to the top of the hill, reciting the national anthem. As they returned, running at a slow pace, Babatunde felt the streams of perspiration running down his spine. Sweat-beads covered his forehead and soon he was even tasting his own sweat.

*

'You'll be thoroughly trained in how to be good soldiers. Soldiers who'll not piss in their trousers at the first whisper of danger,' the commander addressed the recruits on the bank of the Benue river after lunch. 'Among other things, a good soldier must listen and execute the given commands.'

'Yes, commander!'

31

'A good soldier never questions when given a task. His response is always…?'

'Yes, commander!'

'A good soldier never cries, even if it is his commander who dies. Clear?'

'Yes, commander!'

'A good soldier has no pity for the enemy, for the aim of any war is to destroy the enemy. If your mother or uncle is on the side of Gowon, you must show them no pity. If you crush the head of a snake, Biafra stands to benefit.'

'Yes, commander!'

*'Ojukwu bu eze Biafra nine!'*

They repeated after him.

For the rest of that day until dinner time the recruits received training on how to endure heavy loads, and how to swim across a river carrying heavy loads on their backs.


# 12

The previous day's rope climbing left Babatunde's palms bleeding, but his hands were healing well. *I feel in my blood, that one day I will be a great person,* he mused as he climbed down from the bunker bed. *There has to be more to life than being a boy-soldier.*

'Today you are going to do three exercises as we work on your mind,' said the commander.

'Yes, commander!'

They were standing in five rows of twenty boys each, with their backs facing the river. The commander gave them a grin, the first that Babatunde had seen from him. Then he pointed: 'There are snakes under your feet!'

Many of the boys jumped, looking under their feet.

The commander chuckled, and the boys laughed with him.

'It's a two-headed snake called Gowon-Nigeria. Can you picture it?'

'Yes, commander!'

'Now jump as high as you can and crush the head of the snake with the boots of Biafra!'

The boys did as commanded; they were interrupted when the commander shot into the air.

'Listen,' bellowed the commander, 'I'm hard to please. So I'm unimpressed with a lot of your faces. I told you that a good soldier shows no pity for the enemy.'

'Yes, commander!'

'Now let me see vengeance as you crush the head of the snake!'

The boys did as instructed.

'Remember, the snake has two heads. What are you going to do with the other head?'

'Crush it, commander!'

'Now go to that heap of stones. Take a heavy stone, lift it over your head and crush the head of the snake.'

They did as commanded. The commander looked towards his left.

'Instructor, Mad Axe!' the commander called.

'Yes, commander!'

'The machetes!'

The instructor handed them machetes.

'Now go and chop the shrubs. One boy, one tree!'

'Yes, commander!'

'As you hit with your axe, imagine you are chopping the fingers, hands, feet, legs and arms of Gowon-Nigeria!'

'Yes, commander!'

The boys did as commanded and returned to the spot where they stood in front of the commander.

'Now the last exercise.' He paused. 'Instructor Chicken Fun!'

'Yes, commander!' someone responded.

'The chickens!'

Instructor Chicken Fun gave each boy a live chicken. Babatunde was amused and gave Chinua a wry grin.

'Those chickens aren't yours for eating,' the commander explained as Chicken Fun was giving them the chickens. 'They will be taken from you after the exercise.'

'Yes, commander!'

'This is what you are going to do. You are going to cut their throats with your teeth.'

'Yes, commander!'

'When you are done, lift up their heads and shout: "The head of Gowon-Nigeria!"'

'Yes, commander!'

'And when the blood drips, suck it like you are enjoying ice-cream!'

'Yes, commander!'

The boys did as instructed, shouting: *The head of Gowon-Nigeria!*

'*Ojukwu?*' said the commander.
'*Bu eze Biafra nine!*' the boys completed.
Babatunde felt like vomiting.

*

When the week ended, they were able to run up the hill with rucksacks containing stones. They were given stones to lift up and throw down, crushing enemies. In the last session they were trained how to crawl on all fours while holding their rifles with their teeth; they crawled for a hundred yards.

*

'*Attenshun*! Forwaaard march! Left-right-left-right!' shouted the commander, after a burst of gun-fire.

Babatunde was part of the five rows of boys comprising a hundred recruits each. The warm-up continued for about an hour.

'Now is the time for you physically fit soldiers,' the commander said, 'to be trained how to use rifles. The weapons are coming. But while we wait, we are not going to entertain any idle moments. The devil loves idle hands. The synonym for devil or Satan is Nigeria. So, in the meantime we are going to use the gun-shaped wooden dummies. Understood?'

'Yes, commander!'

The recruits used the wooden dummies until the end of the week.

At the beginning of the new week the instructor again stood in front the boys: 'As the arrival of the rifles we are expecting is still delayed, the military high command has instructed the famous blacksmiths of Awka to produce rifles and pistols that can fire cartridges. You will remember that the *Abanidiegwus* have been using Awka-made pistols and guns for years. So we can use the same against the Nigerians.'

A few days later some Awka-made rifles arrived and Babatunde was one of the lucky boys to receive a weapon. Leather-workers designed colourful holsters in which the young recruits dangled their home-made pistols. It was altogether an exciting time for Babatunde and his fellow boy-soldiers.

Just before the end of the day's training the instructor said: 'The weapons can arrive any moment, so you'll soon be trained in how to use the rifles. I mean real weaponry that defends Biafra and destroys the enemy! You'll be holding it like this…' He demonstrated: '*Tako-tako!! Tako-tako!!*' He swung from left to right. '*Tako-tako!! Tako-tako!!*'

## 13

One morning the recruits were told that a consignment of guns had arrived from a country that could not be named.

'You are no longer Nigerians but…?' asked the instructor at the beginning of the training session.

'Proud Biafrans!' responded the trainees.

'Beloved homeland…?' the instructor quoted from the national anthem.

'Of our brave heroes!' Babatunde competed with the shouting voices around him with all the power of his vocal chords.

'Spilling our blood…?' asked the instructor.

'We'll count a privilege!' the boys completed.

The rifles were unpacked and counted and all the recruits watched with wide eyes, their attention distracted by the sight. A small military truck arrived and the soldier who was driving and his mate dismounted and went to speak to the commander.

'Cubs of Biafra,' said the commander, 'to make your hearts tough, as soldiers, we have one more exercise.' He paused and scanned the boys; the soldiers unloaded four bulldogs and brought them to the commander, holding them by their collars.

'We have four dogs and we want four volunteers to come and cut their heads off.'

The boys responded, 'Yes, commander!'

'Now, let the four brave boys come!' said the commander as the soldiers tied the dogs' jaws and legs.

Twenty boys rushed to the commander; four of the volunteers were handed bayonets. Chinua was one of the first boys to cut the throat of a dog held down by ten boys. When he finally cut the dog's head off and lifted it up, the commander, the two soldiers and the boys applauded.

'You have just cut off the head of Gowon and Nigeria,' said the commander as the boys continued to applaud.

The two soldiers took the carcasses away and the boys were handed their rifles. Babatunde held his breath as he received a gun.

'You've been given the weapons of war to defend our beloved Biafra,' said the commander. 'Your duty is to shoot the enemy before he shoots you.'

'Yes, commander!'

The commander paused for a moment. 'Now put down the rifle in front of you.'

They did as instructed.

'When I say, "Kneel down and step!" this is what you must do,' said the commander, kneeling on his left knee and taking a step with his right foot.

'Let me repeat the exercise,' said the commander, 'Kneel down and step!'

The boys did as instructed, and the commander looked round the trainees to ascertain if his instructions were being followed accurately.

'The second step is,' the commander continued, 'hands on the rifle!' He gripped the gun, and the trainees followed his example.

'The next steps are, lift up the rifle and aim at target!'

The commander took aim, and the trainees followed his example.

'Hold your breath!'

The commander held his breath, and the boys did likewise, focusing on their targets.

'And shoot the Nigerians!'

The boys shot at the trunks of the trees. The commander assessed everything thus far.

'You'll do better as you practice more,' he said, 'and you have to learn to be fast.' He paused. 'Now let's do it all over again!'

The boys repeated the exercise.

The commander sighed. 'A good soldier is alert and his senses are sharp, with an additional sixth sense for instant decision. Understood?'

'Yes, commander!'

'A good soldier is awake like an owl, ready to fight, in defence of Biafra and fellow Biafrans, at any time.'

'Yes, commander!'

The commander took a breath. '*Attenshun*! Forwaaard march! Left-right-left-right!' he shouted, and the trainees did as he instructed.

*

It was the beginning of July 1967 and the military head of Nigeria, General Gowon, gave Lt-Col Ojukwu an ultimatum: *Stop your madness or face a full-scale war on 6th July.*

On the same date Ojukwu instructed all the boy-soldiers and young men in the army to be sent to the Apapa airstrip to witness the first air-strike by the Biafran army. Babatunde and the other boys cheered and shot their rifles into the sky as a Biafran B26 bomber ascended the clouds, flashing red lights. The message that the bomber had hit the targets in two towns on the Nigerian soil, Idah and Oturkpo, was relayed to all training camps, and that helped to boost their morale. A day before this date Gowon had sent an army lorry to the border of the 'rebel region'.

To demonstrate to the Biafrans that the new army was capable of defending them, Lt-Col Ojukwu, whose new title was Dikedioramma, shortened to 'Dim', commanded that the soldiers engage in a 'show of might' by driving through some of the towns and villages. Babatunde's heart swelled with pride as he stood chin-up in a truck, lifting up his rifle to cheering crowds. The Biafrans were repeatedly reminded: *You are no longer Nigerians, but proud Biafrans; so report anyone who has a Nigerian spirit to the military or the police.*

*

Babatunde was assigned many non-combatant tasks such as collecting food from the businesses, farms and even homes of well-off sympathisers and sponsors. Only half of the 500 000 boy-soldiers were at the warfront; these were regarded by Babatunde and his peers as the 'real' boy-soldiers. For the first few months it was fun for Babatunde to stand on the back of an open army truck, brandishing his new rifle, time and again tilting his cap over his eyes.

They drove from farm to farm, from shop to shop, collecting bags of garri, okro soup dried leaves, bundles of bananas, plantains and other produce. Sometimes a group of ten boy-soldiers and two adult soldiers walked and waited for the trucks to arrive later. As bags were loaded, Babatunde and his peers chanted: 'This is Biafra land!'

The army lorry which Babatunde was riding in also drove to the freshwater ponds of Gbalam to collect fish. He got his first taste of commandeering when he and other boy-soldiers commanded the fishermen at gunpoint to surrender their baskets full of fish. The adult soldiers were waiting in the truck. Babatunde grinned as a fellow soldier-boy said: 'This is Biafra fish, you'll catch another fish, man!'

*

One morning Babatunde, Chinua and three other boy-soldiers were instructed by the commander to go to the relief centre to control the queues of food-ration seekers. Although it was less challenging than being a truck soldier, Babatunde welcomed the change. They were going to replace the whip-holders, following a rumour that some men offered food parcels to girls and women in exchange for sex.

37

On arrival, Babatunde and his mates were taken to the office of the relief centre, which used to be a secondary school for girls. The centre manager, Felix Okoro, a high school teacher until the war broke out, wore a T-shirt inscribed with 'A LAND OF THE RISING SUN', as he welcomed Babatunde and his mates; he also gave them orientation about the tasks to be assigned to them. 'Put on a smile,' was Mr Okoro's advice, 'Remember, the women are your mothers and aunts.'


In order to be clearly visible, Babatunde and the others had to stand on chairs to monitor the queues. He enjoyed the affection of the women who called them 'baby soldiers'.

One morning they were instructed to tell the people that food parcels were not available because the delivery truck could not arrive at the centre as expected. Mr Okoro said, 'Tell them to try tomorrow.'

The following day the truck again could not deliver the food parcels. So Babatunde and his comrades again had to tell the people to return to their homes empty-handed. On that day the women refused to be turned away.

'We aren't going anywhere today,' said one of the women. 'Baby soldiers, are you aware that we spent the whole night waiting outside the gates?'

'Baba,' said Chinua, 'please go and ask Mr Okoro to come and address these angry mothers.'

Minutes later Babatunde came walking back with Mr Okoro beside him.

'There's no food because the truck carrying our supplies was hijacked,' said Okoro. 'Apologies for the inconvenience, ladies. But…'

'What?' said a woman, edging her way to the front. 'Do you expect us to believe your story? Were there no soldiers to escort the lorry?'

'The soldiers are the culprits; the people who were supposed to protect the lorry have become thieves. So come back on Monday, maybe there'll be food then.'

A woman holding a baby lifted it up. 'Then take him!' She thrust the baby boy into Mr Okoro's arms. 'Feed him until food parcels arrive!'

Very upset, the woman began to walk away as her emaciated baby cried.

'Woman, what are you doing? Come back!' Mr Okoro held the baby with stiff arms.

Other women chided the baby's mother, who continued to walk away. Babatunde rushed forward and overtook the woman. He blocked her way and looked straight into her eyes.

'Mama, please go and take your baby,' he said.

The woman stood with drooping shoulders.

'Please mama,' Babatunde continued. 'It's not Mr Okoro's fault that there's no food today.'

The woman returned, fetched her baby from Mr Okoro and walked away without saying a word. She then stopped, turned and spitt before she resumed her walking.

# 14

The relief centre was finally closed because the Red Cross was unable to deliver food aid, owing to political pressure and fear of military action by the Federal government. Babatunde returned to the task of travelling with the army trucks; this went on until August 1968. He could not admit to anyone that he was getting bored with food collecting. He and the other boy-soldiers were itching to see war, for which they believed they were thoroughly trained. Their rifles were often used for game-hunting, whenever they found themselves near the forests.

During the first week of August, Babatunde and the other boy-soldiers were about to get into a truck for the usual food-collecting chore, when their commander told them that an officer from the military high command was around and wanted to address them.

The commander instructed the boys to stand at ease, holding their rifles with their left hands. The moment the officer appeared from the tent, the boys bent down and put their rifles in front of their toes and stood at attention, their hands on their heads, ready to salute. With military precision the boy-soldiers saluted the officer and stood at attention. The officer sat on a camping chair behind a steel camping table while the commander remained standing.

'Now, rifles up!' shouted the commander.

The boys picked up their rifles.

'Hands on rifles, fingers on triggers!'

The boys did as commanded.

'To your left, *Tako-tako!!*'

The boys swung to their left and simulated gun-fire.

'To your right, *Tako-tako!!*'

The boys swung to their right and simulated gun-fire.

'On your haunches, *Tako-tako!!*'

The boys squatted and simulated gun-fire.

'Bodies flat down, rest on your bellies, and *Tako-tako!!*'

The boys lay on their bellies and simulated gun-fire.

'Now roll to your left and *Tako-tako!!*'

The boys did as instructed.

'Now squat and rifles ready!'

They followed the instruction.

'Now on your feet, feet apart!'

They followed the instruction.

'Now faces up!'

They followed the instruction.

'Rifles ready!'

They followed the instruction.

'Now *Tako-tako!!* To Nigerian bombers!'

The boys released real bullets into the sky. They put down the rifles neatly in front of their toes again, stood at attention and saluted the officer, who stood up, a smile on his face.

'Well done, cubs of Biafra,' said the officer, 'I can see that you are physically and mentally ready to win the war for Biafra. The Nigerian newspapers and Radio Nigeria are lying when they say we are losing the war and that the Federal army has captured Nssuka, Obolo-Eke, Ogoja, and Nkalagu. And they have the audacity to call us rebels! We are freedom fighters for Biafra! We haven't lost an inch of our beloved motherland, Biafra!

'Some of you are yearning to go to the real war, to serve and protect Biafra from the invading Nigerian vultures that take Biafra for a stinking carcass. Biafran cubs, this is your opportunity. As from today you'll no longer do the usual soft duty of collecting food. We want to capture the Midwest region, so we need your soldier power.'

'Yes, commander!'

Babatunde was delighted that his desire to be a 'real soldier' would be fulfilled.

'In order to prepare your hearts finally for what you should expect at the battle front, I want you to do the last exercise. Are you ready?'

'Yes, commander!'

The commander looked towards the truck that was parked behind him.

'Come and stand around this truck.'

The boys stood around the back of the truck, which was covered with a heavy canvas. The commander asked two boys to remove the canvas from the back to the front.

Babatunde held his breath when he saw the feet of men; he knew they were corpses whose boots had been removed.

'Now take these Nigerian dogs out of the truck,' said the commander, 'and put them in a row, face up.'

The boys did as instructed. Again Babatunde took a deep breath as he saw the faces; it was the first time that he had seen corpses.

'You've been trained that a soldier must be brave and show no pity for the enemy.'

'Yes, commander!'

'So, don't think of your father or your uncle when you look at these dead snakes. All you must see are enemies who deserve to be killed I defence of Biafra.'

'Yes, commander!'

'Now go and kick the enemy on their chests and then stand on their heads!'

The boys did as instructed.

'Now piss on them!'

They did as commanded.

'Now hang the corpses from the tree-trunks and shoot them!'

Babatunde saw the face of the dead soldier shaking from left to right as he shot through the chest.

'Take your positions!' the commander bellowed.

The boys did as instructed.

'Round-about-turn! Attention!'

They stood at attention.

'*Ojukwu?*' said the commander.

'*Bu eze Biafra nine!*' *the boys completed.*

'Before you get into the trucks the chaplain is going to pray.'

'Let us pray,' said the chaplain. 'Heavenly Father, we thank you that Biafra is the apple of your eye. We know that You are on our side; we are not the underdog but the bulldog, the top dog on top of the cat. You are on the side of David against Goliath. We ask you to bless His Excellency and his high command. Mighty God, let Your hand use our soldiers to defeat Nigeria and silence her allies. Oh *shababa, rakara-kara! Shababara! Rakara-kara!* The chaplain punched his Bible, looking heavenwards. 'We ask in Jesus's name. Amen!'

'Amen!' said the boys and the commanders.

'Forwaard march! Left-right-left-right!' shouted the commander.

Chests out, heads up, the boys marched.

'Mark time and stop!' The commander lifted his rifle. 'Attention!'

They stood at attention.

'From today as you march, I want you to chant: "Win-the-war! Win-the-war!"'

'Yes, commander!'

'Forwaard march! Win-the-war!"'

The boys marched and leapt into the trucks, chanting, 'Win-the-war! Win-the-war!'

# 15

The following day the Biafran army took part in a fierce battle with the Federal army in the Midwest region. The boys were shooting beside their fathers, uncles and elder brothers. An adult soldier next to Chinua collapsed and Babatunde, Chinua and two other boy-soldiers carried the wounded soldier to the Red Cross ambulance. When Babatunde and the others returned, they heard shouts.

As they rushed closer, they saw the Nigerian army retreating, with red dust billowing. More Nigerian soldiers fell to the ground, and dust and smoke hovered above. Babatunde aimed at the fleeing Nigerians and he counted three soldiers falling owing to his bullets. He heard himself shouting: '*Tako-tako!!*'

The Biafrans chased the Nigerians out of the town. The wounded Nigerian and Biafran soldiers were loaded into the Red Cross ambulances. The Biafrans found ten Nigerian trucks whose soldiers had been killed. They picked up the guns lying beside the corpses, took their rifles and their boots and loaded them into their trucks. As the boy-soldiers removed the boots of the dead Nigerians, Babatunde cast a long look at one of the dead soldiers whose death might have resulted from his rifle. Other Biafran soldiers removed the uniforms of the dead soldiers; in total there were 2 000 of them.

Major Gabriel Okara, the commander of the battle, was applauded and lifted onto the bonnet of the truck. He led the Biafran national anthem, which was sung by the soldiers standing at attention.

'Well done lions, young lions and cubs of Biafra,' said the major, saluting. 'I salute you all for excellent military execution! Please applaud yourselves!'

Some of the soldiers applauded while others lifted their rifles and shot into the sky in sheer excitement.

'They call us rebels,' said the major. 'Today we've taught them a bloody lesson. We are indeed freedom fighters for Biafra!'

The soldiers again applauded while some shot into the sky.

'You've seen the Nigerian dogs fleeing with tails between their injured legs. We are going to call this Friday a Good Friday. Let's celebrate the victory, but at sunset half of you should have a good rest while the other half must patrol this area. I am awaiting further instructions from the high command.'

The soldiers started to stomp about, lifting their rifles, many shooting upwards. Food and drinks were served and high-life music blared from the speakers hanging on the trucks.

*

On Sunday the soldiers attended a thanksgiving service. After dinner, as they all filed into the tent, the chaplain stood beside a wooden altar, holding a Bible in his right hand. He opened with prayer, thanking God for defeating the Nigerian army, and asking for His blessing in the war that Biafrans should win, 'so-that thy people can see that with God nothing is impossible and that the enemy can see that thy hand is upon thy people, they apple's eye, Biafra Amen!'

Before reading scripture, the chaplain played an accordion and sang two Negro spirituals: 'Turn back Pharaoh's Army' and 'Children, we shall be free'. He put on his spectacles and opened the Bible.

'We shall find the word of God from the book of Joshua chapter 6, verse 2 which reads as follows: "And the Lord said to Joshua, See I have given you Jericho, its king and mighty men of valour into your hands."

'As the Lord spoke to Joshua,' the chaplain continued, 'He is today speaking to our beloved hero of the nation, Lt-Col Chukwuemeka Odumegwu Ojukwu, saying, "See I have given you Kano, I have given you Ibadan, I have given you the Fulani grazing land." But we are saying, "Lord, keep those lands, for we are happy to have beautiful Biafra, our promised land. We don't want any extra land, for we don't want headaches. We don't want those bloodthirsty Philistines to give us sleepless nights. So give us Biafra, in Jesus's name!"'

# 16

A third of the soldiers remained in the town while others advanced towards the north and east of the Biafran borders.

Four days later, Major Okpara who was stationed in the Midwest region where the Biafrans had defeated the Federal army, sent an urgent radio message to the commanders in the east and the north: 'Please send three quarters of your men! The Nigerians are coming, over!'

One commander replied: 'We are not afraid of the Nigerians. It's going to be another Good Friday.' He laughed. 'Over!'

That morning in the Midwest region, Babatunde was doing drill with his peers when he saw dust billowing over the hill. Cognisant of the fact that the Nigerian army was coming, he felt his heart beating: *Doom-doom-doom!* The commander looked at him as if he could read his mind.

'Don't be afraid, panthers of Biafra,' said the commander. 'You are well-trained soldiers. Just tell yourselves: no be big problem, you go manage!'

'Yes commander!'

At that juncture the commander's attention was distracted; he was looking in the opposite direction. They saw a convoy of Biafran army trucks emerging from the river half a kilometre away.

The commander chuckled. 'It's going to be another Good Friday for Biafra and another bad Friday for those Nigerians. Are you going to give them another good hiding?'

'Yes, commander!' responded the boy-soldiers.

'Yes, those dogs are going to return to Gowon with tails between their shivering legs!' The commander shot into the air.

'Yes, commander!' roared the boys.

'Yes, let the irons cough death,' the commander continued, 'as one of the army poets once recited. Remember: A good soldier has no pity for the enemy, for the aim of any war is to destroy the enemy to defend Biafra. Are you ready?'

'Yes, commander!'

The commander pointed at the advancing trucks with his rifle. 'Now let's welcome our reinforcements with a win-the-war march and salute.'

'Forwaard march!'

'Win-the-war! Win-the-war!' Babatunde shouted together with the other boy-soldiers.

By the time the Biafran soldiers had been divided into groups of 50, the Nigerian army were shooting flaming rockets at the enemy army. Babatunde saw a rocket plunging into the ground a hundred yards from him. He rolled as he was trained, regained his balance and again stood firmly on his two feet.

'Fall back!' the commander shouted.

Babatunde lay on his back, lifting up his rifle.

He heard missiles whizzing over his head. Thankful that the missile missed him, he recalled his mother's parting words: *May the gods of our clan protect you until you return, Baba.*

Babatunde heard the commander shouting: 'Now stand up!'

Babatunde stood on his feet.

'Advance!'

Babatunde did as instructed.

'Aim and shoot!'

Babatunde shot with his rifle; for hours he heard gunfire rattling and all he could see through the smoke were his fellow fighters. A dust cloud and black smoke rose into the sky in front of him. Babatunde saw boy-soldiers and adult combatants falling to his left and right. He heard bullets hissing past his head. A bullet cut through between his head and ear. He felt blood dripping down his neck.

A bullet hit Babatunde's right shoulder, and he fell on his back; he bled and passed out. He felt arms carrying him and loading him into the Red Cross ambulance. He and ten other boy-soldiers and twenty adult soldiers were rushed to Enugu military hospital in several ambulances.

He was very weak because of loss of blood but he was conscious. A line from the Biafran national anthem crossed his mind: *Spilling our blood we'll count a privilege.*

At the hospital a drip was inserted into his right arm, and he was given an injection. As he fell asleep, he again recalled his mother's parting words: *May the gods of our clan save you until you return, Baba.*

*

The following morning a nursing sister removed his blood-soaked bandage and replaced it with a fresh one. Babatunde groaned and grimaced with pain.

The nurse smiled at him. 'Relax, cub of Biafra, relax.'

He decided to show the nurse that he was no longer a boy but a soldier. After applying a soothing ointment to his shoulder, she looked straight into his eyes. 'Have a good rest, brave Biafra warrior,' she told him in a low tone.

'Thank you, sister.'

As the nurse walked to the door, she turned and looked back at Babatunde:

'Wait a minute; haven't I seen you elsewhere? What's your name?'

'Babatunde.'

'Babatunde Okoronkwo from Ijoto?'

'Yes!'

'Good to meet you! I'm aunt Dorah's younger sister. My name is Minah.'

'Yes, I remember your aunt Minah, but I haven't seen you for many years.'

'I'll be going home later this afternoon. I'll tell your mother that you have been admitted at this hospital.'

'I'll appreciate it, aunt Minah.'


# 17

By Monday afternoon Babatunde was recovering well. He had just returned from the physiotherapist when he saw his aunt, Chimamanda, walking in the corridor that led to his ward. She was his father's younger sister and the mother of his cousin, Nnesinachi. Her husband was an army officer in Kano.

Babatunde and his aunt met at the entrance to his ward and engaged in a prolonged bear-hug.

'I thank the gods of the clan that you are alive, Baba,' she said.

'I also thank the gods, auntie,' said Babatunde.

'Listen, there's no time to waste. Let's go to the village right now.'

Babatunde did not ask any questions. His aunt grabbed him by the hand and walked with him to the doctor in charge and requested his discharge.

*

When they were about three homesteads away from his home, Babatunde saw a truck, onto which his mother, her elder sister and two men were busy loading furniture. As they entered the yard, his mother rushed to them. She embraced Babatunde and kissed him on his neck, then looked deeply into his eyes, holding his hands.

'I thank the gods of our clan for protecting you, my son,' she said, tearfully giving him another tight hug.

'What's happening, mother?' inquired Babatunde.

'We are going to the North, to the place of your aunt, Chimamanda,' said his mother. 'She has persuaded the nurse she works with, who comes from Biafra, to help take us and our furniture to the border of Biafra. There the furniture will be transferred into another truck that has been organised by Chimamanda's husband, the one who is an officer in the Federal army. Do you remember him?'

'Yes, mother.' Babatunde looked around the homestead. 'Where is father?' he asked.

'A few days after you joined the army, he became a member of the village army,' his mother responded. 'A month later the Biafran army took him and other men to Port Harcourt. The town was captured by the Nigerian army two weeks ago. We…' His mother cradled her face in her palms.

'What's wrong, mother?'

'We haven't heard from him since then. It's not known if he's still alive, or…' Tears glinted in her eyes.

Babatunde put his hand on her shoulder. 'May the gods of our clan protect our father,' he said.

His mother wiped her tears away, composed herself and tried to smile.

'And where are my brothers and sisters?' asked Babatunde.

'My cousin, your aunt Nwandu, has taken them. I am hoping that our gods have protected them.'

Babatunde went to help load the furniture. At that moment they were throwing in a few light things such as brooms and kettles.

*

While the driver started the truck, Babatunde and his mother walked to the shrine where they informed the gods of their clan that they were relocating to Kano until the end of the war.

As the truck drove further into the north, it felt strange to Babatunde that what was known as the enemy's land would be his place of refuge. Back in Biafra his uncle, being a Hausa, would be seen as the enemy and torn to pieces.

*

They arrived in Kano at sunset. When they had had supper, his aunt said to him: 'In order to survive in this part of the country there are a few very important things that you should take note of.'

Babatunde's mother was listening.

'First, your name is Ibrahim. Never mention the name Babatunde. *Oya?*'

'Yes, aunt.'

'I'm your mother, as from today, and your mother is your aunt.'

Babatunde smiled. 'Yes, mama.'

Although his aunt was holding the Igbo kinspeople with her left hand and her husband and her Hausa in-laws with her right hand, Babatunde had to hide his identity.

'Your name is?'

'Ibrahim.'

'Good. And I'm…?'

'My mother.'

'And your mother is…?'

'My aunt.'

'Good. I'm going to give you a Koran, and you are going to go to the mosque and tell other boys that you are their brother. Is that alright?'

'Yes, mama.'

'And you are going to be part of those boys; you are going to play soccer with them; if you keep to yourself, you are going to be suspected of being a *sabo*.'

'Yes, mama.'

'And you are going to be part of the boys' militia.'

'Yes, mama.'

## 18

Babatunde spent many afternoons at the soccer pitch near the mosque; he excelled as a striker and was given the soccer name of 'Nigerian bomber'. One afternoon he arrived early at the pitch and started to practice ball control with an old tennis ball. Ismail, the leader of the boy's militia, was the next to arrive. He brought an old soccer ball.

After greeting Babatunde, he looked him in the eyes.

'Whenever I look at your hands,' said Ismail, 'I see many scars, and I suspect that you've been a boy-soldier.'

'Why are you saying that?' Babatunde asked.

'Many people from Lagos are Igbos,' said Ismail.

'My father is a Hausa,' said Babatunde, slightly nervous. 'I was born before my father married my mother. My Mama-Nnukwu did not have boys to do errands for her. So when my father married my mother, she agreed with my Mama-Nnukwu that I should stay with her. But because my Mama-Nnukwu has now passed away, I have come to stay here with my mother and father.'

Ismail touched Babatunde's shoulder. 'Even if you are an Igbo, don't worry. No-one is going to touch you. I'm going to spread the story you've just told me. As long as you are playing soccer with us, you go to the mosque, and you are part of the boys' militia, your life will be safe.'

Babatunde didn't know what to say; he couldn't say 'Thank you', for that would mean that Ismail was right, and that he was an Igbo.

'I hate the face of Ojukwu with all my heart,' said Ismail, 'but I hate him even more for reducing nice boys like yourself to boy-soldiers. Come, Nigerian bomber, let's play soccer! You are the striker and I'm the goalie!'

Babatunde chuckled with relief.

*

One afternoon a next-door neighbour came to the house and talked to Babatunde's aunt.

'Has your son undergone the cleansing ritual?' asked the neighbour.

'Cleansing ritual?'

'Yes. The ritual will purify him from the bad deeds of war and also appease the spirits of those he might have killed; it will open up a new and cleaner life.'

'Can you help with the ritual?'

'No. But I can send a message to the healer and ask her to come and help you.'

*

The following day the woman healer was there to officiate at the cleansing ritual. It had to be done under cover of night.

Babatunde sat on a grass mat in front of the healer who waved a fly-whisk made of an ox tail. The healer raised her voice, invoking the powers of the ancestral spirits of Babatunde's family to help cleanse and purify him of his war deeds. She then took some herbs out of her bag and instructed that they should be boiled and brought to her. When the mixture was no longer hot, she filled a cup and handed it to Babatunde.

'What's the boy's name?' asked the healer.

'Bab...Ibrahim,' said his mother.

'Stand up, Ibrahim,' said the healer. 'Face the south where there is still war. Drink this cup quickly. Don't close your eyes because that can undo the power of the herbs!'

Babatunde did as he was instructed.

'Now come and sit down and face the east,' she commanded. 'The east is the place where the sun comes from. It means the beginning of a new life.'

Babatunde sat on a stool facing east. The healer took out a gourd the size of a hand, put in some herbal mixture and burned it. She instructed Babatunde to inhale the smoke. She opened her bag and searched until she found a plastic container.

'This is a powder of mixed healing herbs.' She looked at Babatunde's mother. 'Bring a basin with water.'

After Babatunde's mother had brought the basin with water, the healer poured in the herbs and stirred it with her fly-whisk.

'Come with me and the boy,' the healer told Babatunde's mother. 'We are going to that hut. He must be naked and stand in a bigger basin.' The healer kept eye contact with Babatunde. 'When we enter the hut, we must find you facing the opposite direction.'

A few minutes later the healer and Babatunde's mother entered the hut. They were carrying a basin in which water and herbs were mixed.

'Ibrahim,' said the healer, 'this mixture is going to cleanse your body of the dirt accumulated during the war. Your mother will pour water from a small basin on top of your head and your neck and shoulders.

As she pours, you must rub the slimy mixture into your skin as far as your hand can reach.'

When Babatunde's mother had poured all the water containing the mixed herbs over her son Babatunde was given a towel; he dried himself and came out of the hut.

'Now the last step,' said the healer. 'All the family members can join me and Ibrahim at the crossroads.' The healer looked at Babatunde's mother. 'Bring the water which your son has washed with.'

The healer walked to the nearest crossroads with Babatunde, his mother and his aunt Chimamanda. When they arrived there, the healer asked that the water be given to Babatunde.

'Pour all this herbal water here,' said the healer, pointing to a spot.

Babatunde did as instructed.

'*Oya*. Now the dirt of war,' said the healer, 'has been dispersed in different directions.'

After the crossroads ceremony, the healer and Babatunde's kinsfolk walked back to the house for a family meal. A goat was slaughtered and palm wine was served. The healer offered some food and wine to the ancestral spirits of Babatunde's family.

*

After the war ended Babatunde and his mother returned to the renamed Eastern Nigeria. His father could not be found among the relatives. After months of waiting and hoping they heard that people who could not trace their next-of-kin should go to the nearest government offices to report their loved ones as 'War Missing Persons'.

Babatunde accompanied his mother to one such office where they found hundreds of women whose sons and husbands could not be found. Babatunde realised that his mother was one of many hundreds of women mourning their relatives; he observed how the women shared their pain and loss. It was painful for Babatunde to see his mother shedding tears. He heard his mother saying, *So, I'll never be able to see my husband's grave?* She asked a question no-one could answer.

As his mother sobbed, he wanted to cry with her. But he recalled his commander's words: *A good soldier never cries, even if it is his commander who dies.*

So he comforted his mother: 'Please don't cry, mama.'

At that moment Babatunde saw several buses offloading women wearing church uniforms and singing hymns.

'Don't worry, mama,' Babatunde offered words of comfort, 'the gods of our clan are with us. I'm going to grow up and help you.'

'Thank you, Baba,' said his mother, giving her son a smile as she embraced him.

Later, his mother joined the church women in comforting other women and handing out food parcels and vegetable seeds.

# PART THREE

## 19

One Monday afternoon, during the New Year's festivities of 1979, Babatunde stood behind a small heap of yams at the end of the village beside the main road to Kano. The five women who hawked next to him had gone to their homes or to the nearest town for a last-minute shopping. He had the last five yams to sell. Over twenty minutes passed without a car stopping to buy. During those idle moments he browsed through a dog-eared copy of Chinua Achebe's novel, *Anthills of the Savannah*, which was prescribed for his Class 12 English literature the previous year.

Babatunde had been hawking at the spot since 08h00 that morning and had sold all of his smoked rabbit meat.

Flipping over a page, he looked up to see a car that had driven past his stall stopping and reversing. He hurried to the driver's side.

'Can I help you, sir?' he inquired, looking at the man whose face was shielded by sunglasses.

The man pointed. 'Four yams please,'

'I've got five left,' said Babatunde, 'so I will give you one yam free, sir. It's your New Year's gift.'

'Thank you very much, young man,' said the customer, taking some crumpled Naira notes from his purse.

Babatunde handed the yams over in a plastic bag and fidgeted in the pocket of his overalls, looking for change.

'You can keep the change,' the man said.

'Thank you, sir,' smiled Babatunde.

'Hey, where have I seen you before?' the man asked. 'Were you one of my students?' He removed his sunglasses.

'*Ewoo*! Teacher Felix!' exclaimed Babatunde.

The man pointed at Babatunde. 'Don't tell me your name. I'll tell you... you are Babatunde Okoronkwo!'

It had taken a while for Felix Okoro to recognise Babatunde, who wore his late father's faded brown overalls and his old grass sun-hat. Felix opened the car door, stepped out and gave Babatunde a firm handshake.

Babatunde laughed. 'You know, teacher Felix, as you said "Four yams please!" I said to myself, "this man's manner of speaking reminds me of teacher Felix."'

'Hop into my car,' said Felix. 'I'll drop you at your home.'

'Thank you, teacher Felix.'

Felix stayed at the neighbouring village of Omarumo, about five kilometres from Babatunde's village. In no time Babatunde was seated in his former teacher's old faded blue Peaugeot 404.

'So what are you doing with your life, Baba?'

'I'm selling yams and the dried meat of rabbits and guinea fowls,' replied Babatunde. 'But I want a proper job.'

'What kind of a job?'

'I don't know. I'm hoping my elder brother who works for Shell Oil Company can help me get one there. But I have been waiting the whole year. Perhaps I should use the talent with which the gods have blessed me.'

'What is that talent?'

'As my villagers would say, I have fingers for yam-planting.'

Felix smiled. 'Yes, I can see that for myself.'

Babatunde chuckled. 'When I was very young I was a farmworker. I was taken to my uncle's place...I remember that day as if it's yesterday. I complained to my mother, *Why is father doing this to me?* She replied, *Perhaps something good will come out of this.* Afterwards, when I returned to my parents' house I wasted no time in planting yams. I was so good with yams that I was soon known in my neighbourhood as the 'yam-boy'. And every year my sisters' children took part in the village Yam Festival and won prizes.

'That's great, Baba!' said Felix.

'But I want to be a better-informed farmer. Uncle Emenike once said a farmer need not know how to read and write. But I can't agree with him, because I've realised that farming is a science. I think I should further my studies.'

'Excellent!'

'I'm thinking of going to an agricultural college in Umudike in Abia State.'

'Go for it, Baba. I will find out information for you.'

Just then they arrived in front of Babatunde's compound. Felix switched off the ignition.

'Listen Baba, why don't you come to my house on Sunday after church?' he said.

'I could come even earlier if you like, because I don't attend church. We worship the Igbo god in my family.'

'Is that so?'

'Yes. I have taken over the *Eze-mmuo* priesthood from my late father.'

Felix gave Babatunde an endearing smile.

'I have a cousin who never stops nagging me to be a Christian,' Babatunde went on. 'Every time she approaches me I give her the same answer: "I will never desert the god of my forefathers."'

'Excellent, Baba!'

'I remember how, during literature classes, you used to encourage us to read Chinua Achebe's *Things Fall Apart* so that we should not turn against our gods.'

Felix grinned. 'I'm delighted to hear that my literature teaching has made a lasting impression on you.'

20

Babatunde related to his family how his former teacher whom he had visited that day had given him some helpful advice. He also told them that he intended to visit the AME church school where he was a pupil many years ago, to see if he could get a job as an auxiliary teacher or administrator.

When Babatunde arrived at the preschool, he was told by the administrator that the principal, Ms Yvonne Adams-Adichie, was not around. He still cherished some hope, as the administrator gave him forms to fill out, until he was told: 'These forms do not necessarily mean that you'll be offered a job.' She also told him to bring letters of recommendation from his former school teacher and from a minister of religion.

Babatunde did not waste any time but took a bus from the school to the village of his former teacher. Fortunately for him, he found Felix at home. On hearing what was needed, Felix disappeared into his study from where Babatunde heard his manual typewriter clattering: *Twa-twa-twa...tjerr...twing!* Minutes later he emerged and handed Babatunde the letter he was requesting.

'Please read it,' said Felix, 'so that I can make corrections where necessary.'

Babatunde read:

> To whom it may concern,
>
> I hereby confirm that I have known Mr Babatunde Okoronkwo since I taught him English at Ijoto High School, where he was doing Grades 11 and 12. He made history at the twenty-year-old high school by becoming the first student to pass English with a distinction. Mr Okoronkwo was one of the most obedient, hardworking and conscientious students I have ever taught. It was really a pleasure to be his teacher. I can therefore

confidently recommend him for any kind of a job or scholarship application.

Yours faithfully,
Felix Kola Okoro.

Babatunde smiled at Felix. 'It's a well-written letter of recommendation. Thank you very much, teacher Felix.'

'It's my pleasure to be of help to one of my students.'

Babatunde stood up, ready to leave. 'I am very much encouraged, Teacher Felix. Can I share something with you?'

'You are welcome, Baba.'

'I feel in my blood that one day I will be a great person. There has to be more to life than standing at the roadside selling yams.'

Felix smiled. 'I like your guts, Baba.'

'Thank you, Teacher Felix. One last challenge is to get a letter of recommendation from a minister of religion. How will I get that if I don't attend any church?'

'Well,' said Felix after a thoughtful pause, 'tell me, Baba, what did you write under the item "Church Denomination"?'

'I left it blank; I wanted to write "None" or put a question mark.'

'Why don't you just write "African Religion"?'

'It's an excellent idea! I never thought of that.'

Felix grinned. 'You can in fact insert an asterisk and then write a remark that your supreme priest of *Eze-mmuo* is unable to write your letter of recommendation because he cannot read or write.'

They shared some belly laughs.

'That was the trick used by my nephew who works at Bata Shoe Company in Lagos,' Felix said. 'Having a terrible hangover one Monday morning he could not go to work. On Tuesday his white boss asked for a doctor's letter. And you know what my nephew said? "My traditional healer is illiterate, so he can't give me a letter."'

They laughed again.


## 21

That Wednesday morning at the AME school, Babatunde entered the principal's office. The young woman sitting behind the desk looked to be in her mid twenties. She rose to her feet when Babatunde walked in.

'Yvonne Adams-Adichie,' she introduced herself.

After introducing himself, Babatunde asked her to repeat her name. To his amazement he realised that she was African-American. He had assumed she was Nigerian. She looked every inch a pretty Nigerian woman, wearing her brightly coloured print dress and matching headscarf.

'So you are the gentleman who asked for the forms yesterday?'

'Yes, ma'am,' replied Babatunde who felt like saying, *please keep talking*. He was totally charmed by her unusual American accent.

She received the forms he handed to her and read through them and the letter of recommendation. Babatunde saw her grin and guessed she had reached the part about his African religion. Studying her face, he felt that her accent complemented her beauty. She was coffee-coloured, with a glowing skin and a pair of piercing eyes fringed by long, thick eyelashes. His keen eye did not miss how the purple colour of her lipstick matched her nail-polish.

'I see here on the form,' said Yvonne, 'that you've written "African religion."'

Babatunde held his breath and nodded.

'What kind of religion is it?' she asked with a grin. 'Do you worship some sort of a god like the sun or the moon?'

'No ma'am. You Christians have Jesus as a mediator or go-between between God and man, while others have Muhammad and Buddha, as my Religious Studies teacher informed me; my people rely on the African gods as mediators. Our ancestors.'

Babatunde felt that from the way Yvonne was looking at him she remained unconvinced.

There was a brief pause during which she maintained eye contact with him.

'I must tell you, Mr...' she paused, glancing at the form to find Babatunde's surname. 'Mr Okoronkwo, I must tell you, that it is against our policy to consider an application from anyone who is not a Christian ... I mean a professing Christian, not just a churchgoer. Because this school has been established by the AME—the African Methodist Episcopal church in the US.'

Babatunde held his breath again, expecting to be told that the interview had come to an end.

'But having said that,' she continued, 'I do appreciate your openness and your truthfulness. Someone too desperate to get a job could have told a convenient lie that he was a church-goer. So, I respect you for your truthfulness. It's what I call integrity.'

'Thank you, ma'am.'

She smiled. 'And it's great that you've passed English with distinction!'

'Thank you, Miss Adams-Adichie.'

Yvonne rubbed her forehead. 'But at the moment... I regret to tell you that we don't have a vacant position, Mr Okoronkwo.' She smiled, as if her intention was to assuage Babatunde's disappointment. 'However, I'll keep your application for future reference.' She shifted her gaze to the forms. 'If we did have a vacant position...' she pointed to the form with her pen, '...this African religion item would be a minus, I must say.'

Babatunde sighed, feeling disappointed. As she told him about her background, he never ceased to be fascinated by her pronunciation of 'Educational Psychology' as '*Ed-yoo-caysh-nul Psychullugy*'.

'Miss Adams-Adichie,' said Babatunde, taking a deep breath, 'I believe I have more pluses than minuses.'

She flashed him a surprised smile.

'And I want to say to you,' continued Babatunde, 'that come tomorrow, you are going to see my face in front of you again.'

She frowned. 'Why would you come when I told you...?'

'I want to volunteer as an auxiliary teacher or something like that, in spite of your query about my religion.'

'Unfortunately we don't have a policy that allows us to hire volunteers.'

Babatunde thought for a moment, pursing his lips. 'I realise you have only women working here,' said Babatunde. 'So the children here need a father figure; someone they can address as "uncle."'

Suddenly Babatunde snapped his fingers. 'And... oh yes! I can also tell them enchanting folktales and teach them indigenous games! That'll be important for their pride as Africans.'

She shook her head, smiling. 'I appreciate what you can offer, Mr Okoronkwo. But I'm afraid we have no vacancy; moreover there are no more classrooms for an extra teacher.'

'Okay Miss Adams-Adich...'

'Why don't you just call me Yvie, and I shall call you Bah-bah-too...'

'You can call me Baba. You know what, Yvie? I don't mind teaching under that iroko tree.'

She creased her forehead. 'Baba, you are really pushing your luck too far. What if it rains?'

'What is rain to an African child and an African teacher? It's no problem. In Africa when it rains children sing, dance and praise the gods in the rain! Listen to this children's rain song, *Ogwogwo mmili takumei ayolo*! '

Yvonne laughed. Babatunde was delighted to see her relaxed face that showed her teeth.

'Having talked to you briefly, Baba, I've picked up that in addition to your excellence in English you are an enthusiastic person. But unfortunately there's no vacant position.'

'You know what, Yvie? Come tomorrow you are going to see my ugly Nigerian face in front of you again!'

Babatunde stood up suddenly. 'Goodbye!'

He opened the door then turned to glance back at Yvonne.

'Can I say one last thing, Yvie? This school is very close to my heart. I'm a former pupil. Please check the records when the first principal, Mrs Johnson, was here and you'll find my name. And what I've achieved.'

# 22

Babatunde waited at the gate of the AME school until the cooks and cleaners arrived at 06h00. It was the beginning of the new week. Waking up at 05h00 that morning, he had recalled his uncle's words of wisdom: *Sleep doesn't buy a cow.*

He told the workers that he was going to volunteer at the school and that if Yvonne had forgotten to tell them, it was not his problem. After a brief discussion among themselves they let him into the yard. He was beaming as he changed into overalls. He had brought a hammer, saw and nails. He asked the women to show him the children's tables and chairs that needed repairs.

Later he went to sweep the dry leaves under the iroko tree. As he dug in the garden, he mulled over how his former teacher had once advised him: *It doesn't help to sit down with hands on your head pitying yourself. The world will laugh at you. The world respects a man who does something about his situation to change the status quo.*

At 07h00 when the children arrived, the aunties were still preparing breakfast. He said to one of the ladies: 'Can I teach the children the game of "The Hyena and the Children"?' At 07h30 when Yvonne arrived, he saw her watching as he had fun with the kids; he observed that she seemed fascinated. Babatunde thought she would come to ask him what he was doing, but she walked away to the kitchen.

A few minutes later she sent for him; he hurried to her office.

Smiling at him she said: 'Baba, I've seen what you're doing, and I can tell you really mean business. I thought you were joking when you told me, "Come tomorrow, you will see my ugly face again." Today I've seen your handsome face, and I realised that the children are enjoying your company.'

Babatunde chuckled. and she continued: 'Baba, you have really made it impossible for me to say no to your request. So I have quickly used my discretion to allow you to stay here as our first volunteer.'

Babatunde was so overcome with emotion that he leapt into the air and clapped his hands.

'Thank you very much Yvie!' he said.

'But I don't want you to waste your time doing gardening, fixing tables and chairs and other menial tasks. I think it is a good idea if you teach elementary English to the preschoolers. I will promote the lady who was teaching the class to take the Grade Ones and I shall focus on administration and do the lesson planning and evaluation; I shall also moderate the tests.'

'I really appreciate it, Yvie!' beamed Babatunde, giving Yvonne an enthusiastic handshake.

'I've also decided to ignore this African religion issue of yours, for now; I hope the problem will somehow be resolved in the future.'

'Thank you indeed, Yvie!' said Babatunde, excitement written all over his face.

*

At the end of the week, as Babatunde strode out of the gates of the school, he saw a blue Toyota approaching. The car indicated, pulled over, and stopped on the side of the dirt road. Babatunde was delighted to see a dreadlocked Odenigbo stepping out of the car. He wore a pair of blue jeans and sky-blue T-shirt with white stripes, his face clean shaven and his eyes sparkling with typical mischief.

Odenigbo slapped Babatunde's open palms, and the exercise was repeated with Babatunde hitting Odenigbo's palms. The two young men bear-hugged and patted each other's shoulders then burst into laughter.

'Is this your car?' asked Babatunde, climbing into the passenger seat as Odenigbo took his place at the wheel once more.

Odenigbo nodded, turning the car in the direction of Port Harcourt.

'My parents bought it for me when I completed my arts degree last year,' he said.

'Great, Ode! Are you still studying?'

'Yes. I'm doing an Honours in Political Science at the London School of Politics.'

'Wonderful!'

They drove until they arrived at a quiet restaurant, talking all the way.

As the order was being prepared, Odenigbo took out two cigarettes and gave one to Babatunde who hesitated to receive it.

'Your first smoking experience?' said Odenigbo, smiling at his friend.

'Yes. I always felt I should start smoking when I grow up; that I should buy my first packet of cigarettes and a bottle of beer when I start working. I don't want to beg for cigarettes or beer.'

Babatunde inserted the cigarette between his lips; Odenigbo lit each of their cigarettes and they puffed at them.

Babatunde smoked with an effort and coughed.

Odenigbo brushed Babatunde's arm. 'You will get used to it, in a matter of days.'

Babatunde continued to smoke, giving a pained smile.

'So what's up? Are you working at that school?' inquired Odenigbo as they sat waiting for their order of jollof rice, plantain and ofe nsala to be delivered.

'Yes. It's my first week as a volunteer there,' responded Babatunde.

'That's good, Baba. Volunteering could open the door to full employment.'

'That's what I'm aiming at, Ode. This reminds me of what Achebe said in *Anthills of the Savannah*, "We praise a man when he slaughters a fowl so that if his hand becomes stronger tomorrow, he will slaughter a goat."'

'You really are a go-getter, Baba!'

'I have no choice, my friend.'

Their meal came.

'Did your people tell you that the other day when I was at your place, I offered your cousin, Nachi, a lift?'

'Yes, they told me. Did Nachi tell you that she's a medical student in Scotland?'

'No, she didn't tell me.'

'Nachi can be modest.'

'She's a beautiful girl. The moment my eyes landed on her tight breasts, my mind just started running amok. You know what I mean?'

They had a good laugh.

Babatunde winked at Odenigbo. 'Have you tried chatting her up?'

'I wanted to.'

'And what happened?'

Odenigbo's smile faded. 'She completely threw me when she wasted no time in asking me, "Are you saved?" I asked, "Saved from what?" She said, "Are you born again?" and I said, "What do you mean?" – pretending to misunderstand her, you know. And she said, "Have you received Jesus Christ as your Lord and Saviour?" I asked, "What's the relevance of that?" And she replied, "It's very relevant. I don't go out with unsaved guys."

'From that moment the short journey felt like a hundred miles. She was quoting Bible verses at me the whole way. I was relieved when she finally climbed out my car at the bus terminal at Kano. She told me, "My brother, I love you with the love of Jesus and I will pray for you to be born again." And I said, gnashing my teeth, "Don't waste your prayer!" I was really pissed off!'

Babatunde chuckled. 'She got involved in that cult of hers at a very young age. Last year she told us that as long as there was hell she would never stop nagging us to quit worshipping our African ancestors. Now she's unceasingly nagging us to accept her Jesus.'

## 23

It was the end of the second week of Babatunde's work as a volunteer teacher at the school. As the noisy pupils raced away at the end of the teaching day, he was packing up his teaching aids when he spotted Yvonne walking towards him.

Smiling, she beckoned to him: 'Baba, please come to the office.'

Babatunde's face brightened; he followed her eagerly, feeling that he was about to receive some good news.

'Mr Okoronkwo,' Yvonne addressed him formally as they sat in her office. 'You have volunteered for us for two weeks now, and I feel I must do the right thing which is to get to know you better. I'm going to do this by interviewing you formally. We can't have someone working for us...volunteering for us...when we know so little about him. Yes, you have completed the application form but we still need to know more about you. Are we in agreement thus far?'

'Yes, Yvie.'

Yvonne looked down at his application form in front of her. 'I see that you have written here under "Additional information" that you were once a pupil of this school in 1962. How old were you?'

'Five years old.'

'Let's take it from here, then. I'm interested in knowing the highlights of your life from six years old until your current age.'

'When I was six years old, I did Class 1 here. I was appointed a class prefect and I was awarded a prize.'

'Excellent, Baba! And then?'

There was a long pause. Babatunde sighed before he spoke: 'When I was in Class 3, my classmates and I received political education from someone in the military about the new state of Biafra to be created. It was 1967...'

'So you were involved in the Biafran War?'

'Yes. When the war broke out in 1967, my Grade 4 studies were interrupted. I was 10 years old when I became a boy-soldier.'

'Really?'

'I'm telling you, Yvie!'

She who was silent for a moment. 'Tell me, Baba, were you not afraid of serious injury? That you could die any minute?'

'No. We were completely sold on the idea of fighting for a sovereign Republic of Biafra. We were highly motivated and well trained.'

As he shared his experiences, Yvonne looked intently into his eyes; he saw her wipe a tear from the corner of her own eye. She gave him a shaky smile.

'Pardon me, Baba, you see that I'm getting a little emotional. I'll tell you why one day.'

'It's all right, Yvie.'

'How did you survive the war?'

He told her all that had happened.

'How did you feel when the Biafran soldiers lost the war?'

'It was very painful. Our great dream as Biafrans was shattered, like a broken earthenware pot. But I was far from it all, in Kano. I stayed with my aunt. It was devastating to see the results of the war. I cried when I saw the pictures of my people dying of famine... they were like walking skeletons ... it was so heartbreaking!

'In January 1970 when the war ended my family moved back to the re-named Eastern Nigeria. For the next six years I concentrated on my education, and in 1978 I completed my Class 12 at the advanced age of 21 years. That's my story, Yvie.'

Babatunde bowed his head, wiping tears away.

## 24

'Let's go back to the beginning,' Yvonne said, when he'd had a chance to recover himself. 'You told me that when you were a pupil of this institution, you were appointed a prefect.'

'Yes, that's true.'

'Tell me about your first day here. What were your impressions?'

'I was surprised that the two female teachers, who looked the same to me as other Nigerians, were not speaking the Igbo language. Later I was told by aunt Florah, a cook at the preschool who came from the same village as my mother, that the teachers were African-Americans. She explained that those were Africans who had been hunted down in the forests and mountains of Africa, loaded into ships and taken as slaves to America. She also told me that the principal of our school, Mrs Johnson, who we called Mama-J, was the wife of Reverend Johnson who preached here on Sundays in a classroom that was turned into a church.'

Yvonne was listening intently.

'To learn that strange language called English that all the teachers spoke,' Babatunde continued, 'was something that never ceased to fascinate me. Mama-J issued an instruction that she didn't want to hear any child speaking Igbo, Hausa, Yoruba or any other Nigerian language. She often said, "If you want to be successful in life, if you want to be a leader, you must learn this language called English. It is the language of strong men who have conquered the whole world."'Every morning before the classes began, we, the learners, were taught a short hymn and instructed to fold our arms to recite a prayer. It wasn't long before I had committed the hymn and the prayer to memory. And, much to the delight of my parents and sisters, I also prayed for supper in English!'

Yvonne chuckled.

'My parents were proud of me; so much so that one evening they made an offering of yam and palm wine to the gods, thanking them for the favour that had fallen on my head. I was squatting next to the shrine, pleased and proud to hear my name being mentioned to the gods.'

'Indeed interesting!' said Yvonne. 'You told me earlier that you were awarded a prize.'

'That's true.'

'What was the prize for?'

'Our teacher had asked us a question: "Who can tell me about the origin of the name Nigeria?" I was the first pupil to shoot my hand into the air, on my feet even before she acknowledged me. I gave the right answer! So after school my teacher took me to the principal, Mama-J. She gave me a hug, wrote something in a Bible and handed it to me, saying, "I'm giving you this book of life. Use it and you'll be successful in your life."'

'Excellent, Baba! And where's that Bible now?'

'Still on my bookshelf.'

'Do you read it?'

as much as I used to. It's gaining dust.'

'Did you used to read it a lot?'

He nodded. 'When I was in Class 12 I liked to study it for the beauty of the language. Our English teacher once told us that there were some examples of good literature in the Bible. I still remember the first chapter of the Book of Job, a dialogue between God and Satan.'

'The Bible is not literature only,' Yvonne said with a spark in her eye. 'Most importantly it's a book of life, as Mama-J once advised you.'

Babatunde smiled. 'How's Mama-J keeping? Are you in touch with her?' he changed the subject.

'She's fine. In fact, excellent. She was about 28 when she came here; she's now over 50. She and her husband have moved from Texas to Ohio. Her husband is a professor of Contextual Theology.'

'I'm pleased to hear that.'

There was a pause before Yvonne spoke again.

'Now that the ice is broken, Baba, I'd like to get down to serious business. Over the past two weeks I have been thinking a lot about your volunteering; I have been observing your performance and your professional attitude towards your work and towards the staff. In view of all these factors, I have decided to put my head on the block by recommending that you should be appointed as an auxiliary teacher on probation.'

'Oh thank you very much, Yvie!' exclaimed Babatunde.

Yvonne grinned. 'Are you sure you are prepared to take up the challenge?'

'No be big problem Yvie,' Babatunde chuckled. 'I go manage. You'll see.'

'This morning I sent off a letter to our head office in the US. I told my superiors that though you are not a Christian, you are a decent African who fears his Creator.'

Babatunde grinned in delight: 'A million thanks, Yvie!'

'I also mentioned that you are considering becoming a Christian.'

'You said that?' Babatunde's grin disappeared. 'But Yvie, how could you dare think that I would ever consider...?'

Yvonne interrupted him with laughter.

Babatunde swallowed the rest of his words: *No, you can't force me to be a Christian!*

'Listen Baba, we can never force or blackmail you to be a Christian,' said Yvonne, as if reading his mind. 'But I hope that one day our goodness may lure you to become a Christian.'

Babatunde avoided her eyes. 'Yes, who knows, I could be a Christian one day,' he mumbled.

The way she was looking at him told him she'd heard the insincerity in his voice.

## 25

The next month seemed to fly by. Teaching a class of 30 Class I pupils was something that Babatunde found highly stimulating. He was so absorbed in his work that he had time for nothing else.

At month end, when Yvonne had given the staff members their cheques, she called Babatunde to her office. She told him that he would get paid a salary for the two and half months' work only at the end of March. She said the delay was due to the fact that their head office was in the US. Out of her petty cash budget, she gave him 100 US dollars, to cover transport and other expenses.

After Babatunde had signed for the money, she invited him to have a cool drink with her.He accepted, smiling as he scrutinised the container. 'This is nice. I'm tasting it for the first time.'

She grinned. 'Enjoy the great American flavour.'

They laughed.

'It's my leadership style to get to know my staff a little better over a drink.'

'I appreciate that, Yvie.'

'I understand that you Africans who practice African religion often offer part of your food to your gods.'

'You know about this?'

'I read books about the world's religions.'

'Yes, it's true.'

'So what is the name of the god you worship?'

'He is called by many names. Some of my people prefer the name Obasi; Obasi-on-high.'

'That sounds very... out of the ordinary.'

'If you don't mind, Yvie,' said Babatunde, 'let's steer away from religion.'

'That's okay. You know Baba, you can't nag or bludgeon someone into heaven; but you can charm him into...'

Babatunde wrinkled his forehead. 'Your Christian charms aren't going to prevail against my gods.'

They grinned at each other.

'But why are you so confident... in fact, so cocky... about your gods?' asked Yvonne.

Babatunde laughed off her remark. 'I have a firm foundation that can't be shaken by the winds of the gods of white people.'

'Why are you so sure that you have a strong foundation that can't be...?'

'I was the Amadioha priest in my family. According to our tribe's tradition, one of the sons, preferably the eldest, is expected to assume the title. For years my father asked my elder brothers to avail themselves for initiation, but the request was like a seed falling on dry ground. They were employed as factory workers in the city and offered many excuses as to why they were unavailable. They told my father that I, as the youngest brother, was a more suitable candidate because I was still young and I stayed with my father.'

'That's an intriguing background, Baba.'

'So when I was nine years old, my father asked for permission from the gods to pass the Amadioha high priesthood to me. Two weeks before the initiation my father asked me to attend the preparatory sessions during which two village elders were present. The elders told me that I was about to take up a serious responsibility and that I should ask the gods to make me brave and strong. During the second week I was given several cups of boiled ground herbs, for purification.

'On the last day of the ritual, which was a Saturday, at midnight, the Amadioha high priest was present. I was given cooked game meat mixed with herbs; I was told it was bitter and that I should chew and swallow it quickly while standing. Later, I was undressed, and some incisions were made on my feet, legs, hands and arms with a razor blade. The Most High Priest of Amadioha motioned towards his leather bag and said, "I am going to take out something out of this bag. It's a Amadioha snake. Boy, be brave like a lion. Don't be afraid, be courageous — for the responsibility of Amadioha priesthood is about to rest on your head. The snake is going to lick the blood on your feet, legs, hands and arms." I held my breath and exhaled slowly as the snake licked my blood and finally crawled away between my legs. I was told to walk around my homestead six times without looking backwards.'

*

Although the money Yvonne had given him was meant for transport and personal expenses, Babatunde shared it with his family. On Saturday morning he took his nephew, Ekene, to the nearest town where he bought him a white school shirt, some underpants and a pair of knee-length socks. He bought himself a wristwatch.

Babatunde also bought his first packet of cigarettes, the menthol brand he'd seen his friend Odenigbo smoking. At school he never smoked publicly. He smoked during breaks in the sanitised sink and cement pit-toilet;

he sucked mint-flavoured sweets thereafter to neutralise the tobacco smell.

As he grew up he learnt that Christians of the calibre of his cousin, Nnesinachi, frowned upon and were offended by people who smoked and drank liquor. He often thought: *I don't want Yvie to tell her superiors in the US that I'm smoking...that could be a minus.*

The cordial relationship between Babatunde and Yvonne motivated him to perform better. During weekends he would find himself wishing he was standing in front of his pupils. He had no doubt that he cherished a passion for teaching.

On the last Friday of March when Babatunde's mind was focused on nothing but his work, Yvonne called him into her office, to hand him his first cheque. It was a dream realised; he smiled as he signed that he had received the cheque, a bluish paper with his name written on it, and gave Yvonne a firm handshake.

*

When Babatunde showed his mother his first salary, she knelt down and thanked the gods. Without delay she suggested that his siblings should be invited for the thanksgiving ceremony.

The shrine made of sticks and adorned with a wooden figure, a monkey's skull, chicken feathers, some snake's teeth and the tusk of an elephant calf, was the focus of Babatunde, his mother, two brothers and two sisters as they stood before it late that Saturday afternoon.

After prostrating herself before the shrine, their mother knelt and gestured to the eldest son to hand her a wooden bowl containing porridge and cooked goat-meat; she took out a handful and transferred it into a bowl on the altar. She passed the bowl back to her eldest son who, after doing what his mother had just done, passed the bowl to his siblings according to birth order, until it landed in the palms of Babatunde, the last born. His mother gestured to him and he knew what to do: hand her the envelope containing his first salary.

'The Great One Amadioha, our gods...' she paused, waving the envelope, '...here is the little fat brought by our son, Baba. Thank you that you have protected him from when he was just a small thing until now that he is a big educated young man, the pride of the Okoronkwo clan.'

His mother went on to thank the gods for good rains, a bountiful harvest and excellent health for all family members. Babatunde kept nodding as his mother was speaking. His mother motioned towards him and he took the cue.

'Obasi-on-high and the gods of my parents,' said Babatunde, 'I am asking you to continue protecting me against witches and wizards of the village as I perform my tasks as an auxiliary teacher. Please help me to make enough money so that I should be in a good position to marry a wife and start my own family.'

## 26

On Monday afternoon Babatunde waited for Yvonne to give him a lift to the city as agreed. He strolled to the toilet where he smoked a cigarette, remembering to suck a mint-flavoured sweet afterwards as he walked towards Yvonne's car.

Before dropping him at the Central Bank of Nigeria, she asked if she could buy him a hamburger and cool drink. Babatunde welcomed the offer.

As the waitress put down the tray loaded with the meal they'd ordered, Yvonne gave Babatunde the kind of smile that made him suspect it would be followed by one of her characteristic witty remarks.

'So how are your gods keeping you?' she asked with a grin.

*I guessed right,* thought Babatunde, smiling and swallowing his mouthful of a burger. 'Very well. And I've already thanked the gods for my first salary.'

'Time will come, Baba.'

'For what?' inquired Babatunde innocently.

'You know what I'm talking about. Your attitude towards Christianity reminds me of the story of an African king ... the king of the Igbos about a century ago.'

Babatunde gazed into her eyes, his curiosity piqued. He thought about the fable of the Lion King that he was so fond of.

'The king often laughed off the attempts of a missionary who kept pestering him to accept the gospel,' said Yvonne. 'Would you be interested in listening to the story?'

'Yes, provided it isn't too long. Tell me Yvie, how do I remind you of the king?'

Yvonne chortled.

Babatunde waved his hand. '*Oya,* go on.'

'Well one day the zealous missionary, out of desperation, handed the king a translated Bible and begged him to read it. The king shook his head and laughed as usual. As the missionary walked to his horse cart the king flipped over the pages of the Bible and remarked: "Ha-ha-haa, I'm going to smoke the whole book."

'The missionary said, "You say you are going to smoke the Bible, your royal highness?" The missionary could not believe what the king had said. And the king replied, "Yes. I'm going to tear off page by page and use it as a homemade cigarette and smoke it." "Please do me a favour, king," appealed the missionary, "Before you smoke each page, read it first. You can start with the gospel of Matthew." The king nodded and smiled as the missionary stepped away.'

'So what happened?' asked Babatunde.

'The king tore out the pages of the Bible and smoked the whole book of Matthew. It took him a month. In the middle of the following month the missionary paid him a visit and inquired: "How far are you, your royal highness?" The king replied, "I am about to finish the book of Mark, because it is shorter than the first book." "Well done!" said the missionary. "Are you still reading every page before smoking it?" "Of course!" replied the king.

'By the middle of the following month the king had finished smoking the gospel of Luke. A few days later the missionary received a visit from the king's guards. They told the missionary that the king wanted to see him urgently. The missionary went to see the king and asked: "How far have you smoked the Bible pages, your royal highness?" "I've started smoking the book of John," replied the king. "But I have only smoked up to chapter two. After reading chapter three I couldn't smoke it." "Why?" asked the missionary. "I stopped at verse 16," said the king, "which says: 'For God so loved people all over the world that He gave his only son, that whoever believes in him should not perish but have everlasting life." To cut a long story short, the king was converted and months later the queen, the king's advisers and some tribes-people followed their leader's example.'

Smiling at Babatunde, Yvonne paused, then said: 'So Baba, what do you think about what I have just told you?'

He shrugged. 'It's an amusing story. But it cannot move me one inch from my African gods. It's fit for kindergarten kids.'

Yvonne laughed.

'Tell me Yvie, why do you have the surname of my people, Adichie?' asked Babatunde, steering the conversation in a different direction. 'I always wanted to ask you this question.'

'I will tell you,' said Yvonne. 'In 1952 my father, Ifeanyichukwu Adichie, went to Atlanta in the US on a Lincoln Scholarship, to study for a Master's degree in English literature. The following year he met and fell in love with a beautiful young African-American woman, Judy Adams. My father married my mother in 1954 and a year later I was born.'

'So you are two years older than me?' asked Babatunde. 'I thought you were two years younger.'

Yvonne had a good laugh. 'Yes, what's the big deal?'

Babatunde just smiled. 'Please continue.'

'Apart from telling us about his family, my father often talked about his best friend, Chris. I later learned that he was referring to Christopher Okigbo, the well-known Nigerian poet. When I was ten years old, we visited my father's family for the first time. I had two brothers who were also with us. My father took us around the country and at last we met Uncle Chris who was an Assistant Librarian at the University of Nsukka. In the evening after supper, Uncle Chris read us some of his poems. I remember my father saying, "Chris, you are writing difficult poems," and Uncle Chris responding with laughter, commenting: "I'm a poet for poets." The next morning Uncle Chris bade us goodbye and within a week we were back in the US. My father and Uncle Chris exchanged letters.

'The following year when I was eleven my father read a letter from Uncle Chris and told my mother, "There's a coup d'état in my country!" "Dad, what's a coup d'état?" I asked, and he replied, "The soldiers have taken over the government." In 1967, towards the end of June—I was twelve then—I was helping my mother prepare supper one evening when my father, who had come from the campus, showed my mother an envelope addressed to him and told her, "Chris has written me a very disturbing letter."

'The following day during supper my mother said to us, "Something has happened in your father's country, Nigeria. Uncle Chris says the Igbos are beginning to talk about secession, which means breaking away to establish their own country. As I'm speaking, the Igbo people from all over the country are going back to the eastern region. Uncle Chris is asking daddy to come home for a short while. So daddy will be going back next week." We, the children, asked, "When will daddy come back home?" And our father assured us, "I could be back after three weeks or even a month."

'When we took daddy to the airport, I had no idea that we were seeing him for the last time. Within a few days he called my mother, and we were delighted to hear his voice; we huddled around my mother as they spoke on the trans-Atlantic telephone call.

'We asked him, "Daddy, are you okay?" and he replied that he was more than okay. We heard him telling mother, "Judy, you might have read in the newspapers that yesterday, on July 1st of 1967, the eastern region under Major General Ojukwu announced its secession as the Independent Republic of Biafra." We were very disappointed when mom told us that daddy would need to extend his stay in Nigeria because many people wanted to speak to him.

'What my father didn't tell us was that he was undergoing military training. Early in August 1967 my mother received a call in the evening. The caller said he was Major General Chinualumogu from the Republic of Biafra. He broke the shattering news that my father had been killed, together with Uncle Chris, at the war front near Nsukka. He said the two had died embracing each other. The man ended by telling my mother that my father and Uncle Chris would be posthumously decorated by the Head of State of Biafra with the National Order of Merit.'

Suddenly Yvonne dropped her face into her palms and began to sob. Babatunde moved close to her and put his hand on her shoulder.

When she had composed herself, Yvonne asked for the bill and they left the restaurant.

She drove Babatunde to his bank and later to the supermarket where they bought some groceries. Babatunde also went to a clothing shop where he bought himself a short-sleeved blue-and-grey checked shirt and a pair of black trousers. He also bought a pair of khaki shorts. The old pair would be Ekene's hand-me-downs, he decided. Thereafter they drove back to the village.

# 27

One morning Babatunde was writing on the blackboard when he looked back to see Yvonne standing in the doorway in the company of Felix Okoro. She beckoned him out of the classroom.

'Yesterday when I walked past the Russian embassy,' Felix said to Babatunde, 'I saw, written on the board at the entrance, "Scholarship available for African students." I went into the embassy for more information, and the first secretary told me that the Russian government is on a recruitment drive for African students. When I told him that I knew of a young student looking for a scholarship, he gave me forms. Here they are, Baba.' Felix handed them to him.

'Thank you Teacher Felix,' said Babatunde, scrutinising them.

'The Russian official told me that to qualify the applicant must win an essay-writing competition. I think that is written on the last page.'

Babatunde flipped to the final page. 'Closing date is the third week of April,' he read.

'That means you have two weeks to prepare,' said Felix.

'Thank you, teacher Felix for thinking of me.'

Felix smiled. 'So what do you think? Are you going to try?' He saw Babatunde's hesitation. 'Perhaps you need some time to consider this scholarship. Why don't you come and see me this Sunday at about 15h00? We can then discuss the matter.'

*

When Babatunde arrived that Sunday afternoon he found Felix alone at his house, reading the newspaper. Felix told him that his wife and children had gone to attend a church meeting.

'So have you made up your mind, Baba?' Felix asked as they had tea.

'To be honest, Teacher Felix, you've really taken me by surprise. At this moment

I'm not sure if I should consider the scholarship.'

'Why? Why would you miss such a golden opportunity?'

'The idea of a scholarship is something I haven't thought about.'

'But you had the whole of Saturday to think about it, Baba.'

'I was interested in agriculture and you suggested teaching. I'm teaching and I'm beginning to like it very much. Now you are suggesting something different: journalism. In a foreign country where the language is not even English.'

'Baba, you are still a young man; it's easy for you to venture into new and different things. You have nothing to lose by trying. Besides, there are too many teachers in the village. Why shouldn't you do something more challenging like journalism? You are a bright boy, and you've passed English with distinction.'

'I haven't even told my mother,' said Babatunde, after a short pause. 'And I know my people aren't going to be impressed with the idea.'

'You know the saying: "If you put a bowl full of food in front of a hungry person and he hesitates to eat it, another person who knows the red eyes of hunger will take it." So it's up to you, Baba.'

After a long pause Babatunde raised his head to look at Felix.

'You are right, Teacher Felix. As I once told you, I feel in my blood that one day I will be a great person. There has to be more to life than teaching children under an iroko tree.'

Felix responded with laughter.

Later, in the bus back to his village, Babatunde recalled what Felix had once said to him: *The world respects any man or woman who does something for himself to change the status quo.*

That evening, standing in the garden of his homestead, smoking, he knew he had to start preparing for the scholarship competition. He decided to go to the Russian embassy on Friday afternoon. His intention was to establish a relationship with the officials and to seek more clarity.

*

Entering the embassy reception area that Friday, the first thing that captured his attention was the life-size bronze statue of a man: 'Vladimir Lenin', he read at the bottom of the statue. Behind the statue was the flag of the USSR, with its distinctive sickle and hammer.

After waiting for some time, he was finally taken by the receptionist to an office, where he met an official. Introducing himself as Yuri Popolov, the smiling official gave him a firm handshake.

'Why do you want to study in the Soviet Union?' asked Popolov, in an accent which sounded strange to Babatunde's ears.

'Sir, it's the only study opportunity available at the moment,' responded Babatunde.

'Tell me,' Popolov grinned, 'If America and the USSR were to offer you scholarships at the same time, which one would you accept?'

'The USSR.'

'Why?'

'I think the science and technology of the USSR is far superior to that of America.'

'That's a brilliant answer.'

Babatunde listened with utmost attention as Popolov enlightened him about the USSR had been empowering African students since the 1920s.

'If you write good essays,' said Popolov as Babatunde got to his feet, preparing to leave, 'you could get the scholarship.'

*

On Saturday, Babatunde stood at the usual make-shift stall at the end of the village, hawking his yams, kola nuts and dried small-game meat. It was the same spot where Felix had met him on New Year's Eve. He wore his new pair of khaki shorts.

As he was smoking, reflecting on his meeting with Yuri Popolov, his train of thought was interrupted by the welcome sight of Felix's car stopping beside his stall. Out of respect, he threw his cigarette down and stamped it out.

He told Felix about his visit to the Russian embassy.

'When you are building a mansion, you start with the first brick. The secret of success is in good preparation,' Felix told him approvingly. 'If you work on your essays diligently and speak well during the interview, you are going to get the scholarship.'

'Thank you for your encouragement, Teacher Felix. A good friend of mine, Odenigbo Nwoye, will be returning from London today. He is an Honours Political Science student. I'm going to ask him to help me with fine-tuning the essays.'

'In life all we see are great people up there; what we don't see are the shoulders carrying them.'

'That's true, Teacher Felix.'

'If you get the scholarship, how long will your degree be? Four years?'

'Yes, Teacher Felix.'

'Time flies, Baba. Four years later you'll be back home and you can join the government as a journalist, perhaps as a speechwriter for the Minister of Information.'

Babatunde chuckled, feeling flattered.

'I'm telling you,' continued Felix, 'you can even join radio or television, who knows?'

# 28

On Sunday afternoon when all the family members were visiting elsewhere, Babatunde heard the sound of a car door banging. When he looked out through the curtain of his study, he saw Odenigbo. Babatunde was eager to share the very important news about his future with the bosom friend he had not seen for over two and a half months.

'I knew I would find you home on a Sunday because you are a man of African gods,' joked Odenigbo. 'So *wuzzup*?' he inquired, typically in high spirits.

Babatunde updated him on everything that had happened since they last met; how he thrived on his job as an auxiliary teacher, and how he always looked forward to standing in front of his pupils.

'That's great; and how's your boss?'

'Yvie is a wonderful woman. The only thing is that she talks a lot about her religious beliefs, but she's not boring. She's not that type of Christian who threatens you so much about hell that when you see them coming your way in the city, you just want to change direction. Yvie has a wonderful sense of humour. You must meet her.'

'I will, very soon. So, I guess you've now found the career you regard as your calling.'

'I'm not so sure. I'm considering changing my career.'

'What do you want to do with your life now?'

'If the gods smile on me, I might go to a university in Russia on a scholarship next year.'

'Is that so? And why have you been hiding this exciting piece of information from me?'

'I only heard about the scholarship last week. The information was brought to my attention by my former teacher, Felix Okoro. He taught me English at high school.'

'For which university is the scholarship?'

'Patrice Lumumba University in the south of Russia. The embassy official said it used to be known as the People's Friendship University. It was established in 1960 and was renamed a year later.'

'You'll be proud to study at an institution named after a great African leader. Do you know about Patrice Lumumba?'

'Not much. I have a hazy idea about him. The Russian official said if I'm successful I will receive full political education.'

'Patrice Lumumba was the first Prime Minister of Congo; he was in power for just a few months and was assassinated by the former colonial power, Belgium, in partnership with the CIA.'

'What's the CIA?'

'The Central Intelligence Agency, an American spy network that is very anti-communist. Lumumba was viewed with horror as a protégé of Russia by the United States who decided he must be exterminated. So he was abducted and assassinated. He was replaced by the pro-Western Mobutu Sese Seko. Lumumba's body could not be found anywhere. Later, a former Belgian police commissioner claimed he had helped to chop Lumumba's body into pieces and dissolved it in acid.'

'*Tufia!* That's terrible!' exclaimed Babatunde.

'Yes! That's why I hate the US. You know, in London, once a year, African and Arab students participate in anti-US protest marches.'

'How do you know all this detailed information about Lumumba?'

'One of my modules is about European powers that colonised central African countries.'

'Listen Ode, to qualify for the Patrice Lumumba scholarship I must win an essay-writing competition. So I need your help, my friend. I've written the first draft. Your knowledge of Political Science will be handy.'

'Have they given you topics? Or must you write what you like?'

'They gave me two topics: the first one is, "Christianity is not a boon but a liability to Africa." The second one is, "Young African Communists can change Africa for the better."'

'It will be a pleasure for me to help a friend,' said Odenigbo.

'Thanks Ode.'

'Those are very juicy topics, Baba. About the topic regarding Christianity, I suggest that we include a famous quotation by Karl Marx: "Religion is the opium of the people."'

Babatunde chuckled. 'Let me get a pen. I must take some notes as you speak.'

'You must prove that Christianity is a pipe-dream,' said Odenigbo, 'a fallacy promising the gullible followers pie-in-the sky, while pragmatic communism believes in the now.'

Babatunde nodded with a smile, writing it all down.

'The great African political thinker and president of the first African independent country, Ghana, Kwame Nkrumah, is another important source. He once said, "Seek ye first the kingdom of politics..."'

'Not so fast, Ode,' said Babatunde scribbling furiously.

'"Seek ye first the kingdom of politics, and the rest shall be added."'

Odenigbo paused before continuing. 'You can see in this statement that the man believed more in the kingdom of politics than in the kingdom of God, which is irrelevant for the realities of life. This towering mind also came up with the term "neo-colonialism"...'

Babatunde continued taking note.

# 29

That Monday afternoon Babatunde emerged from the toilets where he'd been smoking, as was his wont. He was about to head for the gate when he saw Yvonne walking towards her office; he waved at her and she beckoned him over, waiting for him in front of her office.

'How was your weekend, Baba?'

'It was great, Yvie! I'm really excited about life.'

'Your face tells it all.'

'My bosom friend, Odenigbo, paid me a visit on Sunday.'

Yvonne flashed him one of her naughty smiles. 'Is he tall, handsome and rich?'

They laughed.

'Yes, he's tall and handsome, but he's not rich. Ode is studying in London.'

'Wonderful!'

'You must meet the guy, Yvie. He'll be coming to see me on Thursday.'

'I would love to meet him.'

Yvonne glanced at her watch.

'Are you in a hurry?' asked Babatunde.

'Yes, but we can talk.'

Babatunde observed that Yvonne preferred to socialise with him on Fridays. He'd also noted that during the week she consistently kept a professional distance from him, reserving her friendlier manner and smiles for unofficial, off-duty moments.

'Thanks, Yvie.'

'Let's sit in my office.'

They walked in and Babatunde took a seat, leaning forward with his elbows on the desk and his head bowed. He breathed in deeply and said: 'Yvie, there's something I've been hiding from you.'

Yvonne smiled at him. 'What is it? What have you been doing behind my back, Baba?'

'I'm busy applying for a scholarship to go to Russia.'

There was a moment's silence.

'Really?'

'Yes. I didn't want to tell you. What's compelling me now is that you're sure to find out at some time.'

'You've really taken me by surprise, Baba. Tell me, why Russia? Why not the US or the UK? In fact, why don't you apply simultaneously to institutions in the UK and the US?' Yvonne continued. 'I could help you to get into a university in the US.'

Babatunde shook his head. 'My heart is in Russia. And I have a feeling that I'm going to get the scholarship, if I can impress them with my essays.'

'What essays?'

'I'll be submitting two essays on Thursday. My friend Ode will take me to the Russian embassy.'

Yvonne bent her head and held her chin in her hands. 'I took a great risk by employing you here, hoping that our kindness would lure you into becoming a Christian. Now you are becoming a communist.'

'Am I becoming a communist?'

'What else will you become?'

'To be honest, Yvie, there's something that fascinates me about Russia.'

'What is it?'

'I can't place a finger on the exact thing. It's a mystery. I just know I want to go there.'

'Baba, you haven't answered my question. Why don't you apply simultaneously to institutions in the UK and the US? Don't tell me that your heart is in Russia. Please use your head. Get all the facts and take the appropriate decision. What's fascinating to you could in fact be a fatal attraction.'

Babatunde responded with a shrug and a faint grin. She looked straight into his eyes but he turned his head away. He recalled Teacher Felix's words: *Baba, you are still a young man; it's easy for you to venture into new and different things. You have nothing to lose by trying...* 'Baba, are you sure you're taking the right decision?' Yvonne asked, her tone pitched a little higher.

He said nothing.

'I don't want you to find you have blundered. You'll go to Russia and discover when you are there that the food is terrible, the language is strange, the people are unfriendly, and the weather is unkind to your dark skin!'

Again, no words emerged from his lips. When she tried to maintain eye contact with him he avoided her stare.

Sighing, she forced a tired smile out of her tense face.

'Listen Baba, let me not put you under pressure.' She sighed again. 'It is a pity that you aren't going to work with us for a longer time, as I had hoped. But anyway, I'll pray for you. If it's God's will that you should go to Russia, so let it be.'

Babatunde rose from his chair. 'Amen!'

From the manner in which she looked at him he could tell that she sensed his 'Amen' was an empty shell. She stood up too. 'I pray that the next time that you say "Amen" you really mean it. And I pray that if you do go to Russia, you will go there as a Christian.'

'Please don't waste your prayers! Don't bother God, Yvie!'

*

In the days that followed Babatunde and Yvonne never had a moment to engage in a serious discussion. Her head was buried in work. Whenever Babatunde walked to the gate, he was relieved not to hear her familiar voice calling him, or her usual smiling face waiting for him, her hand beckoning him over. He expected to be handed a list of American universities, but that too never happened.

On the appointed Thursday afternoon, Babatunde went to knock at the door of Yvonne's office. He was accompanied by Odenigbo.

'Yvie, sorry to just barge in,' said Babatunde, 'meet my friend, Odenigbo Nwoye. Ode, meet my boss, Yvonne Adams-Adichie.'

Yvonne rose to her feet, her face lit with a smile. Babatunde was delighted to witness his boss and his friend exchanging handshakes.

'Have a seat, guys,' said Yvonne.

'No thanks, Yvie, we're in a hurry,' replied Babatunde. 'Ode is taking me to the Russian embassy. I must submit my essays today.'

Yvonne accompanied Babatunde and Odenigbo to the latter's car.

'Ode and I grew up together,' Babatunde told her.

'We used to live in the same village, playing games together,' added Odenigbo.

Yvonne smiled, glancing at her wristwatch. 'Well Ode, it was very nice meeting you.'

'Likewise. I'm immensely pleased to have met you, Yvie,' said Odenigbo.

'Why don't we meet tomorrow for a drink,' Yvonne suggested. 'Is that alright with both of you?'

Babatunde exchanged glances with Odenigbo then turned back to Yvonne, his thumb upraised.

# 30

By the time they arrived at Madam Anu-nchi restaurant, Yvonne and Odenigbo were conversing like old friends. Yvonne had driven the three of them there in her car. They placed their orders and had drinks while they waited. Before long their meals were placed in front of them. Yvonne said a prayer of thanks for the food and they began to eat.

Odenigbo smiled wryly at Yvonne. 'Yvie, as you were praying you reminded me of a friend from South Africa. He used to joke that the colonialists gave the black man the Bible and taught him how to pray with eyes closed, so that by the time he said, "Amen!" he found that the white man had grabbed his land.'

Babatunde and Odenigbo laughed loudly while Yvonne just grinned.

Babatunde snapped his fingers. 'I should have included that joke in the essay I've just submitted to the Russian embassy.'

'What was your topic?' asked Yvonne.

'"Christianity is not a boon but a liability to Africa."'

'Baba, do you really believe that Christianity is a liability to Africa?' Yvonne challenged him. 'What about the mission hospitals and schools?'

'Slow down, Yvie,' said Odenigbo. 'I knew you would be quick to defend the indefensible.'

'Why do you say that?' Yvonne frowned playfully.

'It's a well-known fact in the village that you are a zealot of a Christian,' replied Odenigbo.

'I take that as a compliment, Ode,' said Yvonne. 'Do you also believe in African religion like Baba?'

'No, I'm an atheist.'

Yvonne looked into Odenigbo's eyes, chuckling: 'Pleased to meet you, Mr Atheist!'

Odenigbo smiled back. 'I take that as a compliment.'

'It's interesting,' said Yvonne, 'that just before the plane crashes, atheists suddenly change their religion.'

'Why should they do that?' asked Babatunde, amused.

'All of a sudden they become Christians,' responded Yvonne, 'pleading with the God of Abraham, Isaac and Jacob to save them from a certain death.'

Odenigbo and Babatunde looked at each other, the former shrugging his shoulders.

'So you African-Americans are comfortable with the idea of adopting the religion of former slave-masters?' asked Odenigbo.

'Well, my people went through very difficult times; to be sane, they had to sing Negro Spirituals; but at the right time God delivered us from slavery.'

'Preach, sistah, preach!' chanted Odenigbo, feigning the role of the zealous churchgoer.

'Hallelujah!' shouted Babatunde.

'Amen!' said Babatunde and Odenigbo almost simultaneously.

The two men slapped each other's palms and burst into laughter.

'Guys, I'm praying for the time when you'll mean your Amens and Hallelujahs,' said Yvonne.

'Pray and waste your prayer,' responded Odenigbo.

'The truth of the matter is that the God of erstwhile slave-masters has become the God of former slaves,' said Yvonne, 'and we have business-like churches that have successful missionary programmes.'

'Like the church that sent you to Nigeria?' inquired Odenigbo.

'Yes, the AME.'

'What does it stand for?'

'African Methodist Episcopal. Do you know that it was started by a former slave church leader?'

'No, I didn't know that.'

'The AME church was established in 1816 in the US because of racism,' Yvonne began to enlighten Odenigbo. 'One day in 1787 the African-American members of the congregation decided to pray in the section reserved for whites, in defiance. When the church officials pulled them off their knees and shoved them towards the "Negro" part of the building, the African-Americans were so offended that they decided to form their own church, the "Free African Society". In 1816 the new church was named the AME, which is today the oldest and largest black church in the US.'

Odenigbo clapped his palms. 'Hallelujah! This time I mean it, Yvie. I must admit, I'm highly impressed with the history of the AME. I think that's the church I could attend, if I become...'

Babatunde suddenly pointed a finger at Odenigbo. 'No, Ode, you aren't going to do that! Remember, religion is the opium of the people!'

'Oh yes! Seek ye first the kingdom of politics, and the rest shall be added,' said Odenigbo.

'Alleloyah!' shouted Babatunde.

'Amen!' said Odenigbo.

Odenigbo and Babatunde again slapped each other's palms, laughing. Yvonne responded with a grim face.

'Okay, Yvie, let's talk about something else,' said Odenigbo. 'Enough of this religion! Did  Baba tell you that he was once a boy-soldier during the Biafran war?'

'Oh yes! And I honour him for having sacrificed his youth for the dream which the Igbo nation hoped would be realised.'

Odenigbo applauded then said: 'Baba told me that your father was one of the fallen soldiers during the Biafran war and that he was posthumously decorated by the Head of State of Biafra with the National Order of Merit.'

'That's true.'

'You should be proud of the sacrifice made by your father and many other gallant soldiers who braved a fierce war and died for us,' said Odenigbo.

Yvonne contained her face in her palms for a moment then lifted her head to look straight into Odenigbo's eyes. 'I'm sorry to be emotional.'

'It's okay,' said Babatunde.

'My dad was,' continued Yvonne, 'one of the first freedom-fighters to be buried in the heroes' acre.'

Odenigbo nodded somberly.

'My mom wanted to take the corpse back to the US. But when she arrived in Nigeria my dad was already buried. The lieutenant-general she spoke to told her that my dad could not be exhumed and that there would be time for emotional matters only at the end of the war.

'She approached the US embassy official who told her that the matter was complicated because the recognition of Biafra was, at that time, indeterminable. So she returned to the US with his belongings. At the bottom of his suitcase we found a copy of Biafra's national anthem, the flag and the minutes of the military high command.'

Yvonne broke off and took out a handkerchief to wipe a lurking tear at the corner of her eye. Babatunde put a comforting hand on her shoulder.

'You don't have to say any more,' said Odenigbo, 'I can see this is digging out painful memories.'

'Please, let me continue,' she responded. 'Talking about it is part of my healing. When I was in high school, I began to research the Biafran war. I read anything I could find — books, magazines, periodicals... I was just thirsty and hungry to know about my father's country... the people, the language, the currency, the geography. I got to know that the motto of Biafra was "Peace, Unity, Freedom" and that the national anthem was "Land of the Rising Sun". When I was doing first year at university, I committed the four stanzas of the anthem to memory.'

'I like that stanza,' said Babatunde, 'the one in which there's a line saying: "Spilling our blood we'll count a privilege."'

'Stanza number two,' said Yvonne.

'Yvie and Baba, will you please recite the national anthem for me?' asked Odenigbo.

Yvonne stood at attention, saluting the imaginary Biafran flag. She recited:

'Land of the rising sun, we love and cherish,
Beloved homeland of our brave heroes.'

Babatunde also stood at attention and continued reciting:

'We must defend our lives or we shall perish,
We shall protect our hearts from all our foes.'

Together, they recited the next lines:

'But if the price is death for all we hold dear;
Then let us die without a shred of fear.'

Odenigbo applauded as Yvonne and Babatunde exchanged firm hugs. Standing up in his turn, he embraced Yvonne and Babatunde, who were both tearful. For a brief moment the three foreheads rubbed against one another.

# PART FOUR

## 31

*Special things seem to happen to me on Fridays*, thought Babatunde as he saw Yvonne coming towards him, holding a red envelope.

'Thank you, Yvie,' he said, receiving the envelope on which was written: *The Embassy of the Union of the Soviet Socialist Republics*. Heart hammering against his ribs, he went to sit on the little boulder under the iroko tree in the schoolyard.

He tore the envelope open, took out a folded letter, unfolded it and began to read it. A sunny smile settled on his face. He laughed and raised his fist, inserting the letter back into the envelope. Then he stood up and hastened to Yvonne's office. He walked in without knocking.

'Guess what, Yvie,' he grinned, waving the envelope at her.

'Don't tell me you've received good news from that red envelope!' responded Yvonne.

'Why not?'

Yvonne grinned. 'Red stands for trouble or ill luck!'

'Wrong! Red is the colour of communism. Listen Yvie, my application for a scholarship to Russia has been approved!'

For a moment she simply stared at him. 'Are you indeed going to Russia, Baba?'

Babatunde raised his fists above his head. 'Yes Yvie, I'm going, I'm going to Russia!'

A warm smile spread across his face. 'Are you rejoicing with me, Yvie?'

'To be honest,' said Yvonne softly, 'my answer is no. It would be dishonest of me to say yes. I'm just uncomfortable with this news. I don't even know why.'

'Your discomfort is based on fear of the unknown, Yvie.'

She looked away for a moment, then back at him.

'You're making me a liar, Baba.'

'Why do you say that?'

'I told my superiors in the US that you are a decent young African man who fears his Creator. Do you remember that's what I once said to you, when I told you that I'd written to our head office regarding your appointment?'

Babatunde smiled, nodding. 'And I said, "Who knows, I could be a Christian one day."'

'I sowed the word of God; the birds came and ate it up. The communists sowed their seed which fell on Baba's fertile soil, and it's clear that the seed is going to yield 60 times as much.'

Babatunde shrugged, feeling uncomfortable.

Yvonne fixed her stare on him. He saw her fist clench: 'You should have said, "Who knows, I could be a communist one day."'

'Does studying in Russia make me a communist?'

'Their goodness is going to lure you to become a communist.'

'I don't know, Yvie. I'm not a clairvoyant.'

'They can be cunning, those people, exploiting the techniques of Pavlov.'

'Who's Pavlov? A great communist?'

'He was a behavioural psychologist. Anyway, that's a topic for another day!'

Yvonne looked into Babatunde's eyes. 'You know what, Baba? I'm going to pray that God should change my heart of stone into a heart of flesh.'

'Alleloyah!' shouted Babatunde with affected holy fervour.

'In fact, God is instantaneously softening my heart.'

'For sure?'

'Yes! So, I'm genuinely rejoicing with you...'

'Thank you, Yvie!'

'Yes, I'm accepting the idea...I'm getting used to the idea, that you're going to Russia.'

'Thank you for that, Yvie! It'll make life easier for both of us. Just assume I'm your brother.'

'Yes, the lost brother, who'll one day come back to his senses and say, "I will arise and go to my father and I will say to him: 'Father I have sinned before heaven and before you.'"'

'Who's my father? The US?'

'Don't talk nonsense, Baba!'

Babatunde laughed.

'Now tell me, Baba: at which university will you be studying?'

'Patrice Lumumba University.'

'Now the communists are going to say, "Can you see how we are honouring your people?"'

The subdued smile on Babatunde's face faded; he contorted his forehead and pointed a finger at Yvonne. 'Listen, Yvonne! You are really speaking like a counter-revolutionary!'

Yvonne grinned. 'If you were a dog, I would say your bark was worse than your bite.'

'You know, Yvie, I got the scholarship because I've made a good impression on the communists. I know my value, and no one is going to undermine my value.'

Yvonne rose from her chair, walked around the desk and embraced Babatunde. 'I'm going to miss you, Baba.'

'Me too, Yvie.'

'I'm going to pray for you. That things should go well with you.'

'Thanks, Yvie.'

'But I'm also going to pray that you should be a Christian,' she said, her smile very bright, 'by the time you go to Russia.'

Babatunde chuckled. 'I told you that your Christian charms aren't going to prevail against my African gods.'

They laughed.


# 32

As he left Yvonne's office Babatunde had two hearts, the first one saying to him: *Rush home to break the exciting news to your people!* While the second heart whispered: *Why don't you first go and inform Teacher Okoro?* He heeded the advice of the first heart. In the bus taking him to his village, he kept saying to himself, *What a blessed Friday!* He took out the red envelope and re-read the letter:

Dear Mr Okoronkwo,
    With reference to your application for a scholarship to study in the USSR, I am delighted to inform you that your application has been favourably considered. Congratulations, Mr Okoronkwo! It's no minor achievement to be selected out of the top five in the short-list of 30 well-deserving applicants. The senior embassy staff will be ready to meet you during the first orientation meeting on Sunday 28th April 1979 at 10h00.
    Yours faithfully,
Leonid Popov,
Second Secretary

Babatunde smiled to himself as he folded the letter and inserted it back into the envelope. Myriad thoughts began to churn around in his head; he wondered if the ordinary Russians were unfriendly as Yvonne had once hinted to him. He felt that the embassy staff was personable enough. He was fascinated by their accents and pronunciation. However, many questions demanded answers: How's their food? Public transport? Health care? University life? Music? Night life? Women? Sport?

When he arrived at his homestead, he found his nephew Ekene digging yams in the backyard.

'Eki, I'll be going to Russia to study at one of the universities there,' he hastened to break his good news to the boy.

Ekene was so thrilled that he immediately went to the next door neighbours' homesteads, looking for his aunt, his mother's younger sister, to share the news. He eventually found her. Half an hour later tens of well-wishers from the neighbourhood had come to Babatunde's homestead.

'We hear that you'll be going to Lashia,' they said as they gave Babatunde congratulatory handshakes.

At sunset his mother was a few homesteads away from the Okoronkwos when she was mobbed by people young and old, saying: 'We hear that Baba will be going to *Lashia.*'

Entering the home yard his mother dashed straight to his hut where she found him with his sister.

'Baba, what is this that I hear, that you'll be going to…what's the name of the country?'

'*Lashia,*' said his sister.

'Why were you hiding such an important matter?' his mother asked in an accusatory tone

of voice.

'I didn't want to speak about the baby before it was born,' he replied. 'If I rushed to open

my mouth and the whole village knew I was applying for a scholarship and months later nothing happened, how would you feel, mother?'

'Yes, they would say he hastened to tan the baby-skin before the child is born.'

'Exactly. So that's the reason I decided to speak only at the right time. Teacher Okoro played a major role in helping me to get the scholarship.'

'Where is *Lashia?*' inquired his mother, 'Is it a city in England?'

'No, Russia is a part of the continent of Asia. It's a great country just like America. They

are clever people there; just like the Americans, they have also sent an aeroplane to the moon.'

'How long are you going to be there?'

'About four years. But I'll be coming home during holidays.'

'How will you be going there? By bus or train?'

'No, mother, it's very far. I'm going to ride in an iron bird.'

'Won't you be afraid that it can crash?'

'No, mother. Our gods are going to protect me.'

'I don't know why my heart is not white-white at this news.'

'What are you telling me, mother? That you don't want me to go there?'

'I haven't heard of anyone going to *Lashia*. Do you know how the people live there?

Eating food you are not going to be used to! Food that can make you ill!' She shook her head. 'Surrounded by people speaking a language you don't even understand!'

'I'll learn the language, mother. I don't want to miss this wonderful opportunity. I must go there, mother!'

'Against my wishes?'

Babatunde kept quiet for a moment, looking down. Suddenly he shuffled towards his mother and put his hand on her shoulder: 'Mother, please allow me to go to Russia. There are many students who are studying in Russia and other countries. To tell you the truth, I didn't want to go there. But Teacher Okoro said, "Baba, there are too many teachers in the village. You are still a young man, so you can still do different things." He also said, "If you put a bowl full of food in front of a hungry person and he hesitates to eat it, another hungry person will take it." Should I go and call Teacher Okoro?'

Babatunde's mother kept quiet for a long moment, gazing at her hands.

'You don't have to call him,' she said. 'If he's behind you and he said all those words, I'll have to go along with him. He's a man I can trust.'

'Thank you, mother!'

## 33

On Sunday Babatunde sat in a soot-black car from the Russian embassy which slowed down as it drew near to his homestead. On both sides of the dusty village street children who saw his face through the open window waved at him and cheered. He waved back at them. When the car stopped and the driver opened the door for him, he stepped out and waved at the boys standing in a half-moon in front of him. Ekene, who was working in the garden, came and stood beside his uncle. Babatunde saw Odenigbo closing the door of his car. For a moment Babatunde scanned the boys.

'It's a car of the Russians!' shouted one boy.

'Yes, that's the car that will take Ekene's uncle to Russia.'

Babatunde laughed.

One boy walked up to the driver sitting in the car and said: 'Uncle, will you please help me to go and attend school in Russia?'

The children, Babatunde, Odenigbo and the driver had a good laugh.

'No, you are too young,' Ekene challenged the boy. 'When uncle Baba goes to Russia, he's going to organise a scholarship for...' Ekene touched his chest with the index finger of his right hand, '...me!'

Babatunde felt Odenigbo's hand touching his and turned to greet him.

He thanked the driver of the embassy car, a Nigerian. The black car that could be mistaken for a hearse cruised along the bumpy dirt road; Babatunde and Odenigbo watched until it disappeared behind a little dust cloud.

'Baba, now I can believe that you are going to Russia,' his friend said. Babatunde responded with laughter. They lit cigarettes and sauntered towards Babatunde's hut.

Odenigbo puffed at his cigarette, excitement smouldering in his eyes. 'So how did it go at the Russian embassy? What was your first impression?'

'My first impression of the Russians was their stern faces; but they soon warm up to you as you talk and they get to know more about you and your goals. They seem to take life's challenges head-on, with unparalleled resoluteness.'

'And how did the session go?'

'It was my first orientation session. When it started I was nervous, but I quickly relaxed as I could see twenty pairs of eyes looking at me from smiling faces, encouraging me with approving nods as I spoke. They outlined the whole process of being a foreign student in Russia. The orientation process will continue for some weeks to come.

'After tea-break I was shown a video of communism and its impact on Africa and the world and how, by contrast, capitalism is a curse and a liability. The last video I was shown was about the 22nd Congress of the Communist Party of the Soviet Union in 1972. This has enabled me to get a clear picture of the communist movement all over the world. I've learned that of the 40 million communists scattered in five continents, only 50 000 are in Africa. I also learnt that the target of the Kremlin is to increase the number to at least 500 000. So as soon as my political education is finished, I'm going to start recruiting the youth. In my neighbourhood the youth are still excited over the fact that I'll be going to Russia. So they are going to be susceptible to my influence.'

'You can also recruit Yvonne!' remarked Odenigbo.

Babatunde winked. 'Oh, that CIA agent?'

They guffawed.

'The leader of the team asked me: "What are you going to do, after you've completed your degree?" I took my time before I replied. This is what I told them: "I'm going to descend on Africa and turn capitalism upside down with the hammer and sickle!" They exchanged glances and clapped their hands. As the applause subsided one of the guys who had not been speaking much said, "But tell us practically what you are going to do." I took a deep breath and replied, "Since I'll be armed with a degree in journalism, I'm going to establish a newspaper to be sponsored by the Kremlin. To be accessible to the working class, the newspaper should be in English and Igbo." At that point I saw them nodding and I added, "The capitalists have been using African politicians like pawns which they are moving around at their whim. So through the newspaper I'm going to conscientise them to frustrate the capitalists." My listeners applauded, smiling at each other and whispering.'

'So you think you've made a good impression?'

'Yes, beyond a shadow of a doubt, Ode! But you share the credit. Had it not been for your contribution I might have put up a mediocre or poor performance. So thank you, Ode.'

'It's always my pleasure to help a good friend!'

Babatunde opened his bag and showed Odenigbo some booklets.

'As you can see,' he said 'these are books about the History of Russia, Farming and Fisheries, Culture, Manufacturing and Government.'

He flipped over some pages and pointed: 'This is the Russian alphabet.'

Odenigbo studied the letters. 'It looks like our alphabet turned backwards and upside down.'

Babatunde chuckled.

'So you are going to learn all these cockroaches?'

They laughed.

'Well, I'm going to spend the first nine to ten months at the language laboratory.'

'What's next?'

'I'll do basic first-year courses. From the second year I'll focus more on journalism. And as a journalist major, I will be required to study Marxism, Leninism and the Theory of Communism, and Atheism.'

'Mh, you really make me salivate.'

Babatunde grinned. 'The ultimate goal is to immerse myself in communist ideology so that I should return to my country as a revolutionary cadre.'

## 34

Babatunde ran into Felix during the third week of November.

'I'm proud of you, Baba. How did your family react?'

'My mother was at first not very comfortable with the idea. But she gave it her blessing when I told her that you are my pillar of support. She trusts you, Teacher Felix.'

'If your mother is happy then the gods will look at you with white eyes.' He paused. 'How time flies,' Felix told Babatunde. 'In a matter of weeks, in January, you'll be flying to Russia.'

'Yes, Teacher Felix. Indeed, the months have not been running at the speed of a tortoise.'

Teacher Felix grinned and patted Babatunde's shoulder. 'Baba, as you spend the last two weeks at your school, be more conscientious.'

'Yes, I'm taking note, Teacher Felix.'

'Never make the mistake of telling yourself that you should slow down or neglect your work because you'll no longer continue to be a teacher.'

Babatunde nodded.

'Always leave the door open,' continued Felix. 'Remember the African idiom: "After drinking from a well, don't defecate into it, because one day you may find yourself thirsty, facing the same well."'

'Thank you for your advice, Teacher Felix.'

That week Babatunde was in high spirits, jovial as he talked to the staff. He felt energy surging in him as he played 'The Hyena and the Children'. He felt a hand tapping his shoulder and when he turned, he saw Yvonne looking at him.

'I guess you've made tremendous progress regarding your trip to Russia,' said Yvonne.

'It's great that I will be going to study in that great country. But one thing I'm going to miss my people and my culture.'

He suddenly broke into the children's rain song, *Ogwogwo mmili takumei ayolo.*

Yvonne grinned.

'Yes, Yvie, I've attended several orientation sessions, which include student life in Russia. I was also given continual political education. Yesterday the embassy sent their driver to collect me at my home. I had supper at the embassy. I was shown the fifth short film on communism, capitalism and the colonisation of Africa. We also had a discussion afterwards. And this is the gist: the communists view the African national independence as a transitory stage. The final objective is the incorporation of the

African nations into a communist bloc, in order to weaken the capitalist imperialist economic system.'

Yvonne shook her head. 'That's a communist pipe-dream!'

'I think it's achievable, Yvie.'

'Impossible, Baba!'

'Because you've confidence in your government's CIA?'

She touched his hand. 'Please let's steer away from this sensitive issue.' She had lowered her voice. 'We both feel strongly about it for different reasons. Okay. Let's focus on the African national independence. For the Christians, independence allows the true unfolding of the individual talents and collective personality of every nation.'

'But religion will remain the opium of the people, as Karl Marx says.'

'Now you are becoming vague and clichéd.'

'The Christianised populations are mere lambs while the capitalist lords are wolves. Let me ask you: didn't your weak Jesus say, "When they beat your cheek you should turn the other cheek, so that your reward in the so-called heaven should be great?'

'No, Baba, you are quoting the Bible out of context.'

'What's the right context? The communist or capitalist?'

'You should simply consult the Bible which Mama-J has given you. Please go and read it.'

'I'm not interested!'

'I sowed the word of God, the birds came and ate it up. The communists sowed their seed which fell on Baba's fertile soil, and it's clear that the seed is going to yield a hundred times as much.'

'Oh no, Yvie! Not again!'


## 35

Although there was a little staffroom adjacent to Yvonne's office, Babatunde preferred to sit on the boulder under the iroko tree when the sky was clear and the equatorial sun unleashed the sharpest spears. That afternoon on the last Friday of November, after class, he laughed aloud as he closed the booklet he was reading.

'Why are you laughing?' asked Yvonne, surprising Babatunde as she spoke from behind him.

'I'm laughing at this story…in fact it's a children's story, which I'm reading from this booklet,' said Babatunde.

He handed her the booklet. 'It's from the Russian embassy. It's a very fascinating story.' Babatunde released a ravishing smile. 'Can I read you the story?'

'Sure, Baba.'

Babatunde took the booklet and began to read: 'A lean and hungry wolf one day met a large, well-fed dog and said to it, "You look very well. I never saw anyone looking more graceful and beautiful. How do you manage to look so well?"

'The dog chuckled at the compliment.

"You seem to live much better than I," continued the wolf, "and yet you do far less than I

do. I'm always moving about looking for food, whereas you seem to live without effort."

"You can live as I do," said the dog, "if only you would do as I do."

"What is that?" asked the wolf.

"What I do is to guard the house at night and keep the thieves away," explained the dog.

"I'm willing to do that," said the wolf, "because at the moment I'm having a very difficult time. The weather is cold and it rains most of the time. What I would not give for a roof over my head and plenty of good food!"

"Follow me," said the dog.

'When they were going along, the wolf saw a mark on the dog's neck and asked what it was.

"It's nothing," said the dog.

"Yes, but tell me," persisted the wolf.

"Well if you must know, I'm tied up in the daytime to prevent me from biting people. It's only at night that I'm let loose. This has an advantage in that it makes me sleep during daytime and makes me a better watchdog at night. As soon as darkness comes, I'm let loose and I can go where I like. My master brings me bones from the table and the children bring me scraps of food. I feed very well and I really enjoy life. What do you think?"

"I'm sorry," said the wolf, "you may keep all you have. I prefer liberty and on no condition would I live the life you are leading."'

Babatunde closed the book, folded his arms and smiled. 'Did you enjoy the story?'

'Yes, very much.'

'What do you think is the moral of the story?' inquired Babatunde.

'I don't know, I haven't thought about it. Perhaps you can tell me.'

'The well-fed dog is the African-American and the wolf…'

Yvonne grinned. 'You can really talk a load of nonsense, Baba.'

Babatunde guffawed. 'Wait, let me finish!'

'Go on,' said Yvonne.

'The well-fed dog is the African-American who is overweight because he's overeating all the hamburgers and chips. And the wolf is Baba, an African-African, who chooses to study in Russia instead of the US or the UK.'

Yvonne shook her head, smiling wryly. 'I remain unconvinced.'

'My mission isn't to convince you, Yvie. It's just to prove to you that the Russians have a sense of humour too.'

'Baba, the Russians have become your heroes, and the Americans are now your villains.'

'Well let Americans choke on Coke!' retorted Babatunde.

'Baba, I've no doubt that the Russians have done a hell of a job in winning you to their side, but I'm not going to give up doing one thing: praying that you should be a Christian by the time you go to Russia.'

'That's becoming a boring song – SOS, Same Old Story. I told you on several occasions that your Christian charms aren't going to prevail against my gods.'

'If you go to Russia before you become a Christian, I pray that God should change you from being Saul into becoming Paul.'

'What do you mean?' He suddenly pointed a finger at her. 'Don't answer me. Listen, I'll go to Russia as a young lion, not as a Christian kid or kitten. Period!'

'I'm getting used to your rhetoric. Anyway, what are your weekend plans, Baba?'

'I'm expecting my cousin Nachi tonight. She's also the type of a Christian that you want to avoid meeting in the city. She's just like you, when she opens her mouth it's Jesus-this, Jesus-that, God-this, God-that.'

Yvonne laughed.

'Well, the less said about this aspect of her life the better,' continued Babatunde. 'She wants to introduce me to a young Nigerian graduate who is an engineer in the north of Russia.'

'Great! You'll have someone you can use as a point of reference. A mentor maybe.'

'Yes, the only problem is that the man is a Christian and he wants to meet me during an evangelistic campaign in Aba.'

'Hallelujah! Are you going to attend?'

'I told my cousin I was going to think about it. I didn't want to commit myself.'

## 36

On Saturday, late in the afternoon, Ekene knocked at the door of Babatunde's hut and told him that his cousin Nnesinachi had just arrived with a man driving a red Mercedes Benz. Babatunde was expecting them.

He had raised the eyebrows of his mother and sister when he told them he was going to attend a church service with his cousin. *You, going to church with Nachi?* his sister had asked. *You who told us that she is a mad woman of Jesus?* They were relieved when he clarified the matter: he was not going to attend church but to meet a fellow Nigerian, Max Akpan, who had important information for him about Russia. As soon as he had spoken to the man he intended returning home.

Babatunde walked to the spot in front of his mother's hut where Nnesinachi and the Mercedes Benz man were standing, chatting to his mother and sister. He greeted his cousin who gestured towards the man beside her.

'Addy, meet my cousin,' she said to the man.

Babatunde introduced himself.

'Adam "Miracle-Boy" Adeboye,' said the man with a smile.

As Babatunde bade his sister goodbye, she whispered: 'Is he Nachi's future husband?'

Babatunde responded with a grin.

Minutes later the red luxury car drove out of the Okoronkwo homestead on the way towards Port Harcourt. Nnesinachi was eager to facilitate the conversation between the two men but Adam did not seem to be in a hurry to open his mouth. Babatunde didn't need to ask if Adam was a Christian or not. To him, Nnesinachi and Adam were speaking a language that was not Chinese but something he could refer to as 'Christianese'. He was informed by Nnesinachi that Adam was an MBA student at a university in the US, and that his father was an export-import tycoon and owner of a beachfront complex, a fleet of German-made cars, motor boats and yachts.

As Babatunde explored the leather seats with the tips of his fingers, he saw Adam eyeing him through the rear-view mirror.

'I like your car, Mr...' said Babatunde, to defuse any feelings of discomfort.

'Thanks, Baba. Just call me Addy,' said Adam.

'I like everything about the car, including the colour: red.'

'Why do you like red?' asked Adam, beginning to warm up to Babatunde.

'It's the colour of communism.'

'Oh, yes, Nachi told me you'll be studying in Russia.'

'That's true. And why did you choose red?' inquired Babatunde.

Adam flashed a smile. 'Well, for me, it's the colour of the blood of Jesus.'

'For us communists, it's the blood of those who sacrificed their lives during the Bolshevik Revolution,' Babatunde replied.

'Yes, they died for Russia,' said Nnesinachi, 'but our Jesus died for the whole world, including the Russians.'

Babatunde chuckled. 'You Christians are a very creative bunch. You can easily stretch your imagination to the moon; frankly, I find your pie-in-the sky religion very nauseating, to say the least.'

Nnesinachi grinned and winked at Adam: 'Be careful when you speak to Baba. He's no longer a rural boy. He has been noticed by the Russians.'

Babatunde laughed. 'Don't be silly, Nachi.'

'We aren't going to argue with you,' said Adam, grinning.

'Because you know you can't defend your religion?' Babatunde challenged him.

'Christianity is not a religion; it's a relationship between God and man,' Nnesinachi contributed.

'It's about how God became man,' said Adam, 'because He wanted to save man.'

'Guys, your reasoning is ridiculous!' said Babatunde. 'And I'm not going to be a captive audience for your virgin-Mary kind of folktales. I have better African and Russian stories.'

Adam and Nnesinachi kept quiet for a while as the Mercedes sped over valleys and hills.

'Addy,' said Babatunde, trying to break the silence, 'I'm a little curious about your middle name, what is it again?'

'Miracle-Boy,' Adam told Babatunde.

'Is it official or just a nickname?'

'It's an official name.' Nnesinachi spoke on behalf of Adam.

'It's a long story, Baba,' said Adam. 'But it's an intriguing story, believe me. I can tell you if you're interested.'

'A few weeks from now he'll be going to Russia,' said Nnesinachi, 'so he'll need a bagful of Nigerian stories.'

'I'm not going to bore you with a long tale, so I'll summarise it. You can believe my story or not, it's your choice, Baba.'

'Please come to the point,' said Babatunde.

'When I was a foetus of six or seven months, in the womb, I was a girl,' said Adam.

'A girl?'

'Yes, Baba.'

'And what happened?'

'My mother—she had given birth to four girls before me, and my father's relatives threatened to send her to her parents. So she visited her pastor and said to him, "Pastor, if you don't pray and ask God to change the gender of this unborn child, I'm not going to leave your office!" The man of God was very embarrassed by my mother's stubbornness.'

'And what happened?' asked Babatunde, genuinely fascinated.

'The pastor said softly: "Okay, I shall pray for you." And he said: "Lord, I'm asking you to change the organs of this baby from that of a girl to that of a boy, as this woman requests. In Jesus's name. Amen!" My mother thanked him and left his office, smiling. Guess what happened? Two months later my mother gave birth to a baby boy! That's why my name was changed from Adelaide to Adam!'

'And that's why he has a pretty face with deep dimples!' added Nnesinachi.

Babatunde shook his head, disgusted. 'You Christians are a crazy bunch! Do you really want me to believe all that hogwash?'

'Yes; with God, nothing is impossible!' said Adam. 'That's why my middle name is "Miracle-Boy".

'Indeed, Karl Marx is right,' said Babatunde, 'religion is indeed the opium of the people. "The people" in this case refers to you Christians. And you expect me to take this cock-and-bull story to Russia? It won't even qualify to be a kindergarten story.'

Adam and Nnesinachi traded looks. Adam put on the indicator and slowed down. They were approaching a blue-and-white tent. Adam parked under an iroko tree next to a mini-bus. About five buses full of singing people had just arrived; as they disembarked they continued to sing, and sort of tap-dancing as they moved forward, stomping forward in two single files.

# 37

At the front of the procession two people unfurled a banner inscribed: 'Forward in Faith Ministries.' Immediately behind the hoisted banner was a brass band. The band and the singers led the march around the tent, creating a festive mood. Before long the place was teeming with thousands of people.

Walking between Nnesinachi and Adam towards the church workers sitting behind tables at the front of the tent, Babatunde repeated the request he'd made earlier, that once he'd finished his discussion with Max, he would be taken back to his home.

'We've no problem with that, Baba,' said Nnesinachi. 'But it'll be a good idea for you to stick around until the occasion is over, in case the guy wants to share something with you later.'

'For example,' said Adam, 'if your guest loves soccer and you meet him at a game, you may watch the match with him, even if you don't like soccer. It's a matter of courtesy.'

'How long will this event be?' asked Babatunde.

'We don't want to lie to you by saying that it's going to be short,' replied Adam.

'Just relax, Baba!' said Nnesinachi, brushing Babatunde's arm, 'it's going to be a lot of fun. You will listen to excellent music and meet very fascinating people!'

Babatunde laughed: 'The same old tricks of the missionaries!'

'What do you mean?' asked Nnesinachi.

'The music and nice people are just a bait for the big fish,' remarked Babatunde. 'Where's the hook?'

Adam and Nnesinachi laughed.

'So I can't promise that I will stay throughout the service,' said Babatunde. 'And where's Max?'

'Take it easy, Baba,' said Nnesinachi genially. 'Max must be on his way. In the meantime, let me introduce you to the pastor of Forward in Faith Ministries.'

Nnesinachi gestured to her right. Babatunde saw a bespectacled man sporting an Afro hairstyle and wearing a purple suit, green shirt and broad, yellow tie, shaking hands with some people forming a short queue.

'Pastor Bennie,' Nnesinachi introduced the flamboyant man to Babatunde, 'meet my cousin, Babatunde Okoronkwo.'

'Benson Okpo,' said the pastor.

A moment later Benson Okpo excused himself and dashed over to meet some VIPs arriving in three Mercedes Benzes. When the VIPs had been led to a reserved section inside the tent, Benson returned to Babatunde, and touched his shoulder: 'Your cousin told me very interesting things about you.'

'What did she say?' asked Babatunde, grinning.

'All I can say is that I've been waiting to meet you,' said Benson.

'Really?'

'Yes! You are an asset, Baba.'

Babatunde smiled in disbelief. *Me an asset?* He mused. *Haven't they told you that I'm a communist? What does a communist and a church-man have in common, Pastor Benson? What can you get from a man who'll keep telling you that religion is the opium of the people?*

Benson hurried off again to meet another batch of VIPs. Babatunde wondered if Max was one of them. People were starting to shuffle into the thousand-seater tent through entrances at the front and back, sitting down on the white plastic chairs.

Babatunde, Adam and Nnesinachi sat in the fourth row from the front. People were chatting in subdued tones around them while Benson and his team checked the programme and the guest list, ticking off the names of those arriving. Fresh flowers were displayed on three tables covered with white cloths. Benson sat down in the row of seats behind the tables. On the left of the tables was a space to be used by the choristers while on the right was the preacher's podium.

Nnesinachi kept craning her neck to see if Max had arrived.

'If Max does not arrive by the time this event starts,' Babatunde told Nnesinachi, 'then I'm free to go.'

'Baba, please take it easy,' said Nnesinachi, trying to charm Babatunde with a smile. 'Max will arrive any moment.'

'I'm not promising to wait for him,' insisted Babatunde.

'Baba, I told you that there's going to be a lot of fun,' said Nnesinachi, 'so please take it easy!'

Adam touched Babatunde's arm. smiling.

'If you think you are going to catch a big fish,' said Babatunde, 'you've made a big-big mistake, Nachi!'

Nnesinachi shrugged and turned to Adam.

# 38

Twenty minutes later when everyone was seated, the entrances of the tent were closed.

Benson rose to his feet and opened the occasion with prayer. Before sitting down again, he said: 'I shall now call king Chinwuba to greet the people.'

The audience applauded and Nnesinachi whispered to Babatunde: 'King Chinwuba is the grandson of a king who smoked the pages of the Bible and became converted.'

Babatunde nodded, recalling the story he was once told by Yvonne.

As the grey-haired man at the front table stood up, Babatunde said to himself: *After this old man has spoken I'm getting out of this place.*

'Alleloyah!' shouted king Chinwuba.

'Alleloyah!' responded the audience.

'My people,' the king bared his palms to his audience, '*Nno nu!*'

'Alleloyah!' responded the audience.

'God is good,' said the king.

'All the time,' replied the people.

'All the time?' he repeated.

The people responded: 'God is good!'

'God alone is more than good,' said the king. 'We Africans are fond of talking about ancestors. God gives us good things but we give credit to the gods. How silly!'

At this point Babatunde became so offended that he felt like standing up and walking out of the place. He cursed the king in his heart: *You silly old man!*

'You know, people who thank the gods instead of God,' the king continued, 'are like children who get food from their father but thank the man next door.'

Babatunde saw people around him laughing and cheering.

'My task is not to preach,' said the king, 'but to prepare the way for the man of God. My real assignment is to greet you, my subjects.'

The king waved his hand. 'Hallo everybody!'

The audience waved back.

'You are most welcome to my area,' continued the king. 'Please enjoy the service. I hope it will make you better citizens.'

As the king sat down Babatunde heard the voices of a choir singing from behind the makeshift stage. He saw ten young women and men singing and tap-dancing as they took their positions in the space beside the tables. The group sang in pidgin English: *My God is good-o!* The audience applauded and sang along: '*He's always by my side, A very good God-o, By my side, by my side!*

Babatunde said to himself: *Now is the moment for me to get out!* At that juncture he saw an albino singer dressed in white robes joining the choir. Babatunde's curiosity was piqued by the sight of the gospel artist, James Okon, whose music he had heard from national radio stations.

Babatunde relaxed in his seat and listened. The audience applauded, cheered and whistled at the end of the item. During the second song, Babatunde no longer felt the urgency to get out of the tent. The audience applauded again as the singers returned backstage. At that moment

Benson stood up, flexed his shoulders, radiated a smile, and stepped to the podium.

'Before I share the word of God,' said Benson, 'shall we all stand and applaud as a way of appreciating God for his goodness?'

Babatunde stood up and applauded, feeling that he was lying to himself. He told himself that he was in fact applauding for the top leadership of the Communist Party during the annual celebrations of the Bolshevik revolution in the Red Square in Moscow.

Babatunde was reminded of the film *Catch them young*, which he had seen at the Russian Embassy. It was about how the communists demonstrated to children that communism was better than God. In the film, a teacher at a kindergarten tells the children: *Now close your eyes and pray that God should give you bread and cheese.*

The teacher then says to them: *Has the god of America given you any bread and cheese?* And the children reply: *No!* The teacher goes on: *Now close your eyes and ask the god of communism to provide bread and cheese.* When the children open their eyes, they see the workers putting paper plates full of bread, cheese, sausage rolls, sweets and cool drinks in front of them. *Can you see now how communism can really provide food while the god of America cannot?* And the children would reply: *Yes, ma'am!*

Benson opened his Bible, suddenly closed it again and smiled at the audience. 'Let me speak to you like Africans. We all grew up listening to folktales. So here is one. A certain hunter went to the forest to kill small game…'

*I must listen to this folktale, thought Babatunde, so I can tell it to the Russians. After listening to it, I will leave this place before they come with the hell-and-suffering scare-stories.*

'He hunted for the whole day and caught nothing,' Benson continued. 'As he returned home he decided to rest under a leafy tree. Lying on his back, he saw an eagle landing in the tree above him. He felt as if the mother bird was talking to its nestling. The hunter scared the mother off and she flew away. He then climbed the tree and found the baby eagle. He looked at it and pitied it. So he took it to his home and put it among his fowls and ducks and gave it chicken feed to eat, even though it was an eagle, the king of birds.

'Five years later a naturalist came to see him, and after walking through his garden, said, "That bird is an eagle, not a chicken!"

"Yes," replied his owner, "but I have trained it to be a chicken. It's no longer an eagle, it's a chicken, even if it measures fifteen feet from wing tip to wing tip."

"No," said the naturalist, "It's an eagle still; it has the heart of an eagle, and I will make it soar high up in the heavens."

"No," insisted the owner, "It's a chicken and it will never fly."

'They agreed to test it. The naturalist picked up the eagle, held it up, and said with great intensity: "Eagle, thou art an eagle, thou dost belong to the sky, stretch forth thy wings and fly."

The eagle turned this way and that way and then, looking down, it saw the chickens eating their food, and down it jumped.'

The owner said: "I told you it's a chicken."

"No," said the naturalist, not prepared to give up, "it's an eagle. Give it another chance tomorrow."

'So the next day the naturalist took the eagle to the top of the house and said: "Eagle, thou art an eagle, stretch forth thy wings and fly." But again the eagle, seeing the chickens feeding below, jumped down and fed with them.

'Again the owner said: "I told you it was a chicken. I hope you'll now forget about your experiment!"

"No, it's an eagle!" the naturalist insisted. "And it still has the heart of an eagle; give it one more chance and I will make it fly tomorrow."

'The next morning the naturalist took the eagle outside the city, away from the houses, to the foot of a high mountain. The sun was rising, gilding the top of the mountain and every crag was glistening in the joy of the beautiful morning.

'He picked up the eagle and said to it: "Eagle, thou art an eagle, thou dost belong to the sky, so stretch forth thy wings and fly!"

'The eagle looked around and trembled as if new life was coming to it; but it did not fly. The naturalist then made it look straight to the sun. Suddenly the eagle stretched out its wings and mounted higher and higher, never to return. It was an eagle, although it had been kept and tamed as a chicken!'

Benson paused and looked around the audience. 'People of Africa, we have been created in the image of God, but the devil has captured us and changed us into his image. But today is the day you are going to look towards heaven like that little eagle and see who has really created you. Eagles, don't be content with the food of chickens, for you are birds of prey! Stretch forth your wings and fly! Fly away from the chickens! Come! Come to God, all of you who are eagles. Brother, sister, *biko*, come to Jesus. *Abeg-o*! Please-o!'

At that moment many people stood up from their chairs and walked forward to stand in front of the preacher.

Nnesinachi felt Babatunde moving next to her as he too stood up and joined the people walking towards the man of God.

She turned towards Adam, clapping her hands. 'Hallelujah! We caught the big fish!'

Adam chortled, also applauding.

Babatunde turned his head and saw Nnesinachi and Adam looking on with interest as he shuffled along with the others towards the front. He was part of the third row, and he kept going until he reached the end of it, close to the front entrance of the tent; at that point he simply turned towards the exit and suddenly rushed out of the tent.

Nnesinachi gasped and turned to Adam: 'Addie, Baba has gone out of the tent. Come, let's go and bring him back!'

'Yes,' said Adam standing up, 'The devil is a liar! This is the day of Baba's salvation!'

They hurried for the exit in search of Babatunde.


# 39

The next morning, as Babatunde sat in his hut, buttoning up his shirt, he heard a knock at his door. When he went to open it he found Nnesinachi and Adam standing there. He was not pleased to see them entering his hut and sitting down on his tree-trunk stools. With tearful eyes Nnesinachi bear-hugged him and patted his shoulders.

'I'm relieved to find you at home,' she said. 'Where were you last night?'

'I slept at aunt Dorah's house in Agbada village,' responded Babatunde. 'Did you come here looking for me last night?'

'No, we didn't come here. We looked for you around the church,' said Adam. 'After failing to find you we went back into the tent and told the church leadership that you had disappeared. So Pastor Benson sent ten young men to search for you. They returned an hour later, empty-handed.'

'They could not find me,' said Babatunde, 'because I was hiding in the branches of a tree next to the gate.'

'The pastor asked us to pray for your safety,' said Nnesinachi. 'Baba, can you tell us why you left the church like that?'

'When the pastor said, "Come to God all of you who are eagles,"' said Babatunde, 'I suddenly heard a voice inside me saying, "Get out of this place and run as fast as your legs can carry you!" So as soon as I had walked out of the tent I sprinted to the nearest tree, climbed it and hid in the leafy branches. I saw you and Adam searching around. And later I saw the men looking for me. I waited until they'd gone back inside and it was quiet again, then I jumped down and ran to the nearest road. There I waited for a lift and fortunately found a truck that was going to my aunt's village.'

'So how do you feel now?' inquired Adam. 'Is there any change in your heart?'

'I'm still myself,' Babatunde said. 'I don't want to become someone else.'

'That's not what we are here for,' said Nnesinachi. 'We aren't trying to change you.'

'What do you want from me?'

'We are here because we care about you, Baba,' Nnesinachi went on. 'You've heard the truth, so we want to appeal to you to choose life, and not death.'

'So if I remain myself, am I choosing death? And what is truth?' Babatunde demanded.

'You are choosing death without realising it,' said Adam. 'God loves you so much that He sent Jesus to be your Saviour. But if you choose to go to hell, it's your choice.'

Babatunde sighed. 'Oh, here we go again! Please stop intimidating me with scary stories!'

'Baba, I told you we are here because we care about you,' said Nnesinachi.

Babatunde stood up abruptly. 'Please stop caring about me! I'm not interested in your religious stuff, okay? You tried to trick me, but your mission has miscarried miserably.'

'How did we trick you?' asked Nnesinachi.

'By telling me that I would meet Max Akpan.'

'You know Baba,' said Nnesinachi, 'you are not aware that by going with us to the tent, you had an appointment with God.'

'So by getting out of the tent,' Adam put in, 'you've in fact missed God.'

Babatunde shook his head. 'Please keep your God. I'm not interested.'

Adam took the car keys out of his pocket and looked at Nnesinachi. 'Nachi, we've taken the horse to the river, but we can't force it to drink.' He stepped out of the hut and walked to his car.

'You are right, Addy,' said Nnesinachi, following him. At the door she stopped and turned back towards Babatunde: 'Perhaps you should have said, "I'm not yet interested in God." But anyway, we are going to continue praying for you.'

'You'll be wasting your precious prayers,' said Babatunde.

He took a cigarette, lit it and puffed at it with a vengeance, staring after them as they got into Adam's red car and drove off, finally disappearing behind a dust cloud.

## 40

Bare to the waist and in his usual pair of khaki shorts, Babatunde stood in the garden in the late afternoon, gripping a smouldering cigarette between the middle finger and forefinger of his left hand and a spade in his right hand. Lost in thought, his attention was attracted by a yellow car stopping in front of his gate. As he examined the car he realised that it was a Peugeot 514, and he wondered who the owner could be. His suspense ended when he saw Nnesinachi stepping out of the car first, followed by Pastor Benson. Babatunde hurriedly took the cigarette from his lips and crushed it out under the sole of his shoe and wiped his lips. He regretted that he had no time to take a mint-flavoured sweet.

'Baba,' said Nnesinachi, when they had exchanged greetings and were in seated in his hut, 'You see I have brought the man of God. Perhaps you'll listen better to him.'

Babatunde saw Pastor Benson smiling.

'Apologies for pouncing on you like this,' said Pastor Benson. 'Can you give us a few minutes?'

Babatunde looked at his wrist-watch. 'Alright. But what new thing are you going to tell me? I already told them, I'm not interested in their religious stuff.'

'I'm not here to win an argument,' said the pastor. 'We are here because we care about you.'

'That sounds familiar,' said Babatunde.

Pastor Benson and Nnesinachi looked at each other. The pastor opened the Bible, glanced at Babatunde and then rested his finger on the book. 'Let me read this verse: It's John chapter 3, verse 16: "For God loved the world so much that He gave His only son so that..."'

'Wait a minute,' Babatunde interrupted him. 'I've already heard about that. I've even seen it on car-stickers. My question is: if God wants to give his only son, what am I expected to do? It's his own business.'

Pastor Benson smiled at Babatunde and shifted his gaze to Nnesinachi.

'What are you expected to do?' Nnesinachi repeated the question. 'To accept him, if you want to.'

'His only Son is the passport to the Father,' said the pastor.

'And if I don't want to accept him?' asked Babatunde.

'It's your choice,' responded Nnesinachi. 'But you'll be choosing to be lost forever.'

Babatunde gave Nnesinachi a frown. 'Just say, "You'll burn in hell." I know it's what you are thinking.'

Nnesinachi responded: 'I'm thinking that you should make the right choice.'

'The right choice according to Nachi's gospel?'

Nnesinachi shrugged and said nothing.

Pastor Benson grinned at Babatunde again before focusing once more on the open Bible. 'Can I quickly read this short verse? "There is no eternal doom for those who trust Him to save them. But those who don't trust Him have already been tried and condemned for not believing in the Son of God. Their sentence is based on this fact: that the light from Heaven came into the world, but they loved darkness more than the Light, for their deeds…"'

'Wait, wait pastor! What kind of justice is that? That I'm already condemned without being given a fair hearing?'

The pastor chuckled.

'It's God's kind of justice,' said Nnesinachi. 'And we can't change it; that's how it works.'

The pastor closed his Bible during a long moment of silence.

'I understand that you've got a scholarship to go and study in Russia,' the pastor said, breaking the silence.

'Yes, that's true,' said Babatunde.

'What a wonderful opportunity you'd be having,' said the pastor, 'if you'd go there as a Christian.'

'Why?' asked Babatunde.

'Because it's a Godless country,' said the pastor. 'And you would go there to be a candle in the midst of communist darkness.'

'The USSR has enough electricity to light up the whole of Africa,' Babatunde moistened his lips with his tongue. 'They don't need a weak Nigerian candlelight.'

The man of God gave Babatunde a grave look; he opened the Bible again and flipped over a few pages. 'Can I read another scripture?'

'No, I'm not interested,' snapped Babatunde. He gestured at Nnesinachi. 'I told her and her boyfriend: "Keep that God of yours to yourselves!"'

'My task isn't to argue with people and force them to accept my God,' said the pastor, closing his Bible. 'Let me tell you one last thing: you can try to run away from God, but He will finally corner you right here in

Nigeria or there in Russia! Ask Saul. He tried to fight against the saints and what happened to him? Jesus blinded him with a bright light and floored him in Damascus. So, you'll encounter your Damascus experience.'

Babatunde lifted up his arm to glance at his watch. 'Pastor, your time is up! I'm not interested in your message. Okay?'

The man of God rose to his feet.

Babatunde looked at Nnesinachi. 'I'm sorry to be rude to your pastor.'

'It's all right, Baba. The time is coming when you will see the light. According to the Bible, the god of this world has blinded you.'

'Blinded me? So I need a guide and a walking stick?' said Babatunde, giving a sardonic smile and glancing at his watch again. 'I think you must preach to those who are interested in your gospel.'

Nnesinachi held Pastor Benson by the hand and led him towards the car.

'God isn't going to leave you,' she called to Babatunde loudly.

'He must mind his own business!' Babatunde shouted back.

He lit another cigarette, stood and puffed at it, watching until the car disappeared.

*

'I didn't want to tell you something yesterday,' Babatunde said to Yvonne that Tuesday afternoon, 'because I knew you would agree with them.'

'Agree with whom?'

'My cousin and her boyfriend. As I told you they took me to an evangelist's tent on Saturday. They imagined they would catch a big fish.'

'What happened?' asked Yvonne, looking interested.

Babatunde told her everything that had happened, including the visit by Pastor Benson.

'Your cousin really cares about you, Baba.'

'That's what they said. It's their well-rehearsed catch-phrase. But I've no doubt that the communists care more about me and millions of others who are presently looking towards the West as saviours. The West who get cocoa from us cheaply and then comes to Africa to sell it exorbitantly as chocolate and coffee.'

'Well, you've strong opinions on certain things,' said Yvonne. 'But you must realise one thing Baba: you can't change the world. But you can change how you want to look at it. The kind of spectacles you are looking through will determine how you see things.'

'So I'm looking through the communist spectacles?'

'I didn't say that.'

'You are implying that.'

'You can change yourself, Baba. You can choose to…'

'Change according to the Christian viewpoint? No I'm not going to do that. I'll go to Russia and get equipped and return to Africa to be part of the solution; not according to *your* gospel.'

'You know Baba, God can use anything to get you. Anything good or bad. He can allow a car accident to happen to you.'

'Are you trying to scare me?'

Yvonne giggled. 'Or He can use a nice dream or a nightmare to get your attention.'

Babatunde shrugged his shoulders.

# 41

'I was in the forest when suddenly I saw a hyena running towards me with menacing teeth exposed. Very terrified, I ran as fast as I could to save my dear life. I thought I had outrun the beast by a safe distance, but I was wrong. Soon, I could hear the paws of the hyena scratching the dry soil behind my heels; when I looked round I saw the dust. I screamed for help, but there was no one to help. I screamed: "God, you are the only one who can help!"'

Completely dumbfounded, Nnesinachi and Adam sat listening to Babatunde, with no idea what he was talking about.

'I was so exhausted that I felt like collapsing. Suddenly I fell into a ditch; it was the size of a grave but very deep. When I hit the bottom I felt as if my legs were fractured. I heard the hyena's roar growing louder and louder. When I looked up I saw the beast that was chasing me staring down at me.'

Nnesinachi and Adam exchanged glances.

'Something very strange happened: the hyena spoke like a human being, saying: "*Hoh-hoh-hoh!* I found what I've been looking for! What a nice supper. In no time, you'll be right in my belly! *Hoh-hoh-hoh!*"'

Nnesinachi leaned forward and said, 'Oh that must have been a terrible dream!'

'Yes, it was very frightening, Nachi. I screamed at the top of my voice and the hyena jeered: "*Hoh-hoh-hoh!* No help is coming! Within minutes, you'll be right in my belly! *Hoh-hoh-hoh!*"

'I started to pray. I can't exactly recall what I said, but I think I pleaded: "Jesus, Jesus!…"'

'A communist pleading, 'Jesus'? I can't...'

'Yes I pleaded "Jesus, Jesus! Please save me! If you are indeed a saviour of people, please demonstrate it now!"'

'At that moment the hyena's face became fierce and really frightening. "You shut up! Don't talk nonsense!" the beast said. "I told you there's no one to help you! You're just wasting your time. And don't call that silly name!"

'I continued to scream, "Jesus, Jesus, please help me!" Suddenly the hyena retreated and disappeared. Breathing out with relief, I stood up slowly. I was amazed that the grave had become shallow. I stuck my head out and looked in all directions.

'I was very relieved to see the hyena was gone. I got out of the grave and said: "Thank you Jesus, that you saved me." I started running, and I kept looking backwards. As I was running, I suddenly fell into a hole. I think it was as deep as a mine. When I reached the bottom, I thought my bones were broken to pieces; I looked upwards, and I saw a huge rock closing the hole, and it became pitch-black and smoggy.

'I felt smoke entering my nostrils, and I choked. I gasped for fresh air and began to cough. The place was very hot, and I was sweating. I shouted: *Jesus, where are you? How can you mislead me? When I got out of the grave and the hyena disappeared, I thought you had saved me. If you are indeed a saviour of people, please demonstrate it now!*

'I screamed for help, shouting until my voice became hoarse, and I cried until my tears dried up. When I had given up all hope, I saw light at the top of the hole, becoming brighter and brighter. The heat and smoke vanished. As the light grew stronger I stood eagerly, expecting miraculous help; I began to smile, tears again streaming down my cheeks.

'Suddenly I heard a voice saying: "Baba, Baba!" And I said: "Who are you?"

'"I am your Lord," the voice replied.

'"Lord, have You come to save me?" I asked with a huge smile. Then I saw the brightest light I've ever seen. Suddenly I saw a man in white shining robes wearing a golden crown and holding a mace shining like diamonds.

'"Those who call me shall not be disappointed," said the man, "but shall be saved from permanent destruction."

'The man stretched out his hand to reach me at the bottom of the hole and pulled me out. I felt as helpless as a little bird. All of a sudden, I found myself on land covered by green-green grass and flowers of all kinds. The man – he looked like a handsome Nigerian man—gazed deep into my eyes, his eyes a colour I can't explain, and very clear, shining like glass. My eyes could not stand the light from his eyes. So I fell on the ground and touched his feet, trying to kiss them and making them wet with tears. I raised my head and asked him: "Who are you, Lord?"

"'I am the same Jesus who appeared to you that day when you were unconscious outside Pastor Ugochukwu's church; that day you ran away when I wanted to take you into my arms of love and peace."

'I replied, "I'm very sorry, Lord."

"'It's alright, Baba, you were blinded by the evil one. Now is the time to come into my arms that have waited for you all these years."

'I continued to kiss his feet, making them wet. The Lord commanded with outstretched arms: "Stand up!"

'I said, "Lord, I'm too dirty to touch your royal robe."

"'I say stand up!" said the Lord with a booming voice.

'I stood up and he embraced me, rubbing my back.

"'You're no longer dirty but clean. You are no longer a slave of the devil, but a child of the king and a friend."

'The Lord held me by my hand and we strolled together in that garden, the most beautiful garden I've ever seen.

'The dream ended abruptly. When I woke up I knew beyond a shadow of doubt that I no longer belonged to the African gods and the god of communism, but…' Babatunde lowered his voice to a whisper, 'to Jesus.'

Nnesinachi clapped her hands. 'Alleloyah!'

'Amen!' exclaimed Adam.

Babatunde bowed his head, covered his face with his palms and sobbed. Nnesinachi stood up and went to put her hand on his shoulder.

'Guys,' said Babatunde as he wiped tears away, 'you can see how very hard I tried to run away from your God. But at this moment I've been cornered and there's nowhere I can go. So your pastor was right when he said that God would at last corner me. And he got me right here in Nigeria. Now,' he looked around and lowered his voice again, 'I want Pastor Benson to help me receive Jesus.'

Nnesinachi lifted Babatunde up by his hands, embraced him and patted his back. Adam stepped forward and also hugged Babatunde.

'For now,' said Babatunde, 'I don't want my people to know about my decision. Let's just go.'

## 42

Babatunde felt that the atmosphere in the car was very different to the previous journey when he'd travelled with them to the church tent. A few days ago he was an arrogant, fire-spitting communist disciple who despised the two Christians, but now he enjoyed their aura and warmth. They had, in less than a week, turned into a source of admiration and inspiration.

Nnesinachi told him that Max Akpan, the engineer who was working in the north of Russia, had entered the tent quietly and sat at the back.

'When we returned to the church after looking for you,' said Nnesinachi, 'we found him standing at the tent entrance. He was very disappointed to hear that you had gone. He sat with us where you were sitting.'

'Why was he so late?'

'He said his cousin's old car had a mechanical problem, and that they had to wait for three hours before they could get help.'

'Will he be at the service today?' inquired Babatunde.

'No, unfortunately. He had to go back to his village to prepare for the flight back to Russia.'

'Oh, what a pity,' said Babatunde.

As Adam swung the steering wheel of the Mercedes to park next to Pastor Benson's BMW, Babatunde's mind replayed what had happened a few days ago when he'd run out of the church; he looked around and saw the tree where he had hidden and could not be found by those searching for him.

They arrived ten minutes before the service started. There were about a hundred people outside the tent, standing in clusters, chatting. It was the same blue-and-white tent as before.

During the church service Nnesinachi was the programme director. This surprised Babatunde as she'd never mentioned anything about it to him.

Lifting up her arms, Nnesinachi led the congregation, singing the Igbo song, *'Imela.'*

Babatunde sang along with ribald excitement, *'Imela, Imela, Eze m oh! / Imela, Imela, Eze m oh!/ Imela, Imela, / Okaka onyekeruwa.'*

Allowing no one to sit down when songs were sung, Nnesinachi encouraged the people to clap their hands and sing lustily.

'If the president of Nigeria could attend this service, how would you behave? Don't give me the answer! King Jesus is in our midst so let's show him how much we appreciate Him! I shall count to three: One! Two! Three!'

The congregants cheered, applauded, whistled and gyrated, clicking their fingers and jumping about.

Minutes later, a special word of welcome was extended to those coming to the church for the first time. Babatunde was one of tens of people who were asked to stand and were welcomed just like King Jesus.

'Now's the time to testify!' announced Nnesinachi. 'Let four people come to the front and tell the world what Jesus did for them!'

Babatunde listened with great attention as four people hastened to the front; he noted that they greeted the congregation in a particular manner, waving and saying: *I greet you all in the name of my Lord Saviour!* And the congregation responded: *Amen!* The content of their testimonies was similar: how Jesus changed their lives from bad to good. The last person to testify went up to the front carrying a plastic shopping bag. She took out a creased, crumpled, grease-stained white shirt and showed it to the congregation.

'Before I met Jesus,' said the woman, 'I was like this shirt. But now after meeting Jesus I became like *this* shirt.' She took out a spotless white shirt and showed it around. 'Because Jesus has removed all terrible stains; Alleloyah!'

The audience applauded, cheered and whistled as the woman went to sit down.

'Family of God,' said Nnesinachi, 'I'm delighted to introduce the man of God, Pastor Benson Okpo!'

Benson was welcomed like a president.

'If your life is bad,' said Benson, 'I can promise you that with God, it will be good!'

'Alleloyah!' said the congregation.

'If your life is good,' continued Benson, 'with God it'll be even better!'

The congregation responded, 'Alleloyah!'

'If your life is better, it'll be excellent!'

'Alleloyah!' roared the congregation.

'If you ask for sugar, God will give you honey!'

'Alleloyah!' said the congregation.

The church members applauded as if they were cheering a hero. Babatunde was impressed. A few days ago he would have dismissed them as having tasted God's opium. But on this day he was enjoying the hallucinogen he had hated with a passion.

'We shall read our scripture from the gospel of Mark,' said Benson, beginning the sermon, 'chapter four, verse three.'

Benson waited a moment for the congregation to open their Bibles. Pages whispered everywhere in the church. Babatunde opened his Bible too. It was the Bible which Mama-J had given him, many years ago.

'A sower went out to sow,' Benson began to read. 'As he was sowing, some seed fell along the path, and the birds came and ate it up. Other seed fell on the ground full of rocks, where there was not much soil; and at once it sprang up, because it had no depth of soil. And when the sun came up, it was scorched, and because it had not taken root, it withered away.

'Other seed fell among thorn plants, and the thistles grew and pressed it together and utterly choked it and suffocated it, and it yielded no grain. And other seed fell into good soil and brought forth grain, growing up and increasing, and yielding up to thirty times as much, and sixty times as much, and even a hundred times as much as had been sown.'

Benson paused as he closed the Bible.

'The word of God is preached daily. And even today I'm still preaching. I'm a sower like the one mentioned in the message I've just read. Now which one is your heart? The path? The ground full of rocks? The ground full of thorn plants? Or the good soil?'

Benson took a breath and smiled at his audience. '"Pastor Bennie, today, I've heard the word, and I want to receive it, because it has fallen on my heart, which is on good soil."' Benson paused and looked around. 'If you've said those words in your heart, please raise your hand.'

The pastor waited as some in the audience raised their hands.

'If you've raised your hand,' continued Benson, 'please stand!'

He waited as people stood up.

'If you are standing, please come to the front and we shall help you to be God's child, and your life will never be the same again!'

Babatunde was prompted to walk to the front, but he hesitated. Looking around, he saw about twenty people stepping towards the pastor; he got up and joined them. Minutes later Babatunde was one of forty people.

'All of you precious people standing in front of me,' said Benson, 'I can assure you that you've made the best decision of your life. Today is so important that you should write it in your Bible, the date on which you chose light over darkness, and life over death. Please turn to your right and follow the lady wearing blue, sister Nachi, and the counsellors. Follow them to the partitioned area at the back of the tent; there they will show you how to receive Jesus into your hearts.

'To the congregation, I say: the Bible says, when one sinner accepts Jesus, there's hullabaloo in heaven. So, come on, let's welcome our brothers- and sisters-in-Christ in African style!'

The congregation cheered, whistled, shouted, waved, clapped their hands and jumped up and down.

Later Babatunde and the new believers returned and stood in front of the pastor.

'Welcome back, new members of the body of Christ,' said Benson. 'I've a few words for you. You are part of us in our journey to heaven. No one who put his hand to the plough and looks back is fit for the kingdom of God. If God calls you and saves you, don't look back like Lot's wife when Sodom and Gomorrah were burning: we all know what happened to her. So don't allow anything to distract you in your journey to the Promised Land.

'Our Lord says, "If your hand puts a stumbling block between you and the kingdom, cut it off, for it's better to inherit eternal life with one hand than to go to hell with two hands. If your eye causes you to stumble, pluck it out! It is more profitable to enter the kingdom of God with one eye than to have two eyes and be thrown into the fire that cannot be put out. If you used to worship the gods, go and destroy the shrine, with its tools of Satan. Last Sunday we burnt the *dibia's* tools of the devil: the snakes, and other things from the kingdom of darkness.

'If you are serious about living a victorious Christian life, you must burn the bridges to your old lifestyle. Yes, any bridge you refuse to burn gives Satan an invitation to re-enter and then destabilise your new life. So go and destroy all the devil's tools.'

# 43

Hours later, Babatunde entered his hut, still reflecting on his pastor's words: *If you used to worship the gods, go and destroy the shrine, with its tools of Satan.* He dropped his jacket on his bed and walked out, rolling up the long sleeves of his shirt; he hurried across to the shrine hut, holding a bottle filled with holy water; he called Ekene who appeared as if he was waiting to be called.

Babatunde led Ekene to the shrine and gestured at that which used to be awe-inspiring components: sticks, an adorned wooden figure, a monkey's skull, chicken feathers, some snake's teeth and the tusk of an elephant calf.

'This,' said Babatunde, 'must be burnt to ashes.'

Ekene gasped in utter shock. 'Are you sure, uncle?'

'Yes, this is the devil's tool. I have just become a Christian.'

'Is that so, uncle? I can't believe it!'

'Listen, Eki, I don't want these evil things to disturb me in my journey to heaven. These tools of Satan are going to oppose whatever God says to me. And what God wants me to do in this family. So I want you to pack them into a plastic shopping bag and tell me when…'

'No uncle! I don't want my hand to shrink!'

Babatunde jeered at the tools of Satan; he looked into Ekene's eyes. 'The Devil is a liar!' he said, his face very serious. 'Okay, look at what I'm going to do.'

He poured holy water from the bottle into his right hand and began to sprinkle the objects of the shrine with it.

'In the name of Jesus,' said Babatunde, 'I neutralise your power, you tools of Satan!'

Babatunde smiled at Ekene. 'Look!' He touched the monkey's skull. 'As harmless as a chicken! Now Eki, pack up these things and when you are done, clean the whole place with this holy water. I'll be praying in my room.'

Just as Ekene put the monkey-skull into the bag, his aunt, Babatunde's sister, Ifeoma, entered.

'What are you doing, Eki?' she asked.

Ekene sighed. 'Auntie, uncle says I should pack all these things into this bag. He said they should be burnt to ashes.'

'What? Burn the tools of our gods? Is he mad?'

'He says he has become a Christian!'

Ifeoma grabbed the bag from Ekene. 'That's not going to happen, Eki! Do you hear me?'

Ekene grabbed the bag back from her. 'Wait, Auntie, let me call uncle Baba. Uncle!' he shouted, 'Please come-o!'

Ifeoma pulled the bag out of Ekene's hand. At that point Babatunde entered the shrine hut, with open palms ready for action.

'Baba, what is this that I hear, that you want to burn the shrine because you've become a Christian?'

'Yes, that's true. So…' Babatunde grabbed the bag and pulled it towards himself. '…I want to burn these tools of Satan!'

'No, Baba, no! If you are indeed a Christian, you must leave the shrine alone!'

As Babatunde and Ifeoma were engaged in a tug of war, pulling the sack containing the shrine objects in opposite directions, their mother entered the hut. After listening to both daughter and son, she persuaded them to discuss the matter with their elder brothers.

## 44

That Monday morning Babatunde arrived at the school at 06h30, an hour before his teaching day began. The cleaners and the women working in the kitchen were amazed to see him. He walked straight to the staff room, which had just been swept and feather dusted; he sat on a chair, took his Bible out of his shopping bag and began to read the gospel of John.

He recalled how Yvonne had said to him: *The Bible is not literature only. It's most importantly a book of life, as Mama-J once advised you.* He smiled as his finger pointed to Chapter three. *So this is the chapter which the Bible-smoking king could not complete?* He read: *A man of the Pharisees named Nicodemus, came to Jesus at night…* He stopped reading and asked himself: *Why did Nicodemus go to Jesus at night? Who was he afraid of? The Jews? Am I going to live like Nicodemus in Russia, because I'll be afraid of the secret police?*

He continued reading: *For everyone who does evil hates the light, and does not come to the light, lest his deeds should be exposed.* He reflected on what he had just read. *If the communists are part of those who hate the light,* he mused, *is it worthwhile going to Russia?* He thought: *I think I should have heeded Yvie's suggestion to apply to some varsities in the US.* He wrote in his notebook then continued to read until he completed the chapter. Again, he scribbled something. When he heard the sound of footsteps—he could tell immediately that they were Yvonne's—he closed his Bible and dropped it back into the shopping bag.

There was a knock and when he answered the door swung open and in came Yvonne, wearing her characteristic smile.

'Yvie, you aren't going to believe what I'm going to tell you,' said Babatunde after they had exchanged greetings.

She beamed a fresh smile towards him. 'Please tell me, Baba!'

'Your prayers have been answered. '

'What do you mean? Have you changed your mind? Are you no longer going to Russia and you are thinking of the US?'

'No, I'm still going to Russia. Haven't you said you would pray for me that I should be a Christian by the time I go to Russia? So your prayers have been answered.'

'I can't believe you, Baba!'

'Believe me, Yvie.'

'Are you pulling my leg? Baba, have you really accepted Jesus…?'

'Yes!'

'Hallelujah!'

She embraced him tightly, kissed his cheeks and patted his back.

'Welcome to the family of God, Baba.' Her words were shrill with excitement.

'Thank you, Yvie.'

'How did it happen?'

'It's a long story. Let's talk after school.'

*

Yvonne invited him to her house where they had a sumptuous lunch. Her maid, who was an excellent cook, was instructed to prepare a dish fit for 'big people'. It was the first time that Babatunde had set foot in her house. He told his rapt, thrilled listener all that had happened.

'This morning when I woke up,' said Babatunde, 'I felt like a new person. I felt as if someone was whispering to me, "If anyone is in Christ, he is a new creation."'

Yvonne applauded. 'Amen!'

'Alleloyah! I felt that my eyes were brand new. It was great to inhale and to exhale, and to taste a glass of water and breakfast. When I look at the sun, the clouds, the sky…all God's creations look very beautiful. The birds chirping in the trees are magnificent, praising their creator. Oh…'

'Hallelujah!' Yvonne exclaimed. 'I'm delighted that you are enjoying every minute of your new life.'

Babatunde smiled radiantly.

'It's such a pity that you won't be working with us,' continued Yvonne. 'I wish you could go to Russia the year after next.'

'To be honest now, I'm not even sure if I should go to Russia at all.'

'Why?'

'How can I live in such an unchristian country, where I can't worship freely?'

Yvonne looked sympathetically into Babatunde's eyes. 'I feel in my spirit that you should go to Russia, Baba.'

'Really?'

'Yes!' Yvonne put her hand on his arm. 'No be big problem, Baba. You go manage!'

Babatunde responded to her pidgin with a chortle.

'Baba, God never makes mistakes. I've no doubt this is according to God's plan. When you drank deep from the river of communism, God was not taken by surprise. He knew that at an appropriate time He would make you a Christian. And you'll be God's tool in Russia.'

Babatunde bowed his head. A moment later he raised his face, revealing tearful eyes as he smiled.

Yvonne rose to her feet. 'I have a verse for you, Baba.'

She picked up a Bible from the coffee table and flipped through the pages.

'Here!' she said 'It's Isaiah chapter 41, verse 13.'

She put the Bible down in front of Babatunde who read silently, nodding as he read: 'For I the Lord hold your right hand; I am the Lord, Who says to you, Fear not: I will help you!'

Yvonne went out, leaving him to his reading; every now and then writing verses into his notebook.

# 45

Babatunde stood at the window of his hut, watching Felix's car slow down to turn into the gate. He felt very uncomfortable, as if he had to meet a person he was owing money to. He felt an urge to instruct Eki: *Please tell Teacher Felix that I'm not well, and I'll speak to him tomorrow!* He recalled how he and Felix had once talked about how they did not like the 'born-again' churches, and about how such churches made inroads into communities that practiced traditional African religion. He also recalled Felix saying: *They cunningly promise our gullible people healing and wealth.* He mused: *Now how am I going to face him and tell him that I now belong to a church of zealots? I'm really embarrassed to meet my former teacher!* Felix was now walking towards his hut; Babatunde went to meet him.

'On Sunday I was looking for you, Baba,' said Felix, after they had greeted each other. 'Your people told me you went to church with your cousin.'

'Yes, that's true, Teacher Felix,' responded Babatunde.

'I must tell you, Teacher Felix, that my life has taken a strange turn… something I never expected or believed could happen to me, has happened.'

'What happened?'

As Babatunde spoke he was amazed that Felix showed no trace of disappointment or discomfort. He merely sighed and released a smile that never flourished to the full.

'I must say you've really taken me by surprise, Baba. If someone told me that you'd collapsed and died, I would get an unpleasant shock. Now you're telling me that you've become a Christian. I can't say you've taken a bad decision, though I do not agree with you this time round.'

'It's okay sir,' said Babatunde softly.

'To be honest with you, you are going to invoke the wrath of the gods for turning against them.'

Felix touched Babatunde's arm as he grinned. 'Okay Baba, let me not pick a fight with you when you are about to go to Russia. I can't say you've taken a bad decision. The circumstances of your life are such that you decided to be a Christian. If being a Christian will make you a better person, I can't stand in your way. So I wish you well, Baba.'

Babatunde stood up and gave Felix a firm bear-hug.

'Thank you, Teacher Felix. But now, I've got a problem: I'm a changed person. What used to be my driving force is no longer part of me. Let me put it this way: it's like I used to be an alcoholic, spending all my money on liquor and my time at the bar. Days later a miracle happens and I realise that I no longer have the desire for the bottle. This is what happened to me.'

'What do you really want to say to me, Baba?'

'I used to feel a consuming desire to be an African communist. I intended to be empowered by the communists and to return to my country as a change agent. Now that the desire is gone, I don't feel like going to Russia. I spoke to Yvie a few hours ago, and she feels that I must go, nevertheless. But all I want to do now is spend more time with Pastor Benson, and be something like his houseboy, until I go to a seminary.'

Felix kept quiet for a while. 'I hear you but I don't agree with you, Baba. I can see that you are very excited about your new belief, but I don't think you should be a pastor. I agree with Yvie: go to Russia. But you'll have to be careful not to embarrass your sponsor.'

Babatunde nodded.

'So you'll have to keep a low profile as a Christian,' Felix went on. 'Your benefactor may turn a blind eye regarding your faith, but the Russian secret police might be a problem. It's all I can say, Baba.'

*

On Saturday afternoon Babatunde sat under the plantain tree and closed the Bible he was reading. He had fasted for the first time. He was alone at home; Ekene had gone to the roadside stall to hawk yams, and his mother, sister and nephews were visiting aunt Dorah in the neighbouring village.

He heard the sound of a car door banging and when he looked towards the gate, he saw Odenigbo. *Oh what a trial I'm going to be exposed to now!* he thought. He removed the Bible from his old desk and put down on the ground. *Anyway, my Lord had to face the devil as he was fasting*, the thought crossed his mind.

Odenigbo approached and took one of the empty chairs which Babatunde had put in front of his desk in case Nnesinachi and Adam visited him.

'How are you?' greeted Odenigbo, without a smile.

'I'm blessed, Ode, and you?'

Odenigbo grinned. 'You blessed? I'm certain you aren't pleased to see this Satan in front of you.'

'Well, I haven't thought of that!'

Odenigbo sat down, took two cigarettes out of a pack, gripped one with his lips and handed one to Babatunde, who shook his head.

'I thought as much,' said Odenigbo. He lit the cigarette, took a few steps away from Babatunde and began to puff at it.

Babatune grinned. 'Listen Ode, if God created man to smoke he would have fitted him with a chimney on his head.'

'Ha! Don't try to be smart o! Did you think of the chimney when you were still a smoker?'

'It's a joke, man. Let's laugh.'

'I won't laugh with you today. Or let me say I'm not one iota impressed with your sense of humour.'

'I'm sorry, my friend.'

Odenigbo continued to puff at his cigarette. 'Anyway, let me move away from Saint Paul.'

Babatunde forced a smile and shrugged.

'All you're seeing,' continued Odenigbo, 'is the smoke of hell. I would have been amazed if you would have touched a cigarette. Rumours abound that you've now become a member of the church of zealots. True or false?'

'I'm not sure if I would call myself a zealot.'

'A spade remains a spade, even if you call it by other name.'

'All I can say is that I have become a Christian. I never thought this could happen to me. It's a long story, if you were interested.'

'I'm not interested in useless details. Baba, I'm very disappointed that the role I played in helping to secure the scholarship has been reduced to nil.'

'What do you mean?' asked Babatunde.

'Listen, I expected you to go to Russia as Lenin's fire-spitting disciple,' continued Odenigbo, 'who four years later would come back to Nigeria to save the masses from the opium of the people. Now you've become an opium-smoker yourself.'

Babatunde said nothing.

'I'm terribly disappointed that you're going to Russia as a wimp and a toothless bulldog!' Odenigbo continued. 'You are like a handsome eunuch going to serve at the king's harem! What a waste!'

Odenigbo stood staring at Babatunde, then turned away from him and walked off to his car.

Nonplussed for a moment, Babatunde stood up and followed his friend.

'Ode, Ode!' Babatunde called. 'Com'n, cool down. Let's talk.'

'Talk what?'

Odenigbo dropped the cigarette stub, crushed it underfoot and got into the car, starting up the engine with loud revs. Babatunde stood with folded arms and looked on as his friend drove off at full throttle, the rear wheels whipping up red dust clouds.

# 46

During Christmas Babatunde's family members met as was customary. His two elder brothers with their children and wives, his sister and her two children, and Ekene were there to enjoy the family reunion. Usually they slaughtered a fattened goat and thanked their gods for having been good to them the whole year. They would put their hands on the goat's head, transferring their ill luck to the animal before slaughtering it. After slaughtering the goat they would collect the blood in a wide-mouthed gourd and present it as an offering to the gods at the shrine. They would then return to the shrine in the afternoon to bring stew with rice or *fufu*.

The family members knew that this meeting would be different because Babatunde was now a Christian. They thought he would be offended by the idea of slaughtering a goat; that he would treat it as a pagan practice.

'There's nothing wrong in slaughtering a goat,' he answered when his mother raised the subject on Christmas Eve. 'What is not right is to thank the gods instead of God.'

His mother was satisfied with his explanation. His brothers and sister had always respected him, as the shrine priesthood was transferred from their father to him. When they heard that he would be going to Russia, they respected him even more.

That Christmas Eve Babatunde went with his two brothers and Ekene, all armed with knives, to slaughter the goat; they would then skin it and cut it up into smaller portions. Laying the goat against the slaughtering tree-trunk, his elder brother turned to Babatunde and said:

'You know, Baba, we don't want to offend you by killing this animal the way we used to do it. If there is a Christian way of slaughtering, please tell us.' His other brother nodded in agreement.

Babatunde folded his arms, closed his eyes and prayed: 'Heavenly father, I praise you for having created goats; thank you for giving us meat, and we ask you to bless it. Amen.'

*

It was Christmas. The preparation of food was a shared task and an expression of appreciation for being part of the Okoronkwo clan. They sat in the shade of the trees on homemade benches, with food plates placed on their laps. The seven adults and eleven children, including Ekene who was the eldest, were about to eat. When his mother turned towards him, Babatunde knew that it was the cue to give thanks.

'You don't have to close your eyes. Let's lift up our plates heavenward.' He paused. 'Bless the Lord oh, my soul and all that is within me. Hallelujah! I thank You Lord for You have in your unlimited wisdom created the goat whose meat we are about to enjoy and thank You for the appetites.' He went on until one of the brothers cleared his throat audibly.

After he had just said, 'Amen,' his eldest brother grinned, 'Do you want the food to get cold?'

His mother broke into a loud laughter and pointed at Babatunde, 'He's the pastor of the family.'

After the meal it was time to discuss what should be done about the shrine.

'Your brother used to be the priest of the shrine,' Babatunde's mother introduced the subject. 'Now he has become a Christian. On the Sunday he became a Christian, he said he wanted to take the shrine objects to his church to be burnt, and I asked him to wait for all of you. According to his new belief, the shrine must be destroyed because it is regarded as a tool of the devil. Ifeoma felt strongly that he should leave the shrine alone. What are you, brothers, saying?'

Babatunde's brothers looked at each other.

'Perhaps it would be a good idea to give him an opportunity,' Babatunde's mother continued, 'to explain to us why he says the shrine is a tool of the devil.'

'Yes,' said Kenechukwu, his eldest brother, 'let him tell us why the shrine should be destroyed.'

Babatunde called Ekene and told him to bring his Bible. When the boy had brought the Word of God to him, Babatunde began to turn over the pages. Then he paused and told Ekene to go to their next-door neighbour and ask for a Bible in the Igbo language.

'I want to ask a question, Baba,' said Nnake his second eldest brother. 'The church that you are attending was brought here by the Europeans, and they have their white Jesus. Tell me what's wrong with us Africans praying our own Obasi and having our gods as intermediaries? This was our way of worship before the first white man came with the first ship.'

Kenechukwu nodded, wearing a smug smile, as if saying: *You gave him a tough question indeed; let's see how he's going to crack it!*

Ekene handed Babatunde the Igbo Bible.

'I'm still young in the knowledge of the Bible, my people,' said Babatunde. 'But all I can say for now is that people all over the world had, and still worship, their gods. Even Abraham worshipped other gods before God who is above all other gods, introduced Himself to him and called him to go to Canaan. Later God made Himself known to Moses and told him to write the ten laws.'

Babatunde paused and looked into his people's eyes: 'Can I read the laws? Then we can discuss these matters later.'

He read the English Bible while Ekene read in Igbo. "'You shall have no other gods before me. You shall not make for yourself a graven image, or any likeness of anything that is in heaven above, or that is in the earth beneath or that is in the water under the earth; you shall not bow to them or serve them; for I the Lord your God am a jealous God.'"

Babatunde turned over some pages.

'Baba, we've heard what you are saying,' said, Kenechukwu, 'but we cannot agree that the objects of the shrine should be burnt. To you they are the tools of the devil, but to us they are a means through which we can speak to those who are in another world, between us and God.'

Ifeoma, looked at Nnake and both nodded in agreement.

'I think we've made a big mistake,' continued Kenechukwu, 'by not worshipping our gods this Christmas because we don't want to offend you before you go to Russia. This is our parents' house, and we want to come here every Christmas to speak to our gods.'

'I agree with Kene,' said Nnake. 'You have chosen your own God over our gods. So you should go and serve your God and leave us alone with our Obasi and our gods.'

Babatunde stayed silent for a while before opening his mouth: 'My people, I have heard you. I told you what God says about the gods. If you want to continue talking to dead people you are making God angry, because He says, "Dead people know nothing and they cannot share in anything under the sun." He also says we should not put our confidence in man because when his breath leaves him, he returns to the earth and in that very day his plans die with him.'

'You may call our gods dead people,' said Kenechukwu, 'but we are happy to continue worshipping them as we follow in the footsteps of our fathers.'

Babatunde gave a wan smile. 'But let me warn you that God is not going to share the same house with the African gods. It's impossible!'

'What are you telling us, now?' Nnake demanded.

'In the Bible it is stated that the snake of Moses swallowed the snakes of the Egyptian magicians.'

'Are you saying that your God is going to swallow the shrine?' asked Ifeoma who had been quiet during the discussion.

'The fire of my God is certainly going to weaken the shrine,' said Babatunde.

'We shall wait to see that taking place,' said Nnake.

<h2 style="text-align:center">47</h2>

During the last days of the year, he spent most of his time at home reading the Bible, studying Russian grammar, and digging in the garden. On alternate weekends he went to sell yams at the roadside stall. He said to himself, *Let me enjoy being a Nigerian, for the time is coming when I'll be in Russia.*

As a result of his busy schedule, the days came and went sooner than expected, and before he knew it it was the last day of December 1980.

On the first Sunday of January it was announced in church that the following Sunday there would be a special service for Babatunde's farewell. Realising that he would be departing from his people in ten days, he decided to spend quality time with his family.

Every morning when his mother asked *How many days are left before you go to Lashia?* he indicated the remaining number of days by raising his fingers. He would spend a moment appraising her troubled smile as she continued with her chores, knowing that she looked away in an attempt to avoid showing her true feelings. Because of his daily chores, the days seemed to come and disappear 'at a speed faster than a donkey-cart', as he once said to his mother.

His daily tasks included packing his bags, reading the Bible and working in the garden. When his mother pleaded with him not to exhaust himself by doing spade work in the casava patch, he said to her: 'Mother,

I just want to enjoy touching and seeing Nigerian soil, for very soon I'll be walking on the Russian soil.'

She smiled at that and left him alone.

*

The second Sunday of the year, the day of the farewell service for Babatunde, dawned finally. Thirty minutes before the service started, Babatunde and his people arrived at the tent in two cars, led by Adam's red Benz. Babatunde saw the smoke of charcoal fires rising behind the tent. Adam told him that an ox had been slaughtered.

Women bustled about, performing chores like peeling potatoes, shredding cabbages and cutting meat, and preparing Nigerian dishes such as Ofe-onubi, Ofe-egusi and Jollof rice. They smiled and waved at Babatunde who waved back. Signs that this was indeed an unusual service included the fact that special guests such as James Okon, the gospel singer, and a brass band had been invited.

Most of the people who mattered in Babatunde's life were there, including Felix and Yvonne. The church yard was full of people, chatting in small groups. As the brass band entertained the crowd, Pastor Benson made sure that everything was in order. After speaking to Babatunde, he walked around greeting the guests, which included the king. Babatunde saw the pastor walking towards a white Mercedes that was busy parking. A grey-haired man got out of the car with the aid of a walking stick.

When the guests were introduced, Babatunde heard that the white-haired man was Prophet Ugochukwu. Looking intently at the old man, he recognised him as the same Pastor Ugochukwu whom he had met sixteen years ago at the age of seven, while working for his uncle. He could still picture that day when he played soccer next to Pastor Ugochukwu's church with his friends.

After the usual 'warming up' choruses and hymns, Benson stood up, smiled and stretched his arms sideways as he opened his palms, 'My people, *nno nu.*'

'Alleloyah!' the congregants responded.

He outlined the programme: a short sermon, a few speeches by some church leaders, benediction, collection of gifts, and lunch. The items would be interspersed with entertainment.

He appealed to those who were going to speak to be brief.

Benson closed the Bible he had just opened, saying: 'I'm not going to read the Bible today. I just want to speak from my heart.'

The people applauded.

Benson turned towards Babatunde who sat next to him. 'Son of Ijoto, you are like Joseph the dreamer, who left his village because his dream was bigger than his small place. Your dream is taking you out of the comfort zone of this village to Russia. That's no small dream. It's a big dream supported by a big God. Hallelujah!'

'Amen!' shouted the congregation, cheering.

Benson touched Babatunde's shoulder. 'But be warned, Baba. Those who have big dreams face big challenges. I always say: "There's a devil at every level." If you don't believe me, please read about the life of Joseph. So, I'm saying: Go to Russia at your own risk. God has something great in store for you, but the devil isn't going to fold his dirty arms. So, you are going to face some trials but you are going to win if you are connected to God at all times. I can assure you that we are going to pray for you, so that you should be protected from temptations.'

The three speakers representing the church spoke next, all of whom had this in common: *Go well to Russia; we shall miss you, and we shall pray for you.*

The king, who was not on the programme, was then asked to say something.

'Son of the soil. I'm proud of you and I want the young people here to follow in your footsteps. My wish is to see you realise your dream in Russia. But my heartfelt desire is to see you coming back to this village to uplift it. Remember that Joseph became a blessing to his own people. That's all I want to say.'

As the king sat down and the people applauded with gusto, Benson stood up, motioning to indicate that the applause should continue. When it finally died down, Benson asked Babatunde to come and bow in front of Prophet Ugochukwu. 'Before I pronounced the benediction, I just want to say: 'May machinations of your enemies be like straw before the wind, like chaff swept away by a gale! May you be like a mighty icheku tree that will resist the storms in Russia. Alleloyah!'

'Alleloyah!' the people cheered.

'I also I see you as rising up as a lioness,' the prophet continued, 'that shall not lie down until she devours the prey and drink the blood of the slain. Alleloyah!'

'Alleloyah!' the people cheered.

The prophet gestured towards Babatuned. 'O chosen one, your head will be adorned with a radiant crown while your enemies are clothed in shame. Alleloyah!'

'Alleloyah!' the people cheered.

The prophet moved closer to Babatuned and put his arms on his shoulders.

'The Lord bless you, and keep you,' said the prophet as he put his hands on Babatunde's head. 'The Lord make His face to shine upon you, and be gracious to you. The Lord lift up His countenance upon you, and give you peace. Amen!'

James Okon then sang Babatunde's favourite song: *My God-o is good-o!*

'Now's the time to bless the son of Ijoto with gifts,' Benson announced.

As the church choir sang, people went up to the table, holding envelopes and wrapped parcels. The envelopes were ripped open and money was counted by the deacons. The wrapped presents were opened, and the congregation was shown shirts, ties, socks and pairs of trousers.

The last person to drop his gift at the table was Adam, who blessed Babatunde a

suit, a wheeled suitcase, a pair of morning slippers and a night gown.

When lunch was dished out, and a queue snaked around the tent. Babatunde shared a special extended table with Benson, Prophet Ugochukwu, his mother, his sister, Felix, Yvonne, the king, and some church leaders.

After lunch Babatunde, Adam and Nnesinachi went to sit on garden chairs under a palm tree.

Babatunde turned towards Adam: 'Thank you for blessing me with a suit and other things.'

'It's a pleasure to be a blessing, Baba.'

'Alleloyah!' said Babatunde. 'And as for this blue-and-grey suit…it's a dream come true.'

Adam grinned. 'Really?'

'Yes.' Babatunde wiped away a tear and gave Adam a hug. 'I once dreamt of myself wearing a blue-and-grey checked suit. I was working at my uncle's farm. In the dream I was walking towards my homestead, and I heard the next-door neighbours cheering, *Baba, you are smart!* When I entered my homestead, my mother and sister complimented me, *Baba, you are smart!*

Babatunde was chatting with Adam when a woman interrupted them.

'I don't have much to give you,' said the woman, 'but perhaps this poster will be of value where you are going.'

'Thank you very much, mama,' said Babatunde, receiving the gift wrapped in brown paper; he unwrapped it and looked at it.

'Wow! A painting of our Lord!' Babatunde gave the woman a searching look. 'Mama, are you sure you want to give me this poster?'

'Yes, son,' the woman replied. 'Take it to Russia. It will remind you of our Lord.'

'It's a precious gift. Thank you, mama.'

'I'm pleased you like the gift,' said the woman as she left.

Babatunde scrutinised the unframed poster-sized oil painting entitled, *My Lord Crucified*. The crown of thorns was deeply pressed into the forehead; blood dripped from the wounds, and from the middle of the palms, from the breast, and from the feet, pinned together with a rough nail.

## 48

The days of the new week arrived and disappeared even faster than those of the previous week. By Thursday Babatunde had finished packing and was counting the hours towards his departure. On Thursday night it was difficult for him to sleep; he was like a child looking forward to an adventure.

On Friday morning—the day of departure - he woke up at 05h00 and read his Bible, as Pastor Benson had advised. He read about Joseph's trials before he became the Prime Minister of Egypt. At 08h00 when his sister gave him breakfast, he told her that he had no appetite. His mother insisted that he should eat.

'I'll eat at 11h00, mother, when I'm hungry,' he replied.

He started to count the hours that remained from 08h00 to 20h00. His mother kept asking him: 'How many hours are left?'

At 13h00 Pastor Benson came to collect him. He had invited Babatunde for lunch. Benson's aim was to impart final words to the important member of his congregation about to fly to Russia.

As they sat at a table in Udala Tree Restaurant, Babatunde realised that he was hungry after all.

'Baba, you're going to Russia, a place that's like a desert,' said Benson. 'So you must learn to survive in the desert. What is worse, you are going to a university, a place dominated by learned pagans and sceptics who'll always be eager to prove that God doesn't exist.'

'Yes, Pastor Bennie,' said Babatunde.

'You must eat the word, Baba. Only the word can keep you strong, like bread and meat which sustained the prophet Elijah.'

'Yes, Pastor Bennie,' said Babatunde.

'So you need to be full of the word,' continued Benson, 'if possible having three meals of the word each day: breakfast, lunch and dinner.'

'Yes, Pastor,' responded Babatunde.

'Your fellow students will enthusiastically persuade you that the Bible is old-fashioned. They'll try to persuade you, "Everybody is doing it, so don't ever try to be Mr Purity." The PhD students in maths will try to prove to you that two plus two equals five.'

Babatunde only nodded, his mouth full of food.

The pastor went on, 'Man shall not live from bread alone, but from every word that comes forth from the mouth of God.'

Babatunde nodded.

'I don't want you to go to Russia as a baby Christian,' Benson remarked. 'And you should please keep in touch with other believers at the campus. You'll know them by their fruits as you get to know them. Remember: when logs burn together, they produce more fire.'

'I agree with you one hundred percent, pastor,' said Babatunde.

'You are like Daniel going to Babylon,' continued Benson. 'So don't conform to their standards. When they give you the so-called rich Babylonian burgers, say, "No thanks!" and stick to your vegetarian meal like Daniel.'

'Yes, pastor.'

'Please read the book of Daniel, and you'll be glad you didn't follow those walking in the broad street of perdition.'

'Yes, pastor.'

'I appreciate that you are going to a foreign country. This means that you'll have to adapt to a new environment, culture food, climate and so forth. But please don't feel overwhelmed for the Bible says, God looks over the way of the righteous. As we say in our country,' the pastor smiled, "No be big problem…'

'I go manage, pastor!'

'Great! You are going to discover three antidotes to temptation: the word, prayer and the company of saints.'

Babatunde nodded again.

'You have a promising future,' Benson went on as a warm smile creased his face. 'I like your high forehead; it testifies to rare intelligence. And those bold eyes of yours—they suggest perception.'

Babatunde chuckled. 'Thank you, pastor.'

'And the fact that you are where you are today confirms that you have initiative and that you're enterprising.'

Late that afternoon Benson dropped Babatunde back at the gate of his homestead. Again Babatunde counted the hours and found that he was left with only five hours before the flight. He was checking that he had not forgotten anything when Ekene knocked at his door: 'Uncle, I just want to find out if you haven't forgotten to pack in the poster of our Lord.'

Babatunde looked from his suitcase to the back of the door, where the poster that he'd put up a few days ago was still pasted. He grinned as Ekene removed it and handed it to him.

'Thank you, Eki!' he said, lightly slapping Ekene's nape. 'How could I forget this precious gift and go off to Russia without it?' He covered the painting with the original brown paper wrapping then lifted up some of the packed clothes and put the painting into the bottom of the suitcase next to his Bible.

Time moved and before he knew it he was left with only one hour before Adam and Nnesinachi arrived to take him to the airport at 18h00.

Finally it was time to depart. Babatunde sat on the back seat of the car with his mother and Ekene. On both sides of the dirt road that led from his homestead neighbours waved to the important villager as the red Mercedes Benz cruised by. *Go well to Lashia,* the villagers shouted, waving enthusiastically.

# 49

At the airport, Adam and Nnesinachi excused themselves from the waiting room and left Babatunde to be alone with his people. A few minutes later Ekene also left so that his uncle could be alone with his Mama-Nnukwu.

'Baba, you should pray for me,' said Babatunde's mother, 'that I should become a Christian like you.'

'Alleloyah! Why do you want to be a Christian, mother?'

'I can now see what the hand of God is doing in your life.'

'It will be as you wish, mother. God is going to answer our prayers.'

His mother bowed her head and when he saw her wiping away tears, he hugged her and comforted her, assuring her that he would travel safely and that he would return home during the university holidays.

Babatunde and his mother enjoyed the peace of being in each other's presence, speaking with long pauses. They recalled many happy moments, including the day he returned from his uncle who lived at Umuahia.

As his mother spoke about how she felt the day, he arrived back home riding on the fender of his brother's bicycle, Babatunde's eyes became moist. He wiped away the tears, reminded of that other day when he, as a boy-soldier, heard his mother saying: *May the gods of our clan protect you until you return, Baba,* and his father saying: *No Baba, you can't cry, you are now a soldier; so you must show your mother that you are going to survive.* For a moment he felt guilty that he was once again about to leave his mother, wondering how she was going to cope without him.

Just after 19h00 Nnesinachi and her 'adorable Addie' returned to the waiting room, walking hand in hand. Ekene was with them. Adam bought some refreshments for all of them. Babatunde now counted the minutes: it was 50 minutes to go before the flight.

The next time Babatunde checked his watch he saw that he was left with only 10 minutes. He went off to the toilet. When he came back, he could not believe his eyes as he saw, of all people, Odenigbo grinning at him.

The two friends embraced. To Babatunde the excitement of seeing Odenigbo again was like on the day when they met at the AME school; the day Odenigbo took him out to a restaurant for a catch-up meal.

Odenigbo gave his characteristic smile, which Babatunde had missed for a while. He was pointing to Babatunde's new lush Afro hairstyle.

'You look different, Baba!'

'I know. I'm hoping my hair will provide some cover against the terrible Russian weather.'

'It makes sense.'

Babatunde saw Odenigbo's face suddenly wearing a serious look, and he wondered what his brain was grinding.

'You know Baba, I feel that the hug I have just given you is like a Judas kiss.'

'What do you mean, Ode?'

'To be brutally frank, I'm not here to apologise for what I have said to you weeks ago.'

Babatunde sighed. 'It's okay with me Ode. You don't have to apologise for...'

'Why should I apologise? I want you to know that although I wish you well as you go to Russia, I haven't changed my mind. I'm like a leopard that doesn't change it spots.'

Babatunde folded his arms as he tried to force a grin.

'And why should I pretentiously wish you well?' Odenigbo continued, 'To be honest, I wish you should have hard times in Russia.'

'But why should you have the heart of a witch towards your friend?'

'Let truth be bitter, but it remains truth.'

'Why should I suffer in Russia?'

'So that you should give up your faith and revert to communism and be a panther Africa should be proud of.'

'Your wish isn't going to happen.'

'It remains a wish.'

Babatunde heard the airport announcer saying: 'Will passengers travelling on flight 650 to Moscow please make your way to the boarding gate now.'

Suddenly Odenigbo grinned. 'Anyway, Baba, let me however, wish you well.'

'Thank you my friend,' said Babatunde with a smile criss-crossing his face.

Odenigbo bear-hugged him and walked away, stopping suddenly: 'Perhaps one day,' he called, 'I'll understand what I don't understand today.'

Babatunde waved, smiling at his friend. Quickly he hugged Adam and kissed Nnesinachi and his mother, hugged Ekene, then grabbed his bag and headed into the Departure area. He turned to give them a final wave, feeling a tear meandering down his cheek.

Heading down the escalator to gate 12, Babatunde saw the huge red aircraft parked about ten metres away; he became short of breath as he scanned the plane from bottom to top. He felt as if the huge iron bird could talk through the 'beak'. Stepping towards the staircase of the plane, he reflected on Benson's words to him during the farewell party: *Son of Ijoto, you are like Joseph the dreamer who left his village because his dream was bigger than his village. Your dream is taking you out of the comfort zone of the village to Russia…*

As the front tyres of the plane left Mother Earth and the head of the giant bird tilted skywards, Babatunde heard Teacher Felix's inspiring words in his ears: *Time flies, Baba. Four years later you'll be back home and you can join the government as a journalist, perhaps as a speechwriter for the Minister of Information.*

# PART FIVE

## 50

The plane Babatunde had boarded flew from Murtala Muhammed International Airport in Lagos, Nigeria to London, where he got onto another airbus going to Berlin in West Germany; there he boarded a bus that took him to Berlin Schönefeld Airport, in East Germany. Six hours later the Russian-made Aeroflot landed at Sheremetyevo International Airport in Moscow. As Babatunde shuffled towards the luggage area, he saw another young African man whom he assumed to be a fellow student.

The two grinned and waved at each other. After transferring his luggage into the trolley, Babatunde waited for his fellow African who was a few paces behind him.

Babatunde smiled at the man. 'Are you a student?'

'*Oui oui, et vous?*'

'Yes, I'm a student too.'

*Good gracious, he's French-speaking!* thought Babatunde, *How are we going to communicate?*

He stretched his hand towards the man.

'I'm Babatunde Okoronkwo from Nigeria.'

'*Je m'appele* Doumbé Khouyaté *en provenance du* Sénégal.'

Babatunde nodded, a smile lingering on his face. 'It's great to meet a fellow African in Russia.'

Doumbé nodded with a grin. '*Oui.*'

As they pushed their trolleys out of the airport building Babatunde stopped and looked about him.

'What problem?' Doumbé tried to speak English.

Babatunde gestured around them, grinning. 'There's no colour here! Where are the people talking and shouting?'

Doumbé gave him a puzzled look.

'Where's the laughter? The noisy hawkers?' Babatunde gestured skywards. '*Ewo*! And look at this vast, freezing greyness everywhere.'

Doumbé grinned and shrugged. They followed the red arrows that led them to a spot clearly marked, 'Collection point for Lumumba Friendship University students.' Eight non-African students also waited there. The microbus arrived, and the luggage was loaded. Babatunde and Doumbé sat next to each other.

'What are you going to study?' asked Babatunde as the bus took them to the main campus.

'*Je vais faire une troisième année en ingéniere civile.*'

'Excuse me?' said Babatunde, his face pleading, *please, not so fast!*

Doumbé raised three fingers, '*troisième année,*' and he enunciated the words clearly, '*en ingéniere civile.*'

Babatunde's face beamed like a pupil getting the answer right: 'Oh, third year in civil engineering?'

'*Oui, et vous?*'

'Journalism.'

'*Magnifique!*'

'So you'll be completing next year?'

'*Oui!*'

They became quiet, their attention absorbed by the Russian architecture, the traffic and people.

Babatunde's face brightened and he pointed. 'Look at the cars! They are so old!'

'*Oui, les voitures sont vrai ancienne!*'

Babatunde looked blankly at Doumbé. 'The what? The voters?'

'*Les voitures.*' Doumbé demonstrated a car's steering wheel and Babatunde laughed at himself.

'I can't believe it!' Babatunde said, 'I'm shocked! Even in my country people don't drive such rickety cars.'

*What I'm seeing doesn't really fit the image of a superpower,* he mused. He had expected the cars in Russia to be far better, bigger and smarter than the old cars in Nigeria.

When they arrived at the office of the warden, they were given different residential blocks. They waved at each other: Goodbye, *Au revoire.*


## 51


For that whole week the first-year students received orientation. During the last week of January the foreign students began language training at a mini-campus. The shuttle-bus took them there every morning and brought them back in the afternoon.

On the first Friday of February Babatunde returned from the language course to find his new roommate, Nikolai Krapov, unpacking his luggage. The Russian was with a fellow country- man, Yuri Yeltsin. Nikolai spoke a halting English while Yuri was more fluent. Yuri asked Babatunde many questions about his country and about why he had come to study at the university.

'How's it going with our Russian language?' asked Yuri.

'Give me three months,' responded Babatunde, 'and I'll be conversing in Russian.'

'I like your confidence,' smiled Yuri. 'The secret of mastering any language is practice, practice, practice.'

'*Da*, I'm going to do that.'

'And don't be shy about murdering the language!'

'*Spasibo*, for encouraging me, Yuri.'

On Saturday as Babatunde emerged from the library with a pile of books gripped under his arm, he felt someone tapping his shoulder. When he glanced around, he saw an African student looking into his eyes.

'I'm Thom Mutesa from Kenya,' said the man.

Babatunde introduced himself.

'When I saw you taking those books as they were stamped by the librarian,' said Thom, 'I felt I should speak to you.'

'I'm glad you did. God has answered my prayer.'

Thom chuckled. 'You speak of God in Russia?'

Babatunde laughed. 'Come, let's sit over there.' He pointed to a steel-and-cement garden bench.

'Now tell me about God and your prayer,' said Thom as they sat down.

'I assume that you are a Christian,' said Babatunde.

'Why?'

'Because Christianity is common in most African countries.'

'You are right, Babatunde.'

'Okay, let me come to the point, Thom. After two weeks in Russia, I've became very disillusioned, and I wanted to return home.'

'Why?'

'I'm not used to the cold weather, the type of food, the language barrier or the unfamiliar land. I missed my people and my language. One day when I woke up I found myself singing an Igbo song: *Ka m bunie afa gi enu.*'

'Will you please repeat that?'

'*Ka m bunie afa gi enu.*'

'It means, "Let me praise your name up high." But even more than that, spiritually I need to worship with fellow Christians. One bangle doesn't make a musical sound.'

Thom smiled. 'I get what you're saying.'

Babatunde grinned. 'I'm delighted that you are a fellow believer. Thom, have you realised that there's nothing to point to the existence of God in this part of Russia?'

'You are right, Baba. I saw a few cathedrals. But there's something strange here. I feel an aloofness and coldness.'

'Yes. There's no warmth. No life. I'm beginning to face the reality of a churchless life. But I'm delighted that I've met you at the right time.'

'Yes, and somehow we have to survive.'

'That's true. You know, I met an old white woman on the plane going to London. When I told her I was going to Russia, she told me to look for an underground church.'

'Where are we going to find an underground church?'

Babatunde shrugged. 'I don't know. Let's come together and pray and read the Bible.'

He glanced at his wristwatch. 'Thom, can we meet tomorrow at your room, for our first meeting of the underground church?'

Several metres away they saw a black male student walking with a Russian female student.

'It's the first time that I see a black and white student together here,' said Thom.

The black student waved to Babatunde who waved back.

'From the body language I can see they are boyfriend and girlfriend,' said Thom. 'Do you know the guy?'

'Yes. His name is Doumbé, from Senegal. He's the first African student I met when I arrived at the airport.'

Thom and Babatunde bade each other goodbye and walked to their rooms.

## 52

On Sunday morning after breakfast, Babatunde strolled to Thom's room, hiding his Bible and the poster of Jesus in the brown paper wrapping. After locking the door he opened the paper wrapping.

'Thom, I've got something very special to share with you,' he said as he took out the poster.

Thom gasped and kissed the poster.

'Where did you get this?'

'From Nigeria.'

'Wonderful! It's great to see a poster of our Lord!'

'Our Lord is attending the service with us today.'

They scrutinised the painting for a moment. The artwork depicted crucified Jesus from the head to the loin-cloth. The head crowned by a wreath of thorns tilted to the right. Blobs of blood were scattered on his face, a faded crimson smudge on the left side of the chest.

'I've seen many paintings of crucifixion,' said Thom, 'They look similar. But this one is unique because Jesus here is a handsome African.'

'Yes. This is our Lord through the eyes of a Nigerian artist, Uche Okeke.'

'I now agree with those who say that the blond, blue-eyed Jesus is the interpretation of European artists.'

'Yes. Because he was born in the Middle East and was taught how to read and write in Africa.'

Thom opened with prayer and they sang in low tones some English hymns which Thom had photocopied. They also read their Bibles and took part in an hour-long biblical discussion.

'I'm missing a lively African church,' said Babatunde as they walked out of Thom's room towards Babatunde's room.

'Me too.'

'I wish our number can increase to three or five next Sunday.'

'We must recruit more believers, Thom.'

'Yes, God will direct us to the right people.'

*

Late that Sunday afternoon Thom and Babatunde took a stroll around the campus. An hour later they sat on a garden bench, enjoying the Russian sun. They were sharing peanuts and cool drinks as they talked.

Their attention was distracted by loud voices nearby. About twenty metres away, they saw five African students standing around a statue. One of the students knelt and kissed the feet of the statue.

'That must be the statue of Patrice Lumumba,' said Babatunde. 'Let's go over there.'

'Perhaps we can recruit them to join our underground church.'

They walked to Lumumba Square at the centre of the university where they found the students looking sombrely at the four-metre high bronze statue.

'Yes, this is indeed the statue of Lumumba,' whispered Babatunde. He recalled the photo of the handcuffed Lumumba standing at the back of an army truck before he was executed.

He and Thom exchanged handshakes with their fellow Africans who were from the Francophone Congo and Rwanda.

With tearful eyes one of the students saluted and addressed the statue in French and the group walked away. Babatunde wanted to ask them about Doumbé, but the language barrier was a problem.

Thom pointed to the student who had spoken to the statue.

'I think he was saying, "I love you, Patrice,"' said Thom.

'That makes sense.'

As they left Lumumba Square they ran into another African student. They rejoiced that he was from another English-speaking country, Ghana. He introduced himself as Kwame Asamoah. After finding out that he was a Christian, they invited him to be part of the underground church.

'No!' Kwame shook his head with a frown. 'Do you want to put our lives in danger? Don't even think of starting an underground church on campus because we'll be watched in whatever we are doing.'

'But God will protect us,' said Babatunde.

'No! I don't want to be part of any Christian meeting. You know that atheism is the official religion here and that practising Christianity in this country is therefore a risky business. How dare you say to the authorities, "You can deport me to my country?" That's knocking at the prison door. So I'll pray alone in my room and read my pocket Bible in the toilet.'

'If you don't want to be part of our group it's okay,' said Thom.

'I just want to collect my degree and return to my country better equipped,' said Kwame. 'And don't tell anyone that I'm a Christian. If you do that, I'll deny as Peter did to Jesus.'

Kwame strode away while Babatunde and Thom exchanged rueful grins.


## 53

The following Sunday afternoon Babatunde and Thom sauntered to Lumumba Square where they expected to meet fellow Africans. There they met Kwame in the company of five students.

Kwame motioned to one of the students: 'He's Hezekiah Ayih from Togo and he's the deputy chairman of the African Students' Union.'

Babatunde and Thom shook hands, introducing themselves.

'It's great to meet such a distinguished young African,' said Thom, looking straight into Hezekiah's eyes. 'Do you want to be part of us?'

Kwame gave Hezekiah a wry smile. 'Hezi, they are recruiting you.'

'Recruiting me for what?'

'Their underground church,' said Kwame, frowning.

Babatunde and Thom grinned.

'Is it true?' Hezekiah asked Babatunde.

'Yes,' said Babatunde.

Hezekiah sighed. 'One thing I can tell you, I'm not a heathen; I know about God, but I

won't have time for any church activity. I've a lot of work to do. I'm a fourth year architecture student and,' he flashed a smile, 'I have a girl-friend to attend to. So my arms are full.'

Another of the students gestured to Hezekiah. 'He's in love with a beautiful Russian girl.'

The rest of the students looked at Hezekiah with awe.

'Tell them about your first experience, Hezi,' said the first student. 'You know what I mean.'

Hezekiah gave a delighted chuckle: 'Oh, it was a marathon of lovemak-ing,' he said, his eyes sparkling.

'You mean an African-Russian marathon?' asked the student.

They all laughed.

*

Engrossed in language learning, Babatunde made use of opportunities to practise Russian with the native speakers who included the library staff, the kitchen staff and other workers.

At the end of the month he received a postcard from Nigeria. He brightened when he observed from the handwriting that it was from Yvonne:

> How's life in Russia? Are you adjusting well? How are the peo-
> ple? And how's the food? Have you met many African students?
> If you have you won't feel very homesick. All of us, the teachers
> and the children, are missing you, Baba. We are recalling the
> good days, especially when you played the 'Hyena and the Chil-
> dren' with the children.
>     With tons of love,
> Yvonne.

He did not hesitate to reply, sent in an enveloped letter:

Dear Yvonne,

Thanks for your postcard. After two weeks in Russia, I wanted to go home. It was cold and cloudy and I missed the African sun for days. And my stomach rebelled against the strange food. Spiritually it felt very cold and dry as I had no fellowship with other believers. To have a one-man church service on two Sundays was something that I never expected.

As I read the Bible and hummed a few hymns and choruses, I was anxious that I would hear a loud knock at my door. I also looked around everywhere to see if there was a hidden camera or microphone. I dearly miss the noisy and active Nigerian Sunday services! When I went to the city, the tall drab buildings, grey weather and the look of helplessness on the faces of the people did not make life easy for me.

My naïve image of Russia as an economic superpower like America came crashing down. Just as I was contemplating returning to Africa, I heard God whispering into my ear: 'I directed you here because I have a purpose in bringing you to this place.' I prayed and God has answered my prayer. He has helped me to meet a fellow Christian from Kenya, and the two of us have established an underground church. We hope that God will send more believers to our group. I'm now positive enough to face the challenges ahead of me. Tell everybody that I love them. And please continue to pray for me.

With love,
Baba.

## 54

Babatunde continued to attend the underground church at Thom's room. One Sunday in March, when he returned from the church, his Bible wrapped in an old newspaper, his roommate Nikolai stood grinning at him.

'I have been observing you, Baba,' said Nikolai.

'Why?'

'Tell me Baba, are you religious?'

Babatunde smiled. 'Why are you asking?'

'Because you don't smoke and you don't take alcoholic beverages or do other things done by most students.'

Babatunde chuckled. 'Well I'm just a well-mannered young man brought up by good African parents.'

Suddenly Nikolai pointed to the plastic shopping bag.

'What are you hiding in there? A Bible? Tell the truth, Baba; Christians say they don't lie!'

Babatunde laughed.

'You are going to be an excellent reverend, Nik.'

Nikolai also laughed. 'We atheists have no reverends. Tell me what you are doing in your friend's room on Sundays.'

'I don't only visit Thom on Sundays. What do friends do when they meet?' asked Babatunde. 'Don't they talk about what they have in common?'

'You give me a clever answer,' said Nikolai in a serious mood, pointing his finger at Babatunde. 'But you are soon going to be exposed.'

'What do you mean?'

Nikolai shook his head and walked out the room.

*

Time passed and Babatunde and Thom completed their basic four months of intensive language training. They would do further language studies individually and consult their tutors once a week. Although Babatunde had long known that Thom would part from him, he was saddened because he would no longer have fellowship with a believer.

One afternoon in May Babatunde was in Thom's room to bid him goodbye. They had had their last underground church meeting. Thom's luggage was neatly packed, and both were standing.

'So, this is the end…call it the death of the underground church?' asked Babatunde sadly.

'Yes, but I'm sure we can still meet, once a month perhaps.'

'It's too little, and too far from now.'

'I know. But it's better than nothing.'

'It's as good as nothing. I don't want to come to your room and find that instead of holding a Bible in your hands you are holding a bottle of vodka and a woman.'

Thom laughed. 'No, that won't happen, Baba!'

'Anyone can fall into temptation or turn into a Judas Iscariot, if…'

'No, that won't happen to me!'

'So, let's not delay in establishing an underground church.'

'I agree.'

Babatunde looked into Thom's eyes. 'Thom, are you promising me that you'll initiate a Christian fellowship without delay?'

'Of course!'

Babatunde gripped Thom's hands: 'Let's pray.'

As they prayed a loud knock at the door interrupted them.

'*Otkroĭte dver' syeĭchas!*' shouted the voice from behind the door.'*Sekretnaya Politsiya!*'

Babatunde and Thom exchanged anxious glances. Thom tiptoed to the door and opened it with bated breath. To his amazement he found no secret police standing there. Craning his neck he saw Doumbé leaning against the wall beside the door, trying to suppress his laughter.

'Dooms! How dare you…?'

Doumbé burst out laughing.

Thom smacked Doumbé's shoulder and led him into the room. 'Naughty boy!'

Doumbé continued to laugh and Babatunde laughed with him in relief.

Doumbé stretched his arms towards Thom. '*K sozhaniyu, chtoby napugat' vas, rebyata!*' He grabbed Thom's hand. '*Proshchay, moy drug.*'

'*Spasibo, moy drug,*' responded Thom, grinning.

## 55

One afternoon Babatunde sat at his table looking out through the window. He preferred facing the lawn that divided the two residence blocks. There was a textbook lying open in front of him, but his mind strayed from the book. His pensive mood was disturbed by the door opening, and in came Nikolai and Yuri. Babatunde realised that the men were drunk. As they staggered closer to him he smelt how they reeked of liquor.

Yuri winked at Babatunde. 'Good gracious! You look so lonely!'

'He should have fun and stop behaving like a monk!' Nikolai teased him.

'Now's the time to enjoy vodka,' said Yuri. 'And *your* women, who are waiting for your arms.'

Babatunde chuckled. 'I don't need vodka and women to be happy.'

Yuri lit a cigarette and puffed at it; suddenly he pointed outside. 'Look!'

Babatunde glanced down and saw a well-fleshed female African student walking across the lawn.

'Look at the tits on that one!' exclaimed Yuri. 'Don't you salivate? I could eat her up if I had her.'

'I had no idea that you were attracted to African women,' remarked Babatunde.

Yuri tittered. 'Don't be a silly man! I'm trying to help you so that you can enjoy life in Russia.'

'I'm not engineered that way.'

'What kind of an African are you?' Yuri asked.

'I'm my type.'

Yuri blew smoke through his nostrils, his eyes flickering with naughtiness. 'Don't you Africans like sex?'

'What?' asked Babatunde, not believing what he was just asked.

'Listen here —' Yuri pointed at Babatunde, 'you've got to be honest with yourself, man. You Africans have a high sex-drive.'

'Who told you that?'

'That's what the Russian girls are saying,' responded Yuri.

Nikolai guffawed.

Babatunde shook his head. 'You've got it all wrong. And if you think this is what it means to have a sense of humour, I must tell you, Yuri, I don't like it.'

'It's a fact, and it has been well documented,' said Yuri.

'Documented by who?' Babatunde challenged him.

'Listen, if a woman sits under a tree an African man will see a woman and not a tree.'

Again Babatunde shook his head, far from impressed.

'Yuri,' said Nikolai, 'he's a strange type of an African this one; he's afraid of women and he hides behind the Bible. He must be a virgin.'

'Are you a virgin?' Yuri asked Babatunde. 'Don't you fear that your organs will be underdeveloped because they aren't used?'

Yuri guffawed and Nikolai joined in.

Babatunde pointed a finger at Yuri. '*Ne glupyĭ chelovek!*'

Yuri and Nikolai continued to laugh as they walked out of the room.

*

It was the third Saturday of June. The following Friday the university would close as the first semester drew to an end. Babatunde was alone in his room as Nikolai was visiting his parents in St Petersburg for the weekend. He was working on his assignments, but his heart wasn't in it. He thought about Thom, missing him sincerely, wondering how he was doing, how he was adjusting to his new mini-campus. As he continued working, he found himself humming hymns and choruses in his Igbo language.

He worked until midnight, planning to wake up at 05h00 to start his day with prayer and Bible-reading as usual. He looked forward to an exciting spiritual moment because he was alone for once and would be free to pray aloud and recite some Bible verses.

On Sunday morning he had just read his Bible and had started praying aloud when he heard a loud knock at his door. He thought of that day, weeks ago, when Doumbé had knocked, pretending to be *Sekretnaya Politsiya*.

'Who's there? Is it Dooms?'

'It's Kwame.'

Babatunde opened the door.

'Are you praying when Russian racists are murdering African students?' Kwame said.

'Who has been killed?'

'Doumbé.'

Babatunde let loose a scream. 'Who killed Dooms? And why?'

'Come with me. We'll get details from Hezi.'


# 56

Babatunde and Kwame rushed to Lumumba Square where about two hundred African students stood chatting in small groups, with more arriving every moment. Hezekiah spoke to four fellow students who appeared to be leaders. Thirty minutes later over 600 students waited for Hezekiah to address them in the arena behind the Lumumba statue. The four students talking to Hezekiah went to join the group and left him standing alone, facing them.

'Fellow African students,' said Hezekiah while another student interpreted in French, 'it is with a broken heart that I must announce the death of a fellow African student, beloved brother, comrade and friend, Doumbé Khouyaté from Senegal.

'Dooms was assaulted by racist thugs while he was with his girlfriend, Vera Politskovskaya. They were driving from the Moscow Ballet Theatre when two cars forced them off the road. One of the men held Vera at gunpoint while four of them assaulted Dooms with clubs, iron rods and sickles. Dooms died of internal injuries and bleeding this morning.

'It seems these racist thugs trailed the couple for weeks, with the help of a security guard at the flat where the woman is staying. Vera says as they left the theatre a man taunted Dooms: "In your country Africans are dancing naked around bonfires." She said although Dooms was angry with the racist, he decided to ignore the man.

'I was with Doumbé on Saturday; we went to St Petersburg by train to attend a meeting organised by the Union of Black African Students. We were accosted by a group of drunken Russians all the way to the train station; they followed us to the coach and demanded that we give up our seats. One of the men said: "In your own country you aren't even allowed to be in the same coach with whites, whereas here you are sitting down comfortably while white people are standing."

'I said to Dooms, "Let's go to another coach," but he said, "This is public transport and no-one should intimidate us or force us to go another coach." So we sat down, but we heard one guy saying: "Africans are noisy and dirty!" "And hypersexual!" another guy added. I grabbed Dooms, pulled him aside and said, "I can't stand all these insults!" As we walked to another coach one of the drunken guy shouted, "These people are spreading syphilis in Russia!"

'Dooms told me when we returned from St Petersburg, that Vera had invited him out to the Moscow Theatre that evening. Fellow African students, it is clear that although officially we are respected by the Soviet authorities who call us comrades, the monster of racism is alive and jumping high among the ordinary Russians. While we don't want to generalise, we can't turn a blind eye to racist attacks inflicted upon us.

'We are witnessing the kind of racist attacks that took place in 1963 when a Nigerian student, Ikenna Nnokwa, was found dead not far from his girlfriend's flat. The question is, how long should Africans be easy targets of Russian racists? That guy over there…Abdul, he's from Somalia, he was recently attacked while the police were watching. I myself have a Russian girlfriend…she is standing over there.' He smiled and gestured towards her. 'Her name is Svetlana Solzhenitsyn. Does that mean that my days are numbered? The last question we must ask this morning is: what kind of action should we take to protest against the racist attacks against Africans in this part of Russia?'

Hezekiah sat down as loud applause broke out. After an hour-long discussion, it was agreed that a Committee of Five should be established with Hezekiah as chairman. The Committee held their first meeting there and then, while other students lounged about and talked in small groups. Forty-five minutes later, Hezekiah was ready to speak.

'Fellow African students, the Committee of Five has resolved the following:

'One! Tomorrow, which is Monday, we are going to boycott classes!

'Two! We are going to take our protest march to the Senegalese embassy and later to the Red Square!'

The students applauded.

'We shall need about ten buses, and the Committee has recommended that Svetlana should organise transport. One last thing – let's prepare posters in Russian, English and French and let's meet here tomorrow at 07h00.'

The group dispersed.

*

By 07h30 on Monday, over 1,000 African students stood around the statue of Patrice Lumumba, some of them looking up at the statue as if drawing inspiration for the day's planned march. More students continued to arrive. Svetlana's was not the only white face there; there were about 50 other whites.

Babatunde observed how festive the mood was and how it seemed as if nothing but action roared in their veins. He hoped that God would answer his prayer: that the march should not end in a bloody confrontation but that an amicable solution to the problem could be found.

Two Senegalese students took slow steps towards the statue, holding a poster-sized photograph of the deceased Doumbé and a funeral wreath. Other students shuffled towards the statue and crowded around it as the two students observed a moment of silence before squatting to place the photo and the wreath at the feet of the statue.

'Long live the spirit of Patrice Lumumba, long live!' shouted a student.

'Long live!' responded other students.

'Away with racism, away!'

'Away!'

The students applauded and shouted slogans. Some waved flags of their countries while others hoisted posters that read: *Stop killing Africans, Crime of Racism Doesn't Pay, Moscow—centre of discrimination, Why Kill Your Comrade?*

At a distance about 50 campus security staff in blue uniforms stood and watched. Two truckloads of Soviet police arrived and armed young constables dismounted and stood in front of their commander. At about 08h30 Hezekiah, who had been consulting with his fellow Committee of Five members, stood in front of the students, a French-speaking student standing beside him to interpret.

'Fellow African students and Russian friends,' said Hezekiah, 'thank you for attending this planned protest march. Let me take this opportunity to welcome our fellow students from other campuses.'

A roar of applause broke out and Hezekiah acknowledged it with a smile and a wave.

'We heartily appreciate your support because we have a common problem: racism. Today history is repeating itself. On 20th December 1963 African students, facing attacks by racists, went on a protest march to the Nigerian embassy and later the Red Square. Following in the footsteps of that gallant generation of African students, we are going to stand in front of the Spasskie Gate at the Kremlin; there we are going to hand over a memorandum – and we will also pose for photographs and give interviews to correspondents of Western newspapers and the BBC. If...'

Thunderous applause interrupted him.

'If the Soviet authorities think that some of us are pawns exploited by the West, it's their problem.'

Another round of loud applause greeted his words.

'They've created the problem because they've ignored it for too long. From the Kremlin we will proceed to the Ministry of Higher Education.'

At that juncture ten buses arrived and parked at the entrance of the university, and the students' attention was distracted for a moment. The Registrar's Private Assistant walked straight up to Hezekiah, whispered to him briefly and left.

'That lady has just told me that the Registrar wishes to speak to the Committee of Five,' said Hezekiah. 'It that acceptable to you?'

'No, they must speak to all of us!' shouted a voice.

'Yes, we should avoid the divide and rule strategy!' someone added.

One of the Committee of Five members raised his hand and Hezekiah acknowledged him.

'Friends, we are leaders, not leaders of tomorrow, but leaders of this historic moment. You've chosen us to lead you and so you should trust us. If the Registrar wishes to speak to us, we should allow him to do so. You can suggest what we should say to him.'

Hezekiah nodded in agreement. 'There you are. What should we tell the Registrar?'

A hand shot into the air and Hezekiah acknowledged its owner.

'Tell him that the march can't be stopped or delayed!' said the student.

Hezekiah and his team talked among themselves in low tones before they went to see the Registrar. A student holding a piece of paper rushed to the spot where Hezekiah had been standing.

The student beat his palms together and raised his hands. 'I've a poem, can I read it?'

'Yes!' the students chorused.

He read:

'Doumbé, bone of our bone / flesh of our flesh /the rain from our eyes / the pain that has become the fruit of our heart / all nourish the tree of our liberation / Mama Afrika lost a son / but the spirit of the son hangs like a necklace / the stubborn spirit hangs like a rain-cloud / the spirit towering like a stone-breaker / an unbreakable tree / that'll be seen by generations/ The young panther pants no more/ but the cat's tigritude rests in our hands / And our toughened fingers can break anything anti-African / the key is in our hands / for a future that cannot be aborted / Can the sunrise be reversed? Long live the spirit of Doumbé!'

The students cheered as their colleague returned to where he'd been standing. They chanted, many of them raising flags or posters, clenching their fists.

Hezekiah and his team returned from their brief meeting with the Registrar and waited in front of the frenzied students. Hezekiah raised his hands and silence descended. 'The Registrar is pleading with us to stop the march, but we told him that we've reached a point of no return.'

Ear-shattering applause filled the arena.

'We told him that the march wasn't against the university,' continued Hezekiah, 'but that it was a statement regarding racism against Africans in Russia, and that we were doing this because history would condemn us if we become fainthearted. He warned us that if things went wrong, we would be held responsible. We assured him that we were responsible, and that's why we were studying in Russia.'

He paused as scattered applause broke out, punctuated by voices calling, *Well done!* Heads nodded and smiles beamed towards him.

'So, let's get into the buses which are going to take us to the Senegalese embassy.'

Hezekiah clapped his hands and students hurried towards the buses.

'One last thing!' he shouted.

The students stood still.

'Fellow students,' said Hezekiah, 'we are going to have a dignified protest march. So no hurling of insults. No destruction of property. If we are unruly and destructive, the men in uniform are going to act, and we don't want to see another spilt drop of African blood. If we are not disciplined, we are going to embarrass our governments and our people, not only from Africa but from the African Diaspora.'

Spirited applause filled the arena.


# 57

The buses cruised out of the campus with the students chanting: 'Long live the spirit of Doumbé!' Clenched fists protruded from bus windows and flags fluttered for onlookers to see. The police trucks trailed the buses, which travelled along Kwame Nkrumah Avenue where many buildings were occupied by African embassies. After the buses were parked, the students stepped out chanting, raising their fists and stomping about.

Led by the Committee of Five, the students chanted: 'Long live, the spirit of Doumbé!' Some of the posters behind the leaders read: "Your silence is too loud!" "Silence isn't golden!" "Are you your brother's keeper?" "Are you deaf and blind?"

Three embassy staff members waited at the stairs in front of the entrance. Hezekiah led the group, walking straight towards a bespectacled, bulky man sandwiched by a male and a female colleague.

'Sir,' Hezekiah addressed the man, 'on behalf of the African students of the Lumumba Friendship University and other Soviet universities, I'm handing you this memorandum for your urgent attention.'

The man received the memorandum, wearing a serious expression. 'Thank you for delivering this document, which the embassy will take seriously. A march like yours should be treated as a legitimate democratic expression, and not necessarily as a form of confrontation. This will receive the attention it deserves and the response shall be duly communicated to you.'

The students returned to the buses, which took them to the Red Square as planned. Hezekiah led the Committee of Five, with other students behind him. Walking up to two sombre-faced police officers standing in front of the Kremlin's Spasskie Gate, they handed the memorandum over in complete silence. The stern-faced officer received it with a stiff nod. As expected, correspondents from Western newspapers and the BBC took many pictures and jotted down notes in their notebooks.

Members of the Committee of Five posed for photographs and gave brief interviews; appointments were made for further in-depth interviews. Soviet plainclothes policemen moved around taking pictures and making quick notes. Thousands of ordinary Russians watched with curious faces from the pavements, shops and apartments.

At the Ministry of Higher Education, the Chief Director received the memorandum and invited the leaders and all the students to Patrice Lumumba Auditorium. Two Senegalese students walked to the front and placed Doumbé's photo and the wreath at the bottom of the podium. A few moments later the Chief Director stood up and introduced the Minister accompanied by three top officials and two representatives of the university-level Communist Party Central Committee.

The Minister rose to his feet and asked the students to stand and observe a moment of silence in memory of their friend.

In his opening remarks he outlined the friendship and brotherhood between the USSR and the African states, and the role that his country had played in the liberation of African countries. His opening statement was met with interjections, angry catcalls and shouts of 'Propaganda!' 'Who are you fooling?' Hezekiah and his colleagues appealed to the students to respect the Minister.

The Minister was focused and refused to be distracted by the angry students.

'I appreciate your anger,' he said, 'but please listen to me because challenges can be solved if the two parties are prepared to listen and understand each other.'

He reiterated that the Soviet Union was sensitive to the African students' experiences in the USSR.

'Remember that the Soviet Union has interacted with African students since the 1920s,' said the Minister. There was a pause while he took a sheet and read a prepared message:

Dear African students,

On behalf of the Soviet People and the Ministry of Higher Education, supported by the Ministry of Home Affairs, I wish to extend heartfelt condolences to the late Doumbé Khouyaté's friends, fellow students and family.

The Ministry strongly condemns this violence against African students. The Ministry further wishes to express sincere sympathy and friendship towards Africans cherished by the Soviet people, to whom feelings of racial inequality or disrespect are alien. We sadly acknowledge that unfortunately even in our socialist society one still encounters isolated hooligan elements through whom hostile attacks on our foreign friends may be unleashed.

Regarding your academic life I'm certain that none of you can say that one of our deans, lecturers, professors or ministry officials have let slip a bad word or deed in relation to you. Lastly, the Ministry wishes to draw your attention to the fact that the foreign policy of the USSR is out-performing the West, China and Israel, with regards to its positive influence over newly independent African states.

Your concerns will be attended to in collaboration with the countries you come from.

We wish you a fruitful stay in our country, and we are positive that in future we are going to interact with some of you as politicians and officials of your own countries.

The Minister flashed a smile towards the students before he sat down. The officials accompanying him applauded.

During the question-and-answer session, it was clear that the Minister had managed to dissipate the students' fury. He even elicited loud applause when he mentioned that the former president of the USSR, Nikita Khrushchev, was a great friend of African people.

The Minister grinned in the direction of Hezekiah. 'I hope you'll appreciate that today we have demonstrated that jaw-jaw is better than war-war, and I hope that you'll also agree with me that a class boycott is therefore unnecessary. African students, please use all available time to study well and become excellent specialists who'll shake off the imperialist yoke.'

Hezekiah asked for a thirty-minute break for the Committee of Five to caucus.

'Honourable Minister, we've listened to your speech,' he said. 'As leaders of these students we've decided to take responsible action that won't see us being cursed by the next generation of African students. In view of the seriousness of our grievances, we have decided that we aren't going to take the risk of suspending the class boycott.

'The boycott will continue until we can see that your government is making some meaningful changes. If we can see that the people who are committing these barbaric acts against African students are arrested and charged within 24 hours, then we will know you mean business, and that will be a good reason to suspend the boycott.

'As we've stated in our memorandum, we want to see your government taking the bold step of re-educating and rehabilitating the offenders. You, the Soviet people who've brought behavioural change to the world through Pavlov, shouldn't find it difficult to positively change the behaviour of your people. And, finally, let me raise a warning: We are going to organise even bigger marches that can only be contained by your army!' He raised his fist. 'Power to African students!'

'Power!' responded the students.

Applause that was as loud as hail hitting corrugated iron, broke out as Hezekiah sat down.

*

The following day, early in the morning, the African students congregated at Lumumba Square, waiting for the class boycott to start. Babatunde was part of the group. Hezekiah asked the students to wait patiently as student leaders from other campuses in neighbouring Soviet republics were also expected to take part in the meeting.

To while away time a Ghanaian student strummed a guitar and led the students in a song he had composed the previous night: *Africa is a giant, not a pigmy/ Africa can bite/ Africa is no toothless dog/ Wake up USSR / Watch the African panther! Africa is a giant!*

As Babatunde was chanting along a student next to him touched his shoulder, pointing in the direction of the library where a sudden noise had broken out.

'Look! A counter-protest march by Soviet students!'

# 58

Babatunde saw a group of about a thousand students, mainly Russian males, led by three Komsomol members, who wore denims and red T-shirts decorated with hammers and sickles. Fluttering the flags of the Soviet Union, the Russians marched straight for the gathering at Lumumba Square.

Hezekiah grabbed a loudhailer: 'Fellow students, we are at a crossroads. We can either make a good turn or a bad one. Let's choose a good turn. Let's not hurl an insult or dangerous objects at the group. Let's be dignified. Let's just stand and look at them. If they attack us we've no option but to defend ourselves.'

Hezekiah's attention was distracted for a moment as he looked towards the gate. Five army trucks cruised towards the square as the Soviet students approached. Armed with sticks and shields, the helmeted soldiers dismounted and divided into three groups that formed a barrier between the two groups of students. The three Komsomol leaders climbed a one-metre-high wall around the statue and stood on it.

'What are these agitators trying to achieve?' shouted the first Komsomol leader. 'They've only put a smile on the fat face of West!'

His supporters applauded.

The Komsomol leader raised a fist. 'Bad apples…'

Two voices from the African side interrupted: 'We aren't agitators! We demand justice!'

'Bad apples must go!' the Komsomol leader continued.

His supporters raised their fists, shouting, 'They must go!'

'Only well-mannered African students who are making use of the Soviet educational aid for the benefit of their countries can stay,' said a second Komsomol leader. 'Agitators must…'

'I'm not interested in staying in a racist country!' someone from the African side interrupted him.

'Agitators must go!' the second Komsomol leader continued.

'They must go!' echoed the supporters.

The third Komsomol leader shouted: 'Those who are ungrateful must go! Only those who appreciate the hosting country should remain! Enemies of the Soviet Union must go!'

'They must go!'

'Agents of the West must go!'

'They must go!'

'If a guest misbehaves in your house what must happen to him?'

'He must go!'

'If a guest undermines you in your house what must happen to him?'

'He must go!'

'What must happen with those who play into the hands of the imperialists?'

'They must go!'

'And we demand that our university authorities must expel the ungrateful, arrogant students who think they can unseat our government.'

The supporters applauded.

'And when these troublemakers are gone, other agitators who may be keeping a low profile must know that we are watching them, and soon this university will be swept clean!'

The supporters applauded.

'They've become excellent pawns of the West,' commented the second Komsomol leader. 'But I ask: can a mosquito injure the Soviet elephant?'

'No!' responded the supporters.

'Our message today is loud and clear: we can't fold our arms when people we've treated as brothers and comrades are now abusing our hospitality.'

'So what are you going to do, pig?' an African student yelled.

A voice from the Russian side responded, 'You must go back to the African jungle, monkey!'

The two groups started to charge towards each other, and the police struggled to maintain order. Expletives were exchanged by both groups. Soon objects were being hurled from each side. The police commander standing on the bonnet of the truck instructed the students to disperse. The opposing groups did not heed the commander's instruction but continued to shout at each other. Babatunde ducked a bottle that was aimed at his head; as he retreated, he stepped on another student who pushed him away; he fell on his face but quickly jumped back onto his feet and ran with the fleeing students.

He saw a group of Russian students manhandle an African student before the police separated them. An African martial arts student attacked a Russian student, and the police pointed a gun at him and arrested him. More African students charged towards the police who were taking the student to the van.

Another police contingent arrived and offloaded masked policemen and tear gas soon billowed. As mayhem broke out Babatunde felt the weight of bodies pushing him violently. He staggered, fell on his back and rolled before he lifted his feet, using them as shields. Gasping for air as teargas got into his eyes and throat, he felt a student falling on top of him; he shifted the body away, raised his torso, leaned with his arms and stood up. He coughed as if he had bronchitis.

*I'm glad that African students' politics and leadership aren't my passion*, thought Babatunde as students fled in several directions. He sprinted for the safety of his room. *My passion is to be the light of the world while I'm in Russia.* Realising that as a result of his soldier's instinct he had survived a life-threatening moment, he was thankful.


# 59


The university authorities closed the institution the same day and students were instructed to go to their homes. Babatunde could not go home, however, as he had already arranged with the authorities to work at the library during the holiday break. He sent a letter to his mother, explaining why he would not be coming home during the June/July vacation. He put on his pair of khaki shorts, to sunbathe in the Russian summer.

Babatunde's duties in the library comprised shelf-packing and registering new books in a notebook. Every morning he pushed a wheeled cart from which he took out the books and placed them on the shelves. He also took damaged books to the binding section for repairs and repacked the ones that had been repaired. In addition, it was his job to place library stickers in the new books.

*

The new semester opened in the middle of July. Babatunde looked forward to meeting fellow students. He was hoping to meet students whom he could recruit for his Christian group. One afternoon he walked towards the Square which had become a popular haunt for African students. There he found about twenty African students surrounding Kwame, half of them new students. Babatunde greeted them; he saw that Kwame was sombre-faced.

'Is there a problem, Kwame?' he asked in concern.

'Haven't you heard that Hezi and the Committee of Five members have been expelled?' Kwame said. 'The university authorities expelled them during the holidays. Students from other campuses who supported our march have also been kicked out.'

Babatunde shook his head. 'I didn't know. I'm really saddened and angry that the future of our fellow African students was sabotaged in this manner.'

'Guys, it's a bloody witchhunt, that's what it is,' said Etienne Kananga from Rwanda.

Babatunde was amazed to hear Etienne speaking English, because he had seen him in the company of fellow Rwandan and Congolese students, who usually kept to themselves.

'Etienne is right,' said Kwame, 'I was passing Prof Kostoglotov's office, and I overheard him saying to his colleague, "What do you think of that student from Mali?"'

'It is very clear that the Soviet authorities are intent on creating this intimidating environment,' said an older student whom Babatunde did not know, 'so that no African student will be prepared to stand out as a leader in future.'

'You're right, Pierre.'

'And the protest march has divided the student body,' said Kwame. 'The African students are also divided and they don't trust one other.'

One of the students looked away from the group for a moment and pointed: 'Look, Svetlana and her friend are coming!'

'So should we then just forget about student politics?' someone was asking as the newcomers walked up to them.

Kwame shrugged and looked at Svetlana.

'Sorry to interrupt,' said Svetlana whose eyes appeared bloodshot, 'I understand what you are going through. Your problem is my problem too, because my boyfriend is from your continent.'

She burst into tears and her friend comforted her.

'They've expelled Hezi,' said Etienne, 'because they can't stand what they regard as inter-racial romance.'

'Don't worry Sve,' Kwame said, putting his hand on her shoulder, 'this is a temporary setback.'

'Thank you Kwame,' she said, wiping her eyes and blowing her nose. 'I'm applying for a passport and during the winter holidays I'm going to visit Hezi.'

'Yes, you should,' said Kwame, patting her arm.

*

When Babatunde went back to his room, he found a letter from his people waiting for him, recognisable by Ekene's handwriting. He tore the envelope open and read:

> We are well and we are missing you. Uncle, you did well by not coming home during the holidays. A strange fire came into the shrine hut and burnt all what you called 'the tools of the devil'— the monkey skull and other things. My two uncles and my aunt are accusing the Christians for being great witches. The next day my Mama-Nnukwu told us that she has decided to become a Christian. So she went to Pastor Okpo. I accompanied her and the man of God helped us to receive Christ. Pastor Okpo sent greetings.

Babatunde smiled as he folded the letter and inserted it back into the envelope.

## 60

One of the journalism lecturers, Ludimila Zavodchikova, a blue-eyed blonde in her thirties, asked Babatunde to come to her office. She was fond of wearing jeans, and Babatunde had found her to be an easy-going person. But although she was known as 'Smiling Ludi', her smile seemed to have vanished lately. Babatunde suspected that the protest march was the cause of the tension.

Babatunde was one of three African students in the journalism class. Slightly anxious, he wondered what Ludimila was going to say to him.

She smiled at him as he entered her office, but it wasn't a genuine smile; only gradually did it stretch until it became a full smile. She offered him a cup of tea, which he accepted.

'I'm glad that you are in my class, Baba,' she said as they sat sipping.

'Thank you, Ludi.'

'Multi-cultural classes are fascinating for obvious reasons.'

Babatunde nodded, 'That's true.'

'Because you are a hardworking student, you'll certainly pass in record time.'

He was one of the most motivated students in her class. She'd impressed him with her innovative teaching of the Creative Interviewing sub-module. He recalled the time she'd given the class a quotation about the importance of asking questions: *He who asks is a fool for five minutes. He who does not, is a fool forever.* On another occasion, during a speech-writing lesson, she gave them a statement which evoked a heated debate among the students: *A good speech should be like a woman's skirt; long enough to cover the subject, short enough to create interest.*

'Thank you for believing in me, Ludi,' he said.

She nodded. 'And very soon you'll be working.'

'I'm looking forward to that.'

'You'll have your own apartment; after saving for a few years, you'll have a nice house.'

'Yes, I would like to have a nice house, which I would share with some of my relatives.'

'Excellent! And I'm sure you would like to have guests.'

'Of course, Ludi!'

She gulped her remaining tea, put the cup back on the saucer and grinned.

'Now tell me, Baba…' Her smile vanished and her face frowned a little as she looked deep into Babatunde's dark-brown eyes, '…if you have a guest and he or she becomes too familiar and starts undermining your hospitality, what are you going to do?'

Babatunde sighed, broke eye contact with Ludimila for a moment, and then resumed it. His thoughts went to the recent Komsomol-led students' counter march.

'I'd ask her or him to leave my house immediately.'

'Any sensible host would do that.'

'I agree fully, Ludi.'

'But not everybody is agreeing with the Soviet hostess. Now let me say it straight, Baba: the university authorities in the Soviet Union have recently expelled the unthankful and arrogant students but now the West is crying "foul!" But wouldn't they have done the same if their visiting students were unruly?'

'They would have done the same, Ludi.'

'I'm sharing this with you because you aren't a bad apple, Baba.'

Babatunde chuckled at her choice of words. 'Thank you, Ludi.'

'I'm not saying that you African students don't have unique challenges. But if you have problems, the Soviet authorities have big ears. We have had African students since the 1920s. The Soviet Union has been offering generous students aid for decades; so for African students to publicly accuse the USSR of racism, is to play into the hands of the West. And as a result they are selling more newspapers and are continuing to exploit the working class.'

Babatunde began to feel very uncomfortable and even guilty for visiting her. He felt as if he was gossiping about fellow African students. *What if someone asks, 'what were you discussing with Ludi?'* thought Babatunde. He made a show of glancing at his wristwatch.

'Ludi, I forgot that I've arranged to discuss our assignment with a fellow student,' he said. 'Apologies for having to leave so abruptly.'

'It's alright, Baba. You can go. I just felt I had to share my sentiments with you.'

'Thank you for sharing your concern with me.'

They stood up simultaneously. Ludimila smiled and offered a firm handshake.

*

For the rest of that week Babatunde went to the library after his lectures, to look for a face he could approach. He set aside 30 minutes a day for what he referred to as his 'kingdom project'. He applied a well-rehearsed 'sales talk': *Hi, I'm Babatunde Okoronkwo, I'm a prince and I would like to invite you to a venue where you can meet my father!* The first student asked: *Who's your father?* And he responded matter-of-factly: *The king of the universe in person.*

He was delighted that the 'sales talk' earned him the respect of a few students who told him that although Christianity was not their preferred religion, they were fascinated by his enthusiasm and approach. On Friday he cornered a student who said his parents lived in Botswana as refugees from South Africa. He was very confident that this fellow believer, who

160

had introduced himself as Muzi, would be part of the underground church. But he was wrong.

'It's a good idea for Christians to meet and pray and share the word,' said Muzi. 'But it's a bad idea in Russia.'

'Why?'

'In this country you can't trust even your mother, brother or your own child.'

'So you are telling me that you don't even trust a fellow Christian?'

'Doesn't the Bible say that Satan entered Judas who betrayed Jesus?'

'It's true but…'

'I don't want to take a big risk. My parents told me that when the top leadership of their movement, such as Nelson Mandela and Walter Sisulu was arrested, the security police used a man known as Mr X, as a s state witness supplied the police with copies of meeting minutes and plans for sabotage.'

Babatunde was very disappointed that by the end of the week he had not caught a single 'fish'. He saw a few African students who reminded him of Thom. That made him miss Thom even more.


# 61

On Saturday morning he wrote in his diary, 21st July 1981: 'To visit Thom at his residence.'

He prayed before he left. *And I know that God won't disappoint me*, he thought as he walked to the bus stop. About an hour later, the university shuttle-bus transported him to the agricultural campus where Thom stayed. He was positive that the following day, Sunday, he would be praying with Thom.

After knocking twice at the door of Thom's room, Babatunde saw the door open and a woman's head protruded. He could not disguise his amazement as he looked into the brown eyes of that beautiful face—a mixed-race face that could be in its late twenties. Babatunde was convinced he must have knocked at the wrong room.

'Excuse me, does this room belong to Thom Mutesa?' he asked.

'Yes.'

'Is he here?'

'Yes.'

'Can I please speak to him?'

'I'm afraid, not at the moment.' She threw him a suspicious look. 'Who are you?'

'Babatunde Okoronkwo. I'm from the main campus. I used to…'

'As I said, not at the moment.'

With a frown the woman put her hand on the door to push it closed.

'Wait—' said Babatunde, 'please let me finish before you slam the door. Tell me, lady, are you…er…' Babatunde faltered; 'How are you related to Thom? If I may ask?'

'He's my boyfriend. Yesterday he threw a birthday party, it was for the whole night, so he's asleep now. And I don't want to…'

'Tell me, are we talking of the same man? I came to see Thom Mutesa from Kenya.'

'Yes, he's the same guy.'

Babatunde sighed and looked down, not knowing how to hide his pained face. The woman again made an effort to close the door.

'Please tell him I'll come here again. Perhaps next weekend.'

She gave him a blank look.

'What's your name?' he asked.

'Why do you want to know my name?'

Before boarding the bus to return to the main campus, Babatunde spoke to three African students that he encountered, who confirmed that Thom had indeed changed for the worse. *I can't believe that Thom is now a child of darkness*, he thought in the bus driving out of the campus gates. He tried to cheer himself: *Judas was disqualified as a disciple but God sent more disciples*, he told himself, *so I trust that God will send someone to take the place of Thom and add even more disciples.*

*

By the end of the week he had still not succeeded in recruiting a single Christian student. After lunch on Friday Babatunde went straight to his room where he lay on his bed. Nikolai had gone to town with his friend, so Babatunde could enjoy the freedom of being alone. After singing some choruses and hymns, he prayed. An hour later he found himself in tears.

Feeling drowsy, he drifted off and soon found himself dreaming, saying something to God. He felt as if someone was rousing him from slumber; he looked up at the ceiling as if he could see someone or something. *Lord Jesus*, he heard himself whispering, *I know You are as near to me as a friend. But I must admit, you seem to be far away, because I'm missing the fellowship with your people. When a trusted brother like Thom is pounced upon by the evil one, then it's a fatal blow.*

*Lord, I wish you can visit me so that I can look at you, and you can look at me with your clear eyes and see what's deep in my heart. Lord, I feel I must do something right now. At this moment I want to feel that you are near to me. I'm asking this because I feel weak and discouraged and lonely in the Lord.*

He paused and looked around his room.

*What can I do Lord?*

He stood up lifted up his arms and sang, '*Ka m bunie afa gi enu*' until his arms were getting tired. He then sat on the bed mumbling a prayer. He raised himself from his bed, put his feet to the ground, stood up and shuffled to the wardrobe, where he opened his suitcase. There at the bottom he found a folded poster: *My Lord Crucified*; he took it out and unfolded it, scrutinising it for a moment before he carried it over to the wall. *My Lord, let me paste this poster of Your crucifixion on the wall.* He kissed the poster. *Jesus, I love You. I feel alone and I don't want this disappointment to lead me into temptation. I really miss You and I just want to send You kisses, Beautiful Handsome Sinless One, Prince of Peace, Rose of Sharon.*

He kissed the poster again and stuck it on the wall. As he stepped back to look at it, a smile spread over his face. *Lord, thank You for Your physical presence in the form of this poster. Thank You for filling this place with peace and warmth. You are the light of the world and I thank You that this dark part of the world called Russia will be further illuminated through this poster and through Your servants. Jesus, I love You, and I'm sending you kisses.*

Babatunde stood like that for a while, continuing to pray, but he could sense that he was no longer alone. He opened his eyes and looked straight into the livid face of Nikolai.

'Are you crazy?' Nikolai shouted, pointing his finger first at Babatunde and then at the poster on the wall.

'What do you mean?'

'Have you lost your mind? I saw you through the curtain. You were moaning, "I love you," like a little girl. I thought that, finally, my man Baba has got a woman. But oh no, I open the door to find you here kissing the picture of Jesus Christ! Listen, you are a disgrace!' Quivering with anger, he wagged his index finger. 'You belong in a madhouse or a cold prison camp!'

Nikolai walked forward and stopped in front of the poster, staring at it before turning back to Babatunde. He balled his fists. 'So you have the nerve to bring this kind of poster to Russia! This is Russia, not America or Africa. Remove it!'

'No, I'm not going to remove it!'

'I say take it away now!'

'It's the poster of my Lord, my King of Kings, my bread of life…'

'Are you trying to preach to me and convert me? I'll tear it to pieces!'

Nikolai darted towards the poster but Babatunde grabbed him by his arm and threw him to the ground.

'You will not touch my Lord's poster!' shouted Babatunde, stabbing his finger at Nikolai. 'Why don't you put a poster of Stalin and Lenin on the wall next to your bed?'

Nikolai scowled at Babatunde, then got off the floor and hurried towards the door, banging it behind him.


# 62

As Babatunde attended his lectures, he felt as if every lecturer and professor was ready to point a finger, warning him: *If you don't stop your Christian nonsense you'll be deported to Africa!* He was relieved when lectures came to an end. After lunch he went to the library where he spent two hours studying Media Studies, Journalism and Russian.

As he walked down the stairs of the building, he saw a mulatto woman walking towards the library. When she was a few paces from him he smiled at her. She smiled back shyly. Babatunde stopped in front of her, offering his open palm, and introduced himself.

'Antoinette Rawlings,' she said as she stuck her hand out, 'From Ghana.'

'Come, let's sit on the bench,' said Babatunde.

They sat down facing each other.

'Antoinette, I've seen you once or twice, but I don't know why I never associated you with Africa. I thought you were from the UK or the US or Cuba.'

She flashed a smile. 'That's interesting!'

He looked into her eyes as if saying: *Great to meet you, please tell me more about yourself!*

'My father was an aeroplane pilot, and he was Scottish,' Antoinette continued, 'and my mother is Ghanaian. She was an air hostess.'

Babatunde briefly told Antoinette about his background.

'Antoinette, you...'

'You can call me Antoh.'

'Okay, call me Baba.'

'Antoh, are you a Christian?'

She chuckled. 'Yes, Baba. Why are you asking?'

'God has made it possible for me to meet you, a fellow believer, at last. For weeks I've been a one-person underground church until this very moment.' Babatunde smiled. 'Now we are going to be two.'

She gave him a smile in return. 'How can you be so sure that…?'

'Please say yes, Antoh! I assume that you are keen to meet other believers?'

She smiled more widely, wrinkling her forehead. 'Yes, I am.'

'If you weren't prepared to be part of the fellowship, then you'd be saying that God has misled me.'

'No, He cannot mislead His children.'

'I'm elated that God has answered my prayer at last! Thank you, Antoh. God is going to increase our numbers.'

She chuckled. 'I admire your enthusiasm.'

'You came at the right time, Antoh. This morning when I woke up I lay on my bed and prayed for an hour, exclusively in tongues, no English, no Russian!'

'Fantastic! He's faithful to answer our prayers at the right time.'

'Yes. I've been alone for over two months, and to make matters worse my only Christian brother has fallen into the devil's snare.'

'Oh what a pity! What happened?'

'All I can say is that he must have been attacked by the enemy when he was at his weakest moment. As a result he has now become a womaniser and a drunk. I don't want to meet with him because I don't want to get hurt.'

'That's understandable.'

'And the guy has a steady girlfriend back home whom he met at a church in his country, and they planned to get married in December.'

'It's a pity. We should pray for him to come back to the Lord and reconcile with his girl.'

'Yes. So the lesson here is that believers should stand united against the enemy.'

'You are absolutely right, Baba.'

'I missed the company of other believers to the extent that this week I cried to God and pleaded: "Lord, please do something this week, or I'm returning to Africa!" I quickly realised that I had said something very silly and I immediately asked God to forgive me. Yesterday I pasted a poster of Jesus on the wall. I had resolved, "At least I can put a picture of Jesus on my wall to encourage myself." When my roommate came into the room, he told me to remove the poster and I refused. We had an argument which became a little physical and it ended with my roommate going away upset.

'Later my door was banged open and in came the local communist party leader and a professor. "What do you think you are doing?" asked the professor. And the party leader pointed his finger at me, saying, "If you keep doing things like that, we'll send you back to Nigeria!"'

'So I was forced to remove the poster. It dawned on me at that moment that I had been very daring. In fact, foolish. I stood at the doorway, looking at them as they left the room. Suddenly the communist party man grabbed the professor by his hand and they spoke in low tones; they returned to my room.'

'The man stretched out his hand, staring at me. "Bring me the poster!" he commanded. I handed the poster to him. He wrenched it out of my hands, intending to tear it apart, but the professor restrained him, and took it. They walked away. I later said to myself, "Devil, you have won round one. But I'm going to win the fight!" That night, just before I slept, I heard the Lord saying to me, "Don't worry about the removal of the picture; just make sure that they don't remove Me from your heart."'

'So how are you going to cope with each other, now that your room-mate has reported you to the authorities?'

'In the morning, I walked over to him as he was getting ready to go and attend his lectures. I extended a hand towards him and said, "Nik, I've forgiven you, and I love you."'

'And what was his reaction?'

'He neither touched my hand nor answered me; he turned away, grabbed his bag and stormed out of the room. But I'm sure things will go back to normal soon.'

*

On Sunday when Babatunde waited for a moment before he smiled when he read an A4-size white sheet written, 'African Studies 101 Students'Session—PLEASE DO NOT DISTURB.' Upon entering he was amazed to find Kwame sitting there and flipping over the pages of a Bible. Babatunde recalled how Kwame had rebuffed his efforts to recruit him weeks ago. Kwame rose to his feet, grinning widely, and gave Babatunde a firm bear-hug.

'So you've succumbed to the feminine charm of your countrywoman?' asked Babatunde.

Antoinette and Kwame burst into laughter.

Babatunde opened the meeting with prayer, and they sang a hymn, *What a Friend we have in Jesus*. Their voices were low, the door was locked, and all windows closed.

'We shall find the word of God from Romans chapter 12, verse 2,' said Kwame. He paused to give the others a chance to find the scriptures.

*Do not copy the behaviour and customs of this world,* Kwame read, *but be a new and different person with a fresh newness in all you do and think.*

They discussed the verse, sang another hymn, and closed with prayer. At the end of the service Antoinette asked: 'What should we pray for?'

'Well, the obvious: that God should send more members.'

'Okay,' said Antoinette, writing in her notebook. 'And what else?'

'Let's pray for unity on this campus,' said Kwame. 'There are still tensions and the students and staff members are divided because of the protest march.'

'Yes, I heard from a student from Tanzania,' said Antoinette, 'that her countryman was involved in a fist fight at the bar. He is nursing a black eye and a swollen jaw.'

As they walked out of Antoinette's room, Kwame told them that he knew of an African student who'd tried unsuccessfully to invite him to join a prayer group, and that he would look out for him.

A few days later Kwame brought a student from Zambia, Jeff Kapemba, who told them that he was the leader of another Christian cell on the campus. Babatunde, Antoinette and Kwame agreed to be part of Jeff's group.

# 63

It was a Tuesday, the last day of July, as Babatunde had noted in his pocket diary. Before he went to attend the first lecture of the day, he looked at the important dates with corresponding events that he had written and pinned on his noticeboard: *Tuesday 30th October—Exams Starting; Tuesday 27th November—Finish exams; Wednesday 28th November—Going home.* He had also written exam dates opposite the subjects, together with the marks he'd scored: *Media Studies (75%), Journalism (87%), Russian (55%), Communication (80%), Business Economics (70%), International Relations (75%).* He was pleased with his performance in Journalism.

Following the first Communication lecture of the day, his lecturer, Ludimila, beckoned him over.

'Baba, please come to my office after lectures today,' she said.

'Okay Ludi,' responded Babatunde, his mind beginning to ask questions: *What have I done now? Can it be the Jesus poster?*

Babatunde had guessed right; the meeting was about the poster.

'I don't want to interfere with your beliefs, Baba,' said Ludimila, 'but when you visit our country, you should know what to expect.'

Babatunde assured Ludimila that he regretted what he had done.

'Honestly speaking, I'm not very offended because you did not put it in a public place. It was in the privacy of your room.' She grinned: 'So if I were a judge, that would be an extenuating circumstance.'

'Thank you, Ludi.'

'Look after yourself, Baba and...' she smiled, pointing at his mouth, '...keep your mouth shut. I would hate to see my best student being deported.'

She told him that one of her colleagues had a problematic student from Malawi, who used to miss extra classes on Saturdays. When he was confronted he confessed that he could not attend them because it was on the day that he called Sabbath. He was ultimately sent back to his country.

*

During the second Monday of September Ludimila handed each student a letter. 'You'll remember that I told you at the beginning of the year that you would be assigned tasks from some departments,' said Ludimila, 'to write or re-write their articles, stories, reports, and so on, as part of your practical training. So tomorrow, please visit the lecturers or professors whose names and office details are on your letters.'

On Babatunde's letter was the name of Professor Isayevich Leonidovich, Head of Rocket Science.

Later that week Babatunde found himself looking at a slim, tall, bearded man in his early fifties, sporting a ponytailed hairstyle, in his office.

Isayevich smiled at Babatunde. 'Please tell me briefly about yourself.' He listened and took a few notes as Babatunde spoke.

After practising how to pronounce Babatunde's name properly, Isayevich switched to English.

'Attending a lot of international conferences has compelled me to learn English,' he said.

'I must say you speak it well, Prof Leonidovich,' Babatunde complimented him.

'Thank you, Babatunde. By training I'm an aeronautic engineer. But ten years later I specialised in rocket science.'

'That's interesting, Prof.'

Isayevich handed Babatunde a file containing typed A4 sheets.

'When should I bring this back to you, Prof?'

'On Monday, please.'

Babatunde stood up, ready to go. 'I can bring it back this Thursday.'

'Excellent! Ludi told me that you are her best journalism student.'

Babatunde was grinning as he closed the door behind him.

*

Two weeks later Babatunde handed the third and last batch of articles to Isayevich, who glanced at the headings: *Aviation History; Fundamentals of Aerospace Engineering; The Relationship between Aeronautical and Astronomical Engineering;* and *The Research, Design, Development and Construction and Testing of Spacecraft.*

Isayevich smiled. 'Babatunde, your effort looks impressive.'

'Thank you, Prof.'

'As a token of my gratitude, I would like to give you this silver ballpoint pen,' Isayevich said, handing Babatunde the pen.

'Thank you Prof,' said Babatunde, admiring the gift.

When Babatunde stood up, Isayevich did likewise.

'I really enjoyed working with you, Babatunde.'

'It's a pleasure for me to exercise a God-given talent.'

Babatunde immediately wanted to put his hand over his mouth; he felt slightly embarrassed that he had mentioned 'God' – something that could show him in an unfavourable light.

'Ludi told me that you aren't a bad apple. I can see for myself that you are indeed a good guy.'

Babatunde smiled, not knowing how to respond.

'What are you doing on Saturday?' asked Isayevich. 'Why don't you visit me? I want to discuss something with you. We can't talk freely at my office because there might be interruptions. So I'll appreciate it if you could come to my house.'

'Alright Prof, I'll come,' said Babatunde, after giving the proposition quick consideration.

Isayevich drew a map to his house on a piece of paper and handed it to Babatunde.

# 64

Arriving at Isayevich's house Babatunde rang the bell and stood waiting to be admitted. *Typically Russian,* he thought, hearing the classical string instrument music that was playing as Isayevich opened the door. A pleasant voice, a smiling face and a firm handshake all made Babatunde feel very welcomed by his Russian host.

'I'm all by myself,' said Isayevich, 'my wife has gone to see our daughter in Kiev in the Ukraine.' He motioned towards the dining table. 'Come, let's have something to eat.'

On the table was a plate of hot toasted sandwiches. After they'd helped themselves to the food, the atmosphere became more relaxed, and Babatunde could finally look around to admire the Russian furniture. *The West has most definitely not invaded Russia*, he thought to himself, staring at a particularly ornate piano in the corner of the room.

'So, Baba, how do you like my household? It's not large, I must say, but it is more than enough for my family. My son is in the army and my daughter works as a nursery school teacher in Kiev.'

'I like it very much, Prof. In my country this would be considered as upper-class.'

After talking for a while about Nigerian life, they moved into the lounge where they ate dried fruit and nuts.

As they talked about various issues, Babatunde kept asking himself: *When are we going to talk about the real item?*

'Now let's talk about an important subject: the reason that I've invited you to my house,' said Isayevich at last, much to Babatunde's relief. 'I know that you are a Christian.'

'How do you know, Prof?'

Isayevich gave Babatunde a grin. 'A young man from the KGB told me.'

Babatunde's eyes widened, and he held his breath.

'No, I'm joking, Baba.'

Isayevich gave Babatunde a moment to recover from the shock. 'Actually I heard about you from the professor who ordered you to remove the poster of Jesus from the wall in your room.'

'Really?'

'Yes. Comrade Prof Ostapenko is one of the five academics who are serving as the 'antennae' of the Soviet Union's top leadership. I'm part of the group, and our task is to see to it that communism is not undermined and adulterated in any way and to coordinate the network of our informers, whose job is to identify students who could be suspected of being agents or pawns of the West.'

Leaning forward, his heart beating fast, Babatunde could not control himself: 'So you want to speak to me,' he said with a tense face, 'because I'm suspected of being an agent of the West?'

'No, no, Baba, relax! Just bear with me and you'll understand why I'm speaking to you today.'

Isayevich paused for a moment, giving Babatunde a faint smile. 'You aren't going to believe what I'm going to tell you.' The professor looked around as if checking whether anyone was listening. 'I'm a secret believer,' he said, in a near whisper.

'What do you mean?'

'I'm a Christian who can't practise my belief openly, for obvious reasons. Comrade Prof Ostapenko doesn't know, and he'll never know, that I'm a secret believer. I'm a member of one of Moscow's underground churches. Whenever I attend the cell, I have to carry notes and posters to give the impression that I'm presenting for the Rocket Science clubs. The reason we have survived so long is because we've a mole in the KGB. In short, that's why I asked you to visit me.'

Babatunde sighed. 'Thank you for confiding in me, Prof.'

Isayevich grinned. 'Just call me brother Ish. Ish is the shortened form of Isayevich. For in God's eyes we are equal.'

Isayevich stood, pulled Babatunde up and gave him a hug and a back-slap. In an attempt to hide his tearful eyes, he turned away from Babatunde.

'I'm sorry, Baba, I'm getting emotional.'

Babatunde laid his hand on Isayevich's shoulder. 'It's alright, brother Ish.'

'Excuse me a moment, Baba,' said Isayevich. He walked from the room and returned holding a photo album.

'These are members of my underground cell,' he said, showing Babatunde a photo of many people.

Babatunde concentrated on the photo.

'This man over here,' Isayevich pointed, 'is the leader, and this is his wife, and their children. You can see here: it's written "Rocket Science Club". Other groups meet under the pretence that they are celebrating their members' birthday parties. People have to be creative to survive.'

'You are precious saints,' Babatunde said, addressing the people in the photo, 'because for you to meet is to risk going to prison or being tortured. I want to honour you, brothers and sisters.'

Babatunde kissed the photo; he was moved to near tears and now it was Isayevich who patted his shoulder.

'Tonight, I'm inviting you to come to my cell,' said Isayevich, 'to meet your Russian brothers and sisters.'

Babatunde leaned forward thoughtfully: 'I'm not sure if I can visit your cell tonight, brother Ish.'

'Please don't disappoint me, Baba.'

'I'm joking, Prof,' he smiled. 'In fact, I've been yearning to attend an underground church.'

Isayevich grinned. 'Great!'

'So it's tonight?'

'Yes. During this morning's prayer I clearly heard God's voice, saying it must be tonight. I can say with certainly that I have peace beyond my understanding that it's the right moment.'

Babatunde hesitated. 'Brother Ish, I must pray about this.'

Isayevich opened his hands and stretched them towards Babatunde. 'Let's pray now.'

They held hands and prayed in low tones.

'Okay, brother Ish, I'll tell my fellow group members. If they have peace about this, they'll attend.'

'Thank you for your willingness, Baba. It's absolutely necessary that you should attend, so that when you pray back in Nigeria with other Christians, you should pray for people whose faces you have seen, whose hands you have touched, and whose shoulders you've embraced.'

Babatunde looked into Isayevich's eyes, reflecting on his other life of a respected Rocket Science professor. *At the campus I'll continue to address you as Prof Ish*, thought Babatunde, *for obvious reasons.*

'Come, let's go into the garden,' said Isayevich, rising to his feet.

Isayevich brought cushions from the house and they relaxed on well-crafted garden chairs made of cast iron. Isayevich observed that Babatunde was so fascinated by the chairs that he could not keep his eyes off them.

'Do you like them?' the professor asked.

'Yes! I'm impressed by the great craftsmanship.'

'My brother-in-law is a welder at Moscow Steel Company. So his hobby is to make garden chairs.'

'One day when I have a mansion and a nice garden,' said Babatunde, 'I'm going to ask him to make such chairs for me.'

'Well, what you're saying could happen,' smiled his host.

They were silent for a while. Then Isayevich said: 'Baba, I guess you were raised as a Christian?'

Babatunde shook head and told him how he had become converted.

'So, how did you become a Christian, brother Ish?' Babatunde asked after telling his story.

# 65

'My career led to my conversion,' said Isayevich. 'Three years ago I went to attend the Rocket Scientists' International Conference in Helsinki. There I met a retired American astronaut, James Irwin, who was one of the guest speakers. He was introduced as "the Apollo 15 astronaut, the eighth man to walk on the moon, and a passionate ambassador for Christ."

'Well, being an atheist, it was a serious problem for me that I should have to listen to a zealot for Christ. So I said to myself: *I'll listen only to the part where he speaks about his experiences during the take-off, the walk on the moon, the spaceship, the return back to earth and the landing. When he speaks about his Christianity, I'm going to sneak out of the room..*

'He spoke well, and I was impressed with his massive experience and knowledge as an astronaut. I gasped when I saw the video of him walking on the moon-soil as if he was airborne. I had seen the picture before but it struck me as if I was seeing it for the first time. When he started speaking about his conversion, I wanted to go off the bathroom as I had decided. But something just grabbed me, saying, *No you can't do that! People here will think that Russians are rude! Stay and listen! Surely listening to him won't contaminate your belief?*

'So I listened to him. I remember what he said as if it was yesterday. When he said: "It's a great opportunity to share an unusual encounter with the Lord some 616 000 kilometres from earth," I continued to listen, though I was still sceptical. But when he said: "I had been an atheist all my life," he gripped my interest, and I gave him my total attention.

'He mentioned two reasons why he became converted. He said the first reason was that something went seriously wrong during the moon exploration. He told us, "All I can say is that God had miraculously taken my soul out of the fingers of death; I survived death."

'I was very curious to know more, and I was disappointed when he said that for further detail, interested people could check out his book and CDs. About the second reason, he said: "Seeing the earth hanging majestically in space reminded me how fragile it is…how small we are in the greater scheme of things…and how big God is."

'At the end of the session everyone rushed to congratulate the great man of the moment and I also shuffled along in the queue. When I finally met him he was delighted to hear that I was a Russian; he invited me for a drink. I wasted no time in finding out how he had survived a heart attack. He said, "Come to my room after dinner." I was thrilled to be able to sit alone with him in his hotel room.

'He said to me: "Apparently when I was suiting up, my water tube kinked, so I wasn't able to get any liquid for the day.' He explained that the temperature on the lunar surface was 150 degrees and that as a result he'd perspired excessively. He lost his electrolyte balance, and the imbalance of sodium and potassium almost triggered a heart attack.

'He said: "I felt dizzy and there was no way the doctors down there on earth could help me. I immediately faced the reality that there was someone who had created the moon sand I was walking on and that he was the one who could save my life at that moment." He said he had prayed like this: "God, if indeed you exist, please heal me now!" After he prayed, he suddenly realised that he had the power to keep on walking; he was convinced that the reason he didn't collapse from a heart attack was because his life was in God's hands."

'It was great spending time with him, and by the end of the meeting we were calling each other Jimmy and Ish. I lied when I told him that I was impressed with how he'd gotten to know God.

'That night, deep in sleep, I had a dream in which I saw an astronaut walking clumsily on the moon; in the next scene the man stood near my bed. I said to him, "Jimmy, is that you?" The man replied, "No, I'm not Jimmy." "Are you perhaps Yuri Gagarrin, the Russian astronaut?" I asked. He said, "Look at me carefully, and you'll know who really I am." He removed the transparent cover from his headgear; I looked at him intently and I could see he wasn't Jimmy. I said, "I don't know you. Who are you?" He disappeared.

'Back in Russia, the same astronaut appeared in my dream again and I quickly asked him, "Who are you?" He said, "Do you really want to know me?" I said, "Yes." He pointed upwards, and I saw an image of the moon. He told me, "I'm the one who made it!" I replied, "No, that can't be!" He didn't argue; he just disappeared.

'The following night the strange astronaut again visited me in my sleep. This time he had removed his headgear completely. So I could see him clearly. The man's regular visits began to irritate me; I opened my mouth, ready to shout, *Get out of my bedroom*! But I only managed to say, "Get ahhh..." when my voice vanished. I touched my throat, wondering what had happened. I lifted my hand with the intention of indicating that he should leave my bedroom, but my arm froze. I didn't know what to do at that moment. I stared at him helplessly, panicking.

'He came closer to my bed, his face shining like gold and his eyes radiating a mixture of blue and red light. Holding a flaming sword, he pointed it towards my chest; I retreated, terrified that he was about to stab me. But he pulled back his sword and said, "I can see that your heart is full of pride, stubbornness, knowledge and other things that are making it difficult for you to accept me." I said to him, "Who are you?" He answered, "I told you last night, but you don't believe that I've made the moon."

'I looked deep into his eyes, which were now sky-blue, and in his hand he was no longer holding a sword but carrying a basket full of flowers of many colours, and fruit. He said, "I'm king of the universe!" I scrutinised him and said, "I know of many kings from many parts of the world, but I haven't heard of the king of the universe." He replied, "I'm King of Kings!"

'I still wanted to ask a question, but he said quickly, "This is your last chance to accept me. You can make a choice that will condemn or save your soul." Shocked by his straightforwardness, I didn't know how to respond.

'He continued, "If you accept me you'll end up in that destination." He gestured, and I looked where he pointed and saw an extraordinarily beautiful botanical garden with a well-manicured lawn and trees which the best Russian visual artist couldn't reproduce, and multi-coloured birds of varying sizes and shapes, chirping and churning out melodious songs on the tree branches; clear ponds glimmered everywhere. As I walked in the garden, hand in hand with the King of the Universe, we arrived at an orchard laden with luscious fruits.

'In the next scene he led me by my hand to a street with pavements made of pure gold; there were houses on both sides. What was strange was the houses were not occupied. I said, "Lord, where are the people?" And he replied, "These dwellings are still to be occupied." Walking along, we arrived at a part of the garden where there were many people, the healthiest people, full of joy, chatting, eating fruit, plucking flowers, catching fish from the crystal-clear ponds and frying them, and doing many other activities.

'Speechless, I was still looking at his pleasant face, when suddenly his smile faded. "But if you deny me," he said in a grave tone, "you'll end up at that place." He pointed under my feet. Suddenly I saw myself standing on the round earth. At the centre of the earth I saw huge flames and a heavy smog, and I heard voices coughing, shouting, screaming, cursing the Lord and crying in a heartrending manner. When I looked closer, I saw people's faces, and I could recognise my mother and other relatives.

'My mother said, with tears running down her cheeks, "Son, change your life or you'll end up at this terrible place!" The scene ended, and I heard myself shouting, "King of the Universe, I don't want to go to that terrible place. Please Lord, I beg you! I want the place of mansions, golden pavements and flowers and fruit! I want the place of flowers and fruit!

I want the place of…!" At that point I felt my wife nudging me and say-ing, "Ish, what's happening?"'

## 66

That evening, Isayevich drove to the gate of the campus where he col-lected Babatunde, Kwame and Antoinette. Jeff Kapemba had declined the invitation, saying, 'We should not send the whole army to one battle. The three of you can attend. If you are arrested, we shall pray for your release or visit you in the prison.'

Babatunde wore his blue-and-grey checked suit. They used two cars to ferry them to the underground church. But they didn't go straight to the venue; they proceeded first to the train station where they pretended to be catching the train. After walking through a tunnel to the other side, they divided up and boarded two cars, which left at different times.

It took them an hour to arrive at the house where the service was to be held. Isayevich led them into a spacious room where they found eight men and ten women. There they waited for three hours for the other worshippers to come, arriving in twos and threes. The room was so dim that it took Babatunde a while to make out the faces around him. Only one small light bulb hung from the ceiling and blankets were draped over the windows to block out prying eyes.

Each new worshipper took his or her place around the central table, and sat with bowed head, muttering a prayer for the safety of the service. It felt good to see joy and peace on everyone's faces. The men leaned against the wall while women sat on the beds, couches and makeshift seats and the younger people sat or squatted on the floor. Isayevich in-troduced them to the host and leader of the group, known as Petroff.

All over the room, faces brightened as they turned in the direction of the newcomers, Babatunde, Antoinette and Kwame; some people said, *We are delighted to see you!* The children kept coming to the guests to feel their kinky hair; their parents laughed and the African guests laughed with them.

'*Ah*, these sweet little angels!' said Babatunde, touching a small girl's cheek.

The group members waited until their numbers had reached twenty-five, packed rib-to-rib in the room. All eyes were directed at the guest as Isayevich stepped forward:

'We are truly blessed tonight to have with us our African brethren who are students at the university,' said Isayevich. 'We in Russia may feel isolated and alone but God has sent these precious saints to us.'

After mentioning their names, Isayevich smiled and added, 'Our dark-skinned brethren are the bright lanterns in dark Russia.'

Everyone laughed; there were exclamations of surprise and joy.

Petroff read one of the letters of Paul where the Apostle encouraged the saints to rejoice in spite of the difficulties facing them. The leader invited the group to suggest other scriptures and to comment as they were led by the Spirit.

Babatunde observed that many people shared the Bibles. As a young girl read, an older woman sitting next to the window suddenly waved at her and she stopped reading. In complete silence they listened to footsteps approaching the house. One of the men looked through the shutters.

'It's a policeman!' the man whispered.

They held their breaths and exchanged nervous glances. The slow footsteps stopped at the door. They all started to mutter something, and their lips made the *bha-bha-bha* of frenzied whispers. They later heard the footsteps going away. Babatunde heard sighs of relief all over the room, including his own.

'Thank you, Lord,' the girl who'd been reading from the Bible whispered. Lifting her arms, she kissed her hands and threw kisses heavenwards.

'Hallelujah!' an old woman added her cheerful whisper.

As the leader sat down again, Isayevich stood up and said, 'Brethren, let us continue to pray for the persecuted church in Russia and other communist countries.'

The meeting lasted for about three hours. Before the leader closed with prayer, he thanked those who'd attended, for their dedication and their willingness to risk their homes, families and jobs. They had tea with toasted home-baked bread and cakes.

Isayevich introduced two young women to Babatunde and his two African companions.

'They are volunteers at a secret Bible factory,' said Isayevich.

'We work in shifts of four hours,' the one called Zoya told him, 'and we sit at a table to hand-copy the Bible.'

'When the copying is finished,' her companion, Salome, added, 'we put it all together and stitch it as a complete Bible. Later we bind it in leather and send the Bibles to the believers as soon as we can.'

'I commend you girls for your bravery and sacrifice!' said Antoinette.

'Are you not afraid of the secret police?' asked Kwame.

'We don't care about the consequences,' Zoya said. 'We care only about the will of God.'

'Amen!' exclaimed Antoinette who high-fived with the girl.

*

Preparing for and writing the examinations caused the sun to run faster than usual, and soon it was time to go home.

Five days before his departure to Nigeria, Babatunde started to pack his bags. He ticked off the days on the calendar pasted to his wall. The day before leaving for home, he spent hours in Jeff Kapemba's room with the twelve underground church members; they had a last service, which ended with a holy communion.

In the morning Babatunde, Antoinette, and Kwame left together for the airport, where they sat separately in the plane going to London. There, they took different planes to their respective countries.

# PART SIX

## 67

A domestic flight in Nigeria took Babatunde to Eastern Nigeria. He arrived at his home at midday. His people rejoiced to see him after almost a year's absence. His mother saw to it that he rested well. Upon waking up he was thrilled to be surrounded by his loving and caring relatives. His mother and nephew wasted no time in firing many questions at him: *How are the people in Lashia? What kind of food do they eat? How are the cars, buses and trains? What kind of money are they using? Do Lashians like Africans?*

They lapped up every word he told them about his life in Russia. Curious next-door neighbours dropped in to hear for themselves how it was there.

As the night wore on, he enjoyed time with his family without fear of intruders. As he later sat alone in the family dining area, he smelt an aroma which he had missed for nearly a year. Salivating, he saw Ekene bringing in a tray containing three utensils: a small silver basin with water to wash his hands; a bowl of okro soup and a plate loaded with two oblong pieces of garri. As he inhaled the tangy aroma of garri, Babatunde found himself salivating again. His mother and Ekene brought their food in and sat in front of him. He said grace, then washed his hands and wiped off the water with a brand-new hand-towel. Although he was in a hurry to eat, he paused for a moment to smile at his mother.

'Mother, I have missed garri and okro soup for nearly a year!' he grinned.

She smiled back at him, 'Enjoy the food, son.'

Taking a piece of garri, he kneaded it, dipped it in the bowl filled with light-brown soup and threw the 'baptised' garri into his mouth. Using both hands he took a piece of fish which lay deep in the bowl, broke it with his left thumb and pointing finger and inserted it into his mouth. As he chewed he saw his mother smiling at him.

'Thank you *nne* for this delicious food,' he said. He continued to chew and dip balls of garri into the steaming okro soup.

After supper Babatunde had tea, which he'd brought from Russia, with his mother and Ekene. Later, he opened his portmanteau and took out some presents: a coat and lady's hat for his mother; and for his nephew, a plastic shopping bag containing a winter hat with ear-flaps, a pair of socks, a shirt and a pair of trousers.

'Thank you Baba!' said his mother, 'I didn't expect any present from a student.'

'I saved money from my monthly living expenses,' said Babatunde. 'Remember, I also worked for a month at the university library.'

Ekene explored the fur of the winter hat with his fingers.

'It's a *shapka* headgear,' Babatunde enlightened his nephew.

Ekene put it on. 'Uncle, is the place very cold?'

'It's bitterly cold,' replied Babatunde, 'especially for us Africans who live near the Equator.'

Ekene continued to feel the texture of the headgear.

'It's so cold,' continued Babatunde, 'that you will feel like packing your bags and returning home the same day you arrive. I still remember that particular day when I could not see the sun; it was so frosty that I shivered and my teeth cried, "ka-ka-ka-kaa!" I had put on my coat already, so I put on two thick blankets but I was still shaking; I felt cold to my bones.'

Ekene grinned. '*Ewu-o*, uncle!'

His mother brought a mirror and Ekene smiled at his reflection.

'You'll not use that hat in Nigeria, but in England, Europe or Russia, if you work hard enough to get a scholarship.'

Ekene chuckled.

Babatunde showed them his photos, taking them one by one out of the envelope. His mother and Ekene bent their heads, focusing with interest on each snapshot. After passing a photo to Ekene, his mother took it back, squinted her eyes and pointed: 'Who is this white woman?'

'She is one of my lecturers.'

'And these two?'

'They are African students and fellow Christians.'

He also showed them his Aeroflot boarding pass.

'So, Uncle, you can speak Russian?' asked Ekene, grinning.

'Yes, I'm now fluent in the language,' said Babatunde, smiling at the curiosity that burnt in Ekene's eyes. 'All foreign students have to learn Russian.'

'How do you say "good morning" in Russian?'

'*Dobroeutro.*'

'Good night?'

'*Spokoĭ noĭnochi.*'

'Spoko…?'

'*Spokoĭ noĭnochi.*'

'*Spokoĭ noĭnochi?*'

'Correct!'

'Goodbye?'
*Do svidaniya.*
'Thank you?'
*Spasibo.*
'Come here?'
*Idite syuda.*
'Please repeat.'
*Idite syuda.*
Highly thrilled, Ekene's smile flourished before he shifted his gaze to Babatunde's mother. 'Granny, can you hear how my uncle speaks Russian?'

Babatunde's mother gave a crooked smile and shook her head. 'I don't think *Lashia* loves you, my child.'

'Why are you saying that, mother?'

'If *Lashia* indeed loved you, you would have put on weight, son.' She paused. 'Now you look…' she indicated something smaller or thinner with her two palms.

'You know, mother, books can make people lean.'

His nephew and his mother burst into lusty laughter.

'When you return to the big school next year,' said his mother, 'I'm going to give you parcels of fufu, yams, kola nuts, garri, anu-nchi and okro spices.'

Babatunde laughed so heartily that his mother saw his molars. Before he went to sleep, Ekene gave him a letter. From the handwriting on the envelope he could tell it was from Yvonne. He tore it open and read the letter. She told him that she had gone to the US to visit her mother, adding that she'd decided to go two weeks earlier because her mother had to undergo an operation.


## 68

On Sunday before the pastor delivered his sermon, Babatunde stood in front of the congregation wearing his blue-and-grey checked suit. He thanked the parishioners for their prayers for him.

'I can assure you, brothers and sisters, mothers and fathers, uncles and aunts,' he said with a jaw-to-jaw smile, 'that your prayers have not been in vain.'

'Alleloyah!' cheered the pastor, leading the loud applause.

'When the Israelite army fought against the Amalekites…' For a moment Babatunde looked straight at his mother who gave him a shy smile;

she was a member of the church now. '…Moses held up his hands and the Israelites began to win the war. But when he got tired and lowered his arms, the Amalekites caused the Israelites to retreat in defeat. We read further in the Bible that when Aaron and Hur supported Moses's arms, the Israelites annihilated their enemy by sunset. So, brethren, thank you for lifting up your arms of prayer so that I could resist the trials and temptations in Russia.'

The congregation applauded with cheers and whistles.

After telling them about his challenges in Russia, a lot of questions were asked. He answered them and received positive feedback from the congregation in the form of nods and smiles.

After the church service Babatunde was part of about twenty guests, including Nnesinachi and Adam, the deacons and the pastor's friends who were invited for lunch. The pastor slaughtered a ram and some home-reared chickens.

A marquee was pitched behind the pastor's house.

'Let's all eat and enjoy and finish our food,' said the pastor, 'and later listen to our guest who will tell us about his life as an African student and a Christian in Russia.'

Later, when all the eating was done, the pastor opened the discussion by saying: 'Yvonne told me about the letter you wrote to her. She said you told her about a church you started on the campus.'

'Yes. During my second semester there, I met two Christians from Ghana. We started off slowly because we had to evade the all-penetrating eyes of the KGB. But we later made an agreement with God, saying, "We know that we are watched and monitored, but no matter what, we are now going to meet for two hours thrice a week."

'We spent 75 percent of that time praying for a miracle. For two months it seemed nothing positive would happen. But then one day God miraculously led us to other African students who were believers. Our faith increased tremendously, and we trusted God to help us avoid detection by the secret police. We chose a leader, Jeff Kapemba from Zambia. We pretended to be African Studies students.

'Brother Jeff encouraged us always to seek the face of God, and to trust that He made no mistake in sending us to Russia. Very much inspired, I prayed in the morning and at night, asking God why He sent me to the Soviet Union. For three consecutive nights the Lord showed me a vision in which I saw myself preaching to thousands of white faces. I said to myself, "No, it can't be true! Thousands of white people, in such a Godless country? How will I be taken seriously by whites who may be put off by my accent?"

'Because I was in doubt, I consulted Jeff; he said I should give him time to pray. A few days later he gave me a written statement about what God had said to him regarding my vision. I read his prophecy so many times that I knew it by heart. He wrote, "God cannot afford to give precious materials to cowards or careless children. God needs people who will not toy with pearls, people who will not give what is meant for the children to the pigs."'

Babatunde paused, keeping eye contact with his pastor. 'So, men of God, I'm looking for confirmation from you.'

Pastor Benson nodded and looked at his pastor friends who nodded back, smiling.

'I can assure you, Baba,' said Pastor Benson, 'we are going to pray for you, and we know that God never makes mistakes.'

'Tell us, brother Baba,' said the pastor's friend, 'how does an underground church really work in Moscow?'

Babatunde smiled. 'First let me explain that there are two groups of churches in Russia and the communist block: the secret or underground churches and the puppet or counterfeit churches. The puppet churches are also known as "registered churches" and they echo the mind and voice of the state, while in the underground church, which is also referred to as the "suffering church", you hear the voice of the true gospel and the Spirit of Christ.'

Some listeners had started taking notes, and Babatunde appreciated that he was being treated with respect.

'The pastors of true churches are known by the state as rebels because they refuse to register their churches. These men of God would see their churches growing to 200 or 300 people. The secret police would choose that moment to take harsh action against the church; the youth would be collected at night and beaten and threatened that if they didn't leave the unregistered church; they would also be sent to labour camps in Siberia.

'Many pastors and leaders were imprisoned. As a result of this harassment, membership would be reduced to as few as 10 or 15. This compelled the believers to become part of the underground church.

'The man who introduced me to the underground church is a professor of Rocket Science at my university. I'll never forget that night when Prof Ish collected me and two university believers, Antoinette and Kwame, in front of the campus gate. Whenever we drove past police cars I became anxious about our safety. Who wants to land in jail when your parents expect you to be safe and studying at the varsity?'

'Inspired by that experience, I continued to attend other services with brother Ish. It was risky and dangerous but I found it impossible to backtrack. I was like a daring drug trafficker. I discovered how the believers improvised very creative ways of spreading the gospel: they used opportunities such as weddings, funerals, birthdays, visiting sick people in their homes and sporting events to evangelise. What was interesting was that a family of four would end up having ten birthdays per year!'

## 69

Babatunde was digging in the garden, bare to the waist in his pair of khaki shorts, when he saw Odenigbo's car stopping at the gate. He threw the spade down, wiped his dusty hands on his shorts and walked to meet Odenigbo as he entered the yard. The two laughed as they stepped towards each other. They embraced warmly, slapping each other's shoulders and looking deeply into each other's eyes, climaxing the moment with loud laughter.

Odenigbo drew back to examine his friend: '*Hei chi m o*! What happened to your Afro-hairstyle?'

Babatunde's close-cropped hair exposed his ears, and he had trimmed his beard and moustache.

'So much hair needs maintenance. Within my first week there, once I'd got used to the weather, I decided to trim my hair.'

'I like it,' smiled Odenigbo: 'The shortness and shiny blackness of your hair looks natural and smart.'

'Thank you, my friend.'

'I thought I should give you a few days to recover from your jet-lag and see your people before I visited you,' said Odenigbo.

'You did well, Ode,' said Babatunde, heading for his hut to change into smart casuals.

Shortly afterwards they drove to Port Harcourt.

As they entered the town and drove past Ogige market Babatunde said: 'Please stop the car!'

'Do you want to buy something?'

Babatunde opened the car door and stepped out: 'No. I just want to enjoy my people.'

Odenigbo joined him and they stood watching the hustle and bustle of the market.

'This past year when I was in Russia, I really missed the colour, noise, movement, energy and exuberance of my fellow Nigerians.'

Odenigbo laughed. 'You are becoming a tourist, my friend!' he said. 'All you need now is a camera and a strange accent!'

They had a good laugh.

'I also felt the same when I returned here after spending years in London,' Odenigbo said.

Next to them two women pounding yams while others roasted peanuts in large cast-iron pans. Babatunde bought two pieces of roasted yam, some roasted peanuts and plantain chips from one of the women.

They went on their way, heading for the harbour where they sat at a corner table in a quiet restaurant facing the water, having drinks while their food was being prepared.

Odenigbo took a swig at his drink and smiled at the friend he had not seen for a year.

'So, how's life in Russia, Baba?'

'Life is great, but there were challenges.'

A vague question deserved a vague answer.

'And how did you adapt to the weather?'

'With difficulty. When I arrived at the airport, I found that the place was colder than my body had ever experienced. But I observed that the local people were comfortable with the weather. They were happily rubbing their hands together and toasting to Marxism with shots of vodka.'

Odenigbo chortled.

'The next day we were taken out shopping by a tall, athletic man we knew as Mikhail. He escorted us to the government-owned store known as GUM, near the Red Square. We were refitted, literally from head to toes: thick cotton underwear, vests and long-tapered leggings. Next, we chose heavy flannel trousers, heavy shirts, jerseys and overcoats. Last but not least, we put on the headgear. I'm telling you, Ode, the way we looked as we left the store, Lenin would have been proud of our contribution to the socialist cause.'

Odenigo laughed again.

He took out a neatly folded newspaper article and showed it to Babatunde who read the caption: 'African student killed in Moscow.'

'I knew the guy,' Babatunde told him. 'His name is Doumbé Khouyaté, from Senegal. He was the first African student I met at the airport. He had a great sense of humour and I think that must have attracted the Russian girl. He was very popular and the chairman of the African Students' Union. I know his girlfriend, Vera; she is beautiful enough to be a model.

'One afternoon, about a week before he was killed, I walked with them. On our way from the library, we met a group of five male Russian students. When they saw us coming, I could see them scheming something. As we were about to walk past them, one of them shouted, pointing at

Vera: "A Russian girl who dates blacks…" And the group responded, "… Is worse than the lowest prostitute!"'

Babatunde glanced at the newspaper clipping. 'I don't want to repeat all that was written in the newspapers.'

Odenigbo stared at Babatunde with a pained face. 'Tell me, Baba, do you think this guy ignored some warning signs? Don't you think he should have been more discreet, to avoid being killed?'

'I think he tried to be discreet, but it was too late. It's clear that the girl's next-door neighbours and the security men at the flats were conspiring against them for a long time. His Senegalese friends said Doumbé told them that when he visited the girl a few days before he was killed, the uniformed police were tipped off. After demanding entry into her flat, the officers rudely interrogated him to embarrass him in front of his girlfriend, who objected and threatened to report them to their superiors.'

Odenigbo shook his head. 'It's sad that a young life should be lost like that in a foreign country.'

'Yes, and this has embarrassed the Soviet Union who are posturing as a loyal comrade of the Third World countries.'

'I didn't know that Russians could be so evil.'

'Russians are not evil people. There are a few bad ones, that's all. You know that sex drive can trigger jealousy which can be expressed negatively in people; such people can get angry and violent; they can even commit murder. I think all over the world men are protective of their women, and they can become extremely jealous when a male from another race or country becomes too familiar or intimate with their women.'

'So this means that you'll be returning to the university,' said Odenigbo after a long pause, 'and staying in Moscow at your own risk?'

'You know, Ode, racists are a small minority; perhaps less than one percent. I choose to focus on the other 99.9 percent of decent Russians.'

# 70

One day Babatunde was preparing to go the roadside stall to hawk yams when Ekene told him that a car was outside. His face brightened when he realised that the visitor was Felix Okoro. For the next hour Felix listened with utmost concentration as Babatunde told of his experiences in Russia. He showed Felix the academic report that had arrived the previous day. Felix studied the results with a smiling face.

'I'm very impressed with your report, Baba!'

'Thanks, teacher Felix.'

Felix tapped the paper with his index finger. 'I see your lowest mark is 65 percent—for Russian?'

'Yes!'

Babatunde took out some of the photos from the envelope and showed them to Felix. After looking through them, Felix went back to a photo in which Babatunde, wearing a red suit, was with Ludimila.

'Who's this white woman?'

'My journalism lecturer, Ludi.'

'What was happening here?'

'She was handing me a certificate of excellence for being the top student in journalism.'

Felix shook his hand. 'You have performed excellently, Baba. Your lecturer must be proud of you.'

'Thank you, sir!'

*

In addition to his chores at home, Babatunde volunteered for the church where he applied his journalism skills to writing church leaflets, newsletters and letterheads. He made time to visit relatives he had not seen for months and also spent time with his cousin Nnesinachi and her boyfriend, Adam, who was now recognised by the church as her fiancé.

During his last Sunday at home Nnesinachi stood with Babatunde beside her fiancé's car.

She smiled and gestured towards a group of girls nearby: 'I overheard one of those girls saying, "I wonder if he has a girlfriend in Russia."'

Babatunde chuckled.

'All eyes are on you, Baba,' said Nnesinachi who winked, '*Wetin* be your problem when you see beautiful women?'

He laughed also because he was fascinated by how she was addressing him partly in pidgin as if she was trying to exclude an eavesdropper.

'You *dey* blind? Baba please come to your senses. *Abeg-o*!'

He shrugged. 'I'm my kind, Nachi.'

'What's your problem because you can now pick and choose?'

'That'll happen in three years' time, Nachi.'

'Why such a long time?'

'My priority is to get an education, a job, money in the bank and a house.'

Nnesinachi narrowed her eyes and gave a wry smile. 'You'll have to adjust your plans when you are bitten by the bug of love.'

Babatunde chortled. 'I'm going to use the most lethal insecticide!'

They both laughed.

'So, as far as you're concerned it's "Seek ye first the kingdom of education and the rest shall be added."'

They laughed again. 'You are 100 percent correct, Nachi. You get what you focus on. So please,' he said with a grin, 'do me a favour. When you observe that a girl is interested in me, just say to her, "That one is a man of books, and he has no time for girls."'

Nnesinachi laughed. 'How can I say that?'

'It's true that all I'm thinking about is books, books, books!'

'And later it'll be boobs, boobs, boobs!'

Babatunde pinched her arm, and they continued to laugh.

# PART SEVEN

## 71

Babatunde returned to Russia where he continued with his degree, and three years went by like a few months, because he studied hard and was very motivated. Attending the underground church once a week also ate up his time and before he knew it days had become months. He used to tell his pastor and fellow Christians that he felt like Jacob labouring for Rachel, the woman he loved with all his heart and mind.

After graduating he was employed as an industrial journalist by the Moscow Steel Company, where he did practical work. To apply his acquired knowledge to a practical situation was fulfilling. Compiling articles, editing the bi-monthly newsletter and writing items about new products were his main duties. He spent most mornings interviewing the employees in order to write stories and profiles; the articles included news about innovative workers, promotions, retirements, long-service awards and items about new products.

Because of the extensive nature of his work, many employees got to know him. During lunch and sometimes after hours, he strolled to the park two blocks from his company, where he read his Bible, far from the inquisitive the eyes of his colleagues. Bible-reading whetted his appetite to evangelise to his colleagues, but he was not sure if he could trust anyone yet. On several occasions he found a fellow employee alone in his office and he told himself, *Here is a target,* but when he opened his mouth, he changed the subject.

He continued to be an active member of Prof Isayevich's underground church. One of the members introduced him to a widow whose husband had been a pastor until his death at a labour camp five years before. The widow lent him her husband's theology books and allowed him the use of his bound lecture notes.

*

Antoinette returned to Ghana after graduating as a medical doctor, while Kwame, Jeff and Etienne remained in Russia and were all employed. The four African men kept in touch with each other over the years.

They visited one another on public holidays, at least three times a year and often spent time together at the parks and botanical gardens, updating each other on events as they shared picnic baskets. Babatunde insisted on playing games when they met, such as hide-and-seek, 'The Hyena and the Children', and other games that would make them remember 'back home' and enjoy the shrill excitement like children.

Whenever Babatunde went back to his country, people peppered him with questions such as: *When are you coming to work in our country? When are you getting married? Are you going to marry a Nigerian girl?* His ready answer was: *When God opens the door. At the moment God still wants me to remain in Russia; I'm awaiting His further instructions.*

His former teacher, Felix Okoro, who hoped that he would work for the government in Nigeria, was disappointed that he was staying on in Russia.

*

One day, in his fourth year in Russia, Babatunde visited Kwame at his flat where he found Jeff and Etienne. As they had tea Kwame put his TV set on; they watched as a bespectacled, bald-headed man in a black suit, white shirt and tie appeared on the screen.

'I like Gorbachev,' said Kwame. 'Since he took over as General Secretary of the Communist Party last year things are changing in this country.'

'Yes,' said Jeff, 'the country is taking a different direction, for the better. His Perestroika and Glasnost policies are affording new freedoms to the Soviet people, including freedom of speech.'

'This is a radical change,' agreed Etienne.

'His economic policies are making provision for private ownership of what used to be controlled by the government,' Kwame continued.

'He did a good thing by repealing the restrictive laws on newspapers,' Jeff contributed. 'And the workers can now talk freely. But not every Russian is happy with his liberal policies.'

'You are right, Jeff,' said Etienne. 'For example, his anti-alcohol campaign is making him unpopular among the ordinary workers who are now paying more for liquor because of increased taxes. My colleague told me that at many bars the men are cursing him between gulps of vodka.'

'I read in *Sovetskaya Rossiya*,' said Kwame, 'that because of reduced liquor sales, the state budget has lost billions of rubles.'

'Guys, Gorbachev's changes are going to benefit the spreading of the gospel,' said Babatunde. 'Because of his fight against widespread alcoholism, I hope that the people will stop drinking and have a thirst for our gospel instead. What do you think?'

'No, Baba, the people will never stop drinking,' said Jeff. 'So we must preach to them as they are drinking.'

'Preaching to them when they are drinking?' asked Kwame, 'No, I don't want to be sworn at by drunk Russians!'

'Or how about an empty bottle of vodka on your head!' said Babatunde.

'Besides, drunks never take any message seriously,' said Jeff.

'Yes,' said Kwame, 'someone is sure to ask if there'll be vodka in heaven.'

They all laughed.

'I think we should continue to pray for Gorbachev,' said Etienne after a long pause.

The others agreed with him.

*

Six months later Babatunde was with his friends in his flat. Kwame entered, holding a copy of *Sovetskaya Rossiya*. On the front page was a photo of Gorbachev standing in front of a podium, with several microphones facing him. The presence of two formally dressed men behind him indicated that he was perhaps in parliament, or at a Politburo meeting.

'What's new from comrade Gorbachev?' asked Babatunde, glancing at the newspaper.

'There's no doubt,' said Jeff 'that he is busy making another important announcement.'

'He's trying his best; he has been bold enough to release thousands of political prisoners and dissidents,' Kwame put in.

'I heard from my colleagues,' said Jeff, 'that he invited Andrei Sakharov to return to Moscow.'

'Who's Andrei Sakharov?' asked Babatunde.

'An intellectual who was in internal exile somewhere in the north of Russia,' said Etienne.

'Gorbachev gave the Russians a finger of freedom, now they are demanding the whole hand,' said Kwame.

'Why are you saying that?' asked Babatunde.

Kwame flipped over a page and pointed to a headline: *Calls for greater independence*. He read the item: *Calls for greater independence from Moscow's rule are growing louder, especially in the Baltic republics of Lithuania, Latvia and Estonia, which were annexed into the Soviet Union by Josef Stalin in 1940. Nationalist feeling is also taking hold in Georgia, Ukraine, Armenia and Azerbaijan.*

'You know why this is happening?' said Kwame. 'Feelings that were suppressed for decades are now being unleashed.'

Jeff and Etienne continued to read the paper while Babatunde went to the kitchen to prepare cool drinks and snacks.

'Gorbachev must be a fireman with many hands,' said Jeff.

'The man's trouble,' said Babatunde, 'is an opportunity for us.'

'Yes, we could travel all over the republics and give the people hope,' said Kwame.

'Friends,' said Etienne, 'Kwame is right. Let's pray that God should open our eyes to the gospel opportunities.'

# 72

Months later Babatunde and his fellow Africans witnessed history unfolding in front of their eyes. Protest marches took place in many republics because of the re-awakening of long-suppressed nationalist and anti-Russian feelings. Pro-independence voices became louder, even among the top communist leadership. Soviet troops were sent to quell multiple uprisings. Estonia and Lithuania led other republics in declaring their independence, an unprecedented act that ultimately led to the dissolution of the Soviet Union.

Following discussions and prayer meetings for several weekends, Babatunde agreed with his friends that it was the right time to quit their jobs and spread the gospel full-time.

For weeks they printed soul-winning material; they packed their luggage, planning to travel from the west to the east of Russia to distribute their evangelistic leaflets and to preach.

For three months they boarded trains and distributed evangelistic leaflets to commuters. They walked around shopping malls and preached at the youth hostels where they lodged.

They also visited old age homes and retirement villages. At one retirement home they led two couples to the Lord. Encouraged by that little success, they decided to stay there longer.

'Whom do you suggest we should approach here?' Babatunde asked the newly converted woman.

'You can try Nikita Kosmolonov,' said the old lady.

Her husband nodded. 'Yes, he could be an easy fish because he's a widower.'

An hour later Old Nikita welcomed Babatunde and Kwame to his small room while Jeff and Etienne evangelised to another couple. Babatunde and Kwame prayed, read the Bible and shared the gospel with him.

'Sir, we've presented the good gospel of our Lord,' said Babatunde, oozing confidence. 'Now, are you ready to receive Him?'

'Receive who?'

'Receive Jesus Christ as your Lord and Saviour.'

Nikita kept quiet.

'Sir, have you any questions?' asked Kwame.

'Is there anything we can clarify?' inquired Babatunde.

Suddenly Nikita stamped his walking stick on the ground in front of him. 'Young man, who said you can impose your West-inspired religion on millions of us Russians who are happy to live as we are?'

Babatunde and Kwame were taken aback. They'd been informed that although Nikita was a former KGB member, he'd become a 'toothless bulldog' in the midst of crumbling communism.

Babatunde took his time to explain to Nikita how Gorbachev's political reforms had made it possible for them to preach because more religious freedom was guaranteed, and that their evangelising confirmed that change was indeed taking place.

'More religious freedom,' added Kwame, 'means that your country will be part of the bigger free world, and that will benefit your country.'

'Benefit *my* country?' asked Nikita in an irritated falsetto. 'My country must be a yes-sir, yes-ma'am of the West? And what do you think Gorbachev must do with the thousands of KGBs? Send them to sweep the streets? Certainly not! They aren't going to fold their arms while America is multiplying itself in my beloved motherland.'

'Well I'm sure, sir,' said Babatunde, 'that the former KGBs can do other nation-building tasks such as crime prevention, tending to patients, farming and so on.'

'A cat will always catch mice,' Nikita insisted. 'And a Soviet leopard never changes its spots. *Nikogda!*'

'But sir, how can that happen when Gorbachev is telling the world that there is religious freedom in Russia?'

Nikita showed his teeth, swallowing spit. 'Listen young men, you are not going to tell us how we must run *our* government.'

'Apologies, sir. We didn't mean to…'

'*Slushat!*' Nikita cut in. 'I'm not interested in your religion. And I want to tell you one thing: You'll know who's really in charge in Russia.' He jabbed his finger at the door. '*Ubiraytes!*'

Kwame stood up but Babatunde hesitated, his open Bible resting on his lap.

'Can we at least pray for you, sir?' Babatunde asked.

'*Nyet!* I'm not interested in your prayer,' said Nikita gnashing his teeth, his rigid index finger quivering with emotion.

*

The next morning as Babatunde, Kwame, Jeff and Etienne boarded the bus that would take them to the next town they observed two black cars with blue lights trailing the bus. When the bus arrived at the next bus stop, the cars overtook it and halted in front of it. A thickset man got out of the car and waved at the bus driver, instructing him not to move the bus. He boarded the bus and, after looking around at the passengers, pointed, grinning, to where Babatunde, Kwame, Jeff and Etienne were sitting.

'*Poĭdem so mnoĭ!*' he bellowed at them and turned to the bus driver: '*Spasibo!*'

Kwame whispered to Babatunde as they shuffled out of the bus: 'So old Nikita has reported us to the KGB?'

# 73

The two black cars entered the gate of a police station where Soviet flags fluttered on both sides on iron masts. Babatunde saw several double- and triple-storey buildings. Towards the back of the yard were higher buildings. The cars parked in front of the tallest building. The two officers led them to a lift that took them to the seventh floor where they were herded into an empty office. One of the officers instructed them to sit on chairs behind two tables; the other disappeared. The first officer sat, stern-faced, at one of the tables, writing on sheets of paper.

'Your passports!' he barked.

Babatunde, Kwame, Jeff and Etienne exchanged glances.

'If you are unwilling to produce the documents,' said the officer with a sardonic smile, 'we know how to make you co-operate with us.'

The four men handed their passports over and the officer began filling in the forms in front of him. Babatunde saw other officers going to and fro in the corridor. A burly officer with bloodshot eyes entered the office with a younger, handsome officer beside him. The two spoke briefly to the officer who had taken their passports then walked out again, the older officer muttering to his companion.

The officer who'd taken their passports completed the forms, inserted each document into a file cover and put them in an *Immediate Attention* basket. A female officer later collected the files and escorted Babatunde and the others to a different office where they waited for a long time.

Two hours later, a well-fleshed officer entered. 'All of you, follow me,' he bellowed at them.

Babatunde and his companions were taken to a different section where they were kept in separate rooms and interrogated for hours. Afterwards they were escorted to the canteen and given food, before they were returned to the first office, where they waited together.

Late in the afternoon, the good-looking officer they'd seen earlier came in, holding the four files; he half smiled as he took a seat facing them: 'Good afternoon, gentlemen.'

Babatunde and the others greeted him back.

The officer scanned the four Africans with his blue eyes before turning his attention back to the files in front of him. He read out the names on the files, making quick ticks as he identified each face.

'Leonid Margelov is my name,' he told them.

'It's our pleasure to meet you, Mr Margelov,' said Babatunde, wondering if his sarcasm would misfire.

Margelov pressed his lips together and raised his eyebrows commandingly.

'I must say, I'm pleased that the arm of the Soviet law has caught you at last,' he said. 'When I meet people who stand against us like yourselves, I know that they will soon realise they are fighting a battle they are certainly going to lose.'

Babatunde glanced at his friends, not knowing what to say.

'Gentlemen, have you benefited from the much-needed Soviet educational aid we made available to you?' asked Margelov.

'Yes, of course,' said Babatunde.

'And now you are fully equipped to help your poor and struggling nations?'

'Yes,' responded Kwame.

'I find it quite interesting that instead of going back to your continent to uplift your people, you are still here, trying to develop us.'

'What do you mean Mr Margelov?' asked Babatunde.

Margelov aimed a sardonic smile at Babatunde. 'Do you think you've been given a licence to go all over our vast country imposing your beliefs on our people?'

'We aren't imposing our beliefs, Mr Margelov,' said Etienne.

'All we are doing is to preach the gospel of our Lord,' Jeff put in, 'and the people can make their own choice.'

Margelov wagged his forefinger at them. 'You are faithfully representing your masters from the West. Pawns of the West bent on hoodwinking our old and helpless people and our youth, promising them heaven on earth if they are gullible to swallow your superstition.'

Babatunde shook his head. 'Whoever thinks we are hoodwinking people with superstition is someone blessed with a fertile imagination, Mr Margelov.'

'Who do you think has a fertile imagination?' retorted Margelov.

Babatunde shrugged.

'Sir,' said Jeff, 'you should appreciate that the gospel we are preaching to your people is life-transforming; it has the power to change a drunk and a prostitute into a respectable citizen.'

Margelov wagged his finger at Jeff. 'What are you trying to do?' He opened the files and took out some documents. 'Gentlemen, let me take this opportunity to inform you that your religious activities have offended the state to the extent that your passports have been confiscated. They have been sent to the judge via the office of the state prosecutor, and in their place you'll be issued with temporary passports. In response to the information appearing on your charge sheets, you are likely to be deported to your countries within fourteen days.'

Babatunde and the others looked at each other, not believing what they had just been told.

'Mr Margelov,' said Babatunde, 'I want to speak to the public prosecutor and the judge. They must show me the law which says the KGB has the authority to stop a bus and arrest passengers purely on suspicion and prepare a charge sheet claiming that the suspects were preaching.'

Margelov stared at Babatunde. 'I can tell you right now, without a doubt, that the court is going to endorse our recommendation, which is that you should be deported for your own protection.'

'No! We are not…'

'Listen here,' Margelov interrupted Babatunde, 'the patriotic Russians, who are happy
with their religion, are angry with you guys.'

'Why would they be angry with us?'

'Because you are imposing a Western religion on them,' Margelov continued. 'They may want to assault or even kill you!'

Babatunde smiled with confidence. 'God is going to protect us, because we have a mission in Russia.'

Margelov pointed at Babatunde. 'You must stop fooling yourself!'

His fist slammed the table like he was swatting a fly. He looked at Babatunde as if hoping to see him flinch, but the man in front of him merely stayed silent. 'That's what's going to happen to you, if you continue to be stubborn,' Margelov sneered. 'Let the Western media say and write what they like about this great country; we, the hands and feet of this proud nation, are going to do everything within our power to protect our people from the influx of Christianity and perverted values. If you continue to be a tick on the buttocks of the Russian bear, you will be surely crushed!'

Margelov creased his forehead. 'You seem to think that the spirit of the West is beginning to influence my country, but fourteen days from now you'll find yourself breathing humid African air.'

He got up and hurried out of the office, leaving them alone.

After waiting for another three hours, they received their temporary passports and were discharged with a warning never to evangelise again in Russia.

# 74

Babatunde took his fellow believers back to his apartment where they prayed. Afterwards he prepared a meal of rice, minced meat and mixed vegetables for them. As they ate, he told them that he felt like packing his bags and returning to his country the same evening.

Jeff shook his head at him. 'I rebuke that spirit of discouragement. You aren't going anywhere! Have you forgotten about your dream in which you were preaching to thousands of white people?'

'You are right Jeff,' Babatunde said, 'returning home now would be bad timing. So I must go when our soul-winning is beginning to bear fruit.'

'It is true,' said Etienne. 'Your people will try to discourage you and plead with you to return home for good.'

'Brothers,' said Jeff, 'we need to be courageous like Saint Paul. You'll remember how at one time he was arrested, landed in prison and was beaten up.' Heads nodded. 'So I suggest that we should fast for a week.'

'I'm positive,' agreed Kwame, 'that God is going to answer our prayers. The same moon that wanes today will give light tomorrow.'

'Amen!' said Jeff.

'And our God is going to make a way in the wilderness and extract water out of a rock!"

They later sang a hymn, *We shall overcome*. Then Babatunde's friends departed.

As they left the flat, Etienne touched Babatunde's shoulder and said: 'Since you can't go home now, Baba, why don't you send your people a letter?'

'I'll do that,' responded Babatunde.

*

A day after Babatunde and the others had completed their fast they went to a special immigration court. During the hearing the prosecutor read the charges, to which they all replied with *Not guilty*. The verdict was that they should be deported within 30 days, once their papers had been processed by the Ministry of Home Affairs. As Babatunde and his friends-in-the-Lord walked down the stairs of the court building, they met Professor Isayevich.

'What brings you here?' inquired Babatunde, elated at the sight of his former professor.

'One of our underground church members received information that you guys would appear in court today,' Isayevich told him.

'I appreciate your concern and you coming here,' said Babatunde, introducing Isayevich to his friends. He told Isayevich about the verdict of the court.

'Did you have a lawyer?' asked the professor.

'No,' replied Babatunde.

'God is our lawyer,' said Kwame.

When Babatunde arrived at his apartment, he found a letter from home. As he opened the door, he also saw a note that had been inserted under the door. He unfolded it and read with bated breath:

> Dear brother Babatunde,
>
> I am Kofi Osei from Ghana. I'm a student at Kiev and I've been sent by Chris Reed of Global Evangelism to find him an English-speaking person who is fluent in Russian to interpret for him. Please visit me at Molotov guest house as soon as possible.
> K Osei.

Babatunde exhaled and re-read the letter. *Perhaps God is going to use this challenge*, he mused as he re-folded the note, *as an opening for other godly opportunities.*

He opened the envelope from home read the letter, written by Ekene as dictated by his mother:

> Dear son,

We are well, but we'll be better when you are part of us again.
You have attended the big school and you are educated. So
please come home. Teacher Okoro says you can easily get employment in the government offices. You have problems because
God is telling you that you should come back home. The pastor
says we should tell you to write to him. The yam garden is missing the touch of your hands.
Your mother,
Chioke.

Still reflecting on the letter from his mother, he walked to the apartment
shared by Jeff, Etienne and Kwame, a block away. He showed them both
the letters and they agreed with him that the invitation to interpret for
Chris Reed was a godly opportunity he should not miss. They all prayed
for him.

# 75

That weekend Babatunde and Kofi boarded an electric tram that took
them to Moscow's Central Railroad Station, Privokzal'naya Square. From
there they travelled by *Elektrischka*, an electric train, to Ukraine's northern
town, Kharkiv. As the train crossed the Russian border, Babatunde felt as
if he was suddenly breathing fresh air, and a burden seemed to fall from
his back. A bus took them to the next town, Poltava, where they disembarked for refreshment and leg-stretching. Their journey continued
through two other towns, Lubny and Brovari. Upon approaching Kiev,
Babatunde saw buildings of many shapes, heights and colours and a variety of green trees.

'What is that imposing statue?' he asked his companion as they drove
past the 'Welcome to Kiev' signboard decorated with the city's coat-of-
arms.

'It's the Motherland statue. It's known as Rodina-Mat in Russian.'

Babatunde held his breath, his eyes glinting with awe and interest.

'On the left you can see the shield,' Kofi continued, 'and on the right is
the sword. It's 203 feet, or 62 metres high.'

'*Ewu-oo*!' Babatunde continued to marvel at the stainless steel statue.
The bus moved on, focusing on a massive white structure comprising a
cluster of oval-shaped buildings with green domes topped with silver
crosses.

'And this architectural masterpiece?'

'It's Saint Sophia Cathedral.'

There was so much to view that he became speechless.

'We are now reaching the centre of the city, as we turn into Chervonoarmiiska Street,' his guide told him. 'The building over there is Saint Volodymyr's Cathedral.'

'Saint Volodymyr's Cathedral,' Babatunde repeated in awe. 'It feels like I'll see the Virgin Mary walking out!'

'It's not Catholic but an Orthodox Cathedral. It's in fact known as the mother cathedral,' Kofi grinned. 'You'd need a month at least to immerse yourself in the aesthetic pleasures dished out by Kiev.'

Babatunde smiled.

*

At the offices of the Baptist Union, Kofi introduced Babatunde to Chris Reed, the American preacher who had taken his 'Crusade for Christ' evangelistic campaign to the Ukraine.

Babatunde rejoiced to meet Chris, a man he found very affable.

'Have you ever been to the Ukraine before?' asked Chris as he led Babatunde to his office.

'No, I've never set foot in Ukraine till now. I must say, Kiev is a beautiful city; I think the parks and statues are even better than in Moscow.'

Chris nodded, grinning.

'I also like the people here, Chris. They seem a lot happier than the Russians.'

Chris shook his head. 'I don't think the Muscovites will agree with you. In fact, they'd be eager to lynch you!'

They laughed.

Kofi brought tea with muffins and they ate.

'I really wish I could live and work in Kiev.'

'Well, Baba, if it's the desire of your heart, then pray and expect God to answer your prayer.'

An hour later Chris gave Babatunde an orientation of what lay ahead; he would be interpreting for two weeks as Chris preached.

The first five minutes of interpreting were a little challenging for Babatunde whose confidence increased as time went on. The brightening faces of the audience seemed to give him feedback, 'You are doing well, young man.' 'Pastor Reed, please pray for a divine intervention,' Babatunde pleaded, before taking the bus back to Russia, 'so that this black cloud of a curse that hangs over our heads should be turned into a blessing.'

Chris responded by touching Babatunde's shoulder. 'Young man, don't lose hope.'

'If a miracle doesn't happen,' Babatunde went on, 'I'm going to be deported to Nigeria, and the devil is going to mock me: "*Hahahaa!* Who do you think you are?"'

'I can assure you, Baba,' said Chris, 'that for the next fourteen days I'm going to be part of your prayer and fasting, and I'm confident that God will never disappoint us.'

*

When Babatunde arrived back at his flat he found a letter from his pastor:

Dear Baba,
　　Greetings. I hope you are well, brother. Whenever a Christian is faced with a problem the question could be: 'Does it come from Satan or God?' I'm certain that through your challenges God is preparing you for a better future. Remember what happened to Job. So, I want to encourage you not to allow the devil to steal your joy or to frustrate your dream. Stay focused like Joseph who believed in his dream even when he was in the dungeon.
　　Remember that God has not promised a storms-free journey. As the Bible says in the book of Proverbs, when the storm has swept by the wicked are gone, but the righteous stand firm forever.
　　Baba, just look ahead and never look backwards. The rearview mirror is small while the windshield is bigger so that you should spend more time looking at where you are going than where you come from.
　　Regards,
Pastor Benson Okpo.

Babatunde was so energised by the pastor's letter that he immediately sat down and wrote a letter to his people:

Dear Mother,
　　I don't think it's according to God's plan that I should come back to Nigeria and look for employment. My people, can I remind you about my dream in which I saw myself preaching to thousands of white faces? I don't doubt that I should preach the

gospel in this part of the world. God is going to use me in a big way. So please give me your blessings.
Baba

A week later he received a note from Chris Reed; again it was sent by Kofi Osei. Babatunde read the typed message:

Hallo Baba,
The Lord has answered our prayers! Just pack your bags and return to the Ukraine. I have a job for you. I am returning to Oklahoma and I want someone I can trust to represent me in the Ukraine. I have just signed a contract with an independent commercial TV station. The person to fill the vacancy should firstly be a Christian and secondly a professional journalist. The only person I know with such qualifications happens to be you! Hallelujah!
Chris

Babatunde was so exhilarated by the good news from Chris that he laughed aloud, kissed the note, and lifted it skywards.

'Thank you, Lord!' Holding his arms outstretched, he swung around and around, shouting, 'Alleloyah!'

He beat his left palm with right fist. 'The Lord has blessed me and filled my mouth with laughter, my tongue with songs of praise.'

# PART EIGHT

## 76

A few days before Babatunde returned to Kiev, Chris Reed called him and told him that he had engaged a lawyer who would see to it that the Ukrainian Department of Home Affairs should send a letter to their Russian counterparts, explaining that Babatunde had got a job in the Ukraine and that he was therefore no longer deportable.

Among the many well-wishers who came to see him off at the Central Railroad Station was Professor Isayevich.

'My daughter is employed as a nursery-school teacher in Kiev,' Isayevich said. 'After you've settled, please visit her; I've told her about you.'

Isayevich handed Babatunde a piece of paper which had his daughter's name, address and telephone number on it.

He looked at Babatunde with misty eyes. 'I am going to miss you, Baba.'

'Me too, brother Ish.'

'Russia will be poorer and Ukraine will be richer. Russia will realise when you are gone that you were indeed an African treasure.'

'Thank you very much for your kind words, brother Ish.'

The two were locked in a tight bear-hug for a moment.

*

After a month as a 'Faith Programme' producer and presenter, Babatunde wrote a letter to his people, telling them how blessed he was, getting a job that offered him a good salary, a car and an apartment.

He also wrote letters to Jeff, Kwame and Etienne, informing them that his stint as an interpreter had improved his speaking skills and his confidence as a preacher. He mentioned that he intended to evangelise part-time. He also told them that Chris Reed had introduced him to the Texas School of Theology, and that he was studying for a diploma in theology through correspondence.

He found his job very fulfilling, often arriving at the office early to start preparing for the day. First, he reviewed the questions he had prepared for his guests; after the interviews, he held meetings with the producers, crew and administrators; writing the daily reports ended his days.

The daily reports were gathered into weekly reports, which contributed to monthly reports. He also met potential sponsors from the UK, US and Europe.

Because he was happy in his job, time seemed to move fast. But as the year tapered towards its end, he was amazed one morning when he awoke with mixed feelings towards his job. He began to ask himself questions such as: *Is this job too good to be true?* A week before Christmas he felt a strong compulsion to write a letter to his pastor.

Dear Pastor Benson,

I am about to take a decision that will certainly shock you and my people. I'm quitting my job at the TV station, though I know many people will disagree strongly with my action. The job is great, and I'm enjoying every minute of it; it's very fulfilling to my career as a journalist and my faith as a Christian.

However, for months I haven't been able to resist the urging of the Spirit to step out of this cozy comfort zone, dirty my hands and plant a church in Kiev. Kofi Osei, a Ghanaian post-graduate engineering student, and I have been part of a cell group. For months now, we have been praying and fasting, seeking God's direction.

Five African students and an African couple are part of the group. One Friday evening as we were praying, a Ghanaian student, Asamoah Anan, prophesied that I should be prepared to walk out of this secure job and take a step of faith, trusting God in His mission to establish His kingdom in this part of the world.

I have already printed the evangelistic tracts which we've distributed at parks and shopping malls, where we preached the gospel. But the Lord has told me on more than one occasion to do the kingdom project full-time. Other believers will work with me part-time because they are still students, and the couple from Cameroon are embassy officials. Please pray for me — but I can assure you that by the time you say 'Amen!' I will be in the streets sharing the good news. This is the best time to reach out to people; people who will be in the more relaxed and jovial mood of the Christmas season. So I want to take advantage of that and tell them how they can receive Jesus whom they are about to celebrate.

Yours in Christ,
BO

PS: I must not forget to inform you that for months I have
been studying for a diploma in theology through correspondence. Chris Reed has introduced me to the Texas School of
Theology. I am doing so well that the Director is convinced that
if I progress at this rate, I could complete this two-year diploma
within a year!

It was a week since he had quit his job; when he came back from his
evangelistic outreach, he found two letters from Nigeria. He could see
from the handwriting on the white envelope that it was from his nephew,
Ekene. He was strangely reluctant to open it; after praying that he should
be strong if it contained bad news, he tore the envelope open and read
with a tinge of anxiety:

Dear Uncle,
     Uncle, granny and the other relatives are angry with you for
quitting a job that gave you a good salary, a company car and an
apartment. They say this year they expected you to come home,
look for a wife, get married and end your life as a bachelor. They
asked the pastor to pray for you. They are convinced that Satan
must have entered your head. They cannot say it directly but I
can say confidently that they will never appreciate your reason
that God has called you to preach in the streets of Kiev in order
to start a church. Please reply to this letter as soon as possible.
     Ekene.

Babatunde re-read the letter like a student determined to pass a compre-
hension test with a distinction.

*I don't want the devil to use this letter to steal my joy,* Babatunde mused as he
folded the letter up and returned it to its envelope. *I'm doing very well in
establishing God's kingdom in Kiev. I am going to heed my pastor's advice that I
should not turn to the left or right but that I should proceed forward.*

He was hugely relieved that the other letter was from Pastor Benson.
After skimming through the usual and familiar Nigerian-correct plati-
tudes and pleasantries, he highlighted the part which he regarded as the
heart and spirit of the pastor's letter:

*But as a man of God who prayed and fasted about your situation, I cannot agree
with your mother—although I appreciate her motherly sentiments. I now stand behind
you as the Spirit has led and guided me. Your people will realise years later that it was
a good thing to focus on God's kingdom, and that the rest will be added.*

*All I can say now is that the journey is going to be very long and the burden will
most of the time be unbearable and in fact back-breaking. But be encouraged and*

*persevere for your sweat will not be in vain. As I ended the fast, the Lord has spoken to me through Isaiah 27 verse 3: 'Sing about a fruitful vineyard. I, the Lord watch over it, I water it continually, I guard it day and night so that no one may harm it.'*

He shouted, 'Hallelujah!' as he folded the letter, a fat smile tugging at the corners of his lips.

Babatunde was pleased with his evangelistic progress: he had distributed many leaflets to scores of people in parks and in the city streets. When he saw a couple passing by with their children, he approached them; before talking to the parents and handing them a leaflet, he smiled, bowed at the children and gave them sweets. His well-rehearsed presentation was: *It's about Jesus whom you are about to celebrate. Please read it in the comfort of your home. There are my telephone numbers. You can call me after you have enjoyed your Christmas. I wish you a merry Christmas.*

# 77

The people received his leaflets and left without saying a word; a few smiled at him. On Christmas Eve Babatunde went to Bessakarabka shopping centre where the shoppers were entertained by a big-bellied, jovial Father Christmas who capered about and ringing his bell in his trademark red and white attire, Taking advantage of the throngs, Babatunde handed out the leaflets to many people who received them without hesitation, rudeness or coldness; some of them smiled at him and wished him a merry Christmas.

As Babatunde left the mall, he saw a tall African man strolling beside an African woman. *Am I dreaming?* thought Babatunde. *This can't be Thom!* He rushed up to the couple, a smile tugging his lips apart as he realised that the man was indeed Thom.

'Baba, what are you doing in Kiev?' Thom yelped, opening his arms. The two men embraced, slapping each other's backs with loud peals of laughter.

'I never imagined I'd see your face again, Thom,' said Babatunde with tearful eyes.

'Well, God made it possible.'

Thom gestured to the woman standing beside him. 'Meet Florence, my wife.'

Babatunde and Florence shook hands.

'What are you doing in Kiev on Christmas Eve?' inquired Babatunde.

'We should have gone back to Kenya,' responded Thom, 'but Florence wants to have a white Christmas experience.'

Babatunde smiled at Florence. 'Yes, I'm sure she will have a special Christmas surrounded by snowflakes.'

Florence chuckled.

'Baba, there's a lot to discuss, so why don't you come to my apartment tonight for dinner?' said Thom as he touched Florece's arm.

When she smiled Babatunde accepted the invitation.

*

That evening, sitting on a zebra-striped leather couch in Thom and Florence's spacious lounge, they sipped juice while Florence prepared dinner assisted by a houseboy who was from Kenya.

'Thom, that afternoon when I looked for you at the campus and I was told, "He drinks vodka and he screws women," I soaked my pillow with tears,' Babatunde told him, lowering his voice so the others should not hear.

Thom giggled. 'I'm laughing at the devil,' he said, putting his glass down, 'because he thought he had won the battle. But he only won rounds one, two and three.'

'Tell me about rounds two and three.'

'It's true, I had become a womaniser and a vodka drinker. One morning I returned from my Russian girlfriend's apartment to find three policemen waiting outside my room. They produced a search warrant. Because I had nothing to hide, I opened my room and stood by as they turned my belongings upside down.

'Suddenly a policeman showed me a plastic container which he had taken from under my bed. "What's this?" he asked. I answered honestly: "I don't know." The officers scrutinised the contents. One of them shouted: "Drugs!" I said: "It's impossible!" Another officer pointed to the cream-white powder and said: "But today, it's possible!" I resisted arrest, screaming: "Someone has put drugs in my room!" I suspected one of the wardens who had access to our rooms; the guy hated me, for dating a Russian girl.

'The officers overpowered me and took me to the police holding cells. At the court I was told to choose: go to jail or return to your country! Within a week I was deported to Kenya. My student aid was cancelled. I was so ashamed of myself that I nearly committed suicide.

'I had no choice but to own up to the embarrassment I had caused my people. I also asked Florence and the church to forgive me. "Please give me a second chance!" I begged in tears. Florence and the congregation did forgive me and I got my second chance. Florence assured me that she was going to stand by me.

'Two miracles happened within six months, believe it or not! A businessman who was a member of the church said to me, out of the blue: "I want to bless you with money that you should give to Florence's parents as a bride-price." Before I could recover from the shock, he said, "I'll also pay for your wedding, the honeymoon, and other expenses." During the wedding, members of my church collected up to 500 000 Kenyan shillings.

'Two months later someone from the Department of Agriculture invited me to their offices. The official said: "We have a scholarship for you to study agricultural economics in Ukraine; your wife can join you."'

'Alleloyah!' enthused Babatunde.

Wananchi, the houseboy, announced that dinner was ready and they went to the table.

'I've told you a lot about Baba, Flo,' said Thom, as he passed a bowl of potato salad to Babatunde. 'Now here he is.'

'Yes,' responded Florence with a sweet smile. 'I'm delighted to meet you in person, man of God.'

Wananchi entered the room with a three-year-old boy who was just waking up, rubbing his eyes.

'Man of God...' said Florence.

Thom touched her arm. 'Just call him Baba, or Mr Okoronkwo.'

'...Mr Okoronkwo,' continued Florence, 'you've made a lasting impression on my husband to the extent that when this boy was born, he said, "Let's name him after two people who made a difference in my life." So our son's first name is Kimathi, which is the businessman's name. And his second name is your name, Babatunde.'

Babatunde smiled widely and then laughed. 'What difference have I made?'

'Your enthusiasm for God has inspired me; I saw you several times in my dreams, and I've no doubt that you were praying for me,' said Thom. 'Now let me tell you a little about my country: the land is vast, and food must be produced; the settler farmers left the country after the Mau-Mau revolution and the uhuru that followed it. My government is so desperate for food security that they invited farmers from South Africa to settle in Kenya. So we Kenyans have to upgrade our agricultural knowledge and skill.'

'That's interesting. So what are you doing at the moment?'

'I've just begun a two-year Diploma in Agricultural Economics, and next year when I complete my studies I'm returning to my country.'

Babatunde told them of his intention to establish a church in Kiev.

'We are going to launch a gospel guerrilla warfare,' said Babatunde.

'It sounds great; go for it!'

'Thank you, Thom.'

Thom assured him of his wholehearted support—spiritually and materially; he also promised to be part of the weekly cell group meetings.

Babatunde spent Christmas with Thom's family at their home. On the 26th December they undertook a six-hour journey to Odessa by the Black Sea. The following day Thom, Florence, the toddler and Wananchi flew to Kenya. Babatunde accompanied them to the airport.

He stood on the airport balcony watching as the Air Kenya plane soared towards the clouds. His eyes watered as he remembered that he would spend the remaining days of the year alone, far from his people. It would be hard to convince his people that he had taken a sound decision in quitting his well-paying job at the TV station, as Ekene had pointed out in his letter. It would be like trying to uproot a towering iroko tree.

## 78

During the second week of January, Babatunde decided to preach the gospel and distribute more leaflets. Around midday, wearing his trademark blue-and-grey checked suit, he strolled towards the entrance to Khreschaty Park in the city centre, leaflets in hand. He was ready to unleash his well-prepared Kingdom sales talk: *Did you have a wonderful Christmas, celebrating the birth of Jesus? Now I want to tell you how you can receive Jesus.* He joined a well-dressed man sitting on a park bench; when he greeted the man, he frowned at him, scanning him from head to foot.

'Please don't disturb my meditation,' the man scowled.

Babatunde apologised and hurried over to a couple crossing the park hand in hand. He expected a smile but the man gripped his wife's hand and walked faster, pulling his wife along with him.

He decided to speak to another couple sitting on a bench further down. Suddenly he heard a voice in him saying: *Hahahaa! You are wasting your precious time. These people don't want your lousy product! You would be happier in a boisterous market in the overpopulated Lagos than in a park in Kiev!*

Babatunde stopped, smacked his Bible and shouted: 'Shut up Satan!'

He came to stand in front of the couple on the bench. They did not respond when he greeted them. The man turned to his partner, gesturing at Babatunde and saying, 'This man is a crazy. That's what I hate about religion.'

Babatunde gave a hesitant smile: 'I'm sorry, *uhm*…it's just…something was disturbing me. Can I…do you mind if…if I join you?'

The man took his wife's hand and stood up to walk away.

'No, please—don't go!' Babatunde pleaded. 'You don't know what you're missing!'

The man stopped and turned back to Babatunde.

'Does this nigger think he can tell us about God?' he sneered. 'Listen, you must go to the jungle of Congo and preach to the monkeys, your cousins!'

The couple strode out of the park. Babatunde sat down on the bench and closed his eyes in dejection. Utterly discouraged, he muttered a prayer before slouching off to the bus terminal to catch a bus home.

After a two-day break he again took to the city streets, where he handed out his tracts; several people received them but a few threw them away. In need of a break, he went to the park, took out his lunch-box and had sandwiches and a cool drink. After distributing more leaflets to people who all seemed to be in a hurry when he approached them, he returned to the city streets. As he stood waiting next to a traffic light, he saw a well-dressed man walking in his direction hand in hand with his partner. Ready with his smile, Babatunde approached them.

'Hallo, my name is Babatunde Okoronkwo. I have wonderful news of how the Lord we have just celebrated during Christmas can be real and live in our hearts. Please take this leaflet and…'

'No, I'm not interested!' the man cut in.

The couple hurried away. Two men who were behind him overtook Babatunde and one of them gestured at him, saying, 'What is this monkey trying to do?'

Babatunde went to the man, bear-hugged him and said with a grin: 'Have you ever hugged a monkey before?'

The man, who looked like a body-builder, grabbed Babatunde by his upper arms and flung him away with such force that he fell to the pavement. As a few shoppers walked over to him he heard a voice inside him shouting, *Get up and fight! Remember that you were once a trained and hardened soldier!* But another disagreed, *No Baba, you can't revenge, for vengeance is mine.* A throbbing pain at his elbow caused him to grimace. *Oh my God, why is this happening to me?* thought Babatunde. *God, are You sure I should be doing what I'm doing? If not, why have You shown me a dream in which I'm preaching to whites?*

An old woman walking by with her husband hurried to him and helped raise him to his feet.

'Are you alright?' she asked him with tenderness.

Babatunde brushed the dust off his suit and forced a smile: 'Yes, thank you, and God bless you, ma'am.'

'Give that monkey some peanuts!' the man who had pushed him jeered loudly as he strode off, laughing, with his friend.

## 79

Babatunde was about to board a bus but he changed his mind and decided to return to the park. He just felt he was not ready to go to his flat. Not in that emotional state. So he trudged all the way to the park where he chose a bench at the corner. He leaned against the back rest and looked heavenward for a moment as if saying, *God where are you at this hour of tribulation?* He closed his eyes, pretending to be drowsy.

*God, are You sure I should be doing what I'm doing?* He did not hesitate to express his feelings. *If not, why have You shown me a dream in which I'm preaching to whites? I wonder what happened to the prophecy that I will be a rising lioness that shall not lie down until she devours the prey and drink the blood of the slain. I really feel like a wounded ram. Didn't the prophet also say I would wear a radiant crown while my enemies are clothed in shame?* He took a long pause. *And what about brother Ish kind words that I will be an African treasure in Ukraine? Look at just what has just happened…*He waited for a moment without getting an answer. *Lord, if you aren't going to walk with me in this journey I can as well pack my bags and deport myself to Nigeria!*

He opened his eyes, divided the Bible into two halves and started flipping over the pages from his right to his left, searching for solace and words of encouragement. His eyes landed on Psalm 27, the first verse: 'The Lord is a stronghold of my life—of whom shall I fear?' He turned a few pages and found verse one of Psalm 25, 'In You Lord my God, I put my trust.' In Psalm 23 he read, 'Even though I walk through the darkest valley, I shall fear no evil…Surely goodness and mercy shall follow me all the days of my life.'

At that juncture he was so comforted that he found himself smiling ear-to-ear. A moment later he burst into laughter. The bubbling joy in his heart resulted in him singing softly, *Imela, Imela, Eze m oh! Okaka onyekeruwa.*

At the end of the song he closed his eyes, still smiling and whispered a prayer which was interrupted by a hand gently tapping his shoulder.

'Are you okay,' Babatunde heard the voice of a middle-aged man with a friendly face. 'I am Pastor Mikhail Turgenev.'

Babatunde introduced himself.

'I have been following you from the spot where an old woman helped to raise you to your feet. I saw all what happened. I was sitting in a restaurant. I had just had my meal and was about to drink my glass of wine when 'Bham!' You were thrown down by one of the rascals. So as you left the spot I wanted to overtake you.'

'Thank you for your concern, Pastor Turgenev. Why did you want to overtake me?'

'I wanted to offer a word of comfort…just to assure you that like that old woman, I did not support the actions and attitudes of those rascals.'

'Thank you sir.'

'Where do you come from?'

'Nigeria.'

'What are you doing in the city?'

'I am establishing a church. God has spoken to me to…'

'God has spoken to you?'

'Yes.'

'Are you sure?'

'Yes. He spoke to me in a dream in which I was preaching to white people.'

Turgenev grinned. 'What if it's the devil, trying to mislead you? The devil can pretend to be an angel of light.'

'No, it's not the devil. It's God. A pastor from my country has confirmed my vision.'

'What is your vision?'

'To establish a big church in this city.'

'I don't think you are realistic. If God is behind you then why is he exposing you to such humiliation I have just witnessed?'

'The devil is working very hard to discourage me, but God in His word is saying, "I am your stronghold and do not be afraid of people or circumstances who are used by the devil."'

'I think you should be man enough to face the truth, that God is clearly telling you that you should just pack your bags and return to Nigeria.'

Babatunde shook his head grinning, 'It's not what God told me.'

'What did God really tell you?'

'To establish a big church in this city.'

'I don't think you need to start a church here because nothing is going to come right. God is speaking to you and you are choosing to ignore the warnings. You would better be a travelling preacher who accepts preaching invitations from different churches.'

'No, it's not what God is saying to me.'

'What is God…? Okay don't waste your breath. Do you really think that people will ever come to a church led by you or stay for that matter?'

'I am not going to listen to the devil's…'

'Can I be brutally frank with you? You can't speak the language fluently and worse still, you have a different skin colour. You have no chance of being successful!'

'I agree with you that…'

'Do you now agree with me that God is telling you not to start a church in this city?'

Babatunde smiled. 'No I agree with you that I have a dark skin. And I may speak broken Russian but my message will be unbroken because the Holy Spirit lives deep inside me. I am therefore confident that in spite of my limitations I will realise the vision that He has deposited in my heart.'

Turgenev laughed with a scorn. 'I was trying to save your time as I see God giving you warning signs.'

'Listen Pastor. I don't walk by sight but by faith.'

'No-no-no! That's not faith but…'

'But what?'

'I don't want you to think that I am disrespectful when I mention the word, 'stupidity' or something in that direction.'

'God can turn my stupidity into something wonderful.'

'The reality you must face is, to be brutally frank again, you are black, you are emotional and you have a hot temperament. Do you really think…?'

'With due respect my friend, I have just told you that I am not moved by what is seen but by faith. What a pity that you are not hot as me! I am going to use my hot temperament to preach the gospel in this city. You must live to see how God is going to use me.'

Turgenev stood up abruptly and looked deeply into Babatunde's eyes before he walked away.

'Yes,' Babatunde continued, 'One day you'll see how God is going to use what you see as problems or weaknesses.'

## 80

'Before Christmas the people weren't hostile but polite. Perhaps it has to do with the mood of the festive season,' Babatunde said, as he updated Thom on his efforts to evangelise in the streets and parks of Kiev; Thom had invited him to his flat during the third week of the New Year.

'But in January,' Babatunde went on, 'people were rude to me, and had no time for me.'

'Why do you think that was?' Thom asked.

'Thom, I have come to realise what these people are thinking when they look at me: "You are black, you have an accent and you come from an uncivilised place. So who are you to preach to us?" I really wonder if I've taken the right decision.'

'No, please don't be discouraged, Baba. You are on the right track. If it's difficult to start with, it doesn't mean it can't be done or that it mustn't be done.'

'You are right,' said Babatunde after a long silence. 'But to be honest with you, I don't feel like going back to the streets and parks of the city again.'

'You don't have to go when you feel like a demotivated combatant. Go out there when you are ready as a soldier of our Lord. Perhaps this challenge is telling you that the strategy is inappropriate even though the mission is spot-on.'

'I see what you mean, Thom.'

Thom snapped his fingers. 'Listen, let's meet in a week. That will give us enough time to fast and pray. On Friday when I come back from the library, I'll pick you up from your apartment. We can have dinner at my house.'

*

Wananchi played with the baby as Florence, Thom and Babatunde had dinner.

'Are you enjoying the food, brother Baba?' asked Florence, frowning a little as she looked at his half-eaten plateful.

'Yes, Sis Flo. You are an excellent cook,' he replied. 'But you know, when one is breaking a fast, one should not fill one's tummy too much. I'll eat more solid food tomorrow.'

'So what has the Lord said to you since we last spoke?' inquired Thom.

'You were right when you said the mission may be excellent but the strategy not appropriate. On the third day of my fasting, God said to me, "Don't waste your time on people who appear outwardly decent; they don't think they need your message. Go out to the streets and alleys and be my hands that touch the poor, the homeless, the jobless, the tramps, the prostitutes and the alcoholics."'

'I have no doubt that that is the right strategy,' Thom agreed, after a thoughtful pause. 'In the days of our Lord the Pharisees rejected his

214

message; they were in fact offended; so Jesus had to reach out to the tax-collectors, the prostitutes and other lowly people. We are behind you, Baba.'

'Thank you, Thom.'

Suddenly Thom winked at Florence. 'This brother should have a life partner, instead of carrying all the load by himself.'

'I know,' said Babatunde. 'And I can assure you that the right time for that is not far away.'

Florence and Thom smiled at each other.

# 81

It's Friday evening and Babatunde was in his flat, looking forward to visiting the city's parks and alleys to implement his new plan the following morning. His telephone rang.

'Good evening,' said a soft old woman's voice, 'My name is Anna Potopaevavich. I met you that day when a ruffian jostled you to the pavement and called you a monkey. Do you still remember?'

'Yes,' said Babatunde, 'I'll never forget that day.'

'Yes. Can I share bad news with you?' said Anna. 'My husband…the old man I was walking with that day, has died.'

'I'm sorry to hear that, ma'am. Was he ill? What happened?'

'Cancer.'

'My condolences, ma'am.'

'Thank you. If you want to attend the funeral service, it will be held tomorrow at Saint Volodymyr's Cathedral.'

*

That Saturday morning Babatunde, accompanied by Thom, boarded a bus that dropped them in Moskovskaya Square. Another bus took them to Volodymyr's Cathedral. Although Babatunde had seen the building before, the place charmed him as if he was viewing it for the first time; he looked on all agape as they walked to the entrance.

Stepping into the building he shuffled along holding Thom's hand, heading for the middle rows of the chapel. He held his breath as he scanned the interior of the cathedral, drinking in the many paintings on the walls and ceiling. The whole cathedral was, in fact, a massive piece of visual art, comprising smaller pieces thematically complementing each other. Babatunde observed that a lot of the pieces were in blue.

Several golden crosses were displayed over the pieces. On top of the largest cross was a painting of Mother Mary in dark-blue robes, cuddling baby Jesus. On other parts of the ceiling he saw paintings of saints with haloes wearing purple robes. In the centre was a painting of Jesus bare to the waist, emerging from a deep-blue tomb with raised arms. As Babatunde stood, absorbed in the feeling of being in heaven, he felt someone tapping his shoulder. A male usher in a blue-and-white uniform led him and Thom to the second row behind the chief mourner and her relatives.

Out of about 300 people, Babatunde and Thom were the only two black faces. Babatunde looked on with utmost concentration as the archbishop, wearing purple and black robes, lifted up a mace; he addressed the congregation who stood to their feet, heads bowed and arms lifted. Six bearded priests wearing brown robes paced around the mahogany coffin, ringing the golden hand-bells which they waved heavenwards at certain intervals.

After the funeral service Babatunde and Thom walked along the back streets of Bessarabka Market, where hobos often went to scavenge for half-rotten fruit and vegetables in the rubbish bins. The two Africans carried tracts which they distributed to the tramps, saying to each one: *God loves you.* Most of the tramps responded with bored expressions. One drunk man grinned, hiccupped and said, *Really?* A few of the tramps read the tracts while others gave the leaflets only a cursory glance before throwing them away.

Ready for home, Babatunde and Thom walked to the nearest tram stop. As they crossed a small park, they saw a hobo sitting on one of the cast-iron benches. What fascinated Babatunde was the fact that the tramp was writing in a black pocket notebook, oblivious to the doves pecking, fighting and mating in front of him.

Babatunde and Thom strolled towards the man and stood in front of him. A little startled, he raised his haggard face and half-smiled at the intruders. He inserted his pen and notebook into a pocket of his greasy jacket and looked at the two Africans, his wary brown eyes examining them intently. They greeted him and he responded with a slight stammer, still viewing them with mild suspicion.

'Apologies for intruding on your space,' smiled Babatunde, 'can we sit with you for a short while?'

'Alright,' responded the man, giving them a shy smile in return.

Babatunde and Thom sat down on either side of him. Babatunde proffered his palm to the man, saying, 'My name is Babatunde Okoronkwo from Nigeria and this is Thom Mutesa from Kenya.'

'I am Alexandrovich Mayakovsky.'

'We are pleased to meet you, Alexandrovich,' said Thom.

'What were you writing in your notebook?' inquired Babatunde.

'Nothing of great importance,' said Alexandrovich, with another shy smile.

'Can we share the good news with you?' asked Babatunde.

'The good news?' asked Alexandrovich, 'What good news?'

'The good news of how God can become your partner,' Babatunde responded.

'How God can become my partner?' Alexandrovich's tone became a little more confident.

'Let's put it this way,' said Thom, 'How God can become your friend.'

Alexandrovich looked puzzled.

'Do you have a friend?' Babatunde asked.

'Not at the moment.'

'If you had a friend, what would you share with him?' asked Thom.

Alexandrovich smiled more widely so that Babatunde and Thom could see his tobacco-stained teeth.

'We would walk together, talk and share food,' said Alexandrovich.

'Great!' said Babatunde.

'In other words,' Thom kept eye contact with Alexandrovich, 'you would share your life with him.'

'Yes.'

'Just as you can share your life with a friend,' Thom continued, 'so God, in the person of His son Jesus, can share your life.'

Alexandrovich looked at his feet for a moment before shifting his gaze back to Thom.

'Food for thought, *eh*?' said Babatunde.

'We want you to be our friend; so can we invite you for a meal?' asked Thom, taking Babatunde by surprise.

Alexandrovich smiled. 'You want to invite me for a meal?' he giggled. 'When?'

'Now.'

Alexandrovich looked at Babatunde, seeking confirmation.

'Yes, you are invited; please accept our invitation,' Babatunde told Alexandrovich who laughed, looking at his hands.

Thom rose to his feet and so did Babatunde. As if they had rehearsed it, they held Alexandrovich by his arms, lifted him onto his feet, and walked with him out of the park towards the tram stop. When the tram arrived, Thom bought three tickets and they sat together in the middle of the tram, all the curious stares in the half-full bus directed at them.

## 82

Florence stood at the kitchen window, astonished to see her husband, followed by a tramp and Babatunde, entering the gate. She was preparing a Greek salad, assisted by Wananchi. Thom led Babatunde and Alexandrovich to a tree in the corner of the garden; they sat on the garden chairs while Thom hastened to the house.

'Flo, we have a special guest,' he said, 'you'll meet him soon. We are still working on him. I invited him for dinner; is that all right?'

She sighed and nodded: 'It's okay, Thom.' She watched him walk to the bathroom, from where he returned holding an old leather bag and hurried back to where Babatunde and Alexandrovich were waiting.

From the bag Thom took out a pair of plastic gloves and handed them to Babatunde, who put them on and started trimming Alexandrovich's hair with a pair of silver and steel scissors. When he'd finished trimming the hair, he cut Alexandrovich's beard. He then applied shaving foam, gave him a disposable shaving blade and took him to the cement basin attached to the toolshed where there was a gardener's toilet and shower. Looking at himself in the mirror, Alexandrovich shaved his face.

Thom walked back to the house.

'Flo,' he said with a smile, 'we are making remarkable progress.'

'I'm pleased to hear that.'

'Now please get me that sky-blue shirt and the navy-blue suit which I said we should bring to give to a needy person in Ukraine,' said Thom. 'The man is having a shower. I'm getting him some clean underpants and a pair of socks. I don't have a size ten shoe for him. But the pair he's wearing is still okay.'

Thom rejoined Babatunde, carrying the clothes, some body lotion and after-shave cologne.

Twenty minutes later Alexandrovich emerged wearing the suit. Babatunde took him over to the mirror where he stood admiring at himself, feeling his smooth chin with his fingers. He turned to smile at his benefactors; they smiled back at him. Overcome, he walked up to Thom and Babatunde and gave them each a hug.

'You are special in our eyes and in God's eyes,' Babatunde assured him.

'Thank you, both of you!'

Thom took Alexandrovich's old clothes and went to a corner of the yard, beckoning to the others to join him. He threw the old clothes into the incinerator, sprinkled them with benzene and took up a matchbox. Alexandrovich touched his arm.

'Please wait!' he said, 'my notebook is in the pocket of the jacket.'

He retrieved the black notebook and transferred it to the pocket of his new jacket. Thom struck a match, threw the flaming stick onto Alexandrovich's old clothes into the incinerator. The three looked on as the smoke curled upwards.

'The old Alexandrovich is dead,' pronounced Thom solemnly. 'Dust to dust, ashes to ashes.' He raised his hand: 'And now the new Alex is born.'

'Alleloyah!' Babatunde shouted.

Alexandrovich embraced Babatunde and Thom, shedding tears.

'Now Alex,' said Thom with a broad smile, 'let's go and meet my family. Lunch is ready.'

As they walked together to the house, it was evident that Alexandrovich still had to get used to the suit he was wearing; he kept flexing his shoulders, touching the lapels, brushing the arms and feeling the texture of the trousers.

'Flo,' said Thom, 'meet our guest of honour, Alex…what's your surname again?'

'Mayakovsky,' responded Alex, smiling shyly at his hostess.

Florence gripped Alex's palm in hers, looking straight into his brown eyes. 'I'm Florence Mutesa.' She motioned towards Wananchi who was standing beside her, holding the baby: 'This is Wananchi. And this is our son, Kimathi Babatunde. Say hello to Uncle Alex,' she said to the little boy.

Alex patted the child's head. The smell of fried potatoes and other vegetables filled the room; Babatunde saw Alexandrovich swallowing his saliva.

When the food was put on the table, Thom prayed and they began to eat. Wananchi kept casting curious looks at Alex who smiled at him. Babatunde observed how vigorously Alex chewed his food, his eyes glowing, and how he was not shy to fill his plate again.

Enjoying every minute, he was the centre of attraction. After the meal, Florence and Wananchi left the three men at the table, returning later to serve them tea with chocolate and a cream cake.

Time passed quickly and soon it was the moment for Alex to leave.

'Alex, it was a great pleasure to have you as our guest,' said Thom.

'Thank you, Mr Mu…'

'Mutesa,' Thom completed. 'But you can call me Thom.'

Alex shook his head, smiling tearfully: 'Mr Mutesa, I don't know how to thank you for…' he brushed the lapel of his jacket.

'You should thank God for leading us to you,' Thom interrupted him.

'We are merely God's hands,' Babatunde agreed. 'It is God you must give credit to.'

Alex nodded, flashing another smile.

'Now Alex, because God has led us to you,' said Thom, 'we want to lead you to Him, so that He can help you to live a better life.'

Babatunde took a booklet out of his pocket. 'We don't want to put you under pressure. But please take this booklet and read it,' he said, handing it over.

Alex took it and read the title: 'Passport into God's Kingdom.' He flipped through the pages.

'That booklet is going to help you understand how you can truly become a child of God,' said Thom.

'Let's meet tomorrow at the park where we found you,' said Babatunde. 'From there we can go to my flat and talk over a cup of tea. Is that alright, Alex?'

'Yes, Mr Kokoro…'

'O-ko-ro-nkwo,' Babatunde helped him to complete his surname. 'But you can call me Baba.'

'I'll wait for you, Mr Oko-ro-nkwo,' said Alex.

'You got it right this time,' said Babatunde smiling.

As they walked towards the gate, Alex suddenly stopped and felt the pocket of his jacket.

'Have you forgotten anything?' inquired Thom.

'I was just checking I have my notebook,' said Alex.

Babatunde grinned. 'Alex, what are you writing in your notebook? I'm curious.'

Alex responded with a bigger grin. 'Lots of funny things. Because I don't have a friend, I talk to myself by writing to myself.'

'Interesting,' said Thom. 'It's healthy to speak to yourself, especially positively.'

'And you'll share those funny things you are writing in your notebook with us one day?' asked Babatunde.

'Yes, I will.'

A block later Thom and Babatunde bade Alex goodbye; they stood looking on as he stepped forward, chest out, head up, his eyes sparkling. Babatunde guessed that Alex could not wait to go and walk with a swagger in the streets in his new guise, in order to be seen by those who knew him as a hobo. He wondered how many people would recognise him.

'I wonder where he's going to sleep tonight,' said Babatunde.

'God will provide,' Thom responded.

## 83

The following day Babatunde found Alex sitting on a park bench, chatting to three tramps. He rejoiced to see Alex reading the 'Passport into God's Kingdom' to curious listeners. After greeting them, Babatunde told Alex to give his friends the booklet if they wanted it. Alex handed them the text and told them that he would see them later.

'So how did it go yesterday?' inquired Babatunde as they strolled towards the bus route, 'where did you sleep?'

'I went to a park next to the Centre of Hope.'

'Centre of Hope?' asked Babatunde. 'It sounds familiar. Where have I heard the name?'

'After the Second World War a nun known as Mother Helena started a soup kitchen for the war orphans. The present venue used to be a church; it was closed by the government many years ago when the leadership clashed with the Ministry of Religious Affairs. The authorities sent the pastor and some of the leaders to prison. It was rumoured that members of the church chose to be part of an underground church rather than become what they called "the state's lapdog".'

'That's an interesting background,' said Babatunde.

'So, the caretaker of the centre was about to close the pedestrians gate when he saw me sitting on the bench. He beckoned me over and as I walked to him I saw curiosity in his eyes. He knew me very well because I was a regular visitor, begging for left-over bread and soup. I slept at the park toilets for many years.'

Alex paused, smiling at Babatunde as if saying: *Are you still listening?*

'So, the caretaker stood rooted to the ground for a short while. Suddenly, he walked towards me, smiling, his hand outstretched to give me a handshake. He asked me, "What's your name by the way?" He did not know my name; he used to call me *brodyaga*.

'He asked me to accompany him to his house and said to his wife, "Do you remember him? He has been sleeping at the toilets at the park for years. Now he's a changed man." He then asked me, "What happened to you?" and I told him all that had happened after meeting you. When I had finished, he winked at his wife and they laughed aloud.'

'So you spent the night at the caretaker's house?'

'Yes. He said I could stay with them for a few days and that he would ask the management of the centre to give me a place that used to be an additional storeroom.'

'Wonderful! Can you see now how the Lord is looking after you?'
'Yes!'

'Now let's talk about the "Passport into God's Kingdom." Have you read the booklet?'

'Yes.'

'And you are ready to do as you were advised in the booklet?'

'Yes.'

'Excellent! Now, whatever I'm going to say, please repeat after me.'

Alex nodded.

'Lord Jesus, I heard Your word and I'm now receiving You as my Lord and personal Saviour. Wash my dirty sins away and make me as white as snow and let Your spirit help me to be Your follower all the days of my life.' Babatunde spoke the words slowly, pausing after each line so that Alex could repeat after him. At the end Babatunde stood up and gave him a firm bear-hug.

'Welcome to the family of God,' said Babatunde with a broad smile.

'Thank you, Mr Okoronkwo.'

'Yesterday Thom said, "The old Alexandrovich is dead, and the new Alex is born."

Is that not so?'

'That's true, brother Baba.'

'So don't look back, Alex. When Sodom and Gomorrah was burning, Lot's wife looked back, and she turned into a pillar of salt.'

Babatunde took his Bible, turned over some pages, and pointed to a passage with his forefinger. '"Jesus said to him, no one who puts his hand to the plough and looks back is fit for the kingdom of God."'

Babatunde spent the rest of the afternoon providing Alex with what he called the 'starter pack'. That included a list of 'dos' and 'don'ts'. He also gave him a Bible.

'Start with the gospel of John,' instructed Babatunde, as Alex sat absorbed in his brand-new Bible. 'That reminds me of an interesting story about an African king who was given a Bible by a missionary. The king turned the pages of the three gospels into tobacco wrapping but stopped as he was about to tear off a page on which John 3:16 was written. I'll tell you the whole story next time.'

'It sounds interesting,' said Alex.


## 84


On Saturday Babatunde was relaxing with Kofi Osei and four West African students when, to his amazement, he saw Alex through the window entering the yard accompanied by five tramps.

Alex knocked at the door and when Babatunde told him to enter, waited in the doorway. Babatunde walked over to him.

'Hallo brother Baba,' said Alex.

'Hallo Alex,' responded Babatunde. "What can I do for you guys?'

Alex flashed a smile 'Can I talk to you?'

'Yes, Alex,' responded Babatunde.

Alex entered, clasping his hands, his eyes focused on where he could find a seat. He waved with a shy smile to the people in the room.

'I'm sorry to bring these guys here,' said Alex in a low tone, motioning towards the tramps standing at the door.

'No problem, Alex.'

'They insisted that I should bring them to you today. The whole week I shared the "Passport into God's Kingdom" with them, and I read the Bible to them. Last week when you collected me at the park you found me sitting with three of them.'

'Oh yes, I remember.'

'Today one of them told me that he was ready to receive Jesus, and I said to him, "Wonderful! But I can't help you, because I have little knowledge of the Bible. You'll need to see the man of God himself on Sunday." I asked him to wait for tomorrow but he said he couldn't wait. And he said, "I want to see him today, the man who changed you."'

'I don't change people, Alex,' said Babatunde smiling. 'It's only God who changes people. Anyway, please let them come in. They are welcome.'

Alex walked to the door and beckoned the men over, and they shuffled into the house with drooping shoulders, their eyes cast down. Their faces appeared not to have seen water for days; their hair was unkempt, their beards telling a story of not having been touched by a razor blade for months. Babatunde, Kofi and the four students greeted the tramps with handshakes.

Babatunde held a quick discussion with Kofi and the others. Two students were sent to the

café to buy three loaves of bread while the other two went to the supermarket to buy disposable gloves, a disinfectant liquid, bath soap, a pair of scissors, a packet of disposable shavers, and five small towels.

'Gentlemen,' Babatunde addressed the hobos, 'we are highly honoured by your visit, which puts smiles on the faces of God and the angels when they see you knocking at heaven's door.'

Babatunde reviewed the 'Passport into God's Kingdom' and also read the Bible to the rapt listeners. Alex noted what was happening around him. Kofi read some Bible verses and asked if everyone understood everything and if they had questions.

The guests were given fruit and fruit juice while the students prepared platefuls of food.

Three of the men asked questions which were answered by Babatunde and Kofi. Alex flipped over some pages in his Bible and offered a few verses. An hour later Kofi and Babatunde led them one by one through the 'sinners' prayer'.

'Brothers-in-Christ,' said Kofi, 'you have taken the best decision of your lives.'

'You've been admitted into God's palace and at this moment a great celebration is taking place in heaven!'

Babatunde applauded and Kofi and Alex joined him. The tramps exchanged smiles and also applauded.

'You are now new creatures in Christ!' Kofi bubbled with joy as he spoke, 'and the old tramps are dead and must be buried when you are baptised!'

Kofi led the applause.

*

On Sunday Thom was pleased to see how the congregation of nine, including the houseboy Wananchi, had increased to fourteen. They held services in the boardroom which had been made available to them by the owner of a marketing company next to the offices of the Kenyan embassy. The following weekend the number reached twenty; each of the tramps brought their friends to Babatunde's flat. After three weeks the boardroom overflowed with converted hobos.

At Babatunde's block of flats the caretaker called him.

'There are too many tramps visiting your flat,' the caretaker warned him. 'The owners are worried that the value of their properties is going to depreciate. And that possible tenants are going to be discouraged by the sight of the hobos.'

Babatunde told Thom about the latest development, and the two agreed that they should fast and pray.

A few days later Alex told Babatunde that he had persuaded the caretaker of the Centre of Hope to arrange a meeting with the board members; the purpose of the meeting was to request the use of an empty church building which could accommodate 150 people. During the meeting, it was agreed that Babatunde's church should pay a monthly fee of 200 AUH, and that the amount would be increased after three months.

Every week more people were added to the church; it was not only hobos who became members. Out of curiosity, relatives of the hobos and alcoholics went to see the black man who had changed the people about whom they had given up hope. Within six months the congregation had over 100 members, and there was a five-piece band.

What also brought people to the church was the healing; nothing as dramatic as the blind receiving sight and the lame walking. Babatunde had 'discovered' the gift of healing by accident. It happened one Sunday when he touched the hands and arms of a former hobo, one of the new members of the church. The man had asked to be prayed for so that he could earn a living. Babatunde touched the man's hand as he was praying. Suddenly the man lifted up his hands and swung his arms, shouting: 'I'm healed! The arthritis is gone!'

The following week a woman suffering from menstrual pains asked to be prayed for. He prayed and touched her belly and the woman suddenly broke loose and cried: 'I'm healed! Fire is burning my belly! I'm healed.' As members of the church applauded, many shouting Alleluiah!, Babatunde waved for them to stop applauding.

He pointed upwards. 'God is the real healer. I'm just the channel. He decides whom to heal, when to heal and what type of illness to heal.'

After the service a woman went over to Babatunde.

'Pastor, my husband is unfaithful,' said the woman.

'Bring his shirt here,' said Babatunde, 'I'm going to pray over it, and he'll return to you!'

Three weeks later, the woman came and stood in front of the congregation to tell them that her husband had returned home and asked for forgiveness for cheating on her for many years.

It was rumoured that young people from other churches flocked to Babatunde's church because they liked the upbeat music and his charismatic preaching style.

Florence was in charge of the Sunday school while Alex was one of two ushers. Wearing a blue jacket, grey trousers, a purple shirt and a red tie, Alex stood at the door every alternate Sunday, smiling and shaking hands with every person attending the service. 'Welcome, enjoy the service,' he would tell them. After the service people would turn and point to him, saying, 'He used to be a bum; we used to see him at the park. Look how he looks now!'

The church was named Centre of Hope Church, with the slogan: *A church expecting the unexpected.* A board of elders consisting of five people was appointed; it included Thom, Olga Ivanov, a retired nurse, Ursula

Raduyev, a retired medical practitioner, Vladimir Sokolov, an accountant, and Gregoriy Yamadayev, an architect.

As it was a church that preached that members should part with a tenth of their salaries, the church funds increased every month. The board resolved that Babatunde should be given a salary

equivalent to that of a high school headmaster, and that his salary would be increased as the church membership increased. Alex received a monthly salary as an administrator. Babatunde moved out of his flat and occupied a three-bedroom house next to the Kiev River. He also bought a silver-grey Volvo.

## 85

One Sunday afternoon Babatunde invited Thom, Florence, Wananchi and Alex for lunch. Florence and another church member had cooked the food. Thom and Florence's son played on the lawn with Wananchi.

'Can you believe that we are in September already?' said Thom. 'How time flies! In December we'll be returning to Kenya.'

'The Lord has sustained us through this challenging time,' said Babatunde.

'Yes. To plant a church and have over 150 members within eight months is no child's play.'

Florence smiled at Babatunde. 'Brother Baba, when we come to your house again, I want us to be welcomed by Mrs Okoronkwo.'

They laughed.

'Jokes aside, Baba,' said Thom, 'Why are you continuing to be a bachelor of a pastor, when so many young women are available?'

Laughter filled the dining room.

'I hope that the Lord will answer my prayer by the time you leave for Kenya,' said Babatunde.

'Hallelujah, Baba!' said Thom.

They shifted their attention to Alex and talked about how the hobos continued to stream into the church.

'Since we are doing very well regarding the hobos,' said Thom, 'I think we should also reach out to old age and children's homes, as you once suggested.'

'You are right, Thom,' said Babatunde. 'This reminds me to visit the preschool where Prof Isayevich's daughter is working.'

*

The following week Babatunde drove to the preschool. The receptionist was not in but glancing round the office, his eyes caught a young woman with a thick brown mane hanging over her shoulders. She sat at a table a few metres from the reception desk, her back turned to him as she spoke on the telephone. When she'd finished speaking, Babatunde rang the bell for attention. The woman turned around and saw him; smiling, she stood up and walked over.

'Good morning, sir,' she greeted him.

'Morning, ma'am.'

'Have you been waiting long?'

Looking deep into her sky-blue eyes, Babatunde was struck by her beauty. 'Not too long.'

'How can I help you?'

'I'm looking for Isabella…I don't know her surname.'

'She is Isabella Arsanov, but she's off sick today. Can I help?'

'I came specifically to see her. I was a student at the Lumumba Friend-ship University in Moscow, where I met her father, Prof Isayevich. When I told him I was coming to Kiev, he said I should come here and say "Hallo" to her.'

She nodded with a smile. 'I'll pass the message on to her.'

Babatunde smiled back: 'Thank you, ma'am.'

He walked towards the door.

'Should I tell her you'll pass here again?'

'Yes, please.'

*

A few days later when Babatunde entered the gate of the preschool, he found the children playing on the swings; others skipped about, chasing one another, shouting and laughing shrilly. He passed a group of boys and girls who, after giving him a quick glance, whispered among them-selves. He wondered what they were saying.

Suddenly a small girl rushed up to him. 'Uncle, please pick me up!'

Babatunde laughed and lifted her onto his hip, stroking her hair. A boy came up and insisted that Babatunde should carry him too; then another girl ran to him and asked for the same favour, and again he obliged. The boy felt the texture of Babatunde's hair, his little hand slipping down to his temples and finally his beard. Babatunde was about to enter the reception area with his small cargo when the woman he'd met on his previous visit emerged.

'Hey, boys and girls,' she said, 'you are burdening the uncle!'

Babatunde chuckled as he put the boy and two girls down, groaning a little, pretending that they were too heavy for him.

'Good morning,' the woman greeted him, with a wide smile.

'Morning, ma'am.'

'You are really the darling of the children,' said the woman, grinning as she smoothed her long hair back to her nape.

Babatunde chuckled. 'I know; children are children, whether you go to China, Timbuktu or Guatemala. They are just little angels without wings.'

She flashed a smile at him. 'It's good to meet you again. Let's go to my office.'

'I have bad news for you, again,' she told him as they sat in her office. 'Isabella isn't here. It's her child who is sick today.'

'That's okay. There must be a good reason why this is happening.'

'You are a positive person. People like you don't stress easily.'

'Thanks for the compliment.'

'I don't know if you are willing to come back here again?'

'Discouragement is not my lot.'

She smiled. 'So what are you doing in Kiev? Studying?'

'I'm planting a church.'

'Planting a church? And where do you come from?'

'Nigeria.'

'Interesting! What's your name?'

Babatunde told her and she introduced herself in turn: 'I'm Yelishaveta Pavlov. So what made you to think of starting a church in Kiev?'

Babatunde smiled, not immediately giving a reply.

'I'm just curious,' said Yelishaveta.

'It's a long story. Perhaps you can listen when I speak to Isabella next time I'm here.'

'When are you coming again?'

'Perhaps in a week. I'm so busy at the moment. Right now I must visit an old age home.'

'What are you going to do there? Pray for old people?'

He grinned at her question. 'We need old folks in the church,' he said. 'Where I come from grey hair is a source of wisdom.'

'That's true. Old people are more stable too.'

He glanced at his watch and said: 'I must go now, Ye…'

'Yelishaveta,' she completed. 'And your name is Bab…?"

'Babatunde.'

'Bah-bah-tun-de. I want to remember it so that I can mention it to Isabella.'

'Next time when I come here, I also want to speak to the children. As you have observed, I'm a friend of children…just like our Lord used to love children.'

'You can do anything else, but don't come and preach to the children here. I don't want parents complaining that…'

'No, I won't do that! I just want to be their friend. I love the children; they remind me of my own childhood. I want to play with them and tell them African folktales.'

Her smile was back. 'Good! I'd love to listen to your folktales too.'

# 86

At the old age home he found the administrator, a woman in her early fifties, standing at the reception desk as if she expected him.

'How can I help you?' she asked after they'd exchanged greetings.

'I am starting a welfare project, and I want to…'

'What kind of welfare project?' interrupted the woman.

'I'll explain it to you in a moment. But let me say first that before I establish the project,' he continued to avoid the word 'church', 'I just want to have a sense of the community; I want to start a working relationship. And one way of doing that is to tell the old folks of Ukraine some stories of Africa.'

The woman smiled. 'Oh that would be interesting indeed. No one has ever thought of storytelling. Which part of Africa do you come from?'

'Nigeria.'

*Oh please don't think I'm going to bring drugs here!* thought Babatunde.

'Great! When do you want to start?'

'I can come tomorrow.'

'Perfect. What's your name?'

He told her.

'I am Nadya Nikolayevna.' She consulted an open diary in front of her. 'I could give you the 15h00 to16h00 slot. That will be after the Orthodox priest has given his members holy communion.'

'Okay ma'am. Can I pray for them after my story?'

'You can preach if you want to. Leaders of various religions visit this place. On Mondays the Islamic Moulana comes here; Tuesdays it's the Orthodox priest; and on Wednesdays a Catholic nun does Bible study.'

'Please give me a Thursday or Friday,' said Babatunde grinning. 'I'll tell a story and preach and pray.'

'I'll give you Friday at 15h00.'

'Thank you, ma'am.'

*

That Friday afternoon, five minutes before 15h00, the old women sat waiting in the hall. They had been told that a black man would come to tell them a folktale from his country. Babatunde entered the hall accompanied by Nadya. An old woman sitting in the front row started to whisper to the women on her left and her right, pointing at Babatunde with a grin.

'Over to you, Mr Okoronkwo,' said Nadya after introducing him and telling the old women the purpose of his visit.

Smiling, Babatunde bowed his head, clapping his hands twice in the gesture of African respect.

'My aunts, mothers and grandmothers, it's a great honour for me to come before you and share a folktale from my country. Who am I to stand before the custodians of knowledge and wisdom?'

He paused and scanned his audience.

'I was told this folktale by grandmother Nwaboudu, the raconteur-extraordinaire. Before she told us the tale she always said: "Remember, my children's children, after I've told you this tale don't tell it to anyone during the day. Fables are told only at night. If you tell them to anyone during the day, you shall surely grow little horns."'

An old woman sitting in the first row smiled at Babatunde and clapped her hands, and other women applauded too. Babatunde thought he had seen that face somewhere but he could not remember where.

'Long, long ago, deep in the forest of Nugwuchukwu, before the white men came to our land,' Babatunde said to his attentive audience, 'there lived a lion who was a king. He had a large kingdom filled by all kinds of animals. One day when he awoke he decided that all the old animals should be killed as they did not work but ate the grass that the younger animals should be eating...'

Babatunde held their attention captured until the end of the tale, when he bowed and then lifted up his hands. The old woman in the front row stood up and led the applause.

Babatunde motioned for them to sit down.

'My aunts, mothers and grandmothers, thank you for listening to my folktale. What is the lesson of the tale?' He paused and smiled. 'You may be old, but in God's eyes you are useful,' said Babatunde. 'It's only the devil who tells people that they are useless because they are old.'

Again the woman in the front row applauded and others followed suit.

'Sarah, the wife of Abraham, was 90 years old when she gave birth to Isaac,' Babatunde continued. 'God didn't say, "You are a useless hag!" No! He must have thought, "Your womb may be old and tired, but I'm going to use it to bless many, many generations!" I am not, however, suggesting that you should have babies at your age,' he said quickly.

The old women guffawed.

'God called Moses when he was 80 years old, and He used him until he was 120 years old. At the age of 85, Caleb led an army and defeated the giant-like Anakim inhabitants of a hill country.'

Babatunde paused and continued: 'I see you as God sees you. I want you to partner with me as I work for His Kingdom. If you feel you can be part of my ministry, I want to talk to you now!'

Babatunde folded his arms and fell silent, looking at Nadya. Again the woman in the front row stood up and led the applause. Nadya gripped Babatunde's arm, leading him towards the door, but he stopped: 'I want to see this mama in the front, whose face looks so familiar,' he told Nadya.

The old woman from the front row walked straight up to Babatunde, bear-hugged him and kissed him on both cheeks. Nadya gasped in surprise.

'I'm Anna Potopaevavich—do you remember me?' the woman said. 'I met you that day when the ruffian threw you to the pavement and called you a monkey. You even attended my husband's funeral.'

Babatunde embraced her and planted two kisses on her cheeks.

'I'm thrilled to meet you again, mama!'

'Thank you very much sir, for your folktale, and for giving us hope that God can still use us despite our age.'

A queue of old women had formed, all eager to shake hands with Babatunde; he had no choice but to give each one a hug. Anna waited patiently.

'Pastor Okoronkwo,' said Nadya, impatient to get back to her work, 'you can find me at the office on your way out.'

'Pastor,' said Anna when all the other women had left, 'I'm inspired by how you told us that God can still use us, just as He did with Sarah and Moses. I don't want to rush into things which I don't yet understand. But I'd like you to meet with me and my friends, so that you can explain to us the word of God and we can have the opportunity to ask questions where we don't understand.'

'Thank you mama Anna for your desire to know more about God,' said Babatunde. 'I'm happy to come here again tomorrow afternoon.'

'Wonderful! But let's arrange it with the administrator.'

Nadya suggested that Babatunde should come before lunch because in the afternoon many of the old people went out for shopping.


# 87

'Once upon a time, there lived a rich man who had two daughters…' Babatunde started his folktale in front of ten women who had gathered to listen to him at the old age home the following day. He'd decided to open the 'soul-winning session' with another folktale to whet their appetites. On his arrival, he had found Anna and her four friends waiting for him in a room where chairs were arranged in a circle. Five other women who were passing by followed Babatunde when they saw him entering the room armed with a Bible.

'One day,' Babatunde continued, 'after enjoying a lunch where the table was decked out with turkey, lamb, vegetables and salads, the widowed rich man called his daughters. Sipping wine, the man smiled as his grown-up daughters entered the dining room.

"Since your mother's death, what do you think about how I'm treating you?" he asked them.

"You are treating us very well, papa," said the eldest daughter.

The younger daughter nodded. "Your treatment is, in fact, excellent, daddy."

The man smiled at them and asked, "Now, how do you love me?"

"Because you have been so sweet to us," said the oldest daughter, "I love you more than honey."

"Well done, girl," said the father; he then gestured towards the younger daughter. "And you?"

"My wonderful dad, I love you more than salt."

"You can't tell me that you love me more than salt, Mothepana. Salt is not sweet!" Her father shook his head, disappointed by her answer.

'The rich man was so upset that he chased his younger daughter away. Years later the elder daughter got married and went to live with her husband in a far-off country. The father remained with his farmhands who looked after his farm, where he had cattle, chickens, vegetable gardens, orchards and crops.

'There was a great drought and the rich man's livestock died in large numbers and the hot sun killed everything that had grown. Ultimately the rich man lost everything. He left his home, taking the last food in the house. He could not even ride a horse or a donkey – they had all died – so he wandered about, looking for a place where he could find food.

'His provision dried up, but he plodded along for many weeks, depending on the kindness of those who gave him a piece of bread and a cup of water. When he thought he would die of hunger and thirst, he saw a farm where the cattle had not died and the grass was green. He collapsed as he finally entered the yard; the servants took him into the spacious farmhouse.

"Here is an old man who is about to die," the servants told their mistress.

'The mistress realised that the old man was, in fact, her father who had chased her out of the house many years ago, but she pretended not to recognise him. Her husband was a successful farmer whose farm was not affected by the drought.

"Give him water, fruit and vegetable soup; also let him have a bath and take him to the guest room to have a nap," instructed the mistress.

'The mistress also told her male servants to slaughter a fattened turkey. "But in separate pots don't put any salt to what you are cooking," the mistress instructed the cook.

'After the old man had taken the first bite of a piece of turkey, he asked for salt. "No, don't give him any salt," the mistress told her servant.

'The mistress turned to the old man and said: "Enjoy the turkey, sir."

"I need salt. I can't enjoy the meat without salt," the old man insisted.

'At that moment the mistress identified herself to the old man: "Papa, I am Mothepana, your daughter."'

Babatunde paused to let his message sink into the hearts of his listeners.

'If we have God in our lives…' Babatunde lowered his voice, no longer speaking in his raconteur's tone, '…we shall be the salt of the earth. We can't do without salt in our homes. Salt is good because it gives taste to meat and it stops meat from rotting.'

Anna nodded in agreement and so did her friends. After that, Babatunde read some verses from the Bible and was asked many questions which he answered to their satisfaction.

# 88

A week later Babatunde was surprised to see Anna and eight other women visiting him at his church office. He was thrilled when they told him that they were ready to be the salt of the earth. The new converts became loyal members of his church from then on.

Every week Anna brought new converts to be taught the word and to be made the 'salt and light of the world', as Babatunde often told them during his Sunday church services and weekly Bible study meetings.

There were several service committees in the church, and the new members were encouraged to be part of the committees. A month after Anna and her friends had become members of the church, a new Feeding Committee was started. The church had decided to feed the unemployed people, and she joined the committee.

One day Anna told Babatunde how her relatives on her late husband's side were not impressed with her faith and how they had not tired of confronting her for attending what they called a questionable church.

'One day when I came back from the Bible study meeting I found a leader of the Orthodox Church, Yuri Gaganov, waiting for me in the visitors' area. He was my husband's distant cousin.

'He said to me, "You are a mother of three children, and you raised them with all your love and care." I wondered what he was about to say. He continued: "So, Anna, how will you feel one day when they are adults and they tell you that you are no longer their mother?" Looking into my eyes, he went on, "And as if that isn't painful enough, your children then go to a stranger and tell her, 'You are our mother!'"

'I said to him, "Yuri, I don't know what you are trying to tell me." I knew full well what he was referring to, but I nonetheless asked him, "Will you please tell me plainly?"

'He said, "I know that you know what I'm hinting at." He gave me a sardonic smile. "The Bible says you can't serve two masters. You can try, you can pretend, but as time goes on, you will spend more time with the master you love most."

'He looked at me to see my reaction then said, "Now let me come to the point. You've been raised as a member of the Orthodox Church. You met your husband in the church and you were married in the church. Your husband died as a loyal member and was buried according to the church rites."

'When I did not reply immediately, he went on: "Anna, it's a known fact that you have become a member of a new church; it's a shame that you are swayed by a mushroom church whose leader is using black magic."

'I was becoming angry now, and I gave him an unfriendly look. Yuri scowled back at me. "Anna, our church is highly disappointed that you no longer see us as your mother. Instead, you are kissing a strange woman. You are telling her, 'You are my mother and I love you.'"

'At last I opened my mouth and said, "So the church leaders sent you to speak to me?" He answered, "Yes. We are trying to help you before it's too late."

'I said to him, "You're already too late, Yuri. And I don't need your help. For me to return to the Orthodox Church would be like a woman returning to a husband who is failing to meet her emotional needs."'

Babatunde grinned. 'And how did he react to that?'

'He stood up and walked out of the room, upset, saying in a loud voice: "Anna I can't listen to your insults!" At the door he stopped and swung back to wag his forefinger at me. "Anna, you'll reap what you've sowed!"'

'He's right – but what you'll reap are the good things,' said Babatunde. 'And if he continues to be nasty to you, he will reap according to his actions.'

*

On Sunday Babatunde and Thom stood chatting in front of the office while Alex and the female usher counted the tithes and offerings. When Babatunde went outside, he found Anna waiting for him.

'Good to see you Anna,' he said.

'Hallo Baba,' she responded.

It had taken her weeks to address Babatunde simply as 'Baba'. She had, out of respect, preferred 'pastor'.

'On Friday,' said Babatunde, 'I almost came to visit you. I was driving past the old age home when I just felt like seeing you.'

'You did well by not coming.'

'Why?'

'The administrator told me that you are no longer welcome at the home.'

'Why? Is there a problem?'

'Yes. She says she has received instructions from above that you must never set foot in the place again.'

Babatunde sighed. 'Have I been declared an undesirable person?'

'Yes. And I have been told to stop recruiting the women. A circular was issued stating that no one is allowed to recruit anyone to their religion. The second paragraph went like this: "We, the undersigned, want to register our complaint that Anna Potopaevavich is actively recruiting us to become members of her church and she keeps on telling us that if we don't cooperate, we'll go to hell."'

'Who has conceived of such an evil thing?'

'Agents of the Orthodox Church. Who else should we suspect? Signatures were collected from the old people and they were tricked into believing it had to do with the improvement of service provision. A woman who claimed to be a journalist from the Department of Social Development said she was writing a short article. But the signatures were used for something else.'

Babatunde shook his head. 'We have all been made to believe that since the fall of communism there is freedom of religion in Ukraine, and that the right to preach is upheld by the new constitution.'

'I sometimes feel that I'm living in a confused country,' Anna confessed. 'Today this is allowed, and tomorrow it's prohibited.'

'Opposition is good for us, Anna.'

'Why are you saying that?'

'It will help us to develop muscles and to grow.'

'Oh, before I forget: the administrator told me that we can't afford to offend the Orthodox Church because they have donated the building that we're in.'

Babatunde paused to consider what he'd just been told.'I think it's about time,' Anna continued, 'that I should go to another old age home.'

'No, Anna, please don't even think of that. Just remain there because God wants to develop your character through a difficult situation. If you can't be a fisher of women in the old age home, you can still do that outside the place. And as you are busy for the Lord at the moment, you'll be a happy person.'

# 89

One morning Babatunde was in his church office when Anna and Alex bade him goodbye and left with two other members to distribute food parcels at one of the parks.

Late that afternoon he was about to lock his office when he saw Alex driving into the yard alone.

'Alex, why are alone? Where's Anna? I expected you and her to be back by midday.'

'It's a long story, my pastor.'

Alex told Babatunde all that had happened at the park.

'We were apprehended and driven to the police station where we were interrogated separately for hours. The officer who questioned me told me: "You are just a pawn of a system you don't understand the workings of." I was too tongue-tied to say anything. Later he said, "You couldn't give us the information we are looking for so you are being released with a warning." I couldn't believe I was free to go. I wanted to ask where Anna was but I was afraid to speak. As I walked out of the interrogation room, I heard the officer call after me: "Do yourself a favour. Stay away from that Nigerian confidence-trickster.'"

While Anna spent the night in the police holding cells, the church leadership held a vigil for her at the church, praying and singing hymns.

In the morning Babatunde, Thom, Alex and two of the women who'd been recruited by Anna waited at the court. Just before proceedings started, Babatunde saw a young man entering the building with a lawyer, identifiable by his gown and the rectangular black leather case he was carrying.

During the brief hearing the magistrate ruled that the state was withdrawing the charges against Anna, without giving reasons.

'Hallelujah! God is great!' chanted Anna, raising her hands heavenwards and throwing kisses upwards with both hands.

'Indeed religion is the opium of the people!' someone shouted from among the spectators audience, as they all left the court.

Babatunde saw the young man hugging and kissing Anna; she held his hand and led him over to Babatunde.

'Baba, meet my only son, Leo.'

'Leonid Potopaevavich,' Anna's son introduced himself, gripping Babatunde's hand with his own.

'This is the man of God I've told you about, Leo,' said Anna.

Leonid smiled at Babatunde. 'My mother talks a lot about you, pastor.'

'Leo is the last-born of my children,' said Anna. 'He's a parliamentary journalist here in Ukraine. My two married daughters live in Kazakhstan and Georgia.'

*

The following day Babatunde visited Anna, who had moved to a new flat.

'Baba, it's good that you visited me at the police station and brought me food,' said Anna with a smile, 'but it would have been even better if your wife was the one who came to see me there.'

Babatunde laughed.

'So, my pastor,' Anna continued with a twinkle in her eye, 'let God help you to meet a woman who'll stand beside you in your life.'

'Tell me what really happened at the police station,' Babatunde changed the subject. 'Alex told me some of it but I want to hear it from the horse's mouth.'

Anna grinned at his choice of words. 'From the horse's mouth? Alright.' She heaved a sigh and launched into her tale. 'We were busy giving the hobos food parcels when suddenly a police van pulled up next to us with a screech tyres. The doors banged open and a police officer marched towards us with a senior officer beside him. "Have you got a licence to do what you are doing?" they demanded. "What licence?" I asked, trying to control my irritation. "A licence from the Department of Welfare. Are you a registered welfare organisation?" the senior officer asked. I don't know why I was so brave—or perhaps, so foolish. I did not want to be intimidated. So I said, "I'm sure you know that we are here representing a church. Our Lord didn't need a licence to help the poor." I saw the officers look at each other. "He once provided bread and fish to feed hungry people," I continued. "The people would have died of hunger if he had first to secure a licence from Pontius Pilate."

'The senior officer turned towards his junior and said, "This woman is hard in the mouth. She knows too much. We are going to have to teach her a lesson. Take her to the van." So the junior officer handcuffed me and led me to the van.

'Then Alex stepped forward and said, "I'm going with her. We are partners in this project."'

Babatunde put his hand on Anna's arm.'I'm sorry this had to happen to you, Anna. I feel guilty that...'

'It's okay, Baba, don't feel guilty or sorry for me. There is a reason why that had to happen to us.'

Anna smiled at him. 'So, man of God, I want to repeat what I said earlier: Get married quickly. You need a life partner! Someone you can share your problems with.' She pointed her finger at him. 'Will you say amen to that?'

'Amen! Alleloyah!' Babatunde laughed. 'God has used you to speak directly to my heart. So please pray for me, Anna.'

'I will pray for you, Baba. But your feet should walk to the woman of your choice, your mouth should speak and your hands should touch the woman of your desire.'

'There's no truth better than this. Thank you, Anna.'

# 90

'The church is growing impressively,' said Thom after the service.

'Yes, we've performed very well, especially among the old people,' Babatunde agreed. 'Anna is doing a lot to promote the church, particularly with her service to the poor; those who are benefiting are flocking to the church.'

'Yes.'

'I think I must now find time to visit the preschool again, the one where Prof Isayevich's daughter is a teacher,' said Babatunde. 'I'll go tomorrow.'

*

When he parked his Volvo next to the gate of the preschool the next day, he saw the children playing on the swings. As he slipped the car keys into the pocket of his tracksuit, he was delighted to see Yelishaveta walking towards him, dressed in a purple tracksuit, her hair smoothed back into a neat ponytail. Struck by her gorgeousness, he caught his breath for a moment.

'I guess that Isabella isn't here again,' said Babatunde once they'd exchanged greetings.

'You've guessed right, Babatunde. See, I've remembered your name,' she smiled, showing her dimples.

'I'm impressed. You can call me just "Baba", Yelishaveta.'

'Okay Baba. And you can call me "Yeli",' she offered.

She then told him some surprising news: 'Isabella isn't here anymore. She sent in a letter of resignation, explaining that she was making preparations to go with her husband to a country in West Africa on a diplomatic posting.'

'I can't complain, Yeli. As I said to you last time, there's a good reason for everything.'

She smiled. 'You're a kind man, Baba.'

He smiled back, then hit his hands together. 'I'm ready for action! Let me have some fun with the children! Let them come!'

'Where do you want to play with them?'

Babatunde looked around the yard. 'Over there,' he gestured, 'on the lawn next to the swings.'

Yelishaveta clapped her hands. 'Come children, come!'

The children ran to them, forming a half moon around Babatunde.

'Children,' said Yelishaveta, 'Uncle Baba is going tell you an African folktale, and he's going to play with you. He loves children. Do you love him?'

'Yes, ma'am!' they shouted in unison.

'Hello children!' said Babatunde, showing his teeth in a smile, 'While *dyadya* Baba is telling you this story, he's going to pause every now and then. That's the opportunity for you to say, "We are listening". In Africa the children say: "*Sala!*" But you can simply say: "We are listening." Is that alright, children?'

'Yes, *dyadya*!' said the wide-eyed children.

'Once upon a time there was a woman who had ten children.'

'We are listening!'

'These children loved wild berries.'

'We are listening!'

Babatunde continued with the story, with the children shouting, 'We are listening!' each time he paused.

'She used to go to plough the field daily, and before she went home, she used to go to the forest to get berries. The children had no childminder. They were looked after by the eldest child. One day their mother failed to bring them berries; she told them that she had been too busy in the field.

'The following day when their mother had gone to the field, the eldest daughter said to the other children: "Let's all go to the forest ourselves and pluck the berries." So they all went to the forest where they found many big and fleshy berries. They started eating, and the more they ate the more they wanted. So they went from tree to tree plucking and eating voraciously. Hours later they found themselves lost in the middle of the thick forest.

'When their mother could not find them at home, she started looking for them; she had no idea where they could be. She first hurried to the next-door neighbours and the relatives who said, "We haven't seen the children!"

'In the forest a hyena saw the children, and she wanted to eat them. So the hyena decided to pretend to be their mother. She could speak like their mother. So she called: "My children, my children, come home!"

'The children said: "We are afraid!"

"Afraid of what?" she asked.

"The hyena!"

"The hyena is not here!" the false mother answered them. "She has gone to nurse her young cubs."

'So when the children tried to run to their mother, the hyena pounced upon three of them, killed them, cut them into small pieces and hung them on a tree as dried meat; she then ran back and waited beside the path where the other children were running and again shouted: "My children, my children, come home!"'

Babatunde paused there, smiling at the children. 'Now, let's play the game.'

They played the game with Babatunde as the hyena. At the end, as the children shouted with shrill voices, asking for a repeat of the game, he turned and smiled at Yelishaveta.

'How do you rate me?' he asked her.

'Baba, you are really the darling of the children! I give you a distinction!'

'Really?'"

'Yes! That was excellent! I've never seen them having such great fun! I really wish some of the parents were here. And I so wish Isabella was here; I know she would be absolutely exhilarated by this African game.'

Babatunde smiled into her eyes, touching her shoulder. 'Okay Yeli. Let me complete the story properly.' He shifted his gaze to the children.

'Listen, children,' said Babatunde. 'The hyena is afraid of the lion. If you walk with God, you won't be afraid of the hyena. If you want to scare the hyena, you must walk with the lion, the lion that loves children.' Pausing for a moment, he scanned the children and said with in a loud voice, 'The Lion of the Tribe of Judah, Jesus Christ our Lord!'

He raised his hand and the children and Yelishaveta clapped for almost a minute. He started to sing a popular Sunday school hymn, and the children stopped clapping and listened to him singing: 'Yes Jesus loves me / Yes Jesus loves me / Yes Jesus loves me/ The Bible tells me so.'

When he repeated the hymn, a few of the girls joined in, and by the time he ended the song all the children and Yelishaveta were singing with him.

Babatunde bowed and stood up straight again with his arms raised, waving his hands.

Again the children and Yelishaveta applauded and shouted. Tears shining in her eyes, she gave him a tight embrace in front of the kids, who laughed, cheered and clapped their small hands together.

# 91

The following week Babatunde returned from an evening meeting to find a letter stuck with a drawing pin to his door. Written by the secretary of the Concerned Church Leaders' Forum of Kiev, the letter invited him to a meeting to be held in three days' time.

Suspecting that the Forum was spearheaded by the Orthodox Church, he discussed the matter with Thom and Florence. Florence advised him not to attend the meeting though Thom disagreed. Her reasoning was that there was no point in arguing with people whose hearts were as hardened as those of the Pharisees of Biblical times. Thom differed with Florence, arguing that if Babatunde could meet the leaders face to face, they would perhaps observe that they did not need long spoons to eat with someone wearing a pair of demonic horns.

On the day of the meeting he drove towards the venue, listening to a cassette; the gospel artist was singing:

> Lord, make me an instrument of Your peace.
> Where there is hatred, let me sow love.
> Where there is injury, pardon.
> Where there is strife, harmony.
> Where there is error, truth.
> Where there is doubt, faith.
> Where there is despair, hope.
> Where there is darkness, light.
> Where there is sadness, joy.

Realising that he was twenty minutes early for the start of the meeting, he decided to visit Yelishaveta at the preschool. The kids mobbed him as expected, pulling at his trousers saying, '*Dyadya*! *Dyadya*! Can we play "The Hyena and the Children"?'

'Hello Baba,' said Yelishaveta, standing in the doorway of her office. 'I heard from the children's shrieks that you were around.'

'I love the children,' said Babatunde, noting the sparkle in her eyes. 'They remind me of my early childhood.'

'Did you have a happy childhood?'

'Yes. But…hm…I will tell you about it next time when I have more time.'

'Have a seat. Can I give you something to drink?'

'No, thank you, Yeli, I'm in a hurry. I'm rushing to an important meeting and I must be there within fifteen minutes. I just felt I had to see you even if only for a few minutes.'

'Thank you for thinking of me, Baba. I know you are a busy man. I need to speak to you too. When you performed "The Hyena and the Children" the other day, you touched something inside of me; so I need a slice of your time if you don't mind.'

He smiled. 'I don't mind, Yeli.'

She gave him a ravishing smile in return. 'Thank you, Baba. Perhaps you can come here tomorrow at 16h00 when I knock off.'

He gave her a tight embrace and walked towards his car parked next to the gate. When he turned for a last look at Yelishaveta, he saw her waving at him. He waved back.

# 92

When Babatunde arrived at the venue, he found twenty members of the Concerned Church Leaders' Forum seated there. After the meeting was opened with prayer, Babatunde saw a tall priest rising to his full height, squaring his shoulders and looking around the room. The man was a commanding figure in his dark suit, crisp white shirt and dark tie. Babatunde guessed he was their spokesperson.

Babatunde thought he had seen his face elsewhere, and sooner than expected, the answer came to him: he had seen the priest during Anna's husband's funeral.

'Concerns have been raised about how some of us here are conducting themselves in an over-zealous manner as they try to increase their church membership,' the speaker said, looking in Babatunde's direction for a moment. 'The purpose of the meeting is to reach a gentlemen's agreement among ourselves as church leaders. I assume that we are all reasonable and respectable, and that none of us wishes to be regarded as a rogue church leader.'

The men around the speaker nodded in agreement.

*Please come to the point!* thought Babatunde.

The speaker scanned his audience for a moment. 'You'll agree with me that straight talk saves time and that it always brings desired results, even if it may be painful to some people.' He returned his gaze to Babatunde.

'Mr...excuse me, Pastor Kokoronko, we all...'

Babatunde raised his hand. 'Objection! My surname is Okoronkwo!'

'Okay, point taken,' the speaker said, waving his hand dismissively. 'We all know that many of our former church members are now attending your church. How do we know this? We have observed from our church records that there's a noticeable drop in attendance; after some thorough detective work, we have traced our lost members to your church. Now, if we are going to have church unity, we must adhere to a gentlemen's agreement. Pastor Oko-ron-kwo, if you are indeed a reasonable man of God and not a rogue of a pastor, you should, for the sake of peace and harmony, return all those members to their original churches.'

Babatunde heard several subdued 'Amens' and saw many of the pastors nodding with smug smiles and grins. He felt like asking, *Gentlemen, where in the world have you seen such a thing taking place?*

The speaker pointed accusingly at Babatunde: 'You have been stealing our sheep!'

Another pastor stood up. 'I support the previous speaker. In my church 75 percent of the youth have become members of Pastor Koko-ro…excuse me, Okoronkwo's church; they say my church is boring and old-fashioned and that his church is modern, the music is nice, and it makes it easy for them to dance.'

Before that speaker had even finished another pastor was crouching in his seat, preparing to stand.

'In my church twenty old women who have been the pillars of my church for many years have joined that man's church,' said the third speaker. 'Now they've decreased the hemlines of their dresses and they sing and jump shamefully high, exposing their knees as if they have taken too much wine.'

The spokesman was on his feet again. 'As far as we are concerned he can keep the drunks and hobos, because after all it was easy for him to manipulate them. But as for the respectable adults and the youth, he must return them to us.'

'Yes, bring them back!' someone else interjected.

As each pastor spoke and sat down heads nodded in agreement. Babatunde was nonplussed. The church leaders were all staring at him, waiting for him to say something; he knew well what it was they wanted to hear.

He stood up slowly to face his accusers, all eyes focused on him. Playing for time, he asked:

'Gentlemen, can I please go to the toilet?'

Now it was they who looked nonplussed. He observed how the spokesman shook his head while others around him nodded, how some of the pastors looked uneasy and frowning, while others whispered and shifted in their seats; one agitated pastor even raised his clenched fist and beat it into his palm.

The spokesman stood up again. 'Gentlemen,' he said with dignity, 'let us not be agitated. In our lives we have come across many challenges. Let him go to the toilet as he requests with three of us escorting him. If he's up to monkey-tricks, then we know which animal we should compare him to.' The remark drew a few sniggers. The spokesman gestured at Babatunde. 'You can go.'

Babatunde walked to the toilet, escorted by three men. He sat on the toilet seat and whispered: 'Lord, please help me. I need your wisdom for this situation. Thank you Lord. Amen.'

Babatunde stood up, opened the cubicle door and found his escorts waiting for him. They accompanied him back to where he was sitting.

Babatunde stood surveying his audience for a moment. 'Gentlemen,' he said, 'we don't steal sheep at the Centre of Hope Church. But one thing we do very well is this: we grow the grass—and we won't deny any hungry sheep who wants to graze it.'

He sat down and awaited their response. Silence hovered in the room; suddenly an angry pastor stood up. 'What do you mean by growing grass?'

Rising again, Babatunde answered him: 'The grass is the Word of God.'

'Are you saying we don't preach the Word of God in our churches?' the angry pastor demanded.

'No, I didn't say that. But we preach the full gospel in our church,' Babatunde responded. 'Jesus said, "Him that cometh to me, I will in no way cast out." Jesus never turned anyone away, and we won't turn away any sheep, either. We are only trying to reach the lost through our sermons.'

'We aren't against your sermons,' said the spokesperson. 'We just want you to return the sheep you've stolen. If you are a decent pastor and not a thief or a rogue pastor, you'll cooperate with us.'

'I'm not going to tell the sheep where they should graze,' said Babatunde, raising his voice. 'The sheep will always go to where the grass is greener. Why don't you make your grass greener? Don't you have enough water and manure?'

'Listen here,' the spokesperson said angrily, 'if you don't cooperate with us, the guilt rests upon…' he shook his finger at Babatunde, '…*your* head!'

'I'm not guilty of anything!' Babatunde replied. 'What I'm doing is putting a smile on the face of God!'

'It's certainly putting a frown on the face of God!' the spokesperson retorted.

The room became silent for a moment until a man at the back stood up. 'Does this pastor know who I am?' the man hissed.

Babatunde grinned at him. 'Sir, who are you?'

'He's a journalist with one of the local newspapers,' another pastor enlightened Babatunde.

'And if you don't cooperate, I'm going to put this story on the front page and ruin you,' the journalist threatened. 'You've no idea what other information I'm going to use that is at my disposal. I've ruined other prominent men in this country and I can do it to you too. In three months your church will be forgotten by everyone.'

'You can write whatever you like,' said Babatunde, unperturbed. 'I've only done what God called me to do and I make no apology for it. Listen here Mr Journalist, wherever the power of God is, the sheep will stay there. Go and write what you like!'

With that Babatunde walked out of the meeting.

He stopped at the door and turned to the group with a grin. 'You don't know what you are missing. You are poorer without me. You don't know that those who know me very well regard me as an African treasure.'

The spokesperson of the group waved an index finger at Babatunde with a scowl. 'Who? You an African treasure?' He opened his lips for a moment as if he would spit. 'I can eat my Bible!'

A mocking laughter broke out as Babatunde closed the door behind him.

A TV journalist waiting outside surprised Babatunde when he pointed his microphone at him.

'Pastor Oko…can you tell us what just happened in there?'

'You can talk to the organisers of the meeting,' said Babatunde.

'I want to know your side.'

'No comment.'

'Pastor,' said another journalist, scribbling in his notebook, 'let's talk about the healing that you do. According to the media and religious leaders, your healing methods are unorthodox and controversial.'

'What do you mean?'

'We've received numerous reports of you shouting at the people as you're supposedly healing them. Why aren't you courteous, kind and gentle like a man of God should be?'

'I become forceful when I deal with the devil because I believe he is the one causing all these sicknesses. And I want to get the attention of those I'm healing so that they should focus on God.'

'But why all this anger?'

'I am angry at the devil.'

'But why then do you punch people on their heads, their shoulders and other parts of their bodies?'

'It is not the believers I am hitting; my real target is the devil. I believe that Satan should not be treated gently or allowed to get away with anything. But no-one is hurt, and the outcome is more important than the method.'

'Recently a story was published that you sometimes kick or touch the women's private parts. Your comment?'

Babatunde shook his head, grinning. 'My methods might be unorthodox but that's an exaggeration. There are women who want me to touch their wombs because they want to have babies. Sometimes, out of respect for their private parts, I touch them with my shoe, not my hand.' He glanced at his wristwatch. 'Thank you gentlemen; now let me go. If you want to speak to me further, you can phone my church office for an appointment.'

# 93

From the meeting he drove straight to Thom and Florence's house. His namesake, the child, was asleep next to Wananchi. He told his friends everything that had happened.

'Well, Baba, no-one said life would be without its challenges,' said Thom. 'The only way of avoiding having to deal with difficult people is to move to another planet.'

'I pity these people who aren't aware how sterile they are,' said Babatunde.

'Yes, they are like clouds without water swept along by the winds.'

'Also trees without fruit.'

'But if God is with you,' added Florence, 'that's all that matters.'

'Stay on course, Baba,' Thom said. 'You don't need the approval of men.'

'Thank you Flo and Thom. I knew that I would leave this place encouraged.'

Florence gave Babatunde a charming smile. There was a mischievous twinkle in her eye, and he knew she was about to say something funny or profound.

'Brother Baba, do you want to be a successful preacher?'

'Yes.'

'Behind every successful pastor there is a faithful praying woman.'

'Amen to that,' said Babatunde.

Thom put his hand on Babatunde's hand. 'You should pray hard, Baba. Cold prayers ask for a denial but it is red-hot prayers which will prevail.'

'Noted, guys. Please continue praying for me,' said Babatunde. 'I think I'm about to get a breakthrough.'

'Hallelujah!' enthused Thom. 'My ears are itching to know more.'

Florence just smiled. Babatunde recalled Anna's advice: *Let God help you to meet a woman to stand beside you. So get married quickly, you need a life partner!*

'You know we'll be returning to Kenya within three weeks,' said Thom. 'So I'll be delighted to meet the woman you are trusting in God for; we serve a miracle-working God, don't we?'

Babatunde took his leave of them and drove back to his house. As the lights of his car shone into the yard on his arrival home, he saw the mulberry tree in the corner of the garden shaking, and immediately knew that something was amiss. Entering the house, he found that he'd been burgled. He soon realised that nothing had been stolen; it appeared the burglars had been disturbed by his unexpected arrival home.

# 94

The following day when Babatunde's Volvo cruised into the yard of the preschool at 16h00, he saw Yelishaveta standing in front of the building with folded arms. She was the last staff member to leave the premises. She was wearing a knee-length red floral dress that showed off her shapely calves.

He stretched across to open the car door for her and she climbed in, squeezing his hand in greeting.

'Nice car,' she said with a smile.

'Thank you. How are the children?'

She chuckled. 'You mean "those little angels without wings", as you once called them? I'm glad they aren't here; they would jump into the car and shout *Dyadya! Dyadya!* – hoping that you would regale them again with "The Hyena and the Children".'

They both laughed.

With Yelishaveta directing him, Babatunde drove to her apartment about thirty minutes away. As they got out the car and walked to the entrance of her building, Babatunde said:

'As I walk beside you, I'm reminded of the days when I was a student in Russia. I recall the incident of an African student who dated a Russian girl. One day the police raided the girl's flat when he was there and inter-rogated him rudely in front of her, in order to embarrass him.'

Blushing, Yelishaveta unlocked her flat, which was on the ground floor. 'How many years ago did that happen?'

'Seven or eight.'

'Well I'm sure things have changed since then.'

'I don't think they have changed that much.'

Yelishaveta left him to make himself comfortable while she went to change. She reappeared wearing a green and white tracksuit and sat on the couch opposite him. His face lit up to see what she was wearing. 'Ah, you have put on the colours of my country's flag!'

'What is your country?'

'Nigeria.'

'Yes, you told me once. Would you like to have tea or coffee, or something cold?'

'Tea, please.'

He looked around the walls of her lounge and saw three framed photos showing a teenage girl and a young woman dressed as a beauty queen and wearing crowns.

'Is that you?' he asked, pointing, as she rejoined him with the tea.

She smiled. 'Yes. There's a long story behind that. That's partly why I've invited you to my flat.'

She put the tray containing two white chinaware cups and saucers, a teapot, honey and biscuits down on the coffee table.

She took a sip of tea, then put her cup down and looked into his eyes. 'Baba, I have invited you to my flat because it would be inappropriate to discuss what I'm going to tell you in a public place.'

He took a draught of his own tea, his focus on her.

'I told you,' Yelishaveta continued, 'that your performance of "The Hyena and the Children" touched something deep inside me. I'm going to tell you now about my background. It's always a journey that's painful for me, but I hope I'll feel better afterwards.'

'I guess that'll be part of your healing,' said Babatunde.

'Exactly!'

They sat quietly for a moment, sipping their tea and eating the biscuits.

'I was raised by Christian parents. My father was a pastor of the Baptist Church in Odessa. But outside our home and the church I was surrounded by communism wherever I went. What I was taught in the family and the church, the world out there waited to 'unteach' me. At school there were very few pupils who had Christian parents. Those of us whose parents were pastors and church leaders were known by our teachers. When

I was in Grade 3 I was eleven years old, and I had a woman teacher who raved about communism.

'I used to sit in class at a desk of three, sandwiched by Svetlana on my left and Lydia on my right. Lydia and I used to attend the same church. The teacher, Mrs Byrda, taught Maths, but she always had what I call 'a commercial break', during which she promoted communism. She used to start by saying: "Communism is wonderful!" And she continued by saying that because the Soviet Union was a great country, America hated us and was jealous of us.

'One day she said to Lydia and me with a sarcastic smile: "Some of you, your parents are Christians, and they tell you that when you die, you are going to paradise. That's absolute hogwash! Poppycock! In communism we believe in the earthly paradise, not in pie-in-the-sky nonsense!"

'Svetlana used to play with me, but the moment she discovered that I had Christian parents and that I wasn't liked by our teacher, her attitude changed. She stopped playing with me, and one day she brought a boy who was known to be a bully to confront me during break. The boy—his name was Khanid—clenched his fists and scowled at me. "If you and your parents are not communists," he said, "why are you in the Soviet Union?" I was very embarrassed, and all I could do was mumble: "But I don't know any other country in the world."

'"Communism is wonderful!" said Mrs Byrda one day. "Here everything belongs to everyone, and there's equality, freedom and brotherly solidarity. Under communism everyone receives whatever he needs. Bacon will fry in every pan."

'Our teacher paused there, to signify that she was coming to a great announcement. All of us waited for what this prophetess of communism had to say. Our expectations were raised to a high pitch.

'Then she said, addressing her words directly to Lydia and me: "and *you* can lick the hot frying pan clean!"

'The whole class sniggered as I stared at the teacher, dumbfounded and humiliated.

Svetlana poked me in the ribs with her elbow and made a face at me; there were jeers from around me. I expected the teacher to come to my defence, but she just stood there smiling smugly, with her arms folded. I jumped up, opened my school bag, took out a ruler and lifted it up with the intention of beating Svetlana on her head. But she shielded her face with her bag; so I beat her on her thigh thrice with all my might and ran out of the classroom.

'My world collapsed. For two days I lay in bed with a high fever, hallucinating: "Mama, I don't want to lick a burning-hot frying pan! I want a piece of bacon!" I cried bitterly. She rocked me to sleep on her shoulder, whisper-singing: *Yes, Jesus loves me / Yes Jesus loves me / Yes Jesus loves me/ The Bible tells me so.* She prayed for me and assured me that everything would be alright.

'I went back to school after two days, expecting the worst. But I was amazed when Svetlana, the girl who hated me with a passion, gave me a smile and shared an apple with me, and the teacher was friendly to me. I thought that my mother's prayer had yielded the best results. I also thought that the teacher and the pupils who hated me must have missed me for two days, and that they perhaps regretted how they had treated me…'

Yelishaveta broke off, surprising him by suddenly standing up and saying, 'Let's have a short break.'

'Alright,' said Babatunde, a little puzzled.

'You can go and stretch your legs,' she told him. 'Take a peek at my garden through the window while I bring something to eat.'

# 95

She hurried off to the kitchen, returning with a side-plate filled with peanuts and dried fruit.

Sitting down again, she continued with her story.

'A year later, when I was twelve years old, the KGB came to our house one Saturday morning. As usual my father was in his study reading the Bible and praying. When my father saw them entering the gate, he called my mother and said to her: "They have at last come for me. Don't worry, Nati"—my mother's name was Natalia—"God will look after me, and He will look after you and Yeli."

'The police instructed us not to speak to my father; they gave him fifteen minutes to pack his toiletries and clothes. He was very composed. I saw no trace of fear or anger in his face as they led him to the police van.

'My mother stood gripping my hand as we watched. I cried and tried to extricate my arm so that I could run to him, but she would not loosen her grip. We walked with him to the police car; I could see my father's lips quivering and I knew he was muttering a prayer. As the police officer opened the car door for him to get in, my father turned to give me a last look. I shouted to the police officer: "Uncle, uncle, please don't take my father away! Please, I beg you!" I continued crying while my mother laid her hand on my head.

'My father said softly, "Nati, Yeli, God will look after you. Don't turn to the left or the right, just stay on course. Read the word and pray every day."

He got into the car with dignity and the door was slammed; the car drove away. It was like a hearse carrying my father's coffin.'

Babatunde went to sit next to her and gave her a warm hug. 'Yeli, if it's too painful, please don't continue. We can talk about it another time.'

She put her hand on his knee. 'It's okay, Baba, I want to continue.'

Babatunde patted her shoulder. 'Are you sure?'

'Yes.'

But when Babatunde continued to look into her eyes, she couldn't hold back her tears.

'Excuse me,' she said, hurrying off to one of the rooms. It was a while before she returned, her eyes still teary. She sat down next to him and he took her hand.

'Are you sure you want to continue…?' he asked.

'Yes!'

Her bright smile on a face that had just released tears reminded Babatunde of sunshine immediately after a cloudburst.

'As they took my father away, I looked into my mom's face and saw tears streaming down her cheeks. I was crying too. She tried to comfort me, singing, *Jesus loves me/ Yes Jesus loves me/ Yes Jesus loves me/ The Bible tells me so*. But I was too heartbroken to sing with her.

'In the afternoon members of the church dropped in at my home. Word about my father's arrest had reached many ears. The atmosphere was very sombre; it was as if my father had died. Most of the people who were there were women. They all said, "Mikhail was a good husband and a good father." They talked about him as people would talk about a dead person.

'In the evening my grandmother on my mother's side came. I kept saying to my mother: "Mama, will they not come for you tomorrow?" and she replied, "My life is in God's hands, my child."

'My grandmother, who overheard me, asked my mother: "If those hawks take you tomorrow, what should we do with Yeli?" My mother answered: "Her life will be in God's hands, mama." Towards midnight, I still had not slept and I overheard one woman saying to my mother, "Nati, if we are seeing you for the last time, we are leaving you in God's hands."

'On Sunday morning after we had had breakfast and I was washing the dishes, my grandmother who had been outside entered and said to my mother, "Nati, they have come for you; I knew that the vultures are hungry."

'As my mother was packing her bag, my grandmother made me sit on her lap, patting my chest and whispering a prayer. When my mother was ready to be escorted to the police van, she came to me and kissed me on my lips, my cheeks and forehead; then she walked towards the policeman waiting for her. Screaming, I jumped from my grandmother's lap, ran towards my mother and clung to her dress, not wanting to let her go.

'A policeman reprimanded my grandmother for not holding onto me; my granny came and took me into her arms while my mother helped remove my hands from her dress. Another officer stopped, turned to me and gave a mean smile, "Your father is going to jail because he loves his Jesus more than you." Granny crouched beside me for a moment and said, sighing: "Father, into Your hands I place her." That was all the goodbye we had before my mother was pushed into a "Black Maria".'

Yelishaveta bowed her head, held her face cupped in her hands and sobbed until she hiccupped, her shoulders shaking. Babatunde patted her arm, massaged her back and then tenderly kissed her on the cheek. As she turned towards him, tears glinting in her eyes, he found her so irresistibly charming that he felt like kissing her right on the lips.

'Thank you for listening to me, Baba,' she said to him softly.

Babatunde smiled and put his hand over his heart; it was as if he was trying to block her eyes from seeing his naked feelings towards her.

'Thank you for sharing your pain with me, Yeli,' he said. 'I'll listen to part two of your life story next time.'

*

Babatunde was very thoughtful as he drove home. When he arrived back at his house, he found that there had been a second burglary. In his bedroom his clothes were strewn all over his bed and the drawers of his wardrobes had been emptied. In his study he found the two four-drawer cabinets opened, and the drawers pulled out; he could see that some files had been taken. He realised that the file in which he kept hard copies of his sermons was one of those missing. He had fortunately saved the information on a floppy disk which was in Thom's care.

# 96

'After my mother was taken, I was sent to a children's home in Kiev,' Yelishaveta continued with her story when they met again. This time Babatunde had taken her to his house.

'What happened to your grandmother?'

'She spent a few hours with me at the home. A court enforcement official allowed her to go there with me.

'In the hours after my mother's arrest, I cried without stopping. Just before sunset, a woman wearing a blue uniform arrived at my home; she told me that she was not working for the police but was a court enforcement official, and therefore a friend of children. She said that the next morning a government car would fetch me and take me to a place where I would live with other children.

'When we arrived at the home children came to welcome me, but I was not yet ready to talk to them. I was still depressed. I didn't want my granny to leave immediately; if I wanted her to, she could stay with me for a week. The overseer of the home, Mama Magdalena, led me and my granny to a room that contained four double beds. She then took us to the dining hall where my granny and I were given lunch; we had arrived two hours after all the other children had finished eating. As I had no appetite, I only ate a big red apple.

'Mama Magdalena left us alone together in the dining hall. We spent an hour there without talking much; I was happy that my grandmother was with me at least. She held my hand and smoothed my palm with hers.

'"Yeli," she said softly, "when I leave you within the hour, God is going to continue to hold your hand. So you won't be alone; God is with you even if you can't see Him. Your parents have taught you how to pray, so continue to do that when you are alone. But even if you are with other people, you can still pray without opening your mouth and speak to God, the father of orphans. What you must know is that God has not forgotten you."

'She kept quiet for a long time, continuing to hold my hand and stroked my palm. One of the female workers at the home came and told my granny that she had five minutes left to spend with me. My granny led me by the hand to the door. On the lawn between the dining hall and my room, she stood looking at me.

'"Yeli, you aren't in jail. You are at the children's home. Some of the world's great leaders once lived in children's homes. Joseph the son of Jacob was in jail but God had not forgotten him. So remember that God has not forgotten you."

'She kissed me on my cheeks and forehead and walked away. I could not shed a tear; it seemed I had cried all the tears out of me. But I did cry when I saw her getting into a bus in the street. As I stood sobbing, I felt a hand touching my shoulder. I looked round and saw three girls who told me that they were my roommates. The older girl held my hand, and another put her hand on my shoulder. The older girl said, "Come with us, you'll be all right. Every child who comes here feels out of place at first, but she soon gets used to the place and have fun."

'And that was what grandmother had advised, but all I could do was to look heavenwards and say, "God why am I here? Why didn't you stop the police from taking my parents? God, have you forgotten me?"

'I started crying aloud and a woman who came to check the toilet rolls heard me and went to call Mama Magdalena. She took me to my room and told me that I should try to be part of the children and that I would get used to the place soon. She encouraged me to make friends. "If you reach out with a hand of friendship, many hands will reach out to you, and you'll be a happier child."

'At the school and at the home everybody went out of their way to appreciate me and to give me affection, but I could not receive love and friendship. It was just too difficult for me to open the hand of friendship as Mama Magdalena had advised me to do. I felt that no-one could love me better than my parents. I didn't stop crying throughout the next day, for the whole week and for the whole month; I missed my parents terribly, and I knew they missed me.

'But as time went on, I decided to love myself. I thought that the best way of demonstrating that was to look after myself very well and to always put on my best dresses. When no-one was looking I used to walk like the models I'd seen on the catwalk on TV; I'd put my hand to my chest, on my waist, and turn my hips sideways.

'One day one of the aunties found me in the toilets pracising my catwalking and she said, "You are going to be a beauty queen one day." From that day onwards people always said I would be a beauty queen. The pain of not living with parents became less as I learnt to appreciate myself and as other people paid me compliments. But there were days when I still missed my parents terribly and the pain became unbearable; I would cry, and no-one could console me. During such moments of depression I kept away from other people.

'One weekend I was alone in the room, crying while the other girls were playing, when I heard a knock at the door. Opening, I found Mama Magdalena standing there with a young man beside her.

"He's your visitor," said Mama Magdalena, leaving us together. The nice-looking young man introduced himself as Nikolai Khodorkovsky; he said he had been a friend of my father's. I was delighted that Nikolai came into my miserable life. At home and at the school the staff liked him, and they allowed him to see me. Whenever he came, Mama Magdalena or the headmistress would smile at me and say, "Niki is here." When he stayed away for a week or a month, I yearned for him, even more than I did for my parents.

'During the first holidays I was sent to live with my guardians. Although they were loving and kind to me, I still missed Niki. My guardians made me forget my religious beliefs completely; they told me that if there was a God, he would have stopped the police from taking my parents. They said I should not cry for my parents because they had done a terrible thing by trying to be gods above the Soviet Union leaders.

'In the evenings before I slept, my guardian mother waved the Soviet flag around my bed and assured me that I would be protected throughout the night. When we had breakfast, they told me that I should bow to the Soviet flag and thank the Soviet Union for providing me with food.

'One Friday the manager of the home told us that the five children's homes in Kiev would hold a beauty contest and that I would represent our home. When Niki visited me he was thrilled to hear I was going to take part in a beauty contest in four week's time. I was pleased when he told me that he would attend.

'It was the happiest day of my life when I was crowned the winner of the Kiev Beauty Contest; Niki came onto the stage and kissed me. I was given three nice dresses and a handbag full of toiletries as well as a cash prize. I was proud of the achievement and wished my mother was around to see me. I kept hoping that she would be released, and that one day I would introduce Niki to her.

'I had a photo in which I was smiling as the crown was put on my head and I kept it safely, to be shared with my mother. More rooms were built in the home and I was one of the girls to have a room to myself. I pasted magazine pictures of older beauty queens on the walls of the room. I did well at school, obtaining over 60 and 70 percent in all subjects.

'When I turned sixteen, I received the shattering news that my parents had died in prison. Mama Magdalena said a government official had brought a short letter which stated that my parents died of a heart attack and cancer. I remember that it was a Saturday morning. She and the staff tried their best to comfort me but I was inconsolable. I did not eat lunch or dinner.

'On Sunday I could not have my breakfast either; I remained alone in my room. Mama Magdalena was concerned. She pleaded with me to eat something; she brought cooked porridge with milk and sugar, bacon and fried eggs, an apple and a pear, but I told her that I had no appetite.

'As I continued crying, my face buried in my pillow, I heard my room door open quietly. I thought it was Mama Magdalena; but it was Niki. He held me gently by my shoulders and let my head lean against his chest. Why did he come at that time when I most needed to see him? The thought that he must have been sent to me by God comforted me greatly.

'Niki started to visit me regularly. He brought me exciting books from the KGB about the vital work of the watchful men of the Tscheka, the state security forces of the KGB. I read voraciously, at times right through the night; there was a vacuum inside me that I was trying to fill. Niki took me to the office of the Communist Party where I joined the Komsomol.

'One day he told me that the Komsomol leadership were thinking of a novel way of promoting the organisation among girls; he said they intended to organise the Miss Kiev Komsomol contest. The contest was organised, and I was crowned Miss Kiev Komsomol. About six months later Miss USSR Komsomol was organised, and I became the queen.

'By that time I'd completed my high school education. Niki took me to the Department of Labour to do a course of my choice. Because I was raised in the children's home I had the desire to work around children; so I chose to be trained as a preschool educator. I stayed at a boarding house owned by the Department of Trade and Industries.

'When I turned twenty, I obtained a Child Minder's and Educator's Certificate. I got employment at a preschool educator near the boarding house. One weekend, Niki came to my room and held my hand: "You look mature and beautiful!" I thought it was an innocent compliment. But he immediately proposed marriage, and I accepted without hesitation. I could no longer imagine a life without him. I was indebted to him after all that he had done for me over the years.

'After the wedding I discovered that Niki had been married before and was divorced. I easily forgave him for not telling me. He had told me that he was a mechanic in a factory. I was never able to find out what he actually did. What did it matter? I was very happy to share my life with him. There was no lack of money.'

## 97

'Three months after our marriage we were transferred to another city.' Yelishaveta continued to relate her story to a rapt listener. 'He told me that the transfer had to do with his work; I asked no questions. We lived on the outskirts of the city. Niki liked to take a walk round the neighbourhood before going to bed. One night as we were strolling we heard someone singing.

'We stopped to listen. The voice came from a little yellow house; I had walked past the house many times on my way to the supermarket. I said to Niki, "Let's go nearer and listen." Someone was singing, accompanied by an accordion: *Yes, Jesus loves me / Yes Jesus loves me / Yes Jesus loves me/ The Bible tells me so.*

'Niki looked at me intently and said, "There are believers in this house." I said, "Oh, she can sing beautifully." Niki said, "Why don't you befriend her?" I asked, "Do you know her?" and he said, "I sometimes greet her when I pass by her home and see her in the yard. She's got a friendly face." I said, "Why should I befriend her?" He replied that while I was looking for a job, it would help me to have a friend so that I should not be bored while he was at work.

'That night I turned from side to side, unable to sleep. I was reviewing my long-forgotten childhood, how my mother used to sing, *Yes, Jesus loves me,* and how she once sang that song to comfort me when I was crying after my teacher Mrs Byrda had said that I should lick a hot frying pan clean because I was a Christian.

I also recalled how my mother sang the song the day my father was taken away by a Black Maria. I recalled the scene as my mother was taken by the KGB, and how my grandmother remained and comforted me as the police van disappeared with my mother inside. So I lay awake until the first sounds of the morning. Finally I fell asleep on Niki's shoulder.

'A day after Niki suggested that I should speak to the "yellow house" girl, I walked past her home. It was in the morning and Niki had just left for work. I was on my way to the store when I saw the girl closing the gate. I recalled Niki saying that she had a friendly face. I was a few metres behind her, so I overtook her and we exchanged greetings. I introduced myself and she told me that her name was Marina Aksenenko. She was also on her way to the store.

'We walked together, and I said to her, "Last night while my husband and I were strolling past your home, we heard a melody through the window. It reminded me of something about my past." Then I said, "You must be a believer, aren't you?"

'She said she was a Christian. I said to her, "My parents belonged to a Pentecostal congregation. They were arrested and died in prison." She expressed sorrow and comforted me. She told me that she had not gone to school because her schoolmates were sent to a farming area to help with the harvest, and that she was excused because she was sick. I told her about my background, including the fact that I was a member of the Komsomol.

'When we returned from the store, I admitted that I didn't know whether there was a God, but that the Christian melodies had appealed to me. They sounded very happy and peaceful. She responded with a smile and I felt that she did not want to enter into the debate about God.

'On reaching her home she asked me if I would like to meet her parents and I agreed. My attention was attracted to an inscription on the wall: "God is Love." Suddenly Marina took up an accordion and sang me Psalm 23. I was thrilled.

'That evening Niki asked how I'd spent my day and I excitedly told him about meeting the "yellow house" girl. I told him everything that had happened and he said: "How were her parents?" I replied, "They are a wonderful couple. They reminded me of my parents." I added: "They invited me to their meeting. Do you think I should go?" And he replied, "Of course you should go. But please, don't even think about your parents. That won't bring them back to life." I was taken aback by his response which I thought was harsh and insensitive but I decided to be forgiving.

'As we were about to celebrate our first wedding anniversary, we were again transferred to another location. A night before I was to part with my fellow believers, the police raided Marina's home and many Christians, including our leader, Tima Stolyarov, were arrested and sent to prison.

'At the new location it took me two months to find a new Christian cell-group. I missed Marina's group, and I desperately hungered for a cell-group. One day I was standing in a queue at the greengrocer when, oblivious to the people around me, I sighed, 'Praise the Lord!' A woman behind me leaned forward and said, "What did you just say?" Embarrassed, I said, "Nothing!" She said, "I heard you!" I said, "What did you hear?" She whispered, "I know you are a child of the King, I'm also one!"

'Later when we came out of the supermarket, she told me that she was a member of a cell-group and she gave me particulars of where she lived.

'At home I kept telling Niki about what happened at the home-cell. When I asked when he would become a member, he just shrugged and smiled lamely, saying, "Time will come."'

'Then, something terrible happened: Niki died.'

'Oh, how tragic. How did he die?' inquired Babatunde.

'He was accidentally shot at a shooting range, where a party was being held. A few people had brought their sons. The kids were shown a TV cartoon show, "The Soviet Tarzan." After the viewing the adults were having drinks when a boy took one of the guns and pointed it at Niki. Everybody thought the boy was just playing. Before they could disarm him, the boy said: "I'll shoot you, America!" and he shot Niki in the head; he was taken to the hospital where he died the next morning.'

'I'm so sorry to hear that.'

'I discovered after his death that he was a KGB operative.'

'How did you find out?'

'Before I answer that question, I must mention that a month before he died, the new home-cell I had joined was raided by the KGB and the leader was sent to prison. How I came to know that he was a KGB officer was this: a former KGB officer confessed it to me, and what he said made sense.'

'Tell me how that happened.'

'There is an old man whose granddaughter was one of the children at our preschool. One day after the parents' meeting he said, out of the blue: "Can I visit you at your house? I have important information to disclose." I said, "No, Mr Chernenko, please visit me here at the preschool." And he said, "But it's very confidential and sensitive." I said, "Then come after the staff and children have gone home."'

'The following day he arrived at the school, driven by a friend. He reeked of vodka, but he insisted that I should take him seriously. He had taken liquor, he said, because he would find it too difficult to speak when he was sober. I said to him, "Okay, speak to me." He said, "I have a confession to make." I said, "Go on." And he said, "Your husband was a KGB officer." I said, "How do you know that?" and he replied, "I was his immediate superior at the local KGB headquarters. His rank was lieutenant."'

'I was shocked beyond words but I tried to concentrate on what he was saying because I didn't want to lose important information. I said to him, "Mr Chernenko, I'm not going to believe you unless you provide more details." He smiled and said, "Did you ever really know his occupation?" I replied, "He told me he was a mechanic."'

'Mr Chernenko laughed and said, "He told you that? Did you ever go to his place of work and find him with greasy hands, wearing an overall?" I replied, "No." He continued, "You don't even have an idea why he was transferred, do you? Let me tell you: we had an important meeting with your late husband. I was there with my three senior colleagues. Your husband said to us, "I'm afraid my wife went too far. She has become a convert, and she has even begun to pray, and she sings the song which she says her mother used to sing to her."

"I said to your husband, "Don't worry lieutenant, you have completed your assignment perfectly, and now it's time to transfer to the south." Mr Chernenko waited as he realised how shocked I was by his confession.

'He continued, "As a Christian you were like a lamb sleeping with a lion. You had no suspicion about the kind of work he was doing, and you told him everything about your meetings. That's why when we interrogated Stolyarov, we knew that members of your group had shared meals." I sighed with shock and said, "Mr Chernenko, thank you for your confession – but tell me, why did you decide to confess all this to me?" He replied: "I don't want to be killed by guilt, and I want to close that chapter of my past life."'

Babatunde touched her arm. 'I understand how betrayed you must have felt,' he said.

'I'm treating the whole thing as part of my history. It was something that had to happen to me, for whatever reason.'

'Yeli, thank you for sharing your history with me.'

'Baba, thank you for listening.' She looked down at her hands. 'For years I have avoided intimate relationships with men.'

'You lost trust in men?'

'Yes.'

'You are going to heal, Yeli. Because you must lead a normal life. You can't live in the past.'

With misty eyes she smiled back at him.

## 98

A day later Babatunde drove to the preschool where he handed an envelope to the handyman and asked him to deliver it to Yelishaveta.

Inside was a note on which he'd written:

Hi Yeli. It was great listening to you and sharing about your past. I am confident that the challenges of the past were a good foundation for your future. You are a strong woman and I admire you. When you knock off, please don't rush to your apartment. Wait for me. BO.

When he entered her office later that afternoon she rose to her feet, a smile spreading over her face. He stepped towards her and they embraced; he felt an urge to plant a kiss on her cheek but restrained himself and instead patted her back. Holding her hands, he looked deep into her eyes; again he had to restrain himself from kissing her on the lips.

'Thank you for waiting for me, Yeli,' he said.

'Thank you for the kind words in your note.'

'You are most welcome. I'm rushing to a meeting. I just wanted to bring you this…' He unwrapped the brown paper parcel he was holding and took out a bouquet of red and yellow carnations. She gasped and clasped her hands.

'To wipe away your tears,' he said handing her the flowers.

She gazed at them silently then leaned towards him and kissed him on the cheek. *Testosterone, I'm not going to listen to you!* he said to himself.

'Thank you so much, Baba,' she said, her glistening eyes darting from the flowers to his eyes and back to the flowers.

'It's my pleasure to be a blessing to you, Yeli.'

*

A few days later Babatunde was with Yelishaveta at his house. He had collected her from the preschool and invited her for a cup of tea. After they had enjoyed their tea and biscuits, he touched her hand and said:

'Can we stretch our legs in the garden?' Holding her hand, he led her outside.

They ambled around his garden, his arm around her shoulders while she hugged him lightly around his waist. He steered her towards the mulberry tree in the corner and stood leaning against the tree-trunk, his hands on her waist, her palms resting on his shoulders.

'Yeli, you've suffered a lot but your life must go on; you can't live in the past. Your needs as a woman must be fulfilled. You have told me that you no longer trust men. But you can trust this one,' he pointed, smiling, to his chest.

A radiant smile lit up her face, and she seemed to run short of breath. 'Really?'

'Absolutely!' said Babatunde. 'One of the proverbs in my language says, "Once you've been bitten by a black reptile, you'll fear even a harmless millipede.'

Yelishaveta chuckled. 'Do you want to tell me another folktale about the harmless millipede?'

He grinned back at her. 'No, I don't have time for folktales now.'

'What do you have time for?'

He stroked the top of her arms. 'Nothing but you, Yeli.'

His hand caressed her back then slid down to her waist; when he touched the top of her bums, she removed his hand.

'Yeli,' he said, short of breath, overwhelmed by emotion, 'I don't know what to say; I don't know where to start.'

She looked deep into his eyes, a smile lingering on her lips.

'Start at the beginning, Baba.'

'We are already in the middle,' said Babatunde.

'What do you mean?'

'Tell me Yeli, is it really necessary to…to tell you that I…I…'

'That you love me?'

He chuckled. 'Yes. How did you know?'

'Sometimes actions can be misleading. So words must set the record straight. Any man can touch any woman. But I'm a woman, and I need to hear you saying…'

Babatunde placed his forefinger firmly on her lips. 'Yeli, I really love you. For me it was love at first sight.'

When she pouted her lips at him, he held her by her head just above her nape; their faces moved closer to each other and gradually until they kissed gently.

'Yes, it was love at first sight,' Babatunde repeated.

'Come on Baba, that exists only in movies and teeneagers' comic books,' she teased.

He chortled. 'No, Yeli. It happened when I saw you for the first time at your office. When I entered you were not facing me. And then, when you turned towards me and I saw your face, your sky-blue eyes, your smile… my heart just skipped and capered about; but I told myself that I was misled by my emotions.'

She raised high-pitched laughter which gave Babatunde a thrill of joy. 'So today you believe that your emotions aren't misleading you?'

'Yes.'

'Baba, are we talking about the same thing? What does loving a woman mean in your culture? We all use the same words but we need to make very sure we really understand each other before getting involved. There will be obstacles. I feel it's a very, very risky endeavour. What do you think?'

Babatunde squeezed her hand, looking deep into her eyes.

'I agree absolutely, Yeli. Across all races and cultures people have common needs. For example, the need to love and to be loved. In spite of cultural differences, if we are attracted to each other we have got to take the risk, just like in business or politics, and hope that the venture will yield positive results. We may make mistakes, but we should be prepared to learn from the experience.'

She smiled and touched his hand. Their fingers entwined, and they gravitated towards each other until their cheeks touched; he could smell her scent which he found very alluring. He broke away from her and looked into her eyes for a moment his eyes ablaze with desire; then bent his neck towards her, his gaze focusing on her lips.

When he bent his neck, targeting her lips she covered her mouth with the palm of her hand. Undeterred, he kissed the back of her hand.

'Com'n Yeli! Don't chicken out!'

They burst into laughter.

Suddenly he kissed her, watching her reaction. Her body language told him that she would not mind a second kiss, so he tried his luck again; but this time she cupped her mouth with her hand and his missile landed on the back of her hand. Again they burst into laughter. He kissed her on her parted mouth, cuddled her and unleashed several kisses onto her cheeks, chin and down to her throat.

She restrained him. They held hands again and looked deeply into each other's eyes, both of them smiling. Again they embraced, and their lips and hands did what words could not do. Then, arms round each other's waists, they sauntered back to the house; this made their walk a little awkward, causing him to stagger, and again they burst into laughter.

*

Parking in front of the apartment building, Babatunde switched off the engine and accompanied Yelishaveta to the entrance of her block of flats; there they embraced and had a long, unhurried kiss. Reluctantly, he took his leave. As the Volvo cruised away from the gate, he hooted and saw her in the rear-view mirror, waving with a huge smile.

He started driving to Thom's place, to share the good news but then changed his mind and instead swung the steering wheel in the direction of his house. He felt he should first thank God alone before he spoke to anyone.

Entering his house, he played a CD and sang along with the gospel artist and fellow Nigerian, James Okon. An hour later he was ready to have his dinner; what should have been a short prayer, *Thank You Lord for the food I am about to enjoy*, became a longer prayer in which he praised and thanked God for sending Yelishaveta across his path. By the time he said *Amen* his food was cold, and he had to microwave it.

*

Late that afternoon when he arrived at Thom's place, he found him watering the flowers in the rockery.

'Thom, I won't sit inside with you today,' he said after they had exchanged greetings. He winked at his friend. 'I want us to talk man-to-man out here.'

'Baba, you're really overflowing with vitality today,' Thom grinned. 'I can see fire in your eyes. What happened to you?'

Babatunde gave Thom a brief account of what had developed between him and Yelishaveta. Thom was exhilarated by what he regarded as an answered prayer item after so many months. He hugged Babatunde and patted him on the back.

'I'm struggling against my feelings, Thom,' Babatunde admitted.

'Baba, I understand what you're going through. You remind me of St Paul when he said, "O wretched man that I am! Who can deliver me from this body of death! What I must do I don't do it, and what I hate to do, I do it!"' Thom paused and then went on: 'Baba, you are a normal human being with a powerful sex drive. You have waited far too long for this.' He put his hand on Babatunde's shoulder. 'Let God tame your testosterone, for it is better to marry than to burn with sexual passion. Be strong Baba. If you are weak, you'll be a man of God up to here,' he put his hand at his navel, 'and below the navel you'll be an ordinary man…'

'Who drinks vodka and screws women?' Babatunde completed.

They burst into peals of laughter.

'Noted, Thomie; there's no more going back. Forward is where I'm going. I've been a bachelor for too long.'

'Florence will be absolutely delighted to hear this exciting piece of news! So what are your immediate plans?' asked Thom.

'I'll take one step at a time. I'll propose marriage soon and inform the board of elders that I'm in courtship with Yeli. But, no…'

'Why do you say "no" when I'm about to tell you how our prayers have been answered?'

'I mustn't go too fast, Thom. Let me ask you to fast and pray with me to make sure that this relationship is from the Lord.'

'We'll gladly do that, Baba. Florence and I will return to Kenya with white hearts.'

'By the way, when are you going back?'
'Within three weeks.'

# 99

Babatunde's last thought as he put his head on his pillow was: *Baba, your days of bachelorhood are coming to an abrupt end!* When he awoke, he felt like a new person: an upsurge of energy made him feel as if his lungs were bigger, his eyes larger and brighter, and his biceps could not resist the itch to lift up weights. He then found himself singing an Igbo song, *Abum onye n'uwa, onye ka m bu n'uwa...*

He knew he was buoyed up by inchoate feelings of being in love. He had a bath and breakfast, his thoughts preoccupied with the woman in his life. Then put on a gold, round-necked, long-sleeved T-shirt, and a pair of brown corduroy trousers. A short while later he was on his way to collect Yelishaveta.

Yelishaveta was waiting for him at the gate as he drove up to the preschool. She had decided to take the afternoon off as the kids were going on a trip to the zoological gardens. He was impressed to see how she had made the effort to dress up for their first outing as a couple. She wore a purple T-shirt that matched her lipstick, a black woollen beret tilted over her brown hair, a light, long-sleeved blue jersey, gold scarf and a pair of peach-coloured jeans.

'Yeli, you look really gorgeous,' said Babatunde, embracing her and kissing her cheek.

She laughed, and he was delighted to hear her carefree laughter.

He told her that as he listened to Nigerian gospel songs, he danced along.

'Dancing? I can't believe it! Why were you dancing?'

'To celebrate our love. You know the way I was dancing...I wish I had made a video! I thought, "Love can really make you silly! It can make a teenager out of a man!"'

She chortled. 'I'm pleased to hear that.'

'Do you want to know the other reason why I was dancing?'

'Please tell me, Baba.'

'I don't want too much energy to lead me into temptation. So I'm expending my energy positively.'

'You are a really smart guy, Baba.'

'Thanks Yeli.'

'I want to start jogging,' she said.

'It's great! Perhaps I could join you on Saturday mornings.'

'That would be nice, Baba.'

Babatunde sneaked a look at her thighs as she sat beside him but resisted the urge to touch her.

'You know, I've been thinking that I should come and park my car at your apartment; and then we can go jogging.'

'Great idea! When can we start?'

'Next weekend.'

'I can't wait.'parked opposite 76 Vladimirskaya Street and, holding her hand, led her to the Casablanca Restaurant.

They ordered crispy Greek salads loaded with olives.

'I never used to eat salads,' said Babatunde. 'Where I come from, the villagers call it food for the rabbits.'

They laughed.

'But a medical practitioner who is on our church board of elders has advised me to eat salads daily,' Babatunde continued.

'Is that why you are slim?'

'Yes.'

'But if my people see you they are going to gossip about me: "He's lean because he has no woman cooking for him."'

They shared another laugh.

'In my culture male obesity is taken as a sign of being well-off,' he said.

'But you are changing the trend.'

'Yes. But to be fair, the present generation is gradually becoming more health conscious.'

After they'd finished their salads Babatunde told the waiter that they were taking a walk around the lake and would then return to the table for a second course.

Holding hands, they sauntered along, gazing into the bushy patch of land around the lake and listening to the birds chirping. Babatunde pulled her towards a park bench that faced the lake. 'Yeli, I want us to take a trip to Odessa,' he said, caressing her.

'That'll be great. I've been avoiding going to Odessa for years.'

'Why?'

'I felt it would evoke memories of my parents. On Sundays after church we used to stroll along the beach there, and we were a very happy family – until that morning when the KGB loaded my father into the police van.'

She covered her face with her hands and Babatunde embraced her, kissing her cheek.

'I'm sorry to be emotional,' said Yelishaveta.

'It's okay, Yeli. It's part of your healing.'

'Thanks Baba.'

She turned towards him tearfully and they kissed.

'When should we go to Odessa?' asked Yelishaveta.

'How about the weekend after next? This Saturday we're going for our jog.'

'Great!'

They returned to their table where they finished their meal without talking much and left after tipping the waiter handsomely.

# 100

On Saturday morning he drove to Yelishaveta's flat to collect her for their first jogging adventure as agreed. She was waiting at the window when his car cruised into the yard of her block of flats.

They headed in the direction of the nearest park; there they stretched their limbs, then lay on their backs and stretched each other's legs; they were ready to hit the road.

As they jogged, facing the oncoming traffic, a motorist stopped beside them in the emergency lane; inside the car were two young men in their twenties. One of them rolled the window down and shouted at Babatunde: 'You ugly baboon!' The passenger threw a handful of peanuts at him.

'Thanks for the compliment!' yelled Babatunde.

Yelishaveta leaned towards Babatunde and kissed him, then she stepped up to the car, her face contorted into a scowl that Babatunde had never seen before. 'You empty-headed racists!'

she shouted at the occupants.

Babatunde pulled her away.

The car sped off and they resumed their jogging. They were going downhill, so they needed less energy. A hundred yards further on the road climbed again and became a little hill.

Yelishaveta breathed heavily through her mouth.

'Let's take it easy,' she said.

They held hands and slowed to a walk. A motorist hooted behind them. *Another empty-headed racist?* thought Babatunde. But it was an old couple in a slow-moving car, cheering them on. Yelishaveta blew a kiss towards them.

*

On Sunday Babatunde sat beside the rostrum listening to the church band behind him singing, *Jesus is the answer.* Looking up, he saw Yelishaveta entering the church. His stomach fluttered as he watched the usher showing her to a seat. He had half expected her to come, but to see her honouring the invitation was mind-blowing to him; he felt like waving to her and shouting 'hallelujah'. Gazing at her as she sat quietly in the back row in her grey two-piece suit, the thought crossed Babatunde's mind: *She really looks like a pastor's wife!* He wondered what was going through her mind at that moment.

'Will all those who are coming to our church for the first time please stand up,' announced Ursula Raduyev, the programme director.

Yelishaveta was one of the people to get to their feet.

'Congregation,' Ursula continued, 'shall we welcome our first-time visitors like the angels would welcome them into heaven?'

She led loud applause. Babatunde waved at Yelishaveta, hoping to capture her attention. After the collection of tithes and offerings, he took up his Bible and stepped towards the rostrum. For a brief moment he felt a little nervous, but soon regained his confidence, feeling adrenalin-driven as he preached his message. He varied his pitch, used his hands to pull and punch at the devil, and moving around ceaselessly.

After the service Babatunde spent about 20 minutes with some parishioners who were eager to chat to him.

'Goodby, praise God,' said Babatunde before shaking hands with the men, hugging the women, patting toddlers and tugging at babies's cheeks.

He then led Thom and Florence over to Yelishaveta who was at the carport, leaning against the back of his car.

'Thom and Flo, meet Yelishaveta Pavlov, my f…' His tongue slipped; he was about to say 'my fiancée' but changed it to 'my visitor'. 'Yeli, this is Thom and Florence Mutesa from Kenya.'

Babatunde's face glowed with a smile as Thom and Florence shook hands with Yelishaveta.

'Thom and Florence are my friends and the pillars of the church,' he told Yelishaveta who nodded with a smile.

After locking the church building, Alex, accompanied by Anna, walked over to where Babatunde and the others were standing. With a sparkle in his eyes Babatunde introduced Yelishaveta to the newcomers. Anna kissed Yelishaveta on her cheeks.

Lunch, prepared by two students from Cameroon and Ghana, was waiting for them when they arrived at Babatunde's house. Florence engaged Yelishaveta in conversation, eager to know more about her.

After lunch Florence helped clear the table and wash the dishes while Anna chatted to Yelishaveta. Alex later offered to take Anna to her apartment.

Thom and Babatunde remained seated at the table, talking quietly.

'Baba, I'm impressed with what I've seen,' said Thom, 'she looks like a humble girl. And she's beautiful.'

'Yes. Last night I had a dream that foretells what I should expect from my people at home. In the dream I had telephoned my female cousin, telling her about Yeli, when all of a sudden she burst out, "No Baba, forget about the white woman! Your suitable woman is waiting for you in Nigeria. A God-fearing woman from your tribe." She then hung up.'

'Well, I guess it's not going to be easy for any of your relatives to accept that you intend to marry a white Ukrainian woman.'

*

The following Saturday Yelishaveta and Babatunde went jogging in the morning and then drove to Odessa in the afternoon. They went to Tavemetta, a seaside restaurant where they enjoyed seafood. As they had tea Yelishaveta looked at the beach.

'Those little girls remind me of my childhood,' she said. 'But I thank God for my family; I had loving parents.'

'You know, Yeli, God knew you before you were born, and He knew how long you would live with your parents.'

'Yes, and I must never think that God was unfair.'

'No! He knows what is good for all of us.'

'Yes.'

'Yeli, your challenges have developed your good character.'

'Thank you, Baba.'

Tears glinted in her eyes and she asked if they could leave the place. They walked hand in hand to his car. Neither of them felt like talking.

As they drove back to Kiev, the mood lightened again. They started to sneak glances at each other, bursting into laughter as their eyes met. Babatunde stole a glance at her shapely legs and put his hand on her thigh. She removed his hand.

'Don't drive and think of love,' said Yelishaveta with a grin, making her tongue protrude.

He put his hand on her thigh again and this time she didn't remove it but put her hand on top of his. Ascending the top of a hill, he saw the signboard for the botanical gardens on his left and slowed the car.

'How did I miss these gardens on our way to Odessa?' he asked. 'Let's go in there and relax.'

She agreed. They went to the entrance, paid the fee and strolled into the gardens. They had bought a fruit basket at the entrance. After a short distance they saw a wooden bench where they sat down and ate the fruit.

Yelishaveta stroked the back of his hand. 'I told you that those little girls reminded me of my childhood. When you saw children at my preschool, you told me on more than one occasion that you loved the children and that they reminded you of your early childhood.'

'That's true, Yeli.'

'Did you have a happy childhood?'

He paused before answering, the smile gradually fading from his face; she continued to massage the back of his hand, looking into his eyes.

He heaved a deep sigh. 'It's a very long story, Yeli.'

'You were available for me when I told a very long story about my childhood. So, I am all ears, Baba.'

'I was an unwanted baby. When I was born my father made it clear that I was not welcome at his homestead.'

'Why, Baba?'

'I'll tell you one day. There's a purpose for every day.'

# 101

To Babatunde it seemed that the botanical gardens and its birds cheered them both. Looking down into Yelishaveta's eyes as she lay on her back, he stroked her forehead and cheeks. He bowed his head and bombarded her face with wet kisses, while his hands continued to explore her temples, her ears, the backs of her ears and her nape. Suddenly she grabbed his hands and raised her torso to sit upright; he did the same.

'Baba,' she said in a serious tone, 'are you really sure that you want to share your life with me?'

With a broad smile he said, 'Before I answer your question, please respond to this question: Yeli, will you please marry me?' He took her hand in his as he asked, 'Will you? Will you be my wife?'

She bent her head and buried her face in her hands while he caressed her shoulders. Then, sighing, she raised her head and looked straight into his eyes: 'Baba, I must say I saw this coming, but I never expected it so soon.'

'Sometimes when God answers your prayers,' he said, caressing her arm, 'the blessing can appear as a shock.'

What was supposed to be the best news in her life seemed to be a source of anxiety. He observed how she lifted her head and looked at the branches of the leafy tree. For a moment he focused on the birds; very beautiful birds with gold, grey and purple feathers and feather-crested heads.

'Let's do like those birds,' he said, with a naughty flicker in his eyes.

She burst out laughing, and he kissed her while her lips were still apart; he tickled her, and she laughed again, trying to disentangle herself from his embrace, but he held her tight.

'Don't try to run away, Yeli; remember, I used to be a hunter, and like a hungry lion I will charge at you, catch you and do this…'

He raised his fingers, imitating an angry fighting cat, grabbed at her ribs with his nails and playfully scratched her; she laughed loudly again. He shushed her with a finger to his lips.

'Yeli,' he said, 'I'm certain I've answered your question: am I really sure that I want to share my life with you? Yes! All that is left is for you to answer my question: will you please marry me?'

Again she hid her face in her hands, tears meandering down her cheeks. Babatunde embraced her and kissed her cheeks where the tears flowed. She restrained him, looking deeply into his eyes. With teardrops still on her face she smiled and offered up her lips to receive his kiss.

'Baba,' she said softly, 'I can't wait to marry you!'

They embraced and kissed again.

*

Thom's farewell party was held at the Goloseyevskaya Hotel, after the church service. It was Thom and Florence's last service and their final Sunday in Ukraine. On Tuesday they would fly to Kenya. During the service Babatunde told the congregation how Thom had been instrumental in planting the church in Ukraine and how he had continued to be a pillar of support.

The board of elders and a few church members attended the farewell party. Alex, Anna and the ushers were also present. After the starters, Babatunde rose to his feet and told the people in front of him how he and the church leadership would miss Thom and Florence; he mentioned that the church would continue to have brotherly ties with Thom and his church in Kenya.

Vladimir Sokolov, representing the board of elders, expressed their heartfelt thanks to Thom for the role he had played. Alex and Anna also thanked Thom, adding that it had been a privilege to work with him and Florence. Babatunde said the last word before he presented Alex and Florence with gifts on behalf the church: books, a laptop and good-quality cutlery. He also handed Thom an envelope.

'After all the hard work,' said Babatunde, 'Thom and Florence deserve a holiday. Remember that in Kenya it's summer. So let them have a sunny holiday during December.'

The guests applauded with smiles.

Thom and Florence received the presents and said that they were honoured to have worked with Babatunde and the board of elders in creating a fast-growing church in Ukraine.

'Baba, I have seen how the hand of the Lord has been with you,' said Thom, 'and I have no doubt that you are on the right path. Please stay on course; don't turn to the left or the right. And don't let success corrupt you.'

His audience clapped in agreement.

'The challenges that we have experienced,' Thom continued, 'were part of growing pains. I have no doubt that this church is going to be a mega-church in Europe; but what we must remember is that the devil is there at every level. But if God is for us, all challenges will be like chaff before the wind!'

Thom sat down to more applause and cheers.

They had the main course, and after dessert the guests dispersed, leaving Thom and Florence, the board of elders, Anna and Alex to remain behind with Babatunde and Yelishaveta.

Anna said to Yelishaveta: 'Yeli, you've hit the jackpot; so don't let it slip through your fingers.'

They all laughed.

'No!' Ursula protested, 'our pastor is the one who hit the jackpot!'

Loud laughter filled the place again. They had tea and cool drinks, and then it was time to leave the hotel.

'Thom, we have heeded your advice,' said Babatunde, 'that it is better to marry than to burn with passion. So we are going to get married very soon, in January.'

'Hallelujah!' exclaimed Thom.

'Amen!' agreed Florence.

'We decided that it would be ideal to marry at a place in the southern hemisphere where it will be summer,' Babatunde went on. 'So we have decided that our wedding destination will be Africa.'

'Nigeria?' inquired Thom.

'No,' responded Babatunde. He grinned at Yelishaveta. 'Please tell them where we intend to get married.'

Yelishaveta opened her handbag, took out a coloured brochure and handed it to Thom and Florence. On the cover was written: *Zambia: one of Africa's most alluring destinations—discover the raw beauty of southern Africa.* Florence turned the page over and they saw a breathtaking picture of misty waterfalls, in the middle of which was the caption: *Victoria Falls—Mosi-oa-Tunya, the Smoke that Thunders.*

'We are going to stay at the five-star Victoria Falls River Lodge,' said Yelishaveta.

'We've decided to combine the wedding ceremony with the honeymoon,' nodded Babatunde. 'Jeff Kapemba is going to marry us. I was with him at Patrice Lumumba university. When I completed my studies, and I was working, we tried to plant a church in Russia, but our efforts were frustrated when we were arrested by the KGB. When I came to Ukraine, he returned to Zambia to start a church. He's also a marriage officer.'

*

Babatunde and Yelishaveta were like a nail and finger; their love flourished, but they lived at separate places. On alternate Sundays they had lunch at her apartment and at his house; they also went out to restaurants. One Saturday morning after their jog, he had a shower at her place and thereafter they went to a hotel for breakfast.

When she inquired about his people, he told her that a month before he had sent several letters home, to inform them about the growth of his church and the challenges he was facing. She inquired about how his people had reacted when they heard that he and Yelishaveta were courting.

'When I broached the topic of a wife in my first letter to my nephew,' said Babatunde, 'I only mentioned that I had met a woman I'm in love with, and he told me that they assumed that she was an African. But he said when they at last became aware that you were white and they saw your photo, they became anxious, wondering if I had not blundered.'

'That's understandable, Baba. If my parents were alive, they would react the same way.'

# 102

Opposition to Babatunde's church did not abate. One Saturday morning when he visited Yelishaveta she showed him a copy of the weekly newspaper, *The Ukrainian Voice*. Babatunde read the story with bated breath. He recalled the day during the Concerned Church Leaders' Forum's meeting when a journalist had threatened that he would destroy the church. The article asserted that people flocked to his church because he used black magic to heal people; the satanic power which he had imported to Ukraine.

'I thought that your detractors would leave you in peace,' said Yelishaveta.

'I don't think such thoughts are going to cross their minds,' said Babatunde. 'Thom is right that there will always be a devil at every level. But my God isn't going to allow them to destroy this fruitful vineyard. He says, 'I, the Lord watch over it, I water it continually, I guard it day and night so that no one may harm it.'

'Hallelujah!' said Yelishaveta lifting up her arms.

They smiled to each other, embraced and kissed.

Because they were truly in love and were talking a lot about their wedding day, time moved fast. Babatunde's church activities also kept him busy. The words on the lips of every church member, big and small, were: *our pastor is getting married*. The known prayer warriors urged others: *pray for the pastor's wedding day*.

A church member went to Anna and suggested donating money for the couple's trip to Zambia. Anna liked the idea and discussed it with Alex, who also supported it enthusiastically. The three then took the idea to the board of elders, who gave it their wholehearted approval; it was agreed that it should be a surprise wedding present to the couple.

*

Early in December Babatunde and Yelishaveta drove to a quiet restaurant out of the city. There he told her that he intended to visit his family in Nigeria. She appreciated that the purpose of the visit was to update his people about their wedding plans.

Yelishaveta put her hand on Babatunde's arm. 'Baba, please tell me about your people. I know so little.'

'What would you like to know, my love?' he said, smiling at her. 'I belong to the Igbo people who live in south-eastern Nigeria.'

He saw she was listening to him raptly.

'One interesting thing about the Igbo; we are very transparent. And please don't ask which tribe is secretive – I don't know. When I was young, I used to hear my relatives saying, "We Igbo people aren't afraid to wash our dirty linen in public." It is said that it's not unusual for Igbo co-wives,' he spoke with a twinkle in his eye, 'to discuss their husband's sexual performance openly at the marketplace.'

She chuckled. 'That's interesting. In fact, it's amusing. Please tell me something about love and romance among your tribe.'

'Let me talk about the girls. When a maiden reaches puberty, she is taken to a specially equipped room known as the "fattening room" or 'fattening pen". There she spends a month. She does nothing other than eating and sleeping. She's locked up in the room and meals are sent to her five times a day.'

Yelishaveta laughed. 'Five times a day?'

'Yes! And she sleeps fifteen hours a day. Her mother is the only woman who is allowed to enter the room. Two hours of her time may be spent on dreaming, thinking of the man she'll meet when she comes out.'

Yelishaveta chuckled.

'Sap of a wild uli wild tree mixed with red clay and oil are applied all over her body. Days later, her body looks as slippery as that of a fish. Her voice thickens, and she starts to put on weight.

'In the village news circulates that a pretty maiden is due to leave the fattening room. The day she leaves the pen, girls of her age-group accompany her to the market. Her eyebrows are painted black and her waist is adorned with multi-coloured beads and as she walks her virgin breasts sway from side to side to attract eligible bachelors. From that moment onwards, she is ready for marriage.'

'Oh that's really fascinating!'

'But the world is changing fast. Girls are now more preoccupied with fattening their brains than their bodies; they want to be different to their mothers.'

'And what should I expect when I meet your people?'

'Expect warmth and love. They were obviously a little shocked and disappointed when they heard that I'm marrying you. But they are getting used to the idea, and they'll accept it fully as time goes on.'

'I hope so; we should continue to pray about this matter, Baba.'

'Absolutely! If you would stay for a long period among my people, other close relatives would help you during the adjustment period. Generally, the qualities desired in a bride are her manners. Physical beauty is secondary. We apply an Igbo proverb: *Agwa bo mma* – "Good manners constitute beauty".'

'Will you please repeat that?'
'*Agwa bo mma.*'
'*Agwa bo mma.*'
Babatunde smiled. 'Yes. Well, other things you'll learn in practice as you interact with my people. And yes, I mustn't forget to tell you that generally we Nigerians…when we speak, our volume and laughter might be too loud for you.'
'Well, your people are now my people,' she said.
He grabbed her hand and kissed it.

*

Before they knew it, it was the week of Christmas. On the day of his departure Yelishaveta and Babatunde spent two hours at the airport restaurant. At the sound of the gong indicating that he must go to the departure lounge, they stood up and embraced, savouring the last sight of each other's faces and tasting a final kiss.
'Goodbye, my yummy Yeli.'
'Bye, Baba.'
As he crossed to the other side he looked back and saw her standing and waving at him. He waved back, kissed his hand and 'threw' it to her; she did the same.

# PART NINE

## 103

Babatunde's plane landed at Murtala Muhammed International Airport in Lagos early in the morning. Without delay he changed to a plane that took him to Port Harcourt International Airport, in Eastern Nigeria. There he found Nnesinachi waiting for him.

'Welcome o, Baba!'

'Welcome o, Nachi!'

They exchanged hugs, kisses and shrill greetings.

'Ah. Long time no see. How you *dey*?' said Nnesinachi

'I dey fine o, I thank God. How you *dey*?'

'Fine Baba'.

Babatunde looked around. 'Are you alone?' he inquired. 'I expected you to come with your fiancé and my nephew Ekene'

'Remember it's the Christmas week; so they've gone to the market to buy a ram or a goat.'

Giving him a bright smile, she scanned him from head to foot.

'I expected to see you putting a kilo or two on your tummy,' she said, 'because according to rumours you are now earning a big salary as a pastor of a fast-growing church.'

He chuckled. 'It's a matter of a lifestyle. I'm trying to be health-conscious.'

'I can see that. How do you manage to…?'

'I eat a lot of salads and I jog.'

She laughed. 'You are really living like a European.'

'Are you suggesting that I'm now becoming an African-European?'

They laughed.

'Can we have something to eat?' asked Babatunde.

'*Oya.*'

They ambled to one of the airport restaurants. He ordered two plates of plantain, vegetables and fish. He had missed that Nigerian dish for a long time.

'I can't wait to hear the truth from you, Baba,' said Nnesinachi, 'are you indeed intending to marry a white woman from Ukraine?'

He grinned, nodding.

'I never imagined,' Nnesinachi continued, 'that the thought would cross your mind to crave white flesh.'

'I never thought I would do such a thing either. Not that it's a bad thing.'

She winked at him. 'Well, I'm happy for you, because you've been single for too long. Some of the villagers were spreading a rumour that you were *okɛ (oke) okporo*.

He chortled. 'No, that'll soon be history.'

'It's good that you've at last found a woman you can share your life with.'

'Thank you, Nachi.'

'It's better to marry a white woman than to wait for an ideal black woman and end up with a scandal on your hands in the interim.'

'Yes.'

'But if I have to be honest with you, Baba, I feel you should have stayed away from white flesh.'

His smiled broadened before he chuckled.

'Is there anything worth laughing at in what I've said?' inquired Nnesinachi.

'I'm laughing because I'm reminded of an African brother who once said that God had a sense of humour in blessing me with a Ukrainian woman.'

'Well I can assure you Baba, our people aren't going to share that sense of humour.'

'I know.'

They finished their meal and left.

*

Babatunde rejoiced to see his mother hurrying forward to help him carry his luggage into the house. He scrutinised her face for signs of tension. But she greeted him cheerfully. His mother was alone at the house as Ekene had not yet returned from the market. Babatunde hugged and kissed her and she led him to his hut, which had been considerably enlarged and refurbished.

'I like how Eki has transformed this hut,' he said, entering and looking around.

'I'm happy that you can see that your money was used very well.'

His mother went out to the cooking shed where she made tea while her son whom she had not seen for months settled into his refurbished hut. The spacious room he was standing in was a well-furnished dining room and lounge. Delegating responsibility to Ekene to choose the furniture had been worthwhile, he thought.

He looked at the wall and saw his framed graduation photo hanging on it. That evoked memories of his university days, and his first negative encounter with the Soviet authorities over the poster of Jesus. He opened a door on his left; it was his bedroom, fitted with a king-size bed, covered with a purple duvet. For a moment he pictured himself and Yelishaveta getting into the bed.

As he returned to the lounge his mother entered with a tray. The next door that he opened led to his study. Ekene had bought a bookcase and put on display the many books that he used to keep in a cardboard box. A table and a chair faced the window. Impressed with what he saw, Babatunde returned to the dining room. His mother waited for him there. He thanked her for the tea, said grace and started to help himself.

'Ogbuishi,' his mother said, addressing him by the middle name which he had inherited from his great grandfather, 'Warrior-hunter who enters the homestead spearing a lion's head; welcome home, seed of Elechi.'

'Thank you, daughter of Okrika, seed of Jumbo,' Babatunde returned, smiling.

His mother smiled. Only adult children addressed their parents with their clan's praise names. He told her how he had travelled in an iron bird that flew high above the clouds. She enquired about the church, and he briefly updated her on the challenges he was facing.

'All I can say, mother, is that the hand of God is upon us.'

'Son, thank you for the letters that you've sent home,' she said, 'and thank you for the money you've been sending regularly.'

'You are welcome, mother.'

'But we've waited and waited to see your face.'

'Apologies for delaying so long before I could come home. Starting a new church is like starting a new business. You can't just hand over to anyone easily unless you've spent time with him and you have confidence that he'll do a good job.'

'I can't complain, because you are doing the work of God.'

She watched him finish his tea; he turned the cup upside down in the saucer as she had taught him and his other siblings. She smiled at him and he smiled back. In the next instant her face had become serious.

'Son, we've heard about your love for a woman from *Lashia*.'

'She's not from Russia mother. She's from Ukraine.'

'Yes, now I remember, Ekene mentioned *Ukereni*.'

She shook her head: 'When I saw a white woman's photo I said, "*Ewoo*! How can he choose a white woman when many suitable girls wait like flowers in the garden of Iboland?" Without delay I went to your pastor and said, "Man of God, please make me understand what I don't think I will ever understand." When I showed him the photo of the woman he laughed aloud and said, "*Chineke! Onye ocha* woman?" He then said to me, "Mama, when you ask for a gift from God, you can't tell him in what type or colour wrapping it must come." He also said, "God is not black or white. He is a life-giving spirit. If you don't want to welcome your son's fiancée because she's white, then you are insulting God.'"

His mother was quiet for a long moment.

'So, mother, you have no objection that I should marry this woman?'

She paused and then went on: 'According to our customs, if you marry you are not marrying for yourself but you are marrying for your people.'

'Mother please answer me. Have you no objection…?'

'Baba, I can't say I'm excited about your choice. Let me now confess that I have been praying that you should change your mind. That the girl…'

'Change my mind?'

'Yes. That the girl's parents would pressurise her saying, "We do't want to see a black face in our house".'

'Fortunately her parents have died a long time ago.'

She paused to wipe a tear that had welled up. 'Tell me Baba, how am I going to relate to *onye ocha* daughter-in-law who speaks a strange language? I was longing for the day I would welcome in this house an Ibo girl like Chimamanda or Chiamaka or Chinelo to whom I would say '*kedu?*' An Ibo bride who would shake the *jikida* waiste-beads and dance,' she gyrated at that juncture, 'to the Ibo wedding songs and loud drums,' she pounded an imaginary drum, 'and later kneel before her Ibo groom. Now you have…' She wiped another tear-drop. 'Baba, *biko*…'

Babatunde gently patted her mother's shoulder, 'Mother, mother, please heed the pastor's advice. If you don't want to welcome your son's fiancée…'

'*Oya*, Baba.' She looked deep into Babatunde's eyes and forced a grinning facial expression. 'Baba, I can't stand against your wish. What can I do? Your pastor gave me a good reason why I shouldn't disagree with you. As things are, I can't say you must marry for all of us. Because you must live and do the work of God in *Ukereni*.'

'I'm sorry mother, for making such a choice.'

'No, you don't have to apologise, son. Because you have asked and God gave what He thinks is best for you.'

'Mother, I can see that you don't want to clash with my choice because you are afraid of God.'

'Son, I am still getting used to your choice. I never thought one of my sons could…'

Babatunde grinned. 'Okay, mother, you'll get used to the idea.'

'I'm not sure if I will…'

'It's a matter of time, mother.'

'Perhaps when I see the woman, my objections will disappear completely.'

'You'll see her at the right time,' Babatunde said. 'And I'm positive your objections will disappear like mist before the hot sun.'

# 104

During the season for *Igba Krismas* the days were eaten until the day of Christmas dawned at last. By the time the sun smiled on the land, a lot had happened at the Okoronkwo homestead. Hours before sunrise, the place witnessed women and men bustling about. Babatunde was awakened by his two sisters and two sisters-in-law talking and laughing loudly and making crockery tinkle. Although he had planned for a quiet time with his Creator, he could not complain. He seemed to hear a voice saying: *Welcome to the hubbubby-hullabalooish Nigerian Christmas; not that dull east European white Christmas!*

He put on his clothes and sandals and strolled to the slaughtering shed where his two brothers and two brothers-in-law had just slaughtered a billy-goat and were skinning it. When he tried to lend a hand, his eldest brother told him to go back to his room.

'You are our brother,' he smiled, 'but today you are our guest, so please relax!'

They continued with their chopping and cutting, reducing the goat into manageable parts to be handed to the women. His younger brother and brother-in-law went off to slaughter a turkey, leaving Babatunde to return to his room.

After reading the Bible and praying, he joined the women in the cooking shed where he began to prepare a bowl of Greek salad.

'*Ewoo*! he's preparing food for the rabbits!' said his eldest sister with a grin.

They all laughed loudly.

'Eating this helps to keep my stomach in check,' he justified.

'*Ahn-ahn*. A prosperous pastor should have a big belly,' chided his sister-in-law.

'Those big-bellied pastors die quicker!' he retorted.

'So you want to live long?' inquired his sister.

'Yes!'

'He wants to live long so that he and the white woman of *Ukereni* can have white hair and hold each other's hands and walk like this…!' said his other sister-in-law, demonstrating as she poked fun at him.

The women guffawed, and he laughed with them. He gave his youngest sister a packet of mushrooms and a recipe and returned to his hut.

Later the women called to say his breakfast was ready. Because he had a good appetite, he ate quickly and finished his food, which included a plantain portion. Hearing the sound of car doors banging, he looked outside and saw his uncle Emenike, taking his time to get out of his old car which was driven by his grandson. Bare to the waist in his khaki shorts, Babatunde walked to meet his uncle who was now in his early eighties. Uncle Emenike's aged face broke into a broad smile as he stood leaning on his walking stick.

Babatunde gave him a firm handshake and hugged him. He led the old man to the spacious veranda where six tables were joined together, covered with white table cloths. His uncle gave a big sigh as he sank into his seat. Babatunde's two brothers-in-law, their wives and children hurried over to greet the great he-elephant.

As the smell of simmering stew-pots and vegetables tantalised their noses, Babatunde inquired about his uncle's health and updated him on his life in Ukraine. His uncle asked many questions which Babatunde answered to the old man's satisfaction.

'I'm really proud of you, nephew.'

'Thank you, uncle.'

'If it were not for my old age, I would come to *Ukereni* and see for myself.'

'You can still come to Ukraine, uncle.'

'*Mba*!' He shook his head. 'I don't want to ride the iron bird. I'm afraid of heights.'

Lunch was served. After a break, cakes and tea was followed by jelly and custard.

Babatunde's sister handed uncle Emenike Yelishaveta's photo, and he squinted his eyes at it. '*Ewoo*! My daughter-in-law is like this…' he raised his index finger, 'nephew!'

'Is she lean, uncle?'

'Yes. Nephew, as it is in our tradition, I sent Ngozi, my youngest daughter, to a fattening pen for the past six months. I waited for you to come home and have a peek at her buttocks and thighs that would have made your blood run to your head. But now you have chosen lean white flesh. What a colossal waste!'

Babatunde laughed along with the others, appreciating his uncle's sense of humour.

'If you can leave her in Nigeria for a month, when you embrace her again you'll feel a real woman ready to keep you warm throughout the European winter.'

They laughed long at that. His two brothers and brothers-in-law went to drink palm-wine under the mango tree, while their wives and the teenage girls helped to wash the dishes and did other chores. Babatunde was left in the presence of his mother and uncle. They chatted for hours, with him doing a lot of the talking; they expressed sympathy as he told them of his trials and tribulations in Ukraine.

'Nephew, when I heard that you intend to marry a white woman, I wanted to share advice with you. I still want to say it, even if it won't reverse your decision.'

'Please tell me what you had in mind, uncle.'

'I wanted to tell you that marriage is a very serious undertaking.'

'I know, uncle.'

'Listen, my nephew, I've observed something about the missionaries who come here from England and America. They raise their boy-children in Africa. But when their sons are old enough for marriage, they send them away to choose girls from their own countries and cultures.'

'I hear you, uncle. It never crossed my mind that I would date or marry someone from a different racial and cultural background. So please forgive me, my people.'

'Well, your mother told me that she now has peace of mind over this matter. I also have peace, nephew. What will it benefit us to keep insisting that you should have married a Nigerian girl?'

'Thank you, uncle.' Babatunde paused. 'My people, the woman of Ukraine and I will be going to Zambia to get married according to the white man's law. We shall then come back home and marry according to Igbo customs. Please give me your blessing.'

'Uncle,' his mother said, 'you can hear for yourself. Your nephew is asking for our blessing.'

His uncle smiled. 'With a white heart I say to you, nephew: let many, many blessings overtake you and dwell in your house.'

'Thank you, uncle and mother.'

Towards sunset, as his uncle was about to return to his village, Babatunde gave him three suits with matching hats; the old man so much appreciated the gift that he kissed his nephew's hands before hugging him.

## 105

Two days after Christmas Babatunde was planning to go to the market after lunch when he heard his mother knocking. She told him that Pastor Benson Okpo was at the door. Babatunde was thrilled to exchange hugs with the man of God he still referred to as his pastor.

'*Chineke bi n'elu!*' said Pastor Okpo who broke into laughter

The two laughed as they looked into each other's eyes and slapped each other's backs.

'Pastor Benson, thank you for having been my advocate when my mother could not appreciate my choice of a Ukrainian woman.'

'It was my pleasure to be a blessing where I could, Baba.'

As they drank fruit juice Babatunde told his eager listener how he met Yelishaveta and how they fell in love.

'I'm delighted that my prayers have been answered,' said Benson.

Babatunde also updated Benson about his church and the challenges facing him, and how he had coped.

'In one of your letters,' said Benson, 'you mentioned that although the church was growing, your trials were increasing.'

'Yes. I told you about opposition from other churches. These guys are beginning to use dangerous tactics; my house has been burgled on two occasions. I upgraded my security but they still manage to get into my house. I suspect one of my next-door neighbours must be helping them.'

Babatunde searched in his bag and took out a folded newspaper.

'Now the enemy is using this latest tactic,' he said, handing the paper to Benson.

*A Nigerian will always be a Nigerian—take him to any part of the world, he will be linked to drugs in some way,*' shouted the headline. *Where does he get his money from? He must be sponsored by Nigerian drug lords—no doubt about it.*

'Sometimes I really feel I've had enough of these attacks,' said Babatunde as Pastor Benson continued to read the article. 'But maybe I should just get used to it,' he answered himself.

Babatunde also handed Benson a copy of *The Ukrainian Voice*. Although the front-page article never mentioned his name, it was clear that the journalist was targeting him. The article presented an argument against healings and miracles; it said that those who believed in healing were not true Christians, and that miracles and healings took place during the apostolic age only to prove that Christ had risen from the dead.

*A true Christian knows that such things ended when the last apostle died,* the journalist stated. *So if someone claims to be gifted in healing, the question is: whose power is he using? God's or the devil's? The answer is obvious. This so-called pastor*

*who, according to many witnesses, has acquired the flamboyant preaching style of rich American pastors, must be watched for he will soon be exposed as a subversive and diabolical agent of the American CIA.*

Benson sighed as he looked up. 'Well, all I can advise you is to do as I wrote in one of my letters,' he said. 'Just stay on course, stay focused on your destination; don't turn to the right or to the left. Remember that it is the tallest tree that gets the most wind.'

'I agree with you, pastor.'

'And also remember that people will always throw stones at a tree that has fruit.'

Babatunde told Benson how the negative newspaper articles had resulted in people flocking to his church out of curiosity and staying on.

Benson smiled. 'I like the boomerang effect!' He glanced at his watch. 'I must go now, Baba. I have a meeting with a young couple at the church office.' He rose to his feet. 'Before I go, let me say this: you'll go through to the other end when the storm abates. Your problems have an expiry date! '

'Amen, I receive your wisdom!' responded Babatunde.

Pastor Benson opened his purse, took out a little card and handed it to Babatunde: 'Read this statement.'

Babatunde read: *Often when we lose hope and are tempted to think it's the end, God smiles from above saying: "Relax sweetheart, it's just a bend, not the end!"*

'What a gem! I must jot it down!'

'You can keep the card.'

'Thank you, Pastor Benson.'

'Now my final word: you'll face problems, but if you stand up in faith, they will be like morning mist that vanishes when the sun shines. Those challenges will be like chaff before a strong wind.'

'In spite of all the challenges I see no big problem man of God.'

'For with God's help you go manage!' Pastor Benson grinned. 'And what is God saying about the fruitful vineyard?'

'I, the Lord watch over it, I water it continually, I guard it day and night so that no one may harm it.'

Laughing, they exchanged bear-hugs ending with back slapping.

# PART TEN

## 106

Babatunde's plane landed safely at Boryspil International Airport in Kiev. He had returned two days after New Year as he and Yelishaveta had agreed. As soon as the taxi had dropped him at his house he phoned her to say he was back and she told him she would come immediately.

Walking to the kitchen, he switched on the electric kettle and returned to the bedroom to unpack his luggage. The moment he heard her knocking, he rushed to the door and opened it; they embraced and kissed; holding her by the waist, he lifted her up and swung her around; laughing, they embraced and kissed again.

He took her hand and led her to the kitchen. There he told her all that had happened during his trip home while they sat on kitchen stools, drinking coffee.

From his bedroom he brought a women's shopping bag made of sisal dyed in many colours. He handed her the bag, which she kissed and hugged before kissing him.

'It's beautiful! Thank you, Baba.'

'Please open it,' he smiled.

She opened the bag and took out a bundle of bead necklaces and some bangles.

'I bought them at the market in Nigeria,' he told her.

She hung one of the necklaces around her neck and inserted her hand through the ivory and copper bangles before taking out a long, brightly coloured strip of printed cloth which she spread in front of them.

'It's called a *lappa*,' he said. 'You wrap it around your lower body like a skirt. It's worn by both men and women in Nigeria. Try it.'

Smiling, she wrapped the cloth around her hips and began to swagger around the room.

He laughed. 'You look gorgeous, Yeli!' Walking over to her, he gave her a long kiss, holding her ear lobes.

She took out the last item from the packet and waved it at him. 'And what's this?'

'It's an *afe itepu*, a Nigerian blouse.'

She turned the purple blouse admiringly from front to back and front again, .

'It's beautiful! Thank you so much, Baba. And this one?'

She was referring to a blue short skirt hemmed with a golden cloth.

'It's an *abada*—a traditional skirt.'

She bent her head to kiss him and they embraced again.

'Let's go and sit in the garden,' he suggested.

Holding hands, they strolled out of the kitchen door into the garden.

'You know Baba, I've been controlling myself all this time,' Yelishaveta said as they sat down on the garden bench.

'Why? What do you mean?'

'Can I share a piece of disturbing news with you?'

He gave her a serious look and sighed. 'What is it?'

'You know, Baba, the devil is trying to wreck our wedding plan.'

'Please come to the point, Yeli.'

'I heard that the Attorney General wants to deport you to Nigeria. I nearly fainted when I heard that.'

'Who told you that?'

'Anna's son; what's his name?'

'Leo.'

'Yes. He said you were discussed in parliament.'

'Me, discussed in parliament?'

They heard a car door banging and Babatunde hastened to the front corner of the yard to look. 'It's Leo and Anna,' he told Yelishaveta. 'Come!'

They went to greet the newcomers as they entered the yard.

'Pastor,' said Leonid, 'your enemies were working very hard while you were enjoying your holiday in Nigeria. Your passport could be seized at any moment. So that your marriage to this,' he gestured towards Yelishaveta, 'beautiful Ukrainian bride should fly up in smoke.'

'On what grounds?' asked Babatunde.

'I'll explain. It all happened in front of me while I was reporting from parliament. An MP from the southern region asked, "How can a black man be a leader in a church where there are 100 percent white Slavs?" He said it's a vote of no confidence in the Ukrainians, and an insult to their dignity. He pointed out that the Orthodox Church, which is recognised as Ukraine's official church, has collected signatures from priests who bitterly accuse you for introducing a corrupted religion in Ukraine and that you are stealing their sheep by cunning means.'

Babatunde remained silent while his three companions looked at him anxiously.

'Another MP mentioned, in support of the previous speaker,' Leonid continued, 'that with your hypnotic powers, you are creating mass hysteria that can lead to a violent overthrow of the government. He says a Nigerian will always remain one: deceitful, tricky and manipulative.'

Babatunde shook his head. 'Do they honestly believe that I have such powers?'

'Yes. A very jealous husband can believe that his wife's lover has the knack to steal her out of bed while he is asleep and return her before he awakes.'

Anna nodded. 'Baba, we must act fast,' she said. 'Leo will organise a lawyer for the church.'

'Yes,' said Leonid, 'I want to get a lawyer who specialises in immigration. While I'm attending to the matter, please collect all the signatures you can from former hobos, drug addicts alcoholics, prostitutes and homeless people for a petition.'

'It's an excellent idea,' said Babatunde. 'We'll start from the church and increase the numbers with others who have benefited from our ministry.'

'I will also ask an MP I grew up with,' Leonid continued, 'to collect signatures from MPs who are sympathetic to Christians.'

'Thank you, Leo,' said Babatunde.

'Yesterday I met the Speaker's wife,' said Anna. 'The couple has a fourteen-year-old daughter who is an epileptic. The woman said to me, "Please tell your pastor to pray for my daughter before he is deported."'

'Okay, I'll pray for the girl,' said Babatunde. 'Tell the woman to bring her to the church on Sunday.'

# 107

On Sunday after the sermon, Babatunde asked the congregation to sing *Power in the Blood of Jesus,* as the mother brought the girl to the 'healing space' in front of the pulpit. As the girl stepped onto the carpet, two church women came to stand behind her. Babatunde prayed aloud, his face contorted, stretching his hand towards the girl's head; he pressed his hand on the girl's head and the girl screamed; he retreated, pointing his forefinger.

'You foul spirit of epilepsy,' Babatunde shouted, 'in the name of Jesus, I command you: come out of her!'

The girl shrieked in terror and fell backwards; a woman standing behind her caught her and laid her down while another woman covered her from waist to ankles with a tablecloth. Babatunde beckoned to the girl's mother, and she walked to where her daughter was lying; the girl's limbs quivered as Babatunde put his hand on her forehead.

'Woman,' said Babatunde, 'healing is taking place right now.'

'Thank you, pastor.'

'Please give me a handkerchief or a tissue.'

The woman opened her handbag and handed Babatunde a tissue.

'I'm going to pray that God should perform a miracle through it. Tonight when she sleeps, put it on her pillow.'

'Yes, pastor,' said the woman, wiping tears away.

Babatunde touched the tissue, prayed over it and handed it to the woman.

*

As the new week started Babatunde instructed the church's senior workers to collect signatures from people willing to join a march against his impending deportation. They went to the parks and other places in the city centre such as bus terminals and railway stations.

*

The following Sunday, the Speaker's wife stood in front of the congregation with her daughter. 'My name is Vera Yakovenko, and this is my daughter, Isadora,' said the woman. 'I'm standing here to give thanks to God. For years my daughter suffered from *petit mal*, a form of epilepsy that affects children. Now she's completely healed.'

Loud applause broke out. The woman gestured towards her daughter. 'Isadora will speak for herself.'

Isadora began speaking in a soft voice: 'As an epileptic I used to be embarrassed by the attacks.'

Her mother gestured that she should speak louder.

Isadora smiled shyly at the listeners. 'I always had to carry a tag stating that I'm epileptic. As a result of the problem, I had to discontinue my ballet lessons. But since the pastor prayed for me I haven't had an attack.' She spread her arms in front of her. 'I'm now completely healed and I'll resume my dance classes soon. Hallelujah!'

'Alleloyah!' exclaimed Babatunde, leading the applause.

The congregants clapped loudly and cheered.

After the service the woman went up to Babatunde who was standing with Yelishaveta.

'Pastor,' she said, 'I didn't want to mention this thing while I was standing in the front. But my husband said I should tell you not to publish the story in the newspapers because it would embarrass him as the Speaker.'

Babatunde laughed aloud.

'Your husband will, sadly, come to realise that good news can't be suppressed and the media will soon look for Isadora,' he said.

'You are right, man of God. I pity your detractors because they don't know that this country is richer because of you.'

'Alleloyah!'

'Those who are trying to deport you aren't aware that they are sending away someone who is an African treasure for Ukraine.'

She gave him a bear-hug and left with tearful eyes.

*

That evening Babatunde's telephone rang; he answered, thinking the call was from Yelishaveta.

'We know that you are using voodoo to make people believe they've been healed,' said an anonymous voice.

Babatunde had a strong urge to interject, but he held his tongue.

'You are taking advantage of gullible people with your hypnosis to make them…'

'Who are you?' Babatunde interrupted. 'Can you talk about specific cases?'

'I don't have time for that,' the voice went on. 'But let me educate you. The scientific term for your kind of healing is the "placebo effect". The patient can experience genuine pain relief after being prayed for. But the relief is short-lived and the patient soon returns to the original condition.'

'I asked for specific cases and not generalisations!' said Babatunde.

'Listen, don't think you can buy time to stay in the country. I can tell you that your days before you return to Nigeria are getting fewer and fewer.'

'Don't try to intimidate me!'

Babatunde banged the receiver down. A moment later the phone rang again and he ignored it. He dialled Yelishaveta's number, but it was engaged. It remained engaged for a long time. He was upset that he could not speak to her. After supper and a shower he went to his bedroom where he lay on his bed trying to sleep. But he could not sleep as his mind was working overtime. He tried to figure out who had called him. How had the man got his telephone number which was not listed in the directory?

When he finally did fall asleep, he dreamed that he was walking hand in hand with Yelishaveta in the botanical gardens – the same gardens where

293

he had made his marriage proposal. They were having a good time, and she was laughing at his jokes. Suddenly ten uniformed men emerged from all directions and stood around them. The armed men broke them apart. She screamed as the men overpowered them and forced them into two separate cars.

Babatunde was driven to an airport where an Air Nigeria plane was about to take off. He was sweating because he'd wrestled with the men and his voice was hoarse from shouting at them. He realised that he was the only passenger. Sitting next to the window as the plane rolled over the tarmac, he saw Yelishaveta waving at him from below; he wondered what had happened to the armed men who had abducted her.

'Baba, how can you leave me in Ukraine and go to Nigeria?' said her strident voice. 'Do you still love me?'

'Yes, I love you with all my heart, my liver, my pancreas and other parts of my body,' he shouted.

The air hostess tapped his shoulder and scowled at him, warning him to keep quiet. He stood up, pointing his finger at the hostess. 'Shut up!'

She tried to slap him but he pushed her away and walked to the cockpit. Two armed security men overpowered him and handcuffed him.

In the next scene he felt strong arms pushing him into a dungeon and he heard the sound of a door being latched; he found himself in a dimly lit place full of cockroaches, reeking of urine and faeces. Suddenly the door opened, and he saw Yelishaveta standing between stern-faced warders.

'Baba, now that you have a criminal record,' she said, wiping away tears, 'you are surely going to be deported.' She burst into tears. As he hurried towards her urgently, his adrenaline in overdrive, one of the warders kicked him with a heavy-duty boot on his stomach, and he fell down grimacing.

The nightmare ended. He was hot, and he felt beads of perspiration covering his forehead. The sweat that had built up at the back of his neck trickled down towards his buttocks. He got out of bed and went to dial Yelishaveta's number again, but her phone was endlessly engaged.

The next morning after breakfast he went with Alex to the city parks to collect more signatures. In the afternoon he drove to Yelishaveta's preschool.

'Yeli, why was your phone engaged all the time last night?'

'Why did you ignore my call?' she demanded.

He told her his reason for not picking up the phone. She responded that she had removed the handset of hers because she had also received a scary call from a stranger.

'The man jeered, "That baboon of yours will be in Nigeria soon,"' said Yelishaveta. 'I couldn't sleep after the call, and I cried all night.'

She burst into tears.

Babatunde embraced her. 'God sees your tears, Yeli.'

'Thank you, Baba.'

'Last night I was so depressed after the call that I completely forgot God's promises,' he told her. 'But this morning I was comforted and encouraged by the message on the card that Pastor Benson's had given me: "Relax, my child; it's just a bend, not the end!"'

# 108

Worry over his possible deportation to Nigeria, which would wreck his wedding plans, caused Babatunde to lose his appetite and sleep. He felt better during the day, when he was encouraged and comforted by Yelishaveta and the church leaders, but at night the demons never ceased to try to steal his joy. As a result he lost two kilograms. He made no effort to regain the lost weight but instead maintained it.

One evening as Babatunde and Yelishaveta were enjoying a meal at a quiet restaurant when she put her hand on his arm, 'Honey, you need to eat more potatoes so that you can put on a kilo or two.'

He gave a rapturous sigh. 'I'm okay, Yeli.'

'You told me about a fattening room for girls in Nigeria. Is there one for men like you?'

They had a raucous laughter.

'Please remember what you once told me,' she continued. 'About a fruitful vineyard. Do you think God isn't watching over it?'

'No! He is watering it and guarding it day and night.'

'And no one is going to harm it!'

They held hands, gravitated towards each other's lips and exchanged a quick tender kiss.

*

For weeks Babatunde and the other church leaders continued to collect signatures and by the time the day of the hearing dawned, 10 000 people had appended their signatures. That Friday morning, two hours before the hearing was due to start, four busloads of church members cruised out of the church yard, heading for the park behind the civic centre. Babatunde and the leadership travelled in three kombis in the front of the buses. Other leaders, including Anna and Alex, had already put up a makeshift stage and prepared the sound equipment. When Babatunde and the rest arrived at the park, the church band was performing.

Babatunde was impressed to see several hundred shoppers standing around the stage. Others lounged around the park while some had opened their picnic baskets. The supporters got out of the buses, waving placards.

Three protestors carried banners which read: "Hands off our Pastor!" "Why deport such a useful man?" and "We love our Pastor." The organisers of the march distributed leaflets to the bystanders who included journalists. Although the church had appointed a spokesperson for the day, the journalists went straight to Babatunde, pens, notebooks and microphones at the ready.

'What is the purpose of this demonstration, pastor?' a female journalist asked Babatunde. In answer he gestured to a group of church members wearing orange T-shirts. 'Those people over there are former hobos, alcoholics and homeless people who have come here today with their family members; they are here to demand an audience with the prosecutor.'

'What do they want to tell the prosecutor?' another journalist asked.

'You can speak to them,' said Babatunde. 'Or perhaps you should wait for the programme to start.'

An hour later as the band still performed, the number of onlookers had increased to a few thousands.

After the church leaders had given a short history of the church and its achievements and outlined the purpose and programme for the day, a woman sitting in the front row on the stage hastened to the microphone with a huge smile.

'My name is Tanya Tolstova,' said the woman. 'I am a former prostitute who was dying of cancer. One evening during a special healing service at the church, I was taken there in an old wheelbarrow. Some kind Christians had found me wasting away in the municipal toilets where I was abandoned to die.

'When the Christians told me about the healing service and offered to take me there in the wheelbarrow, I was overwhelmed by the kindness shown to me. At first I objected because I was sure there was no hope for my ruined life. I had spent years in prostitution and I felt nothing but guilt and shame. But the Christians convinced me that God sent His Son into the world not to condemn the world, but so that the world through Him might be saved.

'Lying there on the wheelbarrow, I listened to the pastor speaking. I experienced bitter sorrow and remorse for the wasted and abusive life I had lived. When those who wanted to receive Jesus were invited to the front, I felt I had nothing to offer Christ but a deteriorated and hopelessly incurable body. I could therefore hardly believe that God loved me enough to forgive me and impart a new life to me.

'A Christian who was sitting next to me smiled at me and, as if she could read my mind, said softly, "Sister, only believe." At last the profound realisation of God's immeasurable love dawned upon me as I began to cry out to Him for His mercy and I received Him into my heart. I found myself weeping with joy, peace and thanksgiving. I looked up at my new friends and reached out my bony arms to their strong hands… and I got up onto my feet—for the first time in months…'

Loud applause broke out.

'As my friends and I wept and thanked God together, I was so overcome by joy and peace in my soul that I forgot about my cancer-ridden body. In a few moments I realised suddenly that the large cancerous growths had disappeared and my legs and arms were strong. With tears streaming down my cheeks, I raised my emaciated arms towards heaven. My entire lifestyle has changed since that day.

'So,' she turned and looked at Babatunde, 'I am indebted to this man of God. Now, if he is deported to his country, what is going to happen to all the other people who are in my former condition? Should they be left to die the way it nearly happened to me? Today…'

Shouts and cheers interrupted her.

'Today I am standing here to say to the authorities, please withdraw the charges, if there are any. Why must the case be withdrawn? Because our pastor is a very useful person to this country. I am a perfect example of how God is using him to change a lot of us hobos, drug addicts, prostitutes and drunks into better people. The government must in fact thank him instead of treating him like a rogue and a criminal.' The audience again applauded and cheered. 'Ukraine is richly blessed because of Pastor Babatunde! He is indeed as we all agree an African treasure!'

The woman returned to her seat as the thunderous applause went on. Babatunde rose and went to give her a hug. As the band performed, Babatunde and the church leaders descended to the lawn in front of the stage. The programme director announced that the march would proceed to the court building.

Babatunde felt someone touch his shoulder and when he turned he saw a former wrestler who had become one of the ushers at the church and was known as Holy Bouncer.

'Sir, can I lift you up on my shoulders?' he asked.

Babatunde responded by laughing aloud as the muscular man inserted his head between the pastor's thighs, holding him firmly by the hips and lifting him up. The people cheered and applauded.

From Holy Bouncer's shoulders Babatunde had a good view of the thousands of marchers. He heard the crowd chanting as they clapped their hands rhythmically: "Hands off our Pastor."

The people marched around the court building, coming to a halt at the foot of the stairs. At that moment the church's lawyer was having a meeting with the prosecutor. At last a court official came to meet Babatunde who had dismounted from the wrestler's shoulders to be handed several pages of documents comprising various demands and lists of signatures.

The official told Babatunde and the three officials who accompanied him that he was going to consult his superiors and that they should wait. For over an hour the people continued to wave their placards, chanting, 'Hands off our Pastor.' 'We demand a withdrawal of the case!' Many foreign and local TV and print media journalists filed up to interview Babatunde.

The lawyer later came back to tell the people what they had been waiting to hear: the case was withdrawn!

Babatunde leapt up in triumph, raising his hands and shouting 'Alleloyah!' before he was again whisked off his feet and carried shoulder high. The people applauded and cheered as if they would never stop. Babatunde waved at them, his eyes focusing for a moment on Yelishaveta who was one of the loudest cheerleaders.

'I don't have much to say except to thank you all the church leadership, the members and the supporters. Thank you all for showing the authorities that your feet can talk louder than your mouths. In Africa we say a mouth can cross a river in floods. We also say, "One person alone cannot move an elephant, but the whole village can." Your action is here to be seen by the whole world. Today we have won another round against the devil. But the enemy always bounces back. So let's be prepared for more trials in the future. But one thing I am sure of is that you won't allow to be overwhelmed by the forces of darkness. Our attitude is: No be big problem?'

'We go manage!' the people roared.

Babatunde raised a clenched fist as he led applause. 'Alleloyah!'

The jubilant people celebrated victory by singing and stomping about for another hour with Babatunde, all smiles, looking down from Holy Bouncer.

# 109

The following day Babatunde and Yelishaveta began preparing themselves for their wedding and honeymoon in Zambia.

They went out to restaurants to relax, unwind and reflect on all that had happened. These outings included places which Yelishaveta had never visited, such as Tokyo and Swing-Bar Restaurant where she listened to the music of the American jazz icon, Louis Armstrong, for the first time.

They went on several shopping trips, where they bought a camera, binoculars, walking shoes, shorts and sun-hats. Babatunde also bought a pair of faded-green khaki shorts with a matching short-sleeved shirt and a green sun-hat. The old pair would become Ekene's hand-me-downs, he decided. They went to clothing shops where they each bought new outfits, helping each other to make the right choices.

Officially, he was still on special leave. As a result there was no need to stress about revising and polishing the Sunday sermon or other church business.

On Friday afternoon they boarded an electric tram which was outfitted with soft red seats, tables and a kitchen. They visited a cottage area on the outskirts of Kiev that was famous for hosting iconic visual artists, writers and celebrities. On their return they passed through the forest of Puscha Vodytsya. As they munched pizzas, Yelishaveta put her hand on the back of Babatunde's hand and whispered, 'Baba, I have something very exciting to share with you.'

He brushed her thigh below the table: 'I'm all ears, Yeli.'

'Someone in our church…let me call him or her an angel, because he or she prefers to be anonymous, bought us two tickets for a boat trip along the Dnieper River tomorrow afternoon.'

'That's wonderful! There is no better way to relax and forget our challenges than on a boat trip.' She leaned towards him, offering him her lips and they kissed.

*

On Saturday afternoon the couple sat hand in hand in the restaurant section of the VIP Class Boat called Silver Breeze, savouring every single moment. As the boat glided over the Dnieper waters, they fed their eyes to 'stomach-burst' level – as Babatunde's people would say. The sights of Kiev included Kiev-Pechersk Lavra, Arch of Friendship, Podol (Lower Town), Metro Bridge, Moscow Bridge and Trukhanov Island, and the

English, German and Polish-speaking guides were kept on their toes for two hours.

Babatunde and Yelishaveta's mouths were not there for eating only but also for chatting, especially about their intended honeymoon, and of course for kissing. As they sat later on the open-air deck, their faces beaten by a cold breeze and Yelishaveta's brown hair tossing in the wind, they agreed that the new wedding date should be Valentine's Day, and that they were going to dress in white on their big day in Zambia.

# PART ELEVEN

## 110

The early morning flight from Boryspil International Airport in Kiev proceeded to Livingstone Airport in Zambia. An empty seat between Babatunde and Yelishaveta afforded them space to turn towards each other as they chatted.

A flight attendant served them breakfast and as they ate, the pilot's voice came over the

intercom, mentioning the altitude and that they were now passing over Egypt.

Upon landing, a micro-bus took them to Victoria Falls River Lodge. The passengers disembarked, walking on a red carpet. Babatunde heard the sound of drums and saw six girl dancers and five boys pounding drums of different sizes; the girls wore traditional dancing skirts and had dancers' rattles tied to their ankles. The girls sang: *Tunaliwane chiwano.*

'What are they saying?' Babatunde asked the porter.

'It simply means "we are pleased to see you all".'

'What language is this?'

'It's Luvale.'

From the reception desk, where they had booked into separate rooms as Ms Y Pavlov and Pastor B Okoronkwo, hotel porters accompanied them to their quarters. The couple had agreed to follow these rules rigidly: *thou shalt not enter his/her room; thou shalt not smooch, but thou shalt wait until tomorrow.*

They relaxed in their rooms until 18h30 and then headed together to the dining hall where they had a delicious and enjoyable dinner. They were the last ones to leave the dining hall.

After dinner, wearing tracksuits, they walked around the hotel under the clear moonlit sky, holding hands and chatting. Suddenly Babatunde broke from her hold and said, 'Yeli, let's play "The Hyena and the Children".'

'Are you serious Baba?'

'Yes, why not? You are the children, and I'm the hyena. Come, let's have fun.' He gestured. 'Go and stand there.'

She walked away from him, laughing, and then turned and faced him.

'My children, my children, come home!'

'We are afraid!'

'Afraid of what?'

'The hyena!'

'The hyena has gone to nurse the cubs.'

She tried to run past him; he was about to grab her when she suddenly backtracked and he missed her. She ran in circles, feinting several times, with him trying to catch her without success; at last he overtook her and grabbed her by her hips and they fell and rolled on the lawn, guffawing. Babatunde heard someone letting out a chuckle. It was the night-watch on duty.

'You people are funny, man,' said the night-watch, laughing.

Babatunde and Yelishaveta chuckled with him.

'Baba, shall we jog around the tennis court?'

'Sure Yeli, that will help to dissipate our energies further.'

After stretching their limbs in a warm-up, they jogged around the tennis court. They then strolled back to the hotel where they took a lift up to their rooms. Babatunde left her at the door of her room. 'Goodbye Yeli; see you tomorrow.'

She kissed her hand and 'threw' him a kiss; he did likewise.


# 111

When the Valentine's Day sun rays invaded Babatunde's hotel room through the curtains, he smiled at the thought that he had only a few hours left to spend as a single person. The day they had waited for and chafed for had dawned at last.

His smile increased when he saw Yelishaveta getting out of the lift on the ground floor to join him at reception; in a frenzy of enthusiasm he embraced her tightly and gave her an explosive kiss.

Babatunde asked the hotel manager to see to it that their belongings were moved to the new communal room that he had already booked. As they sauntered to the dining hall, their arms around each other, the hotel manageress hastened to them and put garlands of red roses and red tulips around their necks.

On their way outside after breakfast, they met a hotel worker leading in an important guest: the marriage officer, Jeff Kapemba, accompanied by his wife, two church elders and their wives. Babatunde rejoiced to meet Jeff again. After he'd introduced Yelishaveta, the two men briefly reminisced about their experiences at Patrice Lumumba Friendship University.

The hotel worker led Babatunde and his guests to the corner of the dining hall where the marriage registration and solemnisation would take place. Jeff asked for Babatunde and Yelishaveta's passports in order to complete the marriage certificate. When the witnesses had signed the certificate, it was handed to Babatunde who showed it to Yelishaveta. The couple hugged, kissed, held hands and smiled at each other. Jeff asked Babatunde if they were ready to proceed and he answered in the affirmative. Jeff gestured that the couple should move closer to him.

'Babatunde Ogbuishi Okoronkwo, will you have this woman, Yelishaveta Sofia Pavlov, to be your lawful wedded wife, to live together in the sacred bond of marriage; will you love her, honour her, comfort and keep her in sickness and in health and, forsaking all others, keep yourself only for her, so long as you both shall live?'

'I will,' responded Babatunde, smiling into Yelishaveta's eyes.

'Yelishaveta Sofia Pavlov, will you have this man…'

'I will,' said Yelishaveta, after Jeff had repeated the marriage vow to her.

'Now please face each other and say the following words. Where I pause, it's your opportunity to repeat what I have said.'

Jeff looked down at his book to find the passage he wanted.

'Entreat me not to leave you…or to turn from following you…for where you go I'll go…and where you lodge I will lodge…your people shall be my people…and your God, my God…where you die, I will die, …and there I shall be buried…May the Lord do so to me…and more also if even death parts me from you…'

Jeff looked up. 'By the authority and power vested in me,' he said, 'in the presence of these witnesses, I'm delighted to pronounce you husband and wife.'

Babatunde and Yelishaveta embraced and kissed while the witnesses applauded.

He smiled at her, 'Now I can address you in my Igbo language as "*Nwunye m.*"'

'"What?'

'*Nwunye m.*'

'Which means?'

'My wife.'

She offered her lips, and they kissed and elicited African exclamations, cheers and rapturous applause from the witnesses.

The newly weds and their guests enjoyed a sumptuous meal. For hours at and off the table the guests were regaled with a love story recounted with an infectious enthusiasm. Just before they parted Jeff held the couple by their hands and pronounced a final blessing 'May gladness and laughter overtake your marriage, everlasting joy crown your heads.'

# 112

As she took her time to undress he was more than eager to lend a helping hand. He heaved a sigh thinking of how his taste-buds are going to savour the moment he has awaited for years. The more he explored her body the more he groaned with libido whose sluice gates wanted to burst. He exclaimed in his heart, 'Ewoo! This is the moment for my stout stick to stir the sweet fountain of her womanhood! To plunge my well-honed teeth in the luscious Ukrainian apple!' He salivated like a ravenous eater who could not wait to gobble up a gorgeous ripe papaya in front of him. He tried to reign in his manhood with not an iota of success.

'Nwunye m,' he gave a radiant smile as he gestured towards the bed whose coloured linens were perfumed with myrrh, aloes and cinnamon, 'Come, let's drink deeply of love till morning; let's enjoy ourselves with love!'

It was a long and sensual afternoon of lovemaking. After taking his time to 'get into' her, he was in no haste to reach Mt Everest summit. And when it happened he was overcome by a strong emotion—an ecstasy at being able to connect intimately with her, at being able to elicit such a powerful reaction from her. Exhausted, they slept until dusk.

Around 04h00 Babatunde was roused from sleep when he felt tender fingers making circular movements around his navel; her hand slipped under his underwear down to his pubic area and then his manhood. Getting aroused gradually he turned towards her, stretched his hand and touched where the waist met the top part of her thigh. She tugged him closer to her. He embraced and kissed her voraciously. After exploring his waist her hand moved towards his bottom. Completely aroused he mounted her. She astonished him when she lifted her knees and pressed his back with two hands. When she suddenly tickled his balls, he accelerated his thrusting movements which made him feel like a jockey riding a horse that was outrunning her competitors.

As he recovered from his erotic hangover, he felt her hand touching his forehead; he smiled as her ring finger explored his upper lip, his chin and his Adam's apple. Lying on his back, he looked up at her as she looked down at him. She touched his chin. 'Baba, I was used to your beard and moustache; you look different now you are clean shaven.' He felt her hand playing with his hairy chest and smiled.

'It's my honeymoon look, *nwunye m*,' he said, lifting his face towards her face so he could kiss her.

She offered him a tender kiss in return.

Realising that they had missed dinner, they dialled for room service. They ordered toasted ham and cheese sandwiches with tea and yogurt for dessert. While they waited for the food, he held her hand and prayed. The memory of their first moment of lovemaking the previous night was etched in Babatunde's mind.

They had a common bath and then shuffled onto the balcony wearing pyjamas, night gowns and slippers. Babatunde cuddled Yelishaveta and planted kisses on her neck, cheeks and finally her lips. He pinched her buttocks and pulled her back into the room, leading her to the bed where they quickly undressed and got between the sheets, making love and sleeping until the morning; then they had baths and made love again.

*

There was no idle moment during their honeymoon holiday. They started off with a visit to the mighty Victoria Falls. In the afternoon they boarded the Flying Fox, a cable with which one slid across a 30-metre deep gorge. Other activities included a visit to the David Livingstone Museum; an Elephant-back Safari; and a visit to Chief Mukuni's Village where they bought a variety of curios. They joined a cruise across the Botswana border and ended on a high note by taking a helicopter flight over the Victoria Falls.

On the day of their departure, as the shuttle kombi took them to the airport, Babatunde gave the hotel a last look. He felt Yelishaveta's hand squeezing his hand. He turned towards her and kissed her tenderly on her lips. When he scanned her body towards the knees he delighted over the fact that she was putting on the *abada* which exposed her thighs. He pinched her thigh. As she chortled, he planted a kiss on her parted lips.

# PART TWELVE

## 113

Back in Ukraine, on a cold afternoon, Babatunde drove them home in his car, which had been parked at the airport. They were engrossed in a postmortem of the honeymoon when his attention was suddenly distracted.

'Is there a problem?' asked Yelishaveta.

'I'm watching the black car behind us which I suspect has been trailing us from the airport.'

'Are you sure?'

'I just have that strange feeling…'

'Why don't you slow down?'

Looking in the rear-view mirror, he kept quiet.

'Can you see the car's occupants? What do they look like?'

'They're wearing dark glasses.' He continued to watch in the mirror. 'Okay, let me turn left at this traffic light.'

He glanced at the mirror. 'The car is still following us.'

'Alright, Baba, make a U-turn here and let's see if the car follows us.'

After driving in the opposite direction for a block or two, they resumed the route to their house. Babatunde didn't see the car again.

At their house two young men from the church opened the gate. Babatunde said to Yelishaveta: 'Something must have gone wrong in our absence.'

'How do you know?' she asked.

'I can read it on Igor's face. He's always cheerful and he should be pleased to see us back home.'

Yelishaveta shrugged.

'Thank you guys for looking after our house while we were on holiday,' said Babatunde as Igor and Ruslan pulled their suitcases into the house.

'It was a pleasure,' said Ruslan.

'But sir, we've bad news for you,' said Igor. 'Burglars broke into the garage.'

'Is there anything missing?'

'Only a toolbox.'

'How could it happen? I've installed an alarm system,' said Babatunde.

'We were baffled too, pastor,' Igor responded. 'The alarm didn't go off. We don't know how it got deactivated.'

Babatunde and Yelishaveta looked at each other. After checking the house and finding that nothing else had been taken, Yelishaveta prepared soup and they all ate. Babatunde had missed home food. It was Yelishaveta's first meal that she had prepared for him.

'You are such a good cook, *nwunye m*,' said Babatunde, asking for a second serving.

Yelishaveta chuckled. 'Remember, I supervise the staff to cook well-balanced meals for the children.'

After the two young men had left, the couple had a nap, and thereafter made love on his bed for the first time.

*

The following day after breakfast, they went to do their first shopping as Mr and Mrs Okoronkwo. They went to the vegetable and fruit market, walking beside each other, picking items and dropping them into their trolley. Babatunde sensed several pairs of eyes staring at them. *I appreciate your discomfort*, he thought, *your eyes might be stumbling on an African-Ukrainian couple for the first time; but I hope you'll get used to us.*

After they had lunch, they drove home. On the way back from doing their shopping, he passed the spot where he had first met Anna, when the young Ukrainian man had called him a monkey and pushed him to the pavement; he wondered how the hooligan and his friend would react when they saw him with Yelishaveta.

As Yelishaveta was new to the house, she set to work to change the way things were in all the rooms. He was happy to go through the adjustment process with her, observing how she preferred to press the toothpaste tube at the end rather than in the middle; how in the morning she did not like to kiss unless she had first brushed her teeth.

Babatunde delighted in the feminine touches his new wife brought to their home. Suddenly there were fresh flowers on the table and all his socks sat neatly paired in his drawer. He especially loved the African throw rugs she hung over their small couch to brighten up the usually drab Eastern European furnishings.

They liked eating out and driving between towns. However they were sensitive to the fact that travelling as a black-and-white couple could be migraine-inducing for those who saw them. So they decided to stick to the big cities instead of heading to the rural areas where they would be more likely to encounter stares, glares and snide remarks.

The last day of their holiday was a Sunday; they went to the church where Babatunde would not preach but would attend as a guest.

## 114

When the service began, Babatunde and Yelishaveta sat in the elders' section. The preacher for the day, Vladimir, asked the congregation from the pulpit to give Babatunde and Yelishaveta a rousing welcome. Wearing a Nigerian kente-cloth suit, Babatunde rose to his feet together with Yelishaveta who, for the first time, had put on *afe itepu* and wrapped around her waist the ankle-length Nigerian print that Babatunde had brought her. The two smiled and waved as the congregants stood up, applauding, cheering and whistling.

Ready to deliver the sermon, Vladimir stepped up to the lectern. Babatunde observed Vladimir smiling at him and wondered what he was about to say. Vladimir turned to the church band and gestured with his right hand. The band played a fast-paced tune. Babatunde saw a group of dancers led by Isadora entering the stage, waving pieces of purple, blue and white cloth.

At the end of the item Isadora led the dancers in a bow while the audience applauded with gusto. As the dancers walked off into the wings, Isadora remained alone on the stage. The leading vocalist of the church band sang:

*Lord, make me an instrument of Your peace*
*Where there is hatred, let me sow love…*

Babatunde looked on open-mouthed as Isadora danced along to the singing, interpreting peace, love, pardon, harmony, truth, faith, hope, light and joy through the movements of her body and limbs.

At the end of the performance, the church members rose to their feet, applauding and exclaiming at her excellence. Vladimir called to Isadora to come and stand beside him, a huge smile on her face. Vladimir lifted her hand in acknowledgement while the applause and cheers went on.

'As a way of thanking the Lord for healing her,' said Vladimir, 'Isadora has established "Isadora's Dancers", to serve the Lord with their bodies and souls.'

Another burst of applause broke out as the dancer walked back to where she'd been sitting.

*

The church membership continued to increase; people who knew Yelishaveta became members, and those who knew Alex and the other changed hobos also joined the church. Other new members came out of curiosity because of the newspaper articles critical of the church.

The feeding scheme for unemployed people also swelled the church membership. As a result, the current church building was extended with marquees on two sides, where latecomers stood viewing the preacher on huge external screens, his voice emerging through powerful speakers.

Around June Babatunde decided to write a letter to Pastor Okpo:

As the Fruitful Vineyard continues to thrive phenomenally, so does opposition. Other churches are continuing to make wild accusations about how I'm stealing their members and how I'm making promises to gullible people.

The Orthodox Church has even written negative newspaper articles, warning the people that our church is a sign of the last days, where false churches brought by false prophets will mushroom. I'm also accused of forcing my members to part with ten percent of their salaries; they say I'm hypnotising the followers to do as I please.

But these articles have piqued the curiosity of the readers, who are continuing to flock to our church; as a result membership has soared to 4 000. As new people come, we have three services on a Sunday, and the church has relocated twice to bigger premises. People just want to come and see for themselves what's going on; they even defy the deadliest winter cold, wind and snow.

There is a new development: I'm getting new visitors who attend for reasons other than spiritual. Police officers, psychiatrists and doctors are attending our services, looking for evidence that they can use in future against my ministry. Please continue to pray for us. I am enclosing some of the photos which Yelishaveta and I took in Zambia.

With much love,
Baba.

## 115

The church continued to grow. Yelishaveta had charmed the leadership to welcome the suggestion that, 'Fruitful Vineyard' should be added to the name of the church. The new name would then be 'Centre of Hope - Fruitful Vineyard Church.' When membership reached 6 000, the leadership decided to hold a special thanksgiving function. During the service the church band played, and the members rose to their feet, clapping hands, jumping with joy and singing aloud—'making a joyful noise to the Lord', as Babatunde had quoted from one of the Psalms.

Right in the front, next to the pulpit on the elevated stage, Babatunde stomped around with arms raised heavenwards, wearing a yellow three-piece suit. He saw Alex handing Anna a piece of paper. Anna hurried to the stage and handed the paper to him; for a brief moment he stopped dancing as he perused it. Then he crumpled up the paper, stamped on it with both feet, and continued stomping about.

Suddenly the attention of the parishioners focused on the church entrance at the back. Babatunde saw ten police officers standing in the aisle near the door. The singing and dancing stopped, and all eyes turned towards the police who stared at Babatunde.

Babatunde grinned. 'Today we have special visitors; they are welcome to be a part of us if they can dance to our kind of music.'

Babatunde's comment drew titters from church members. He saw the police commander talking to Anna and Alex. The latter followed the police as they walked out of the church. Babatunde told the church that he would present a brief sermon because it was a day of celebration.

After the sermon the congregants dispersed and went to sit on the lawn outside the building; they had been asked to bring picnic baskets so that they could relax and have something to eat. The church served ice cream and cool drinks. As Babatunde and members of the board of elders strolled to the marquee to have a fork buffet, Anna and Alex joined them.

'The commander said they are on a routine inspection,' reported Alex, 'and that they will return if necessary.'

'They are just trying to intimidate us,' said Babatunde.

After the meal Babatunde observed that Alex was jotting something down in his black notebook.

'Alex, what are you writing in there?'

Alex smiled at him. 'I just want to capture thoughts before they disappear.'

'When are you going to show me what you are writing?'

'One day I'll tell you.'

*

After attending a meeting with the board, Babatunde drove home that evening. He was alone at home as Yelishaveta was away attending a women's conference in Odessa. As he drove into his yard, he saw in the rear-view mirror another car pulling into the yard behind him, very close

311

to his rear bumper. Two figures stepped out of the car and strode towards him. Switching off the engine, he opened the car door and got out, his eyes fixed on the two men. He gasped when he realised that they had covered their faces with balaclavas; it was too late to retreat back into the car. The men pointed guns at him and he lifted his hands up.

'What's happening? Who are you?' asked Babatunde, shaken.

One of the men searched the pockets of his trousers while his mate kept the gun pointed at his head.

'I said who are you? What do you want from me?' Babatunde demanded again.

'We are on a serious mission,' said the man on his left.

'What mission?'

'To kill you,' responded the man on his right.

'Why do you want to kill me?'

'You are disturbing our peace.'

'Who are you? Listen, will you please remove the balaclavas so that we can talk face to face.'

'Are you crazy? Do you think I'm covering my face for fun?'

'Who sent you?'

'You know you've many enemies.'

'I love my enemies, as the Bible…'

The man gnashed his teeth. 'Shut up!'

Babatunde sighed. 'You are targeting the wrong man. I'm your ally.'

'Nonsense! Now give us the car keys!'

He gave them the keys. The man opened the boot and gestured towards Babatunde with his gun. 'Get in!'

'Please guys, let's talk! If you want money…'

'Get into the boot!'

Babatunde hesitated for a moment, thinking of putting up a fight; the soldier-boy in him threatened to erupt, but the instinct for self-preservation prevailed. As he put one foot into the boot, he heard the sound of a police siren. One of the men kicked his buttocks before hurrying back into the car which drove away at a high speed. Weak with relief, Babatunde took his foot out of the boot and looked down the street. It was strange that the man who had taken the keys had thrown them on the ground. A police patrol car with flashing blue lights was slowing down in front of his yard. Two young policemen stepped out.

The one on the driver's side smiled at him. 'Is there any problem, pastor?'

'Do you know me?' Babatunde asked.

'Yes, we know you, pastor,' the policeman responded. 'We are aware of the good things you are doing in the community.'

'Thank you, officer,' said Babatunde. He told them what had just happened.

'Would you like to open a docket?' asked the other officer.

'Is it really necessary?'

'Absolutely necessary,' said the first officer. 'Reporting it will help our police antennae to pick up information for your safety.'

'Alright officer, I'll cooperate.'

Babatunde drove behind the police car to the police station.

# 116

'I was driving past when I saw Yeli in the garden,' said Alex, greeting Babatunde with a handshake before sitting down. 'She said you were here.'

'What have you got for me today, Alex?' Babatunde asked.

'Something interesting is happening in the church, pastor. Five of our former hobos told me they've met women of their dreams at the church.'

'Wonderful! And what about you?'

Alex chuckled. 'I'm like Apostle Paul: no woman in my life.'

'Well if the bug of love has been unleashed in the church, it will get you.'

Alex laughed. 'I'm joking pastor. Actually I'm seeing Natasha, a former alcoholic.'

'Alleloyah!' Babatunde rose to his feet, laughing and clapping his hands. 'I've been suspecting that. Yeli is going to be thrilled when I tell her.'

'For weeks Natasha has been helping me to count the church collection,' Alex went on. 'One day, I just touched her hand, and when I looked into her eyes, I knew she was the woman God has kept for me.'

Babatunde smiled. 'I'm going to conduct a group wedding ceremony one day!'

'Amen, pastor,' Alex laughed. He took an envelope out of his pocket.

'Pastor, I have a letter addressed to you,' he said, handed it over. 'I found it in the church letter-box.'

Babatunde looked at the envelope; on the back was written: *Department of Welfare and Social Development.*

'I must go, pastor,' said Alex, car keys jangling as he stood up.

Babatunde wagged his finger: 'On your way to see Natasha?'

Alex laughed. 'Yes, pastor. See you on Sunday.'

Two hours later Yelishaveta called to him that food was ready, and he joined her in the dining room. He told her about the letter he had just received.

'According to the official they've received several complaints from concerned parents that the church is confusing the youth and destabilising parental roles.'

'What do they mean? ' inquired Yelishaveta.

'The letter says the church is causing the youth to be rebellious against their parents and that they are behaving strangely because they've been brainwashed. It says that the parents are threatening to take the church to court.'

'Let them take us to court!' said Yelishaveta, 'God is on our side!'

'The letter ends by saying that the state is going to appoint professionals such as psychologists and social workers to investigate the matter.'

'I think you should speak to the youth,' Yelishaveta suggested.

'Yes, I'm going to do that.'

*

On Sunday Babatunde and Yelishaveta went to speak to members of the executive committee of the youth church.

'Guys, what's happening?' asked Babatunde. 'Why do you think this letter has been written? Do the authorities have genuine grounds for their complaints about your negative behaviour?'

No one answered him for a long moment; some of the young people looked at each other while others stared at their feet.

'I can guess why this is happening,' said a girl known as Yelena. 'Many of us have stopped watching TV and are no longer dating.'

'That's right,' added another youth called Sigrid. 'And some of us have begun to criticise the ungodly behaviour of our peers and family members.'

## 117

At the beginning of the new week Babatunde received a phone call that his uncle, Emenike, had passed away. He immediately packed his bags and the following day flew to Nigeria.

After the funeral, when his relatives asked why he had not come with his wife, he told them that she would come back with him later for a traditional wedding.

The following Saturday morning he returned to the airport, boarding a plane to London from where he took another airbus going to Moscow. There he found a plane ready to take off for Kiev.

As the plane descended to the runway, his thoughts were on Yelishaveta; he had in his luggage a lot of things that he knew would satisfy her food cravings: raisins, nuts, chocolate and fresh green grapes. He'd missed her radiant smile and looked forward to kissing her on her bulging tummy, and spoiling her with tons of love.

After disembarking he hurried to the conveyor belt to collect his luggage. To his chagrin, he could not find his suitcase, so he went to the lost luggage counter to inquire from the airport official there. The woman asked him to sit down while she telephoned someone. Five minutes later, a young woman entered the office and asked him to accompany her to a different office. He did so and realised that he was in the office of the security chief. The woman, who told him that she was the PA to the security chief, handed him his suitcase and apologised for the inconvenience.

Then she gave him a grave look. 'Sir, Mr Arsanalov would like to speak to you.'

'Why does he want to speak to me?'

She shrugged: 'I have no idea, sir.'

She escorted him to where her superior sat.

'Mr Arsanalov, why do you want to speak to me?' asked Babatunde after they had exchanged greetings. 'Am I a threat to the security of the state?'

Arsanalov grinned. 'Relax Pastor Oko…'

'I have no time to relax,' Babatunde cut in, 'I'm in a hurry to get home to my house. I haven't seen my wife for some time. And she's pregnant. So…'

Arsanalov nodded. 'I understand. In fact, the people who are keen to speak to you are the police.'

'The police?'

'Yes, the police intelligence.'

'Why?'

Arsanalov shrugged. 'I can't say. I don't know why they want to speak to you. When they make this kind of request we don't ask why. I'm just doing my job of handing you over to them. If you don't…"

'Am I being suspected for any wrong doing?'

'They should be able to tell you that, Pastor Okoronkwo. If you cooperate, I'm sure you will see your wife before long. But if you don't…'

Babatunde frowned. 'I have nothing to hide, Mr Arsanalov. So please take me to those guys.'

A short time later he found himself in an interrogation room. A middle-aged police officer who was lighting up a cigarette, puffed as he stared at a black man facing him. Babatunde, had declined his offer of a cigarette.

The officer, who had introduced himself as Gromyko, grinned and said: 'I have been told you are in a hurry.'

'Certainly; I've no time to waste, my wife is waiting for me. And she's pregnant.'

'I have my work to do, just as you have your own type of work to do,' said Gromyko with smugness. 'I don't know how long it will take us to get what we are looking for. But when we are done, you'll be free to go to your house.'

'What are you looking for?'

Gromyko searched around his table and took up a folded newspaper, unfolding it to show Babatunde the headline.

Babatunde read: *Drug dealing soars at Boryspil International Airport.*

'What has this to do with me?' he asked, annoyed.

Gromyko handed him the newspaper. 'Please take a moment and read this paragraph, to get a proper context.'

Babatunde read: *Illegal trading of drugs at Ukraine's biggest airport has more than doubled in the wake of an influx of Nigerian drug peddlers. The kingpins are yet to be unmasked. In the last two weeks, six young men, all Nigerians, have been arrested for carrying luggage in which drugs had been expertly hidden. During interrogation most of the suspects said they were tricked into taking luggage to Ukraine, and that they were promised jobs at the docks in Odessa.*

Babatunde sighed as he handed the newspaper back to Gromyko.

'Again, what has this to do with me?'

'I was coming to that. One of the suspects told the investigators that he was taking the luggage to Pastor O.'

'So, I'm that Pastor O?'

'We need to determine that. That's the purpose of this investigation.'

'If I can give you a telephone directory from my region in Nigeria, you'll have a lot of work to do. You'll come across many surnames such as Okara, Okoro, Onyekachi, Ojukwu, and many others. So you are wrong to assume that...'

'I'm just doing my work, Mr Pastor O.'

'I'm not Pastor O. You know my full surname, Mr Gromyko.'

Gromyko grinned. 'Noted, Pastor O-ko-ro-nkwo.'

'So what do you want to know from me?' inquired Babatunde.

'I was just doing the introduction. Four other officers are going to do in-depth interviews with you.' He paused and gave him a stern look. 'I doubt if you will be able to see your pregnant wife tonight.'

## 118

Babatunde was held for another day and night. The following day the newspaper headlines shouted: *Nigerian pastor arrested for drug dealing.*

On the third day of his incarceration, hundreds of members of his congregation protested in front of the police headquarters, armed with posters saying, *Our pastor not guilty; 'Release the Man of God; The Devil =a liar; Hands off our Man of God; Don't touch our African Treasure.* Another poster the print of two open palms with these words added…*off our gr8 Pastor.*

The fifth day saw thousands, who regarded themselves as God's army, besieging the court building opposite the police Headquarters; as they continued to sing and chant biblical slogans, Babatunde finally emerged from the court.

'Allelloyah!' shouted Babatunde, waving his hands.

'Hallelujah!' the people responded.

Yelishaveta rushed to him. He moved forwards and took her into his arms. He pressed himself against her, mumbling, *nwunye m.* She buried her face into the nook between his neck and his shoulder. They embraced and kissed. He touched her tummy, bowed his head and kissed it; she leaned her head on his shoulder. The church people applauded, cheered and whistled as he was led to a van whose canopy had been removed; Yelishaveta stood beside him and cuddled his arm.

Babatunde told the cheering crowd that the charges against him were withdrawn because of lack of evidence. He thanked them for praying for him.

'For all those days in there,' Babatunde went on, 'I tasted neither water nor food. Like Queen Esther I was fasting. I wasn't complaining to my God. *Mba!* Like Paul and Silas, I was praising God, for I knew that my arrest was done for a heavenly purpose. The devil may try all tricks in his dirty bag, but he's not going to destroy our…' He paused as he gently squeezed Yelishaveta's hand.

'Fruitful Vineyard!' Yelishaveta completed. 'For the Lord says…' she raised her arms towards the audience.

'I, the Lord watch over it,' said the members of the congregation in unison. 'I water it continually, I guard it day and night so that no one may harm it!'

'Allelloyah!' shouted Babatunde, leading the applause.

Scores of journalists besieged him, eager to interview him as he stepped down from the van to get into a white Mercedes Benz.

'Pastor Okoronkwo, are you going to sue the state?' asked a female TV journalist.

Babatunde laughed aloud. 'I'm laughing at the devil. To answer your question, no.'

'Why?'

'I'm doing what my Lord, Jesus Christ, would have done. I bless those who are trying to make life difficult for me.'

*

After they had had their dinner, Babatunde told Yelishaveta about his uncle's funeral,

'When I saw my uncle during Christmas, I didn't know that I was see-ing him for the last time. He was my father's younger brother. I feel guilty because I didn't do much for him. Three suits and three matching hats is all that I gave him. He deserved far more than that. When I worked at his farm, he taught me work ethics that made me who I am today.'

'I can see that he means so much to you, Baba. Tell me about your stay with him.'

'I still remember that morning, the first Saturday of January; I was helping my mother to gather the laundry. I and the next-door neighbours' boys of my age were about to head for the stream where we would all bathe and then wash our clothes, when my father suddenly appeared in the courtyard and summoned me.

'*What does he want?* I asked myself as I dropped the bundle of laundry and hurried across the courtyard. *Father has been quiet these past days. I won-der if I have done something wrong.*

My father motioned to me and I followed him to his toolshed where two strangers were waiting. I looked from one face to the other, uncer-tain what all of this meant and feeling very juneasy.

"Son, these men are working for my brother Emenike who lives in Umuahia," said my father. "I am sending you to live with your uncle and help him at his farm—these men will take you there."

'I stood rooted to the spot, stunned by the unexpected news. I was about to ask a question when my father continued: "When I was a boy, my father sent me away to work on a farm. So I feel one of my sons should have the same experience I had."

'In my mind the question screamed: *What about my schooling? I must do Grade 2!* But I remained silent, staring at the floor and scraping the dirt with my toe."'Your uncle will take you to school, and you will work on the farm part-time," said my father, as if he could read my mind. I looked straight into my father's eyes for a moment and then continued to scrape dirt with my toe. I felt like saying: *Father, I'm going to miss you.*

"'Go get your things together," my father said brusquely. "You'll be leaving right away—don't keep these men waiting."

"'Yes, father," I answered in a barely audible voice. Retreating from the toolshed, I strode across the compound towards my sisters' hut. My mother and sisters were waiting impatiently to begin their trek to the river.

"'What is it, son?" my mother asked, puzzled by my sombre face and the hurt look in my eyes. I stood in front of her, folding my arms. She motioned that we should sit on the rough bench.

'Father says I should go and stay with uncle Emenike, and work on his farm,' I told her.

As mother and I sat staring at the shrine across the room, the significance of the words sank in. It would mean separation from my mother, who had such great affection for me. I would be living with people I had never even met.

'Why is father doing this?" I asked, searching my mother's face. "Is he getting rid of me?"

My mother replied, "Perhaps something good will come out of this."'

'I like the fact that your mother was positive,' said Yelishaveta, 'despite…'

'Okay, Yeli,' Babatunde interrupted her, feeling tears welling up in his eyes. 'Let's not talk any more about it for now. I will tell more in the future.'

Yelishaveta brushed his arm with her hand and kissed him.

'When we are through with the traditional wedding,' Babatunde continued, 'I want us to visit my uncle's farm.'

'I will appreciate that.'

'What will always remain deeply etched in my memory, is how he once said to me when I was with him on a hunting trip: "Wake up Baba, sleep doesn't buy a cow!"'

*

319

During the meeting of the board of elders Vladimir presented a progress report: he informed them that the church membership had reached more than 15 000 people. Applause broke out among the members.

'So we are planning to hold a jumbo thanksgiving occasion next month, to celebrate our phenomenal growth.'

Another burst of applause followed.

'One important thing that we should pray for,' Vladimir continued, 'is a permanent building that can accommodate 25 000 people. We've applied to the city council, but we aren't getting a positive response.'

'I heard a rumour,' said Babatunde, 'that councillors who have strong links with the Orthodox Church are saying, "Over our dead bodies! They aren't going to get a plot!" So it seems we are going to continue moving from place to place.'

On the agenda was further discussion on a community project to be established in Nigeria.

*

It was a week before the church thanksgiving celebration; Babatunde was preparing to go to the church office. As he was about to close the door of his study, Yelishaveta handed him a letter.

'Alex has just given it to me,' said Yelishaveta.

Babatunde tore the envelope open and unfolded the note inside. 'It's a reply from the Department of Welfare and Social Development.' He smiled at her: 'Honey, you were right that God is on our side. The Committee of Professionals came to the conclusion that nothing abnormal could be noted in the health or psyche of the youth. Allelloyah!' said Babatunde.

'Hallelujah!' responded Yelishaveta, equally thrilled.

# 119

The thanksgiving celebration took place as planned. The congregants were asked to bring their picnic baskets, and the church provided cool drinks and ice cream. As usual the church band played, and the members rose to their feet and worshipped. Before Babatunde presented his sermon, he announced that the Centre of Hope - Fruitful Vineyard Church intended to establish a project in Nigeria.

'We are blessed to be a blessing,' he added.

The parishioners rose to their feet and applauded.

Vladimir presented a detailed progress report on the church and how it had grown from seven members to 16 000; he mentioned the challenges facing Babatunde and how he'd soldiered on; and how a certain Alexandrovich Mayakovsy, formerly a tramp, was the first convert. The church members applauded and looked around for Alex, but he was nowhere to be found.

Babatunde told the church members that because the city council was reluctant to give the church a plot, he didn't know what they should do. 'Does anyone have any suggestions?' he asked.

After a long pause Anna raised her hand. 'We should organise a march to the city council offices, pastor.'

The congregation applauded.

'Are you in agreement with Anna? And are you sure you are going to support the march?' inquired Babatunde.

'Yes!' shouted members of the congregation, standing up and applauding again.

'Okay,' said Babatunde, 'the board will prepare a memorandum to be handed to the mayor at a date to be announced.'

After a short sermon Babatunde told the congregation that the board of elders had recommended that a group wedding ceremony should be conducted. Before the congregation had recovered from the shock of the surprise announcement, Babatunde turned in the other direction and gestured with his right hand.

Ten brides wearing snow-white wedding dresses emerged with their grooms beautifully contrasting with black suits and white shirts. As the couples walked towards the centre of the stage the church members rose to their feet, applauding and cheering with 'stomach burst' joy.

After the noise had subsided, Babatunde conducted the group wedding ceremony. Alex and Natasha were among the couples.

'I wish you a happy honeymoon,' Babatunde told the newly weds as the congregation applauded once more.

When the other couples descended from the stage, Alex and Natasha remained standing.

Alex marched to the microphone: 'I thank God for how He touched Pastor Babatunde, to come and speak to me one day when I was a hobo sitting on a park bench,' said Alex, wiping away tears. Natasha gave him a tissue and held his hand.

'To cut a long story short,' Alex went on, 'you can all see how the Lord has transformed my life; from having nothing, today I own a well-furnished house and a car; from being a nobody, today I am somebody-in-

Christ and God has provided me with a…' he turned to look at Natasha, '…sweet, wonderful life partner.'

The congregation applauded loudly.

'Now, as a token of appreciation, I am going to read a short poem in honour of the man of God, Pastor Babatunde Okoronkwo. Although…' He was interrupted by a thunderous applause. 'Although it takes only a few minutes to read the poem, it took me some time to create it. For months I jotted down notes in this…' He took out a black pocket notebook from his jacket pocket and lifted it up for them to see, '…this notebook.'

Babatunde jumped up. '*Ewu-o!*' he exclaimed, clapping his hands.

Alex grinned. 'Thank you pastor for your enthusiasm.' He cleared his throat and said. 'The title of the poem is, "African treasure".'

Like Abraham, Pastor Babatunde left his village in Nigeria,
Following the footsteps of the Holy Spirit,
Thirsty for God, desperate to be God's hands and feet in
Ukraine,
Like Jesus his Lord and Master, he became a friend of the ho-
bos,
the homeless and prostitutes, and a father to the fatherless;
Filled with God's bread, he hungered to be God's blessing
to the poor and the jobless.
From Africa, fired with passion, he came
to be the smile of Jesus to those with no ray of hope.
Armed with the brightest light, he came
to destroy the works of darkness in Ukraine;
He is an African Treasure, an African flower never born to blush
in the African sun but to be a sweet fragrance and to bear plenti-
ful fruit for Ukraine and the world.
Behold the garland kissing the neck of Ukraine to fill Russia
with envy!
African Treasure, touched by God's fire to change
a prostitute into a saint, a drug addict into God's addict, an alcoholic into a sober soul.
Oh African Treasure, blessing of the world,
may you see many, many sunrises and moons.
African Treasure, whose deeds are taller than Mount Everest's
peaks
And deeper than the sea. Hallelujah!

Alex bowed to the congregation who applauded like hailstones on a zinc roof. Natasha swung towards him and kissed him fervently.

'Allelloyah!' exclaimed Babatunde, hurrying up to give Alex a firm hug; he lifted Alex's arm up and the congregation continued to applaud. He raised his hand to quieten them.

'Thank you, Alex, for this wonderful poem which you've dedicated to me.' He paused smiling at Alex. 'He has been writing it for years in a black notebook. Alex, I feel honoured to have a poem written about me. But,' he pointed heavenwards, 'all credit belongs to Him. It's by His grace that I am what and who I am, so I don't want to be treated like a god.' He gave Alex a smile. 'Thank you once more, Alex.'

Applause followed Alex and Natasha to their seats.

After the service as people dispersed to eat from their picnic baskets, Babatunde went to Alex and said: 'Alex, what a surprise! I didn't know that you are a poet.'

Alex chuckled. 'I'm trying…'

'You aren't trying, Alex, you are excellent!'

Alex laughed.

'I'm interested to know how you started writing poetry,' said Babatunde. 'But don't tell me now; go and enjoy your honeymoon, and when you return, Yelishaveta and I will take you and Natasha out for lunch.'

<h1 style="text-align:center">120</h1>

'It all started when my mother took me to Moscow Stadium to listen to Russia's well-known poet, Yevgeny Yevtushenko,' Alex told Babatunde, Yelishaveta and Natasha as they sat together in Anna Amakhtova Restaurant.

'I was fourteen years old, one of 14 000 people sitting in that stadium. I still remember that it was in 1953, the year Stalin died. Yevgeny Yevtushenko had made a name for himself as a poet of the young people. I was so inspired that the following year I made my literary debut with a satirical poem about a boy gangster. My mother, a high school teacher, played a role in my early literary success. I was the only child and my father died when I was ten.'

'Tell us more, please,' said Babatunde.

'After completing high school I followed in the footsteps of my icon, by becoming a student at the Literary Institute. While I was still at school, my mother introduced me to the poetry of Anna Akhmatova and later

Lydia Chukovskaya, whom I studied at the Institute; I was also exposed to the poetry of Alexander Blok. During the Institute's Friday night poetry readings, I became popular as a performer, and I soon made a name for myself as "another Yevtushenko". I left the Institute to do a teacher's diploma but my heart remained in poetry.

'My mother encouraged me to complete the diploma. Holding the certificate in my hands, I handed it to my mother and said, "Mama, you wanted me to qualify as a teacher; there's the piece of paper, you can keep it. I'm going to hit the road as a poet." My mother didn't argue with me. She only said, "You can follow your heart; perhaps in a few years you'll decide to follow your mind."

'I was invited to many events, and one day I was lucky enough to meet my icon, Yevtushenko. I was flattered when he gave me a warm handshake and congratulated me for following in his footsteps. He was delivering a paper, "Writing Under Stalin's Shadow." I had been lucky to attend the seminar at Poesi Instituut. He shared a word of advice, "If you want to write great poetry you must drink and be drunk with great poetry." Before he left he whispered, "Read also poems circulated as underground *samizdat*."

'Encouraged, I was inspired to write more poems; I began to receive invitations and a few months later I performed all over Russia. The Russians were consuming poetry, at clubs, factories, universities and theatres. I owed my success to the path that was paved by Yevtushenko. At times I found myself performing in three venues a day when Yevtushenko was absent, accepting invitations abroad. He used to visit France, Cuba, the United States and Great Britain. I aspired to reach the heights of his success.'

Alex paused and said, 'Any questions so far?'

'Yes,' said Babatunde. 'I cannot connect your success with the fact that you became a hobo.'

'I'll get to that,' said Alex. He went on: 'I got emotionally involved with a beautiful girl, Lydia Latovsky who worked at the ticket office of the Moscow Theatre. I met her when I was performing there.

'We got married and Lydia persuaded me to look for a career that was safe and secure and not as controversial as poetry. She said to me, "If you become a great poet you must know that popularity comes with dangers." She showed me a literary journal which had published an article about Yevtushenko.

'I began to understand that many Soviet literary critics were inactive during the last years of Stalin when poetry was almost dead. Because of the oppressive politics they became hostile towards young Yevtushenko—they hated the manner in which certain journalists from the West wrote about the poet; these newspapers said Yevtushenko was a confident young poet who could not be dictated to by the Russian authorities. I read more hostile articles written about him in many literary journals.

'Lydia persuaded me to go back to teaching. So I talked to my mother and I was lucky to get a teaching post at the same high school. Yevtushenko kept a low profile and worked very hard, publishing two books in quick succession. He was invited to the International Poetry Festival in Holland. From there he went to England and the US.

'During his stay in one of the American cities, he commented that he felt good that he was there speaking his mind, presenting his poems directly to the consumers of poetry; he stated that for a long time Soviet poetry was relayed to the world by political commentators whose interests were not primarily literary.

'After Yevtushenko had returned to Russia and was invited to perform at varsities and theatres, I went to see him again; his poems were about hypocrisy and seeking truth. At a club he read a poem entitled, 'Who's fooling who?' I think he was extremely daring – or he was drunk. The literary critics now hated him with passion; they branded him "Russia's Angry Young Poet".

'A government newspaper wrote that he was brainwashed by America and that he had become an anti-communist rebel. His audiences began to shrink and he found himself performing only at clubs. The universities and theatres also boycotted him. I heard rumours that the KGB had visited him and warned him that he was playing with fire. We also heard he was told that his passport might be confiscated if he didn't "stop the nonsense".'

'As pressure on him was increased by the Soviet authorities, young unknown poets and poetry lovers rallied around him. I wanted to be part of the "Friends of Yev". But Lydia could not agree that I should go near such "unpatriotic people". One Saturday night when she was at the theatre, I went to one of the clubs where I heard Yev was performing. Friends who had not seen me for months bought me a lot of liquor and I got drunk.

'As Yev read his poems, I cheered the loudest. At the end of the session I joined his table and congratulated him between swigs of beer. I also told the club owner that I was itching to read a poem and he agreed. After reading my own version of "Who's fooling who?" I told my listeners that I supported Yev when he said in the US that the Russian poets must speak for themselves and not rely on the Soviet authorities to speak on their behalf. I received loud cheers and applause.

'Two days later my photo and the story of my performance of "Who's fooling who?" at the Literaturuaya Café appeared in *Pravda* newspaper. The caption was: "Anti-Communist rebel number two." When Lydia saw the article she confronted me: "How can you be so foolish?" I told her that I wasn't sorry about what I had done as I believed that history would prove me right. She warned, "When that history proves you right, you'll be staying alone, because I'm not going to share a bed with an unemployed fool."

'I thought she was just being overly emotional. "Who says I'm going to lose my job?" I said to her. She didn't answer me. That night she slept in another room. The following day a captain of the KGB visited my school and spent hours with the principal. By the end of the week I was without a job. That same weekend, Lydia took her belongings and walked out of the flat without a word. A car was waiting outside. On Monday I went to the theatre, but the security guard told me that he was instructed to deny me entrance. "Who gave you that instruction?" I demanded. "The Security Chief, and he must have received it from people above him."

'The man put his hand on my shoulder and said: "Young man, let me tell you nothing but truth: the instruction comes from the principal dancer. He sent a memo to the Security Chief about you." "Why is the principal dancer against me?" "He has been having an affair with your wife, and it's been going on for months."

'I was mad with anger and I wanted to break everything in front of me. I wanted to get hold of Lydia and tear her to pieces. The same evening, I received the shocking news that my mother had died from breast cancer. After my mother's funeral, which Lydia didn't attend, I returned to the flat to find new occupants inside.

'I went to the caretaker's flat, collected my belongings and left the place, with no clue where I was going. It was very hard knowing that Lydia was warming the bed of the principal dancer. I went to the factories where I used to read my poems, but no one wanted to see me. It was like I was stinking. I hated Lydia and all women. I hated all men I thought were successful. In all such men, I saw the principal dancer making love to Lydia. I was very bitter.

'I was subjected to mood swings, uncontrollable anger and depression; I started to abuse liquor, thinking that I was drowning my troubles. I became dirtier and dirtier, for I no longer cared for myself. I hated my stupidity in allowing myself to be cheated. I wondered if the principal dancer had a bigger and better penis than me. Before long, I had degenerated into a greasy, stinking hobo. It's fortunate that suicide never crossed my mind, because that day you would never have found me on the park bench and told me about God.'

Alex bowed his head and sobbed. Babatunde stood up and went to comfort him.

'I'm sorry, pastor,' said Alex, 'these are tears of gratitude.'

Babatunde patted his shoulder. 'It's okay, Alex.'

## 121

As the car approached the gate of his house Babatunde did not decelerate.

'Why are you driving past our house?' asked Yelishaveta.

Babatunde sighed. 'I have a gut-feeling that there is something suspicious about the red car behind us.'

'Has the car been trailing us for a while?'

'Yes. Since the filling station at Chernenko street. I did not want to tell you because I didn't want you to panic.'

'Should we drive to the police station?'

'It won't be necessary. I'll call the detectives who are handling our case. Let's drive around the suburb and see if the car is following us.'

Much to their relief the suspicious car changed direction as they headed towards the nearest police station.

*

The following week, the march to the offices of the mayor of Kiev took place. Early that morning Babatunde left Yelishaveta lying in bed. She gave him a tired smile as he laid his hand on her bulging stomach and kissed her.

'It's a pity that you can't walk beside me today,' he said. 'I'll tell my fellow pastors that my wife is heavily pregnant.'

'Thank you, honey,' she grinned.

'Have a good rest, *nwunye m.*'

Babatunde started to head for the door then changed his mind and turned back. 'There's something very important I need to talk to you about, Yeli.'

'What is it?'

327

'It's about our child's name.' He sat on the bed beside her. 'Because it's going to be a boy, I would like his name to be *Okechukwu* which means "God's creation".'

'That's lovely.' She gave him a bright smile. 'And if it were a girl, what would her name be?'

'*Chiamaka*, God is beautiful.'

*

The Centre of Hope - Fruitful Vineyard Church march attracted 50 000 people from all strata of society: the poor and rich, scholars in their school uniforms, former drug addicts and alcoholics, ex-prostitutes and tramps, beggars and even some people in wheelchairs. Although the march brought city traffic to a standstill, it was well organised. A hundred church marshals wearing purple and sky-blue T-shirts, assisted by the metro police, manned the streets and guided the marchers to and from the mayoral offices.

Three hours later Babatunde, flanked by Vladimir and Ursula, handed the memorandum to the mayor's secretary. Speaking through a megaphone the official announced that the city council would respond to the memorandum in writing within fourteen days. As the official walked away, Babatunde took the microphone.

'Thank you for this wonderful support,' he said. 'You'll be informed of the mayor's response. And if it's not positive we are going to organise an even bigger march!'

The audience applauded for a long time before dispersing.

# 122

One afternoon Babatunde chaired a fundraising committee meeting at his church office; the discussion went on until evening. All the participants went off until only Babatunde and Alex were left. As Babatunde was locking his office, the telephone rang, and he unlocked the door again.

'Should I wait for you, pastor?' asked Alex.

'No, you can go, Alex. I'll see you tomorrow.'

'Okay, pastor.'

The long telephone conversation came to an end at last and Babatunde hurried off towards his car. Bright headlights shone in his eyes; looking towards the gate he saw a car entering. He thought it might be church members wanting him for something so he waited before getting into his car. Everything suddenly went dark as an electricity blackout hit the area. The car headlights were switched off and, blinded by darkness, he heard a car door banging and someone hissing, 'That's him!'

Bright torchlight shone in his face.

'Hands up!' came the instruction.

Babatunde put his hands up, his heart thumping with anxiety and fear. '*Tufia*!' he exclaimed. 'Who are you?'

He heard quick footsteps and saw figures surrounding him.

'Shut up!' a hoarse voice said from behind him.

'Oh, so we meet again,' Babatunde joked, trying to placate his would-be assailants.

'We've got you today!' the voice said.

As the torch swung, he made out two guns directed at his head, lined up with military precision.

'Gentlemen, let's talk,' Babatunde pleaded. 'What do you want from me?'

'Your life.'

'What wrong have I done?'

'You know. And don't talk so much!'

Babatunde heard the click of metal.

'Please, gentlemen. Don't shoot!'

'Shut up!'

A second voice said: 'This man is a witch!'

A boot kicked him in his midriff and he staggered backwards and fell down. An iron object smashed viciously into his head and body. He felt blood flowing down his face and behind his ears just before he fainted.

*

'I almost lost my life last night,' Babatunde told Yelishaveta as she sat beside him on the hospital bed, massaging his arm and the back of his hand. 'I was amazed that I didn't try to fight back and save my life. Remember, I was once a soldier.I now realise that years as a Christian have softened me. The attackers pointed guns at me, and I heard the sound of the weapons being cocked. I mumbled, "Father, into your hands I am leaving my soul. I waited for the shots but for some reason they didn't pull the triggers — maybe the guns jammed. That's why one of the assailants said I was a wizard. So they hit me and kicked me instead. I thank God that He spared my life, Yeli.'

'Hallelujah!' She embraced him, leaning her head on his shoulder and began to sob.

She stayed with him until it was time for the doctor's visit then left, telling him she would bring the fruit and books he had requested when she returned.


# 123


'Pastor, you must have bodyguards,' said Igor who, with Ruslan and two other youth members, had come to visit Babatunde that afternoon. 'In America all the entertainers have bodyguards.'

'No, I'm not comfortable with that idea,' said Babatunde. 'Let Americans do things their own way.'

'Pastor,' said Ruslan, 'your life is precious.'

'You are an African treasure as Alex wrote in his poem about you,' said Igor.

'I know,' said Babatunde.

'If the board of elders do not agree with us to provide you with bodyguards,' said Ruslan, 'we, the youth, are going to be your bodyguards. We have started with martial arts lessons.'

'I appreciate your concern and your love, Igor,' said Babatunde, 'but let God be my bodyguard.'

Suddenly Igor grinned. 'We know pastor that with God's help you go manage!'


*


Within two weeks Babatunde had recuperated completely. Yelishaveta persuaded him to attend the martial arts lessons that the youth had started. The board of elders established a security department and created a full-time position of security chief for Holy Bouncer, who hired two bodyguards. The young men in black suits, their eyes shielded behind dark glasses, their waists bulging with lethal weapons, could be seen accompanying their pastor wherever he went. Holy Bouncer, with his trademark ponytail, beefed up the security in person whenever necessary.


*


Upon his discharge from the hospital the board of elders showed Babatunde a letter from the Mayoral Council Member for Infrastructure. He smiled when he read that the council would include the matter of the church premises on their agenda for the following month.

'Let's pray and fast for the project,' he said, handing the letter to Ursula.

In the next few weeks church life became very hectic for Babatunde and Yelishaveta. She often accompanied him to community and civic events, though at times she preferred to remain at home to be available for him when he returned. As the pastor's wife, she knew that her prime responsibility was to support him and add value to what he was doing as a man of God. She decided to do a Bible correspondence course, and she also supervised Sunday school. Whenever the children sang *Yes Jesus loves me*, the couple held hands and exchanged smiles.

Because of their active lives, time moved fast. Babatunde exchanged letters with his people in Nigeria. Soon they were left with only a week to go before their departure for Africa. They began to pack their bags.

# PART THIRTEEN

## 124

Babatunde breathed the humid air of Port Harcourt as he and Yelishaveta walked hand in hand down the gangway of their plane. It was 10h00 Nigerian time. When they entered the arrivals hall, they found the air conditioner out of order. Babatunde saw the sweat-beads forming on Yelishaveta's forehead.

'Welcome to Africa!' he grinned, fanning her face with his passport.

After their passports were checked, they walked to the luggage section from where they retrieved their wheeled suitcases and headed for the exit. Babatunde heard a young man calling: '*Oga, oga*!' He ignored him and walked on. Another young man lurched towards Babatunde's luggage, also shouting, '*Oga, oga*, need a taxi-o?'

'How do these people know your name?' Yelishaveta asked. 'Is Oga your other name?'

Babatunde laughed. 'No, "Oga" is a pidgin word which literally means "my master",' he enlightened her.

They waited at the exit, Babatunde searching among the faces that passed them; suddenly he pointed. 'There's my nephew, Ekene.' He shouted: 'Eki!'

Ekene saw him and hurried towards them, a huge smile illuminating his face.

'Hallo, uncle Baba.'

'Eki, *kedu*?' said Babatunde before giving his nephew a bear-hug.

Ekene held Yelishaveta's hand in both of his and bent his neck respectfully.

'Your aunt,' Babatunde told him, 'Yeli. And this is my nephew, Ekene.'

Ekene relieved Yelishaveta of her luggage.

'Let's have something to eat,' said Babatunde.

They headed towards a restaurant.

'Eki is a very responsible young man,' said Babatunde. 'He transformed my little hut into a nice house. I only sent him the money, as you'll remember, and he organised labour, bought building material, chose the paints and looked for furniture.'

'That's wonderful!' said Yelishaveta.

Ekene nodded and smiled at his new aunt as he chewed his food.

'He has completed a diploma in civil engineering,' said Babatunde.

'Fantastic!' responded Yelishaveta, all smiles.

Babatunde looked at Ekene. 'Eki, my church intends to start a community project in the village. We want to install a water reservoir in the village so that the people can irrigate their vegetable gardens and fruit trees. If our people can produce their own food, then we have won the war against poverty.'

'That will be wonderful, uncle.'

'Not only that,' Babatunde continued, 'but we also want to build a preschool here; any educationalist will tell you that the foundation phase is very important.'

'Yes, uncle,' said Ekene, nodding.

'So the church is going to build a structure that can cater for a hundred learners as a start,' said Yelishaveta. 'We'll increase the number every year; the children must get a quality education.'

'And the teachers should be paid well,' Babatunde continued, 'and the classrooms well equipped, with excellent teaching aids, including computers.'

'That will be wonderful, uncle and aunt,' said Ekene with a smile.

'We are blessed to be a blessing to our people,' said Yelishaveta.

'*Ẽeyi!*' said Babatunde. 'Eki, I can now confirm that you've been appointed the projects coordinator of the church in Nigeria. So you are going to be the hands, legs, eyes and ears of the mother church in the Ukraine.'

'*Daalu*, uncle,' Ekene said in appreciation, clasping his fingers together.

## 125

As Ekene led them to the car Yelishaveta stopped suddenly and looked at the traffic passing by in the street.

'Are there a lot of Nigerian women driving?' she asked.

'Yes, they do drive,' said Babatunde. 'But remember that our cars are left-handed, so we drive on the right side of the road.'

'Oh, I see,' said Yelishaveta.

Ekene gestured towards a blue BMW loaned by Pastor Benson and they got in. Babatunde tour-guided Yelishaveta from the airport to his village as they sat together on the back seat. Thirty minutes later the car drove into the home yard and parked beside Babatunde's enlarged and refurbished hut; scores of neighbours stood in their homesteads, looking on with curiosity.

Babatunde heard a woman calling to another in Igbo: "There's a white woman from *Ukereni*!" He chuckled and walked to the house to meet his mother who was standing at the door, her face crisscrossed with smiles. He kissed his mother on both cheeks and turned towards Yelishaveta: 'Mama, meet my wife.'

His mother held Yelishaveta's hand with both her hands and bowed her head a little.

'You are welcome, wife of my son,' she said.

'Thank you, mama,' said Yelishaveta.

After focusing on Yelishaveta's bulging tummy for a moment, his mother grinned at him. 'Son, I'm overjoyed that your wife is…' She indicated pregnancy with her right hand.

The couple had a good laugh.

'I'm thrilled that,' his mother continued, 'people will now see for themselves that you aren't *oke okpor.*'

'Alleloyah!' Babatunde exclaimed.

Babatunde was delighted that his mother met her daughter-in-law wearing an *afe itepu.*

His mother spent over two hours with them, listening to him telling about his challenges as a pastor and how he was coping. Whenever he mentioned something bad, she touched her right cheek, exclaiming, "*Ewoooo!*" and "*Eyaaa!*"

Women from the next-door homesteads dropped in and sat in the courtyard in front of the cluster of houses; his mother sat with them and shared her son's success over a cup of tangerines. She entertained no inquisitive questions about Yelishaveta, but the women made it clear that they would not leave the place until they had glimpsed the white woman from *Ukereni*. As if Babatunde could read their minds, he asked Yelishaveta to stretch her legs with him in the vegetable garden behind his house.

Yelishaveta tied her wrapper over her night dress, knotted it under her arm and joined Babatunde.

'Baba,' his mother called him, 'your mothers are eager to meet their daughter-in-law.'

'I was coming to greet them,' smiled Babatunde.

'*Gudu morni*!' '*Gudu morni*!' '*Gudu morni*!' the women raised their hands before switching to Igbo.

Babatunde bowed with a smile and exchanged handshakes with them, '*Kedu nu?*' He said as he held Yelishaveta's arm.

He stretched his arms as if he was about to embrace someone. '*Nno nu.*'

One woman grinned as she pointed to him and Yelishaveta 'Now we see you no *oke okpor.*'

The women broke into loud laughter.

He then introduced Yelishaveta who waved and smiled at her in-laws.

They walked to the garden a woman wearing a threadbare wrapper with a scarf tied around her head stood; she pointed at Yelishaveta exclaiming, "*Chineke meeee!*"

'What is she saying?' inquired Yelishaveta.

'She's saying: "Good gracious!" She's telling her peers how pretty their daughter-in-law is.'

'*O maka!*' said one woman pointing at Yelishaveta.

'What are they saying?' Yelishaveta asked.

'They say you are beautiful.'

Yelishaveta laughed and took Babatunde's arm.

# 126

'Tomorrow after breakfast I'm going to hand you over to my female cousin, Nachi,' Babatunde told Yelishaveta as they had their supper. 'She'll be like your handbag or your crutch; she'll walk around with you because many next-door neighbours can't wait to meet you.'

'Alright, Baba.'

'This will give me time to be with my nephew and to meet other young men of the village. And remember, the day after tomorrow is our big day.'

'How could I forget?'

An hour later as they retired to bed she asked him, 'How do I say "good morning" in the Igbo language?'

'*Ibola chi.*'

'*Ibola chi,*' she repeated, "'And good night"?'

'*Ka chifo.*'

'*Ka chifo,*' again she imitated him, 'And "good morning, mama"?'

'*Ibola chi, nne.*'

'*Ibola chi, nne.*' She repeated it three times, grinning, before kissing him.

*

In the morning as breakfast was being prepared Babatunde took Yelishaveta for another stroll in the family vegetable garden. She stopped and looked around her. 'I like the weather, cool and cloudy,' she said. 'I expected it would be very hot in Nigeria.'

'It's now the dry season called *harmattan*,' Babatunde told her.

'Harma-what?'

'*Harmattan*, a dry season during December and January. Later the sun will appear and it's going to be hot.'

Babatunde motioned towards the garden. 'Igbos are mainly farmers; in fact an average family in Iboland does not buy food in the market. We use what is obtainable in the family garden or farm.'

'What do you call these plants?' inquired Yelishaveta, pointing.

'These are yams. And those are coco-yams, and over there,' he gestured, 'are cassavas.'

She squatted and touched the plants, then stood up and looked around again. 'What are those trees with broad leaves? Banana trees?'

'No. Those are called plantains. They are bigger than banana trees. Their fruit is bigger. We fry them and…'

'Fry them?' she asked in a surprised tone.

'Yes, we fry them, and they make a delicious meal.'

They returned to the dining room where they had breakfast, comprising okro soup and pounded yam.

'It's delicious,' said Yelishaveta after tasting a spoonful.

'I hope you aren't just trying to humour me, *nwunye m*.'

They had a good laugh.

Nnesinachi was the first relative to enter Babatunde's homestead. After introductions she smiled and switched to the Igbo language. 'She's a beautiful girl. Look at her dimples! I could pour a cup of tea into them!'

Babatunde and Nnesinachi burst into laughter. He touched Yelishaveta's hand. 'She's saying you are pretty.'

'Thank you,' smiled Yelishaveta.

Nnesinachi switched to English. 'But I've a feeling that she has a golden heart too.'

'Thank you, Nachi,' said Yelishaveta.

'Come, Yeli,' said Nnesinachi, 'let's go.'

Babatunde watched the two women walking off to the back of the courtyard where the smoke of a charcoal fire billowed.

Some time later they were back. Yelishaveta went to sit with Babatunde under the shade of a palm tree. Nnesinachi came towards them holding a tray with tinkling glasses and a jar of fruit cocktail juice. She took the tray back to the house, leaving them alone.

Babatunde took Yelishaveta's hand and gestured towards a group of young women and girls busy with some chores at the corner of the homestead.

'Come,' let me show you how garri is being processed,' he said.

'What is *garri*?'

'It's our staple food; it's rich with starch.'

He led her over to the young women and they exchanged smiles. Babatunde pointed to three girls peeling cassava. 'This is the first stage.' He led her over to two young women pounding cassava: 'That is the second phase. And over there,' he gestured, 'they are pressing the bag with two poles to drain the water out. They then dry it in the sun, and the final stage, as you can see, is when they roast it lightly in those cast-iron pans.'

'It's wonderful to see how women can make their own food,' said Yelishaveta.

*

That evening after supper Babatunde and Yelishaveta put on their pyjamas, ready to retire early to bed in order to waken well-rested for the important day.

He lay in bed watching her as she applied beauty lotion to her body. Before she joined him in bed, she opened her handbag, took out a piece of paper and gave him a broad smile. 'Honey,' she said, gazing from him to the paper in her hand, '*A fum gi nanya.*'

Babatunde chortled. 'Who taught you that?'

She laughed: 'You can guess.'

# 127

The morning of the big day dawned. After breakfast, Nnesinachi arrived with her husband Adam. She was appointed by the family as the 'bride's dresser'. She took Yelishaveta to a guest hut while Babatunde remained in his hut, chatting to Adam, the 'groom-dresser'.

Yelishaveta relaxed on a sisal stool covered with a goatskin while Nnesinachi checked that everything they needed had been made available as arranged with the family.

Nnesinachi handed her a piece of paper. 'Yeli, I have written the Igbo words on this paper, so that you can refer to them whenever you want to remember your big day.'

'Thank you, Nachi!'

Nnesinachi asked Yelishaveta to remove her clothes, leaving only her panties on. She handed Yelishaveta a shallow jar containing ointment.

'That is called "*Nzu*", a white clay. You will be beautiful with *Nzu* covering your body. Please apply it.'

Yelishaveta did as instructed. Nnesinachi showed her two pieces of orange African print punctuated with green flowers.

'Now I'm going to cover your upper body and your waist area with these pieces of *Akwete*.'

'As you can see,' Nnesinachi continued, 'this print has been sewn in such a manner that it fits you comfortably in your pregnancy.'

Nnesinachi tied the print around Yelishaveta and smiled at her.

'Look at yourself in the mirror over there,' said Nnesinachi.

Yelishaveta admired herself in the mirror.

'How do you feel?'

'Great!'

'Excellent! *Oya*. Now let's attend to your head. After people have seen your face they will look at your head.'

She showed Yelishaveta the headgear, comprising red beads that were like chalk pieces joined together. She put it on Yelishaveta's head and hooked matching oblong earrings into her ears. Smiling, she said, 'You look beautiful. Please go and look at yourself in the mirror again.'

Yelishaveta looked at herself and responded with a gorgeous smile.

'Are you pleased with how you look?'

'Absolutely!'

'Now please come over to me.'

Yelishaveta did as she was told.

'Lift your arms.'

Yelishaveta lifted her arms.

'Now let me fasten these three rings of *Jigida*, the waist beads, around your waist.'

Nnesinachi then took up a pair of bangles and put them on the bride's wrists.

'Please wave your arm.'

Smiling, Yelishaveta obliged.

'A well-dressed Igbo woman is incomplete without this clutch bag. Hold this *Akpa Aka*, and swagger around with it.'

Yelishaveta chuckled and swaggered.

Nnesinachi handed her a white fly-whisk with a beaded handle.

'I think our elders believed that this chased away bad luck and brought good luck at the same time.'

Yelishaveta laughed as she waved the fly-whisk.

'Yes, have fun, Yeli!'

Yelishaveta shuffled over to the mirror again where she continued to admire herself.

'Now, the last thing: for your bare feet you need these *Akpukpu-Ukwu*, the indigenous sandals.'

Yelishaveta put the sandals on and walked around in them.

'Now you are ready to join the groom. Let's go. But first let me show you how you should walk to your husband. '

'Will I manage?' asked Yelisahveta.

Nnesinachi touched her shoulder. 'Yes, you go manage, baby! Come, now it's an opportunity to learn.'

Moments later Nnesinachi led Yelishaveta by her hand. 'Now go for it baby!'

Yelishaveta waived her arms in the air, shaking her hips so that the jigi-da beads rattled and clinked above the wrappers beneath. The guests clapped and the drummers beat their drums.


# 128

When Nnesinachi and Yelishaveta entered Babatunde's hut they found him wearing a 'two-piece'—a long-sleeved shirt and a pair of trousers of the same colour: blue with zigzagging green strokes. The shirt was em-broidered with green at the neck and sleeves.

Thrilled at the sight of him, Yelishaveta pointed to the red hat on Ba-batunde's head.

'And what do you call this hat?' she asked.

'It's called *Okpu Agu*, the traditional Igbo men's hat.'

'You really look stunning!' said Yelishaveta.

Adam hung a necklace of white coral beads around Babatunde's neck and gave him the tusk of a young elephant to wield. By the time the bride and groom were fully dressed, the relatives had arrived and waited in the courtyard where a marquee was pitched. Ekene operated Babatunde's video camera throughout the proceedings.

Nnesinachi led Babatunde and Yelishaveta to twin chairs draped with white cloth.

His uncle, Abednigo, stood up and smiled at Babatunde before shifting his glance to Yelishaveta.

'Fine woman,' said a male relative who was not very sober, 'look how say even sun dey follow you!' As the people laughed, he added: 'Even sun sabi say dey fine!'

'Some people, you wonder if God was sleeping when he made them,' said a female relative who was also not sober. 'But you, you are beautiful. God was definitely not sleeping when he made you, Alleloya!'

The banters provoked loud peals of laughter from the people who applauded.

'*Nawa-o*!' uncle Abenego exclaimed.

A male relative pointed to Babatunde. 'We bought a cow with a calf kicking in the belly!'

Loud laughter and applause broke out. 'Now people can see that you aren't *oke okpor*, as they were gossiping. A man without a woman is hardly a man.'

The people applauded again.

'Nephew,' his uncle continued, 'in a genuine Igbo traditional wedding, the heads of the two families consult their gods at their shrines. The girl's father tells the family or clan-god, "I thank you for having protected my daughter until she's a young woman ready for marriage. Bless her womb so that she can have plenty of children for her new family. Let her go in peace, and let her husband's gods be her gods."

'The boy's father also goes to the shrine and speak to the gods, "I thank you for having protected my son until he's a young man ready to start his family. We now welcome a new family member, my daughter-in-law." The Amadioha priest goes to the village shrine to thank the gods for the new marriage.

'Because you are a man of God, things will be different. However, some good things in our culture are still relevant today. You all remember that in Iboland much importance is attached to kola nuts; so we are going to break a kola, not for a visitor or a guest, but for our daughter-in-law.'

His uncle gestured towards a male relative who stood up with an old leather-bag flung over his shoulder. The man opened the bag and handed the kola nut to his uncle who waved it around before kissing it.

'This is clear evidence that the kola doesn't contain any poison,' said his uncle, and the people applauded.

He handed it back to the male relative who cut the kola into smaller pieces which he put into a wooden bowl; the man handed the bowl to Babatunde's uncle who took out a piece and waved it around.

'He who brings a kola…?' said uncle Abednigo.

'Brings life!' shouted the others in reply.

He handed the bowl to the male relative who walked over to where Babatunde and Yelishaveta were sitting; the man bowed and handed the bowl to the groom who held his bride's hand and stood up with her. He smiled at her and gave her a piece of kola, keeping one piece for himself.

He then inserted the piece into her mouth while she did the same with him. His uncle led applause.

'She's now part of the family,' said his uncle, 'and she'll bring life with her womb.'

His uncle gestured towards the relative who took a goatskin containing palm wine; the wine was poured into ten small drinking gourds which were passed around: first to his uncle, Babatunde and Yelishaveta and then to the older relatives.

Suddenly all eyes were on the bride; Nnesinachi gestured towards Yelishaveta who took several steps walking away from the groom holding a beaded gourd containing wine; she turned towards him and then walked towards him, kneeled before him and handed him the gourd; a raucous applause broke out as he received the gourd; he then drank under her watchful eye and smiling face.

Babatunde's uncle raised his gourd. 'Let's drink to the good health of their marriage,' he pronounced, 'and may the couple live long in order to see their grandchildren. Amen!'

'Amen!' others responded.

His uncle drank. Babatunde gave Yelishaveta the gourd and told her to drink from it; she drank and returned the gourd to him; he also drank. The people applauded and other relatives lifted their gourds and drank.

'It's now my pleasure,' said his uncle, 'to call upon the man of God, Pastor Benson Okpo, to bless the couple.'

Pastor Benson shuffled forward holding an open Bible.

'According to the Bible,' he smiled, 'a man shall leave his parents and cleave to his wife, and the two shall be one flesh.'

The pastor flipped over some pages of his Bible; he raised his right palm over the bowed heads of the couple. 'May the Lord bless, watch, guard and keep you in the strong marriage bonds. May the Lord make His face shine upon your marriage and be gracious to you. May the Lord lift up His countenance to you and give you peace in your marriage until death separates you. Amen!'

'Amen,' others responded.

The pastor smiled at the couple. 'The groom may kiss the bride to demonstrate to all witnesses today that he loves her as his wife until death takes one of them.'

As Babatunde and Yelishaveta kissed, the people applauded, cheered and filled the place with Igbo exclamations. Food was served and thereafter the couple mingled with the people. Nnesinachi brought many relatives, who surrounded Yelishaveta.

'They all want to meet the woman of *Ukereni*,' Nnesinachi told Yelishaveta. The relatives exchanged handshakes with her. Babatunde introduced Yelishaveta to his former high school teacher, Felix Okoro and to his old friend Odenigbo Nwoye. Later Babatunde and Yelishaveta joined their relatives who were sitting under the plantain tree.

Suddenly one woman broke into an Igbo song which was immediately accompanied by robust hand clapping as other women tap-danced and formed a circle. Talking drums emitting a *kidi-ki-doom* sound, soon embellished the song.

## 129

A day before the couple returned to Ukraine, Odenigbo took them to Port Harcourt. After they had lunch, comprised of garri and okro soup at a seaside bistro, he drove them to the bustling Juba Junction flea markets near the suburb of the university town. There they strolled around the stalls looking at the prints; Babatunde bought Yelishaveta two colourful ankle-length wraps, necklaces and bangles.

As they were about to get into the car, Babatunde gestured towards a yellow three-wheeled motor-bike fitted with a sail canopy.

'Hey, what's that?' he inquired. 'I've seen several of them crisscrossing this part of the city.'

'They are called Keke-nappep,' his friend replied.

'*Keke*-what?'

'*Keke-nappep*.'

'When where they brought to the country?'

'About six months ago. They were imported from India. They are the smallest taxis in the country. As you can see, they carry a passenger in front and two or three at the back.'

'How much are they?'

'Fifty naira. Do you want to have a ride, *nwunye m.*"?'

'Yes, of course!'

Odenigbo thumbed down a Keke-nappep. Babatunde and Yelishaveta boarded it and sat in the back with Odenigbo taking the front seat. As the 'Keke' careered and made a U-turn, the couple burst into loud peals of laughter and waved, while Odenigbo took photos with his cellphone. The Keke-nappep sped away and took a trip around the Juba Junction.

# EPILOGUE

After spending what they referred to as their 'second honeymoon' in the Cape Verde islands for a week, Babatunde and Yelishaveta returned to Ukraine.

A week later, they packed their bags again, for their planned return to Nigeria. Their intention was to launch officially the projects which the church had established in the country. They would be accompanied by members of the board, Alex and his wife Natasha. In Nigeria there would be no need for the bodyguards who should instead guard Babatunde's house 24/7 until he and his entourage return to Ukraine.

On the appointed day they boarded the plane from Kiev to Lagos. From Lagos they took a local flight to Port Harcourt where Ekene waited with the driver of a 12-seater microbus. When Babatunde saw the sky-blue kombi with purple stripes, he smiled at Yelishaveta. 'Look!' he said, and she smiled. They knew it was the vehicle which their church had sponsored, for its colours were those of the church: sky-blue symbolising heaven, and purple for royalty. They stepped closer and read the letters inscribed in bold blue on both sides: *Sponsored by Centre of Hope - Fruitful Vineyard Church, Kiev (Ukraine)*, with the slogan, *A church expecting the unexpected,* written on the front and back of the vehicle.

The other guests came and stood around the kombi to appreciate what their church had done. Babatunde stretched his right hand towards the car and blessed it.

Babatunde and the guests were driven to his village, Ijoto, where they were introduced to his mother who was pleased to meet them. When it was getting dark, the guests were transported to a hotel in Port Harcourt while Babatunde and Yelishaveta remained at his hut.

*

In the morning Ekene collected his uncle and aunt after they'd had their breakfast; he took them to a small filling station at the end of the village where they found the other guests, including Pastor Benson who was with his wife in their Mercedes Benz.

Ekene presented the day's programme: to drive to the reservoir that supplied water for the vegetable gardens and then proceed to a few of the gardens to view the harvest.

In part two of the programme, they drove to the preschool which was to be opened officially. Entering the gates, they saw drum majorettes welcoming them. Babatunde pointed to the huge silver letters inscribed on the gate: *Yelishaveta Okoronkwo Preschool.*

As the cars cruised into the yard Babatunde saw the village women's dance troupe. It comprised about 30 women in blue, ankle-length prints fastened around their waists, their breasts covered with blue cloths, leaving their shoulders and biceps exposed. They wore yellow headscarves and their ankles were like walking percussion as they had tied home-made rattles on them.

The dignitaries had just arrived, and the women were welcoming the chief and the governor's wife with a dance item. When the leader of the dance troupe saw Babatunde and the other guests, she blew a soccer whistle, bowed and spread her arms apart; the women then formed a guard of honour, continuing to sing and presenting a well-rehearsed dance repertoire.

The principal of the preschool led Babatunde, Yelishaveta and the guests to their chairs. Babatunde turned to watch the children who were singing and stomping about to the rhythm of the drums and clapping. One of the teachers pointed to Babatunde and said to the children, '*Oga* is the uncle who has built this place.'

The children ran to Babatunde who picked up a boy and a girl while the others raised their hands to him, their voices shrill with excitement.

Yelishaveta touched Babatunde's shoulder. 'I know you love the children.'

'Yes. They remind me of my early childhood, as I once told you.'

The principal asked the children to continue with their dress rehearsal. She walked up to Babatunde and Yelishaveta and introduced them to the chief and the governor's wife. The principal, who was also the programme director, asked Pastor Benson to open with prayer. She then declared the occasion officially open, and acknowledged the chief, the governor's wife, Babatunde, Yelishaveta and guests accompanying them. Pastor Benson rose to his feet, holding an open Bible.

'We shall read the word of God from Proverbs 18, verse 16: "A man's gift makes room for him and brings him before great men."'

He closed the Bible and paused for a moment. 'We are here today at this preschool because of someone's idea. Our brother, son and uncle, Babatunde Okoronkwo, followed his dream. Because he never failed to use his talents and gifts from God, important people are here today; they had to honour the invitation and celebrate with us.

'If you are utilising your talent, you are like a man or woman who lights a lamp,' Benson continued. 'The lampstand gives light to the whole house, the whole village, the whole city, and the whole state and country. Where he comes from in Ukraine, he is known as an African treasure.'

He flipped over the pages of the Bible. 'This brings me to the last verse I'm going to read. It's from Matthew chapter 15, verse 16: "Let your light shine before men; let your good deeds glow for all to see, so that they will praise your heavenly Father."'

Benson sat down as the chief stood up. 'Many of our sons and daughters have been swallowed up by big cities and we never see them. Those who come back home are doing good things for their families, but rarely for their villages; some die of strange diseases and they return to their villages in coffins. But you, Babatunde, chose to use part of your blessing to bless your village. Because...'

Raucous applause interrupted him. He smiled and continued.

'...Because of what you've done, the people can see that God has hands and feet.' He paused as he looked in Babatunde's direction: 'Thank you, Ogbuishi, warrior-hunter, who enters the homestead spearing a lion's head.'

Loud applause followed as the chief sat down. Rising to his feet, Babatunde thanked the chief and the governor's wife for attending the event.

'My people, it's by God's grace that I was able to achieve what you can see here today. Alleloyah!'

'Alleloyah!' responded the people.

Babatunde motioned towards the buildings. 'This is a small, humble way of saying to my people, "Thank you."'

Pastor Benson led the applause.

'Now we have four classrooms, each used by 25 pupils. The best is yet to come. We want to double this number next year. I'm blessed to be a blessing.'

'Alleloyah!' The chief led applause.

'As I'm receiving from God with two hands,' Babatunde continued, 'another hand must give. Alleloyah!'

'Alleloyah!' the audience echoed, clapping, cheering and whistling.

Babatunde sat down and the programme director stood up.

'Now is the time,' he said, 'for the dignitaries and other guests to have a look at the buildings.'

Ekene led the tour of the four classrooms, the kitchen-cum-pantry, dining hall, activity rooms, library, sick-bed room, storeroom, staffroom and principal's office with a reception area. He also took them to the area at the back of the classrooms where there were swings, and to the vegetable gardens.

Ekene handed over to the principal who invited the guests to the dining hall where lunch was ready. After lunch a leader of the troupe went to Babatunde and Yelishaveta and said: 'Can we greet the woman from *Ukereni?*'

'She's daughter-in-law of the village,' said the troupe's leader, while other women shuffled forward in single file to give Yelishaveta firm handshakes in turn.

The principal instructed one of the teachers to ask the children to present the first item. A wave of excitement burst through Babatunde's eyes as the children sang and stomped about.

At the end of the item he applauded exuberantly as he turned to Yeilshaveta. 'It was the children's rain song, *Ogwogwo mmili takumei ayolo.'*

Nodding, she gave a vague facial expression.

He touched her arm. 'By the way there's no such thing in Ukraine.'

The next item was a traditional Igbo dance. Babatunde and Yelishaveta held hands and were enchanted as the nimble dancers wearing loin-cloths and their seedpods anklets rattling.

The audience applauded and cheered at the end of the first rendition. The sequence of the second and last piece ended with loud pounding drums. Suddenly Babatunde felt Yelishaveta pulling her hand away from his; when he turned towards her, he saw her grimacing and massaging her stomach.

'Are you in pain, Yeli?' he asked, touching her belly.

Leaning back against her chair, her head arched backwards, she groaned softly.

'Should I take you to hospital?'

He put his hand on her belly and muttered some words. A moment later she grabbed his hand, straightened up, brightened and gave a weak smile.

'Honey, the pain is over,' she whispered with a smile. 'The baby was just dancing.'

Grinning with relief Babatunde bent his neck and kissed her belly. 'Okechukwu was taking part in the celebration!' he said.

They laughed and kissed. Those who witnessed the touching of the black and white lips applauded, cheering and whistling.

The chief waved his beaded stick, exclaiming: *Chineke meeeeeeee!*

Babatunde grabbed his wife's hand, and they rose to their feet, bowing; the applause resumed, ending only after they waved and sat down.

*

The following day after breakfast Babatunde, Yelishaveta and the guests drove to his late uncle's farm, as promised. Basking in the Nigerian sun, the men were dressed in shorts. Babatunde wore his pair of faded-green khakis with a matching short-sleeved shirt and green sun-hat.

With the help of the farm manager he located the land which used to be a cassava and yam garden. The place had been turned into an orchard filled with paw-paw, plantain and banana trees. A smile tugged at the corners of Babatunde's mouth.

'Why are you smiling?' inquired Yelishaveta.

He pointed. 'Look, *nwunye m*! The scarecrow!'

Yelishaveta wore a puzzled expression.

'They've covered it with that tattered, faded blue-and-grey chequered blanket. It used to be my blanket when I lived with my uncle!'

Yelishaveta grinned. 'I understand why you are sentimental.'

Babatunde grabbed her by the hand, pulled her closer to him and kissed her. They walked on further.

'My cousins taught me the farm work, starting from the basics to more challenging chores; they told me that in weeks to come I would learn how to sow and harvest the groundnuts, yams, cassava, okra and other crops.

'My life at my uncle's place was not always a source of pain, suffering and drudgery. For example, there were many moments of absolute joy that I shared with my cousins. I still remember how one evening a girl cousin older than me, Adaobi, said: "Let's play school, and I'm the teacher!" "I'm the principal, Mr Okoro!" said Nnamdi, my older boy-cousin.

'As we continued playing, I climbed the paw-paw tree and boasted: "I am now in a high school!"

'I had no idea that one day I would acquire a university education. So, I thank God for what I went through, for He made my life richer, turning my tears into a victory song, my sadness and heaviness into celebration and dancing, the bitterness of an aloe into the sweetness of honey, and my lemons into lemonade.'

*

The cock-crow took Babatunde down memory lane, reminding him of when he'd worked at his uncle's farm. *Wake up Baba, sleep doesn't buy a cow!* He raised his head, stuck out his hand and pushed the blue bedsheet down to his chest, making an effort not to disturb Yelishaveta. Sitting up on his buttocks, he raised his knees, stretched out his arms and cupped his mouth to stifle a yawn.

Although the room was cold, and the air was dry thanks to the Nigerian Harmattan weather, he woke up bare-breasted, wearing only pajama shorts; he took up a light gown, covered himself, shuffled towards the door and opened it gingerly. As he surveyed the compound yard, he took in deep lungfuls of the fresh morning air and watched streaks of light brightening the eastern sky. He then strolled to the pit-toilet at the corner of the homestead. It was quiet, the only noise being that of his mother pounding yam in the cooking-shed.

After emptying his bladder, he sauntered back to the hut, inhaling the air that he had missed for so many months. Re-entering the room, he climbed back onto the bed, inserted his feet under the sheet and pulled it up towards his knees. Sitting on his buttocks, he smiled at Yelishaveta's serene face, her hair smoothed back and tied into a ponytail. When he touched her forehead, she woke up, wiped her eyes and looked at him blankly.

'*Ewu-oo*! You are so pretty even when you are asleep, *nwunye m*,' he whispered, gripping her ear lobe with his lips.

She laughed and lifted herself up to cuddle him; he reciprocated, giving her a tender kiss.

'Daughter-in-law of the Okoronkwos, *Chineke meeeeeeee!*'

# Acknowledgements

My heartfelt thanks to:

Trinity Broadcasting Network for showing a programme about Pastor Sunday Adelaja who inspired the conceptualisation and the writing of the novel whose initial title was, 'African Treasure.'

Professor Henning Pieterse, former head and co-ordinator of the Unit of Creative Writing, Department of Afrikaans, University of Pretoria, for his patient guidance when the novel-in-progress, *African Treasure*, was a 'creative contribution,' and a PhD Creative Writing thesis.

Professors Nhlanhla Maake and Femi Shaka for their critique and input as external examiners when the novel was a 'creative contribution' in and PhD Creative Writing thesis.

Fellow students of the Unit of Creative Writing for their critique and input as I submitted chapters of the novel-in-progress fortnightly.

Elana Bregin who edited *African Treasure* before it was sent to the external examiners.

To the following authors, whose biographies, autobiographies, and novels, I consulted during the research and writing of this novel: Ruthanne Garlock, *Fire in His Bones – the Story of Benson Idahosa*; Elechi Amadi, *Sunset in Biafra*; Chinua Achebe, *There was a Country*; Hermann Hartfeld, *Faith Despite the KGB —what Christians face in the Soviet Union*; Jamala Safari, *The Great Agony and Pure Laughter of the Gods*; Chimamanda Ngozi Adichie, *Half of a Yellow Sun*; Chimamanda Ngozi Adichie, *Purple Hibiscus*; Chinelo Okparanta, *Under the Udala Tree*; Letepe Maisela, *The Empowered Native*; Sunday Adelaja, *The Man that God will use*; and T.L. Osborn, *How to be Born Again*.

David Nnanna Ikpo, a doctoral candidate at the University of Pretoria, who read parts of the novel to ascertain that they were 'Igbo-accurate.'

Ms. Trudie Joynt and Ms. Desiree Homann who edited the early draft of the novel-in-progress.

Mark McFaddyn, Sulis International's editor, for believing in the manuscript and cherishing enthusiasm in publishing the novel.

Sulis International's team: production, editorial, marketing and supporting staff for putting their industrious hands to the plough.

My wife, Sibongile, for her patience and kindness when I was present but absent at times owing to me attending to this manuscript.

My sons, Ramaswaile and Bafana-Bafana, for bearing with me when I was at times an absent father.

And finally and most significantly: my Creator, *Modimo, Ramatla-ohle, Makgona-tšohle,* (God Omnipotent Doer-of-All Things) for lending me the breath of life, and for blessing me with excellent health and wisdom. Hallelujah!

Nape `a Motana

# About the Author

Nape `a Motana is the author of three novels, *Fanie Fourie's Lobola*, *Son-in-Law of the Boere*, *Hamba Sugar Daddy*, and a non-fiction work, *Sepedi Proverbs*. His poem, 'Love Conquers All,' is published in The *2017 New England Poetry Anthology*. *Fanie Fourie's Lobola* was adapted into a movie which won the Jozi Film Festival and Seattle International Film Festival Audience Choice Awards. *Hamba Sugar Daddy* was adapted into a stage play.

*Babatunde's Heroic Journey: From Nigeria to Ukraine via Russia*, is his fourth novel, a project which was submitted for his Ph.D. Creative Writing at the University of Pretoria.

Nape has worked as a social worker, journalist, and a copywriter. In the 1980s he worked as a poet-playwright, short story writer, and an anti-apartheid activist. He lives in Pretoria, South Africa, and is married with four children.

*

If you enjoyed this book, please consider leaving an online review. The author would appreciate reading your thoughts.

*

**Follow Sulis International Press**
Subscribe to the newsletter: https://sulisinternational.com/subscribe/

Follow us:
https://www.facebook.com/SulisInternational
https://twitter.com/Sulis_Intl
https://www.pinterest.com/Sulis_Intl/
https://www.instagram.com/sulis_international/

# A Glossary of Igbo, Pidgin and Russian Words

Abanidiegwus (Igbo): armed robbers.

Abeg-o! (Pidgin English): I beg you.

Abum onye n'uwa, onye ka m bu n'uwa (Igbo): I'm in the world, and who am I in the world.

A fum gi nanya (Igbo): I love you.

Agbada: A Nigerian loose-fitting garment that reaches the calves; it is worn by men and women.

Anu-nchi (Igbo): bush meat.

AUH: Ukrainian currency.

Biko (Igbo): Please.

Brodyaga (Russian): hobo.

Bunie ya enu (Igbo): Lift him high up.

Chi m o! (Igbo): My God!

Da (Russian): Yes.

Daalu (Igbo): Thank you.

Dee (Igbo): (pronounced 'Day') uncle

Dibia (Igbo): A traditional healer derogatorily referred to in other parts of Africa as a witch-doctor.

Dikedioramma (Igbo): Beloved hero; a widely celebrated man.

Dyadya: (Russian): uncle.

Ẽeyi! (Igbo): Yes.

Ewoooo! (Igbo): exclamation of pleasant surprise.

Eyaaa! (Igbo): exclamation of pleasant surprise.

Fufu: A Nigerian type of starchy food which is an equivalent of mealie-meal.

Imela, Imela, Eze m oh! Okaka onyekeruwa (Igbo): Thank you, thank you, my king, great and mighty Creator.

Igba Krismas (Igbo): Celebration of Christmas

Ka m bunie afa gi enu. (Igbo): Let me praise Your name up high.

Kedu? (Igbo): How are you?

Kedu nu? (Igbo): How are you guys?

Komsomol: a member of the Communist youth.

K sozhaniyu, chtoby napugat' vas, rebyata! (Russian): Sorry to scare you guys!

Mama-Nnukwu: (Igbo): Grandmother.

Mba (Igbo): No.

Naira (notes) Nigerian currency.

Nawa-o! (Igbo): Epression of sursprise.

Ne glupyĭ chelovek! (Russian): Don't be a silly man!

Nikogda! (Russian): Never!

Nkowe-oma (Igbo): Good man / fine man.

Nna m o! Nna m o! (Igbo): My father! My father!

Nne: mother.

Nno nu (Igbo): You are all welcome.

No be so. Na so. (Nigerian Pidgin): Not like that. But like this.

Nyet! (Russian): No!

Obi (Igbo): the large living quarters of the head of the family.

Ogu-akwukwo (Igbo): literally and sarcastically means, 'book reader.'

Ojukwu bu eze Biafra nine (Igbo): Ojukwu is the king of all Biafra.

Ojukwu nye anyi egbe ka anyi nuo agba! (Igbo): Ojukwu give us guns to fight a war!

Okɛ (oke) okpor (Igbo): Male woman.

O maka (Igbo): Very beautiful.

Otkroĭte dver' syeĭchas! (Russian): Open the door now!

Oya (Pidgin): Okay.

Onye ocha (Igbo): A white person.

Poĭdem so mnoĭ! (Russian): Come with me.

Proshchay, moy drug (Russian): Goodbye my friend.

Rubles: Russian currency.

Sabo: a Nigerian civil-war time jargon for a saboteur.

Sekretnaya Politsiya! (Russian): The Secret Police!

Shababa, rakara-kara! Shababara! Rakara-kara! This represents praying in 'tongues,' a spiritual effort which cannot be rendered in any earthly language.

Slushat! (Russian): Listen!

Spasibo (Russian): Thank you.

Tank: Thank you.

Tank sah: Thank you, sir.
Tufia! (Igbo): God forbid!
Ubiraytes! (Russian): Get out!
Ude-aki (Igbo): dark brown oil extracted from palm kernel. Also known
    as 'kernel lotion.'

www.ingramcontent.com/pod-product-compliance
Lightning Source LLC
Chambersburg PA
CBHW050616170726
48283CB00001B/264